Praise for *Eyes Turned Skyward*

"*Eyes Turned Skyward* is a p—
emotional, familial, generatic   eir
right to soar. Spitfire aviatrix   try
during World War II as a Women's Airforce Service Pilot, her
fury when the women pilots are sidelined will echo through the
decades to her own daughter, Kathy, a nurse struggling to care
for the frail, aging, angry mother she has never really understood.
Alena Dillon's poetic prose and complex characters will linger
long after the last page is turned!"

—Kate Quinn, *New York Times* bestselling
author of *The Diamond Eye*

"In *Eyes Turned Skyward*, Alena Dillon has masterfully woven together dual timelines and complex characters in an engrossing
and emotional story that celebrates the contributions made by
WASP members while also demonstrating how their sacrifices,
losses, and lack of recognition by the government impacted their
lives following the war."

—Lorraine Heath, *New York Times* bestselling
author of *Girls of Flight City*

"*Eyes Turned Skyward* brings the bravery and tenacity of World
War II's Women Airforce Service Pilots front and center, which is
exactly where this inspiring story belongs. Engaging and honest,
this bighearted book also explores the contemporary challenges
and joys often found in marriage and family life."

—Elise Hooper, author of *Angels of the Pacific*

"Dillon has written a compelling and moving dual-timeline story about the lasting ramifications of misogyny, grief, and the histories we don't know about those we love the most. Filled with laser-sharp insights on motherhood, caregiving, and ambition, *Eyes Turned Skyward* is a rich and unforgettable story that reveals the exquisite humanity of family members in all their faults and glory."

—Marjan Kamali, author of *The Stationery Shop* and *Together Tea*

"Readers seeking a nuanced portrayal of mother-daughter dynamics as well as a soaring portrait of courageous women during wartime will find much to love in Dillon's (*The Happiest Girl in the World*) latest."

—*Library Journal*

Praise for *The Happiest Girl in the World*

"A brilliant and often heartbreaking account of a young girl striving to live a complicated dream, *The Happiest Girl in the World* probes the tragedy of the at-all-costs mentality that fuels Olympic performances."

—Blythe Lawrence, coauthor of Aly Raisman's *Fierce: How Competing for Myself Changed Everything*

"*The Happiest Girl in the World* is a searing look at elite gymnastics and the lengths an athlete will go to reach her goal. Dillon writes a harrowing story about how hope can be saddled with burdens and how sacrifice can wear down the soul. Timely and spirited—I devoured this book."

—Elissa R. Sloan, author of *The Unraveling of Cassidy Holmes*

"*The Happiest Girl in the World* is a tender reflection on the importance of second chances, the ways in which both courage and cowardice can break a person, and what it takes to make yourself whole again."

—Meghan MacLean Weir, author of *The Book of Essie*

"Propulsive, transfixing, and disturbing. I could not set the book down. Harrowing and fearlessly honest, *The Happiest Girl in the World* is a haunting read because it couldn't have done justice to its subjects—fictional and real—any other way."

—PopSugar

"As she did with the Catholic Church in *Mercy House*, Dillon lays bare the sins of the U.S. gymnastic world and all those who enable this sport. . . . Dillon sticks the landing with this layered book about abuse, drive, family expectations, and trauma."

—*Library Journal* (starred review)

"Whether readers can name every Olympian gymnast from the past 40 years or can't tell a Yurchenko from a Mustafina, Dillon's latest novel will enthrall. A natural next read for fans of Hannah Orenstein's *Head over Heels* (2020) or the Netflix documentary *Athlete A*."

—*Booklist* (starred review)

"Dillon (*Mercy House*) explores the dark side of elite gymnastics in her engrossing ripped-from-the-headlines latest. . . . Dillon's nuanced treatment makes for a stirring and complicated picture. . . . Dillon's excellent psychological drama will stay with readers."

—*Publishers Weekly*

Praise for *Mercy House*

"A life-altering debut featuring fierce, funny, and irreverent women who battle the most powerful institution in the world. This is the book we've all been waiting for."   —Amy Schumer

"Never underestimate the power of a group of women. Fierce, thoughtful, and dramatic—this is a story of true courage."
                    —Susan Wiggs, *New York Times* bestselling author

"In *Mercy House*, Alena Dillon gives us one of fiction's more un-likely lovable heroines: elderly, dynamic Sister Evelyn, whose tale—and that of her housemates—is as unexpected as it is mov-ing. This is a thoughtful, accomplished debut."
                    —Therese Anne Fowler, *New York Times* bestselling author
                    of *Z, A Well-Behaved Woman*, and *A Good Neighborhood*

"[A] stirring, fiery debut. . . . Dillon balances her protagonist's righteous anger with an earnest exploration of Evie's faith and devotion to justice and community service. This uncompromis-ing story will light up book clubs."   —*Publishers Weekly*

"Dillon's debut novel is heartwarming to its core. With a widely di-verse cast of supporting characters, author Dillon brings Bed-Stuy to life. Realistic in scope and pious without being preachy, *Mercy House* will appeal to fans of Naomi Ragen's *The Devil in Jerusalem* (2015) and Autumn J. Bright's *Lovely* (2017)."   —*Booklist*

"Dillon's debut novel is heartwarming and easy to read, it never glosses over the history of abuse and sexism in the Catholic Church. . . . Those interested in religious fiction will also appre-ciate a simple narrative tackling complex church events. Perfect for reading groups."   —*Library Journal*

Eyes Turned Skyward

Also by Alena Dillon

Eyes Turned Skyward

A Novel

ALENA DILLON

WILLIAM MORROW
An Imprint of HarperCollinsPublishers

P.S.™ is a trademark of HarperCollins Publishers.

EYES TURNED SKYWARD. Copyright © 2022 by Alena Dillon. All rights reserved. Printed in the United States of America. No part of this book may be used or reproduced in any manner whatsoever without written permission except in the case of brief quotations embodied in critical articles and reviews. For information, address HarperCollins Publishers, 195 Broadway, New York, NY 10007.

HarperCollins books may be purchased for educational, business, or sales promotional use. For information, please email the Special Markets Department at SPsales@harpercollins.com.

FIRST EDITION

Designed by Diahann Sturge

Library of Congress Cataloging-in-Publication Data has been applied for.

ISBN 978-0-06-314476-7

22 23 24 25 26 LSC 10 9 8 7 6 5 4 3 2 1

My daughter and this story briefly passed one another as she began to multiply while the last of these words were released, so this book is dedicated to her, as well as to the WASP.

Once you have tasted flight, you will forever walk the earth with your eyes turned skyward. For there you have been, and there you will always long to return.

—LEONARDO DA VINCI

Prologue

July 1943
KCMI Radio 1340 AM
Kansas City, Missouri

FROM SEA TO SHINING SEA, FROM FARMS AND CITIES ALIKE, women are trading skirts for overalls and fascinators for bandanas, leaving housework behind and putting dances and party-line gossip on hold in order to join the workforce and lend a helping hand in the fight against Hitler.

Uncle Sam's daughters are impressing us with their competence and determination, accomplishing what we once thought only men could. The gender formerly known as the weaker sex is performing man-sized jobs with expertise and grace. They are operating lumber mills, rigging parachutes, testing tanks and the latest machine guns, manning antiaircraft batteries, and working in defense factories—all without even chipping their nail polish.

Despite their sensitive dispositions, women have shown themselves to be surprisingly hard workers and quick learners. They've acquired new language and skills; many are now as familiar with industrial tools as with their grandmother's recipe for apple pie. Given just a few break allowances to freshen their lipstick, women can play an important part in the war effort.

We salute the girls who are already contributing and call on the rest of you ladies out there to do your part. You've all seen Norman Rockwell's painting on the cover of the *Saturday Evening Post*, of a girl named Rosie with a riveting gun in her lap and a foot resting on Hitler's *Mein Kampf*. We need more real-life Rosies on the home front to help us win this war.

Are you doing all *you* can to bring your brothers, neighbors, and sweethearts home safe?

Chapter 1

November 2009

AS KATHY BEGLEY ENDED THE PHONE CALL ACCEPTING her first job in twenty years, she felt a rising that she encompassed but was also floating atop. She was her whole self while simultaneously being contained inside herself, rushing up toward the crown of her head.

To be deemed capable after so long, and to know their bank account would be augmented after months of painful deductions, was uplifting. But there was a contradictory grounding too, a weight in her heels, because now she would have to tell her husband. It wasn't that Neil was a male chauvinist, at least not in the traditional sense. He just wanted to be enough. He'd been that once.

Neil was holed up in his office—was it cruel to call it that after so much unemployment, or cruel to stop calling it that?—where he'd held private court since the night six months earlier when he'd stepped off the commuter train, his tie hanging around his collarbone like an undone noose, emanating whiskey and derailment. After he slept off his hangover, he launched into mania, updating his resume, creating a LinkedIn account, calling headhunters, and feeling out former work contacts and old buddies. There were a few phone interviews, but most applications went unanswered. The middle-aged were considered too expensive, set in their ways, and temporary. Job leads were exhausted and his fervor faded, yet he remained in self-imposed isolation, occupying himself well into the night scrolling Facebook, scoping out golf clubs he wouldn't buy, and watching classic Patriots plays on YouTube, as if he wasn't allowed to abandon his desk until he was bearing good news. Kathy added a cushion to his chair and ferried him coffee every morning. He spent more hours in the house than ever before, yet seemed permanently absent, or abducted by a dejected stranger. She missed her husband half-consciously rubbing her feet while they watched sitcoms; his broad hunch when he washed the dishes; his weekend uniform of moccasins, knee socks, and basketball shorts; and the ritual sharing of his post-jog clementine, whose peel he shucked away in one piece, a rose shell work of art.

She paused outside the office door to give Neil time to close his Solitaire window, thus protecting the illusion of his perpetual state of work, but also so that she could gather courage. She hadn't even disclosed to him that she'd been applying. Such an admission would suggest she'd lost hope in his prospects, and maybe she had, or maybe they were just that desperate.

Neil had been the one to insist on their four-bedroom colonial with wide-planked floors, a butler's pantry, transoms over the doorways, and cast-iron radiators, in Lexington, Massachusetts, a town of white-spire churches, shaped topiary trees, overflowing window boxes, black lantern streetlights, and art galleries, as well as historic renown. It was where the shot had been heard round the world, with grave-yards dating back to the 1690s and a reenactment of the first battle of the Revolutionary War each Patriot's Day. Neil had been raised closer to Boston, and though he was thankful for what his father, a bus driver, had provided, he envisioned a more sophisticated life for his children. He put aside any personal ambitions to pursue the dream life of owning a charming home in an upscale suburb. A good school system was worth paying for, and their house was a utility they'd use every day, he'd promised. He'd set them on that high ledge, where they'd teetered for twenty-five years, Neil putting in long hours and Kathy budgeting their finances. They drove sensible cars, skipped vacations, and lived well below the means of their neighbors, saving any extra income for home repairs and the kids' tuitions. With seven years left on their mortgage and property taxes hovering over twenty grand, Neil's layoff had finally toppled them. They were nose-diving, and without health insurance, but Kathy was about to restore equilibrium.

Neil palmed the mouse and faced the screen. Three frames hung on the wall over the computer: a photo of him and his brothers outside Fenway Park, his MBA diploma from Boston University, and artwork from Journey's album *Evolution*, featuring "Lovin', Touchin', Squeezin'," Neil's half-joking request for their wedding song, which would have been fair grounds for Kathy's father to thump him in front of 125 of their closest friends and family. It was midafternoon, but a half-drunk Stella sweated on the bare varnish, askew from the coaster she'd placed at his elbow.

He wore the same MIT crew neck sweatshirt he'd had

on for days. His coppery hair was dark and bedraggled. He hunched like a man melting, as if his former identity was puddled at his feet. Kathy empathized; she too was familiar with abrupt redefining.

Kathy had, for the most part, reveled in being a full-time mother. When Noah and Fiona were little, she napped alongside them, their faces so close their eyelashes brushed hers with every slowing blink. Later, she cut their meat, tied their shoes, and strapped on kneepads. She hopped from birthday parties to lacrosse games to debate competitions. She tracked their ever-changing predilections and stocked her pantry, tuned her car radio, and bought Christmas presents accordingly. She spent two decades trailing her children's orbit, setting her emotional barometer to their heartbreaks and celebrations, assuring them that they were perfect exactly as they were.

Surely there was jelly-in-hair, sneaker-eternally-missing, just-eat-the-damn-broccoli, bone-deep weariness. But those frustrations were insignificant when held up against electrifying joy, and completely shed once they packed their cars and drove away, and the precious chaos of a busy home dwindled to stillness.

Noah and Fiona still lived within thirty minutes, but even so, their departure from their home felt like limbs being severed, or maybe like the very opposite, as if Kathy had been appointed with too many arms, all dreadfully empty-handed. So she'd rearranged furniture, organized closets, and acquired enough plants to stock an industrial greenhouse and which she tended to the way she had her children, by rotating, repotting, and watering them to death.

She wanted to remind Neil that she was also navigating middle-age aimlessness but was afraid he'd explain exactly what made his situation different: their children's launch was inevitable, and a positive outcome that indicated her success as a mother. What did the hacking of his career say about him?

"I got a job," she said.

His shoulders cinched back as if he'd been jabbed between the blades. "As what?"

Kathy shifted her jaw to release a satisfying pop. She'd worked as a nurse from before she met Neil to when their second child was born—thirteen years of experience. Even when she wasn't practicing, she still renewed her license the morning of every other birthday, updated her certifications, and fulfilled her annual requirement of fifteen hours through school clinics and blood drives.

"As a nurse in a gynecology office," she said, dragging her words over gravel. But then she forcibly picked her pitch back up. "Working for Dr. Smith, who seems like a really nice guy."

"Guy?" He rotated enough for her to see his under-eye circles, looking like bruises she wanted to press ice against. "What kind of man chooses gynecology?"

She wasn't sure whether Neil was implying that caring for female anatomy was only possible if a doctor was strictly interested in the gender clinically, or if choosing a female specialty was creepy, and Dr. Smith must be *too* interested in women. If she pushed her husband for clarification, he'd likely scramble, unsure of his own meaning. The remark was just a toehold to grab, a desperate thing to say to detract from Kathy's accomplishment because it hurt that it hadn't been his.

"All of my gynecologists have been men," she said, and then wondered, briefly, why this was the case.

"What's the salary?" The answer was built into the walls of his tone. It wasn't a question. It was a challenge.

Kathy's compassion flickered, and beyond it she noticed Neil's balsam-scented aftershave had been replaced by his natural perfume—heady and tart. Feather barbs fanned his eyes and silver pencil strokes flecked his strawberry-blond eyebrows. Defeat aged a person, she supposed, and in this case, made him kind of an asshole.

But she wasn't interested in an income contest. Okay, maybe she was a little—only to correct his attitude. She folded her arms over her heart. "It's better than nothing."

Then, regretfully, she unfolded and sat on the edge of his desk so he could see her openness. This wasn't about one besting the other. It was cooperation. They were a team. She cooked dinner and he cleaned up. She stocked the house and he covered home repairs. They had built their lives together and had equal say in matters of importance. If Neil didn't welcome her contributions, then their partnership was a hoax, just how they described it in good times or when the parameters of the roles were clearly defined and limited. Maybe being partners didn't mean doing your fair share in all things, but knowing your part and sticking to it.

Still, Kathy softened her cruelty. "It can serve as a stopgap until you find your next step."

"Why don't we put my balls in a jar and make it official?"

"Let's keep everything right where it is," she said. "You're making too big a deal of this. It's just work."

He sounded as if it was taking great effort to remain measured. "It'd be one thing if you were going back for personal fulfillment, or to keep yourself occupied, but you're only doing it because I can't. How am I supposed to look myself in the mirror knowing that?"

She could take umbrage that her work was categorized as folly rather than necessity, but she longed for her husband's smile the way the winter-buried longs for spring, so she made a play for it, wagging her finger in overdone farce. "Let me carry the load for once. There's nothing wrong with women being breadwinners, Grandpa."

Neil flattened his hands against the desktop and considered them as if they didn't belong to him. Lately, the sight of Kathy's own caused her to pause. Finding bloated fingers and skin gathered into wrinkles around her knuckles, she'd think, *No, those are my mother's.*

He said, "If you didn't think there was anything wrong with it, you would have told me you were applying."

Kathy would have appreciated some acknowledgment of her prudency in keeping at the ready all these years. She would have liked some congratulations, reassurance, and support. After all, she was feeling fragile too; what would happen when everyone discovered her nursing muscles had atrophied? She could easily dwell on Neil's stinginess of spirit, a juxtaposition of childishness and machismo, but it was up to her to remain steady, wrap her arms around her husband's brittle pieces, and keep them from falling apart.

The chorus of the Dixie Chicks' "Not Ready to Make Nice"

strained through the pocket of her jeans, a joke ringtone Neil had programmed for Kathy's mother's phone number. It was a well-timed reminder that Neil once had a sense of humor. The ditty juxtaposed their mood, and Kathy hoped it could knock their tension off-balance, act as a reset. But Neil's annoyance only appeared to batten down, as if her mother was just one more unpalatable item he'd been served.

It was likely a daily ping for Kathy to change a burnt light bulb, refill the bird feeder, or unclog a slow drain, since Peggy often treated Kathy more like a landlord than a daughter. Kathy pinched the phone to silence it and continued, "I liked being a nurse. I'm excited to go back. You didn't even like your job, so what's the issue here?"

Neil's hand, which over the years had swung a bat, changed diapers, cupped the back of her head, sealed business deals, and then carried his briefcase home, lifted off the desk. It hovered and then, having nowhere to go, dropped back down.

"I liked having a reason to get up in the morning," he said, hoarsely. "I liked being of some goddamn use."

The term "heartsick," though mawkish, was apt, because it indeed felt as if the organ inside Kathy's chest went sore and fevered. She moved to place her hand over his, to offer consolation, but also to orient him. Maybe hers would seem more familiar than his own. If nothing else, the gesture could say, *Here you are and here I am, right beside you still.* But then the country melody resuscitated from her pants.

It was unusual for Peggy to call twice in a row. Her needs were recurrent, but not so persistent. Even Neil looked to

Kathy's pocket for an explanation, his mouth pressing down. She took that as permission to answer.

"Katherine?" Her mother sounded small through the speaker, her normally theatrical voice constricted and detained, as if on the other end of a hose. "I seem to have fallen."

Chapter 2

September 1943

PEGGY BORE DOWN THE MOWED PATH, HER EYES ON THE horizon, where the sun quivered like a drop of molten gold. Corn husks crunched below her feet. When the crops dropped away into open field, she whipped to her right and stopped short to behold her Model A.

"It's my name spelled out on her registration papers," her daddy would say. "My crop-dusting business she works for."

"Go ahead and tell me I don't love her best."

Her plane didn't care what she was wearing, if she talked too loud or out of turn, how she laughed, or if she didn't laugh at all. It never minded if she lost her temper or wasn't ladylike. It didn't complain if she visited too often or not enough. It was there either way, waiting for the next time, when it would listen and not ask anything of her in return. It was a companion, an anesthetic, and a thrill. She wasn't satisfied testing new recipes or sewing patterns like the other girls in town, or even by stealing her daddy's bourbon, speeding down country roads, and parking on Lover's Hill, like the boys. Instead, she was called to higher altitude, where she could look down at the world where she never quite belonged and see the town of Longmeadow like a toy village she could pick up, put away, and leave behind.

She laid her hand on the wood of the lower left wing, greeting her beloved like a horse. Then she cranked the cowl and the engine revved to life. Peggy grasped the wing and hoisted herself into the open-air cockpit. She eased the throttle forward and the plane yielded. The corn husks swayed, waving her off like women bidding goodbye to sweethearts at the bus station.

As the plane raced ahead—twenty-five, thirty-five, fifty miles per hour—she didn't need to check the speed indicator in the control panel; she felt the acceleration in her body, could read it off the farmland. When she reached seventy miles per hour, she wrapped her fingers around the yoke and pulled back, lowering the flaps. The plane's rounded nose looked up. For a moment, the back wheel was the only contact Peggy had with the earth, a toe remaining in reality. But then it too lifted off, happy to be carried higher, to soar, to fly.

Peggy was eight years old when her daddy lifted her by the armpits and dropped her into a cockpit. "The instructor said a plane is no place for a little girl, that you'd be too scared. I told him, 'Not my Peg.' Are you making a liar out of me?" her daddy asked. She didn't know how to tell him that she wasn't scared, she was grateful, so she just shook her head and brushed tears from her face. They left the ground, Peggy on her father's lap and the instructor in the bucket behind them, and she was gifted something she didn't know that she'd desperately desired. The boys at school didn't let her play red rover, insisting she join the girls in hopscotch, and she burned the Lazy Daisy Cake in home economics. Her father promised that her feeling of restlessness was because she was special, but she'd been starting to think it was just loneliness, and that she was destined to be unhappy. But now here was the wind, stealing her breath. Her feet were off the ground and her head was in the clouds. The whole thing was a miracle. Her father had handed her a discovery, a potential to go anywhere, to be anything. She could fly, for God's sake.

By the time Peggy was in high school, she managed the Model A better than her father, but his crop-dusting clients wouldn't abide a young woman spraying chemicals on their livelihood. She was a feisty little thing, to be sure, but they weren't willing to hand over their farm to a girl, no matter how pretty. Her value began and ended with what they saw before them: thin eyebrows arched over eyes the shape of a setting sun, cheekbones high enough to create a cavity beneath their ridges, lips that could turn from sweet to cruel, and thick auburn hair that she, with her daddy's permission, tucked into her cap when she did his crop-dusting from then on out.

Peggy had watched with interest this last year as her former classmates packed their suitcases and left for positions in defense industries. It was unprecedented, women doing the work of men. She was tempted to join the tide, imagining the power of a riveting gun inside her grip, assembling a plane bolt by bolt and releasing it into the sky. It would be something to be surrounded by planes, but it would mean leaving her Model A behind, and staying grounded. That just wasn't her brand of adventure.

Then came the call. Male pilots were needed overseas so,

for the first time in history, women were being trained to perform domestic flight duties on military aircraft. Peggy had to be one of those pioneer fly girls. If not her, a misfit in all other spheres whose body chemistry only properly calibrated at a thousand feet, then who? This meant traveling seven hundred miles to Sweetwater, Texas. She loved her parents, particularly her daddy, but not more than she loved the idea of herself as a Women Airforce Service Pilot. There was so much evil, and with her special skills, she could do some good—more importantly, she could be *seen* as someone who could do some good. The possibility made her electric. She might just combust as lightning.

Her desire wouldn't be enough in itself, no matter its unwieldy size. Only eight percent of applicants were being accepted. She fit the age, education, and flight qualifications, but she still had to pass an army physical and a written exam, and be personally interviewed by Jackie Cochran, the first solo woman to win the Bendix aeronautical racing trophy, a speed demon, and the most impressive female pilot of all time.

Although Peggy had been scarfing down more than her share of fried Spam and victory cake in preparation, she was still two pounds below the weight requirement. She could fail the physical. There was a swirling inside her at that thought, where excitement eddied against nerves. She'd be damned if she missed this opportunity by the heft of a bag of flour.

Peggy was soaring five hundred feet in the air now. Who knew when she'd be back in this plane, in this sky, overlooking this town? She took in the neighbor's farm scattered with cows, bored by another muggy day; a sunflower field that carpeted all the way to the horizon; and the general store, gas station, and post office that made up Main Street.

The people here, who always looked at her askance as that bony gal with the pretty face and wind-whipped hair who would never find a husband, would either, in a week's time, eye her like they'd been right all along, or she'd prove what she'd known from her very first flight—that she was destined for a higher purpose.

Peggy rocked the aircraft, wagging her wings.

* * *

The coach bus was crowded with travelers lending themselves to the great effort. That's what Peggy was after too, but beneath the top layer of intent was a more substantial crust. Maybe she wasn't so unusual, and those around her with their hard suitcases, shirtwaist dresses, and puffed sleeves were chasing the same fulfillment.

The ride was rutted, clammy, and endless. By the time they reached Texas, the interior reeked of their cloying collective armpit. Peggy staggered into the morning and gulped air that was too hot to be called refreshing, but at least it was new. She was parched, and the tan and grass-tufted terrain appeared to be in the same state.

"If you're looking for a ride to Avenger Field, go on and join the other livestock." The driver of an open-air cattle truck hitched his thumb toward the back of the vehicle, which was occupied by a group of women wearing an assortment of wrinkled swing skirts, one in a pair of pants. They could have been farmhands or factory workers. Or, just as easily, they could have been pilots. One mooed, and others snickered.

They filled two benches in the bed of the truck, ten women in total, the sum of their possessions at their feet between the rows. They glanced, greeted, assessed, presumed, and perhaps, like Peggy, predicted who would make it and who wouldn't. The truck rumbled to life and Peggy's knees knocked into a pair beside her.

"I hear the written exam is impossible," a redhead said, her hair weaved into plaits.

"Only if you're unqualified. Then you shouldn't be let in anyhow." When this priss finished speaking, her mouth set as if around a lemon.

"I'm just plain itching to get into a Fairchild. Those are the trainer planes." This woman's face was like a front door swung wide, inviting the whole neighborhood in, and the song in her words made her sound a bit like Scarlett O'Hara. "Y'all can call me Georgia, after the peachy state from which I hail."

"Peggy," she said with a finger wave.

The remaining recruits sounded off. When they were through, Georgia hooked one leg over the other and kicked back, treating the hard bench like a lounge sofa. She wore loose-fitting trousers, which Peggy had never seen on a woman, and tugged free the pack of cigarettes she'd tucked into her waistband. They were Chesterfields, whose magazine advertisement touted, *What smokers want on the war front and on the home front.*

Georgia said, "So we are the gals out to save the day. Not a bad looking group, for a bunch of sky skirts."

The truck's wheels rustled the dirt road into rusty clouds, making it seem as if the riders were being trailed by a horde of gnats. Up ahead, a white farmhouse interrupted the cropland. Paint peeled from its clapboard and curled like rows of frightened caterpillars. Two older women were rocking on the sagging front porch. One husked corn in practiced pulls and dropped bare cobs into a steel pot while the other worked two needles and a ball of yarn. Neither appeared happy to see the cattle truck.

"What crawled up their broad behinds?" Georgia asked.

"We are a truckload of women being shipped to a military base," another woman explained. "They think we're prostitutes."

Chapter 3

November 2009

I SEEM TO HAVE FALLEN, PEGGY HAD SAID. IT WAS A RIDICU-lous notion: Kathy's mother, who always knew just what she wanted and was already on course to get it, unsure about her own state of upright.

"Fallen?" Kathy asked.

Then Neil was on his feet, his hand inside Kathy's, leading her out of the office and down the stairs. He snatched the keys from the counter, she grabbed her purse, and they were in the car, backing out of the driveway, passing a yawning green lined with majestic oaks and bistros with gold-stamped nameplates, crossing the town line into a neighborhood five miles away and adjacent to the last air force base where Colonel Mayfield had been stationed.

They might have overlapping genetic material, but Peggy was the petite to Kathy's stocky, the adventurous to her cautious, the bold to her timid, and the outgoing to her introverted. As a mother, Kathy favored transparency, preparing her children for what to expect at the doctor, if their parents left for the evening, or if routines would be interrupted. Peggy sprung things on her kids, ripped off the bandage, disappeared without warning, and sometimes flew into mysterious moods.

There was the time Peggy was driving them to their father's military promotion ceremony, and the boys poked and smacked one another in the back seat until Peggy swerved to the side of the road, thrust the Volvo into park, and fled down a passage through a cornfield, leaving four shocked children terrified their mother might never return. Then there were the many evenings Peggy agitated by the window until her husband pulled into the driveway. She was at his car door before the engine died, her hand reaching for the door handle as if to say *My turn.* What was she running from on those days—or toward?

While Kathy discouraged her kids from leaving their comfort zones, assuring them they were loved not for what they did but because they were, Peggy was a motivator, particularly when it came to her daughter. *Make more jokes. Audition for the lead. Wear bolder lipstick. Ask that boy out. Dream bigger. Don't stand so awkwardly. Act brave and that's what the world will see.* Peggy was a woman who'd gone straight from her father's house to her husband's house, yet she insisted her daughter be a bra burner.

Peggy flung feelings like flour onto a countertop but kept the why of them to herself. Kathy justified her outbursts and staunch opinions with the pressure of being a military wife, tossed about the country, having to constantly make new connections, explore new towns, and settle children into new schools, all while releasing her husband into the line of duty. But there was also the possibility that her mother was just emotionally stunted, unsure how to process and express feelings in an even, healthy way. Kathy didn't know if that was genetic or socialized, but she saw bits of her mother's wildness in her two older brothers, so Kathy strived for emotional fluency, not just for her own mental health, but for her children.

The two women saw through different lenses and moved through life accordingly, but Peggy was still her mother, the woman who tied rag curls in Kathy's hair every night the year the trend went around her school, who gripped her by the shoulders when a boy called her Dumpling and swore they'd get her into bikini shape by summer (they didn't), who cheered louder than any other parent at her softball games, who quizzed her for every test, who threw dance parties with signature mocktails on her children's birthdays, and who flew planes for fun.

Kathy needed her mother to be all right, yet she knew from her geriatrics clinical rotation that falls at her mother's age often resulted in hip fractures, which heightened susceptibility to infection, blood clots, internal bleeding, stroke, heart failure, and compromised social engagement, increasing a person's risk of death within six months by fifty percent.

The stench of scorched canned soup hit Kathy as she pushed through her mother's front door, as tangible as a physical obstruction.

Her mother, eighty-seven and always less than 120 pounds, yet never striking Kathy as delicate, was contorted on the carpet below her peach couch, gazing up at the photograph grid of her family, the phone dangling by its cord off the end table.

The woman who charged her daughter's burly coach to demand Kathy get more playing time, the only air force wife with a pilot's license of her own, who picked up her family's belongings every two years and moved wherever the military sent them, gardening to set down literal roots and painting and arranging so their strange houses felt familiar, who cared for four children single-handedly when her husband was on assignment—this force of nature—had been reduced to a pile of crepe skin and willowy bone.

A tribal drum pulsed in Kathy's ears, but she couldn't give in to panic. She repressed her daughter identity and summoned another. It was out of use, but still she hoped it would rise.

Neil disappeared into the kitchen, presumably to address whatever was burning on the stove, as Kathy knelt beside her mother. She pulled a breath in through her nose and released it out her mouth, to steady herself as well as to provide a calming model for her mother to emulate, though Peggy didn't. Her regal posture had curled into prostration. Her silver hair, swept into its signature bouffant bun, was crushed and frayed, with wisps falling against her cheek. Peony pink lipstick had smeared into her smile lines. She winced and her high-pitched whimpers sliced through the pulp of Kathy's confidence.

Peggy was wearing a long-sleeved blouse and pants, so it was hard to tell if there was any bruising, but Kathy searched the fabric for bloodstains, and her trembling fingers skimmed her mother's limbs to check for obvious breaks. As she approached the hip, Peggy cried out. The faucet turned on in the kitchen, and water hissed against heat.

"Did you roll off the couch?" Kathy asked.

"For God's sake, I'm not a child," Peggy said, her voice

straining through pain. "I slipped down the stairs. It's these damn loafers. No tread."

Kathy had bought Peggy a belt clip for her cell phone, so she could carry it with her at all times, as well as a medical life watch, neither of which were on Peggy's person.

"How'd you manage your way across the living room?" Kathy asked.

"You don't have to be a soldier to army crawl. This old bird still has grit—talons and a sharp beak too."

Neil emerged from the kitchen, his hands propped on his hips. He seemed to take up more space than he had in a while. "How's it going there, Peggy?"

"It's dandy there, Boston," Peggy said, mocking his accent. "Thanks for asking."

He's got the tall part down but is lacking in the dark and handsome departments, Peggy had said of Neil when she'd first met him. *That oblong face. It makes him look like a potato. Maybe you really are what you eat.*

More damning than his look and speech (Peggy never had time for the Boston Irish) was the way Neil took Kathy at her word, accepting who she was rather than who she could be. It probably didn't help that he'd drowned his nerves with cheap beer at Colonel Mayfield's air force retirement party and puked in their bushes. *Be careless with every other aspect of your life, Katherine Mayfield, but don't you dare settle for a drag-racing, tailgating, spud-faced husband who can't even hold his liquor,* Peggy had screeched.

Kathy didn't settle for a husband, but she sure as heck married Neil, who was more provocative than dashing, more wily than commanding, and more brash than brave, but who was also steady and accepting. She even found his wounded quality appealing, because while he protected her, he would need protecting too. Besides, no one could deny his eyes, two glimpses of sky sheltering a private mind.

"We need to get her to the hospital," Kathy told him.

"Don't you call an ambulance," Peggy said through clenched teeth. "This house is in no state to be seen."

"They aren't coming for a dinner party."

"I don't need the spectacle. The flashing lights will get the neighbors gossiping about the old crone who got carted off."

Neil watched Kathy, awaiting her signal. Peggy had been a locomotive earlier in her life—all boiler, pistons, and searing whistle—but at some point even the fieriest engines lost steam, and with it, agency. It was the natural order of things. This was Kathy's decision. Still, Peggy's stare narrowed into a demand and then opened as a plea.

Kathy's reflex was to judge herself unqualified, but wasn't she resuming work as a medical professional on Monday? She better get qualified.

"We have to stabilize you," Kathy said.

They needed a bolster to wedge between Peggy's legs and rope to bind them. Kathy and Neil hunted for materials while Peggy volleyed suggestions from the ground. "There are pillows in the linen closet. Don't even think about using my mother's quilt. She was crotchety at the end, but that doesn't mean her heirloom should be shoved into one."

The linen closet barely contained its torrent of cloth. Bed sheets gushed from the shelves like white rapids. Towels frothed in the corners where they'd been balled and stuffed. A down blanket cascaded overhead. Kathy's mother hadn't been the tidiest of the military wives, but she'd packed and relocated enough that keeping her belongings organized had become habit. She was cleanly, even if only for appearances. This streaming disarray of cotton and terry was as off-putting as entering Peggy's house and finding another woman wearing her chinos.

"What the hell?" Kathy asked as a prescription pill bottle rolled across the parquet.

"The kitchen was the same," Neil whispered behind her. "Dishes were piled in the sink, and God knows how long that soup had been left on the burner. I haven't joined you on a Peggy visit in a while. Is this what she's been like?"

With her brothers plane rides away, Kathy was the boots on the ground, appointed to stop in for a weekly lunch, take Peggy grocery shopping, and accompany her to her husband's grave. Kathy thought she'd been doing her part, and then some. She'd typed instructions for the computer and tacked it to the wall as reference. She'd taped off remote control buttons so Peggy wouldn't switch the language setting in her desperation to watch *The Good Wife*. She touched base daily. But maybe she'd been going through the motions without really being present, too distracted by her own domestic turmoil to notice her mother's steep decline.

Kathy opted for a wool military blanket and closed the door against the chaos that smelled of powder and mildew. She eased it between her mother's legs and then fastened tassel curtain tiebacks around her ankles, knees, and waist.

"Are you bringing me to the hospital or taking me hostage?" Peggy asked.

"You're the one who didn't want to call an ambulance."

"I'm teasing," Peggy said. Then she searched for Neil, standing above them. "Your wife would have made a fine field medic. Did you have any idea she was so resourceful?"

"She surprises me every day," Neil said, and Kathy didn't know if she heard tautness only because she'd been listening for it.

Peggy continued, "How does the saying go? 'Never underestimate the way men underestimate women.'"

Kathy should have completed her kidnapping with a mouth gag.

"I don't underestimate Kathy," Neil said, his words sifted through his teeth.

With every other part bound up, Peggy rolled her eyes. "Agree to disagree."

Neil could have thrown his arms up and let Peggy fend for herself, and Kathy wouldn't have blamed him. Instead, he lowered his towering body and slid his arms beneath Peggy's slight shoulders and linen-clad knees. He counted off to prepare a woman who'd rejected him, and then he hoisted them both to his feet.

If Peggy weren't in his arms, and if Kathy weren't worried about uncapping the scab of their fight, she might have grazed her lips over his, as gentle as a flower petal, and said, "The house and the town aren't important. It's you. It's always been you."

Neil carried Peggy through the front door with Kathy in tandem bracing her mother's legs. In such proximity, Kathy caught a whiff of her mother, who had once smelled of vanilla and ground pepper. Now there was something beneath, fusty and overly sweet, like turned fruit. Had everybody in Kathy's life renounced personal hygiene?

They passed the twiggy azalea bush, dormant this time of year, where Neil had retched the night of her father's retirement party. *You can't count on him to take care of you. He can barely take care of himself,* Peggy had screamed after the guests had dispersed, her cheeks flushed by rage and her own share of amaretto sours.

Now here he was, taking care of her.

The next few hours dragged and then rushed ahead in the syncopation of crisis. There were bright lights and stiff chairs, intake forms and blood tests. Neil left, returned with some necessities, and left again. There was so much waiting, and then Peggy was wheeled away for her X-ray.

Peggy had fractured the femoral neck bone of her hip. The mortality statistic of geriatric breaks reverberated in Kathy's head. She was a fifty-three-year-old woman, but also a girl whose mother might die. Of course her elderly mother was nearing the end of her life; Kathy shouldn't be so discomfited. But Peggy's presence had always seemed so permanent because, to her, it was—Kathy had never known a world without Peggy in it.

In her hospital bed, Peggy cocked her chin, as if to defy her circumstance. Her cheekbones gave her face the topography of rolling hills; her eyes, once searing, had been doused by milk; her hands, once sure of themselves, trembled; and her skin, which she'd tanned under the sun of so many southern states, now seemed pale and prone to tearing. When Peggy's lips worried as caterpillars, Kathy realized with plunging dread that her mother was fighting back tears.

"It can no longer be denied. I'm officially an old lady," Peggy said, with stagey inflection. She patted the pendant on her chest—a silver slab on which an etched sunburst was dotted by pearl—as if to ensure it was still there, which it always was. "I suppose you should update the boys. They'll want to know what's become of their mother."

Peggy referred to Kathy's brothers in the manner they always did, as if the three middle-aged men were precocious scamps the women were equally charged to care for and admire.

Kathy intended to call her brothers, but not in front of Peggy. She wanted to be franker than her audience would allow. But her mother wanted family beyond Kathy to bear witness to her suffering, so Kathy texted her own children. They preferred their communication that way, in the form of abbreviations and emojis rather than trading voices, which she tried not to take personally.

Noah's response, while nearly instantaneous, startled Kathy. "I'm sorry to hear that. I hope she recovers quickly." He might have been emailing a coworker rather than the woman who wiped his backside until he went to kindergarten, potty-training an entire year later than his peers. Was his novel professionalism leaking into all avenues of his correspondences, or was the connection between them thinning? They used to be so intimate: sharing ice-cream cones, reading in bed by the beam of a flashlight, and then, when he was in his teens, canoeing together down the Concord River, their comfortable quiet punctuated by paddle plashes. Then again, once upon a time, Kathy had idolized her mother. That had complicated, petered, and with the burden of care-taking, staled. How long before Kathy became just another chore on her children's list?

Fiona's text saved Kathy from wallowing. "Oh no! Are you with Gammy now?" When she answered yes, her cell phone began to ring with "Brown Eyed Girl."

"It's for you," Kathy said, extending her phone. It was like getting to pass her mother a scoop of sunshine.

Fiona's sympathy poured through the speaker into her grandmother's ear. It was invigoration by proxy to be re-minded that a piece of oneself existed out in creation, radiant and dynamic. Kathy watched Peggy's lips warm, but some-thing kept them from spreading fully. Perhaps it was pain—she contained splintered bone, after all. But Kathy wondered if it was something more, something, perhaps, like longing.

Chapter 4

WALT DISNEY DESIGNED THE MASCOT THE WASP ADOPTED, a sprite with pilot goggles and angel wings. Her name was Fifinella, and she was the first to welcome the recruits atop the wooden Avenger Field sign. The land behind her stretched flat and brown, as if God had sliced all the hills at their base and sprinkled the surface with cinnamon sugar.

"So this is the Cochran Convent," Peggy said.

As the women unloaded, a plane cut across the stark Texas sky. Peggy turned her palm against the sun and watched. But wait, wasn't the nose too high? Then the plane dropped sideways in a dead, hollow drop. It was falling, surely, and she pressed her lips together against the inevitable explosion. Peggy couldn't test after witnessing such catastrophe. She'd have to go home, marry, and have babies. This unlikely adventure would end before it had the chance to begin. She grasped for the sky, as if she had the power to right the plane and save her fate, but then the plane recovered on its own and continued evenly, relishing another hot lazy day.

"Good morning, pilots." The husky voice came from a woman in a blue military uniform.

The purpose of this endeavor was for women to serve not

husband or home, but country. Peggy arrived knowing this, yet evidence of the phenomenon—a gal dressed as if to be part of the U.S. Army Air Forces, the very picture of authority and egalitarianism—still sent goose bumps down her arms. And this wasn't just any gal. She was the heroine of the air, the trophy-winning, record-breaking director of the Women Airforce Service Pilots: Jacqueline Cochran. Some women revered Greta Garbo and Joan Crawford. Peggy was a fan of theirs too, but here was her icon.

Cochran continued, "Too many men assert that women, as a rule of our gender, are unequal to the task of safely and skillfully carrying their aircraft into the sky. These men may never believe otherwise or won't admit their misconceptions. For the few who stood behind us in this effort, a rigorous application process is the only proof of competency to show their peers. We've received thousands of applications, and they continue to pour in. A fraction of them are invited here to take the exams. A fraction of those are welcomed into the program. A fraction of those complete training. The odds say you will not make it to the graduation ceremony, but the fact that you are here in the first place suggests something I've known from the start about female desire and ability—something I trust the world will come to know soon enough. Even if we can't employ your services, I thank you for coming and proving me right."

THE HALLWAY TO the doctor's office was crowded with WASP hopefuls pacing or chatting. They wore dresses or victory skirt suits, bold reds and yellows or faded patterns, purchased for the occasion or, as in Peggy's case, repurposed from old curtains. Berets and small veiled hats topped delicate curls. One woman's hair was pinned into such a tall bouffant, she must have been using it to meet the height requirement.

A woman with buckteeth leaned against the wall. "E, F, P, T, O, Z." When she noticed Peggy watching, she explained, "I'm memorizing the letters for the visual exam."

Peggy had the dizzying sensation of having just stopped spinning. These women wanted what she wanted, and they were willing to fight for it, to lie for it.

She followed the wall until she reached the restroom, turned the faucet on full force, and cupped water to her lips. It tasted metallic, but she slurped until her belly distended against her rib cage.

"Did they not have enough to drink where you came from?"

Peggy had been so intent on filling her stomach, she hadn't heard anyone come in after her. With a stray stream trickling down her neck, she looked up to see Georgia, the southern woman from the cattle truck.

Georgia wasn't necessarily beautiful. Her upper lip lacked definition and her jaw was square. Her figure was buxom but robust, a body that could accomplish good work. But her eyes were an earthy shade of green, her stance was relaxed, and her mouth was upturned, as if she was comfortably herself in every room and conversation, and pleased to be there. Peggy had the sense that she could tell this woman anything, and the urge to do just that.

"I'm terrified I won't make weight," she admitted.

Georgia nodded as if she'd suspected this all along. "You

are a tad on the stringy side. A total showstopper, to be sure, what with that bone scaffolding, but not much meat hanging off. If we were stuck on a desert island together, I'd saw off my own leg before dining on you."

A laugh choked out Peggy's throat. "What am I supposed to do? I can't go home."

"Why, are you on the lam?" Georgia asked, her eyes shimmering. "Please tell me you bumped off your husband. I love a good murderess. I promise to take it to my grave."

Peggy could have told her that she didn't have a husband, dead or alive, and not just because she wasn't interested in marriage, but because no man in town wanted her. Everyone agreed she was attractive, but she was also mulish and sometimes hotheaded. They wanted a wife, not a pretty project. There wasn't time to go into that. Peggy had little use for sympathy. She wanted a solution.

"I need to be a part of this," she said.

Georgia's mischief softened and solidified into something else. Unlike the boys at home, she, it seemed, appreciated a project. "We'll just have to put more weight on your slight little person."

"But we have to undress for the exam."

"Were you planning to get as naked as the Lord made you? That's one way to win over the doctor."

"Where could I hide anything?" Peggy asked, and when Georgia's gaze fell pointedly to her chest, she asked, "My bra?"

"I wasn't suggesting we stick items where the sun don't shine, but you make a fair point. Those dainty cups won't hold much. You'll have to wear mine."

Before Peggy could object, Georgia was reaching behind her back, unclasping, shimmying, and freeing her bra from beneath her button-down shirt. Peggy yipped a laugh and accepted the hefty offering by its strap.

"Forget airplanes," Peggy said. "We should use *this* to sling-shot soldiers across the Atlantic."

"They wish."

Liberated from their bullet-shaped cages, Georgia's breasts jounced. Peggy fought to keep her eyes above her collarbone. "What will you wear?"

Georgia rolled her shoulders back and grinned. "A shirt and a smile, honey."

More modest than her new friend, Peggy ducked into a bathroom stall for the switch. The seams hugged her body but the satin cups deflated around her small breasts. In search of fillers, she parted the mouth of her purse and rummaged through its contents: handkerchiefs, gloves, hairpins, her bus ticket, perfume, a compact mirror, two shades of lipstick, an extra pair of underwear, and her coin pouch.

Peggy pulled the underwear over her existing pair, stuck all the hairpins against her scalp, folded the handkerchiefs, and tucked them into the bra along with her gloves. Then she unzipped the coin pouch, which contained thirteen dollars in singles and a handful of coins. She peeled back the bra and emptied the coins into one side. They jangled, cold. There was still plenty of room.

She wanted to demonstrate to her new friend that she too had ideas and audacity, so she exited the stall and continued past Georgia, her confidence a summons. To her relief, Georgia followed.

Peggy approached the first woman she saw. "Do you have change for a dollar?"

"Just seventy-five cents."

"I'll take it."

Georgia caught on, and together they made their way down the corridor until each of Peggy's bills had been exchanged for heavier currency. Then they returned to the bathroom and fed her bra like a slot machine, coin by coin, until they were laughing so uproariously they bowed beneath the strain.

Georgia gripped Peggy around the shoulders and pulled her upright. "Stand tall or all our work will clatter to the floor."

Peggy couldn't remember a time she'd laughed this hard. It was an unexpected treat to trade joy with a stranger, but Georgia had an ease and familiarity about her that made Peggy feel as if she'd known her for years.

She waited for the last quake to shudder through her, and then she asked, seriously, "Do you really think I can fool the doctor?"

"I met the man and, if you ask me, his cornbread ain't quite done in the middle. Besides, it's all in your confidence. Act brave, and that's what the world will see."

The neckline of Peggy's swing dress pulled across her suddenly full bust. The metal was warming against her body and felt foreign and clunky, but also like a strange kind of armor.

She exhaled so forcefully her lips bloated. "How do I look?"

"Like a little over thirteen bucks," Georgia said. Then she

unfastened her necklace and moved to secure it on Peggy. "One final touch."

Peggy stepped back. "That looks like a family heirloom."

"It's just a parting gift from an old beau. Knowing that cheapskate, he stole it from a junk sale."

Peggy's posture relented. She held still while Georgia swept her thick unruly waves across one shoulder and clipped the hook through its eye. The pendant was indeed heavy, a silver rectangle two inches long, edged in engraved rope, the flare of a compass rose at its center, the stationary needle a tiny pearl.

"You should keep it," Georgia said. "It suits you."

PEGGY'S PIECEMEAL BREASTS protruded like the masthead of a ship, and she followed where they pointed down the hall. *Act brave, and that's what the world will see.*

An hour later, she was at the front of the exam line, her heart a frightened bird in her chest. The office door swung open, and a girl rushed out, crying into her hands. The doctor emerged behind her in a white coat and stethoscope, a head mirror strapped to his forehead. "Next?"

Peggy glided forward so her bra wouldn't rattle.

The doctor gestured to the exam table. "Put that smock on. I'll make notes at my desk to give you privacy."

Peggy reached for her dress's zipper and spoke loudly to camouflage any clanging. "You wouldn't believe the bus ride I had down here. It was so full, I had to sit on my luggage case in the aisle. You might be wondering why no gentleman offered his seat. Well, it was mostly women. I guess it's like the president said, 'Never before have we been called upon for such a prodigious effort. Never before have we had so little time in which to do so much.'"

"Name?" the doctor asked from his desk.

"Franklin Delano Roosevelt."

"No, your name?"

"Lucky for you I know that one too. Hey, that rhymed. Margaret Lewis."

He switched on a lamp beside her head. The light reflected in his head mirror and blinded her. He manipulated her chin until she dropped her jaw. "Ever experience bouts of hysteria?"

"No," she said, wide mouthed.

He propped open her eyes. "How tall are you?"

"Just under five five."

"And weight?"

She remembered Georgia's advice about confidence. "A couple over one hundred."

He ran his gaze over her. "I have a knack for figures, and I'd say you are in the nineties." He indicated the physician's scale, and she approached it as she would a firing squad.

The doctor slid the small balance into the eighties and then slowed to a tick. Peggy begged the needle not to lift. She wondered if the coins would leach onto her skin and stain. Even if her nipples turned lizard green for life, it'd be worth it if she passed this test and flew planes professionally. If she could be taken seriously as a pilot, like Amelia Earhart and Jackie Cochran, she didn't care if she grew scales.

The doctor slowed in the midnineties, expecting the beam to lift. The next pound was her true weight. Peggy dug her heels into the platform, as if the pressure might help. The balance didn't budge but, with the next ascent, the needle awoke, and her stomach plummeted like that plane she'd spotted earlier that day. The doctor paused to let the scale find equilibrium. He slid the weight forward. The needle twitched higher. He nudged it another whisper and the needle settled horizontally.

"Ninety-nine point seven. I'm sorry, Miss"—he glanced at his clipboard— "Lewis. We have strict protocols."

"Please," she said, and seized his forearm. "Don't send me home for this. It's too silly a reason to live with."

"I'm sorry—"

"What I'm short of in this room I far exceed in all other areas. The flight requirement is three hundred hours and I have over a thousand. I aced the written exam. Not a question wrong. I was born to do this. Don't tell me I can't over a fraction of a pound."

"Like I said—"

She squeezed harder. "Think of the stateside boys who want to get into the action and come home heroes. I could do that for them."

She was on high alert and noticed every micro movement— the small flare of his nostrils, a twitch around the eyes. His firmness was thawing.

"My nephew is ferrying planes in Los Angeles," he said, and she knew she had him. "I suppose ninety-nine point seven could be a flat one hundred on a different day."

"And it would have been had I not lost my lunch at a rest stop." She craned to watch as he scratched that perfect round number in the designated column, and then she slumped her relief, forgetting her cargo. A nickel clattered on the scale platform and she covered it with her big toe.

"I won't let you or Uncle Sam down. I'll make all of America's uncles proud."

PEGGY HUSTLED TOWARD where Georgia waited down the hall, her eyes enlarged around the magnitude of her disbelief that their plan had actually worked. They didn't exchange a word, but Georgia skimmed her fingers inside Peggy's palm in a covert offer of congratulations. Then they ducked into the bathroom, where Peggy emptied her counterfeit amplification and downsized to her rightful bra, her hard-earned relief already expiring, because her interview was next.

A map of the United States of America with pushpins decorating its face hung behind Jackie Cochran. Books were lined like soldiers in floor-to-ceiling cases, interrupted only by golden trophies of winged women who clutched eagles to their chests. If she weren't feeling so antsy, Peggy might have appreciated that back at the doctor's office, she'd been a walking version of this prize, just another woman on the air base with metallic breasts.

As it was, she knocked on the doorframe ready to vomit. "I'm here for my interview?"

Cochran's hair swooped over her forehead and curled at her nape. "Are you asking me or telling me?"

"I wouldn't be brazen enough to tell you anything, ma'am."

"I think you're more brazen than you let on." Cochran laid her pen parallel to her sheet of paper. Her sultry eyes, smooth skin, and pretty mouth were strengthened by a prominent nose that set her eyes far apart and attributed fortitude to her expression. "The WASP organization values three qualities above all others. Skill, authenticity, and determination.

Skill, because what we're doing requires talent. Authenticity, because most doubt we can do it, so the second substantiates the first. And determination, because that's the most important attribute, not just in pilots, but in all people."

Cochran waited there, measuring Peggy, perhaps expecting her to break. "Yes, ma'am."

"Your chart says you weighed in at one hundred pounds flat. That's a lucky number." Cochran plucked a pack of Lucky Strikes from her desk drawer and shook out a cigarette. Then she pressed the top of a brass propeller plane and released a flame from its engine. "What'd you do? Bloat with salt? Sew magnets in your underwear?"

Peggy's belly swam with sick dread. "No, ma'am."

"Your country needs women, and you seem more than willing to be needed, but there is a weight requirement for a reason. You have more than your share of skill and determination. If you hope to stay, I expect you to become authentic. I'll be checking your weight before we put you in a bomber. You can take that to the bank."

Peggy warmed beneath the glimmer of clemency. She wanted to promise that she *would* take it to the bank, and while she was there, she'd deposit her coins and leave with the real thing, but then she'd have to admit her fraud, so she only said, "Yes, ma'am. I'll do whatever you say, eat whatever you put in front of me. Road kill armadillo, if you have it."

"I'll see about adding that to the menu," Cochran said, wit wriggling from behind her sternness. "For now, welcome to Class 44-2."

Chapter 5

November 2009

VISITING HOURS ENDED, AND KATHY WAS RELUCTANT TO leave her mother alone in the hospital, cracked and disheartened, but also grateful she didn't have any other choice.

As she drove home, she sifted past impressions of present-day Peggy, an old woman who relied on her, to the days when her mother was a hurricane: the first carouser on the dance floor or swimmer to dive into a watering hole; the block-party organizer, even when she was new to the neighborhood; and the prettiest and most charming wife on every air base. Peggy hadn't delegated. She did, and without anybody's help. She ironed clothes, weeded, and chopped wood. She made dinner and Halloween costumes. She ran their household—though not always happily. Kathy often overheard her mother fume to her father, *What am I supposed to do while you zip off to thirty thousand feet? Knit booties and mix Kool-Aid?*

Her force had eroded into grumpy stubbornness, but perhaps it had now deteriorated past that into something more critical. Nobody as proud as Peggy was going to admit she shouldn't live alone. It was up to the children. Kathy thought she'd bear the grief of her mother's relinquished autonomy almost as poignantly as Peggy herself.

The house was dark, shut down for the night. She had assumed Neil would stay up to greet her, hear the latest update, and offer consolation in the form of company and Oreo cookies. That's what she would have done for him. That's what she *had* done for him, through his father's decline. But it was after eight, her husband was depressed, not to mention peeved and bruised about her job, and perhaps he had done enough that day.

She found her way without turning on the lights, retrieving a quilt and carrying it through the kitchen and out the French doors onto the back patio. Neighboring houses glowed as floating candles, and the sky was flecked with stars. The night shivered up her arms, but living in places like Montana and North Dakota had made her resilient to winter. That was just one of the many skills she'd acquired touring the country. She'd learned to slip into a new classroom unnoticed, to roll clothes into a suitcase rather than fold them, and how to be outside in all weather. There was nothing quite like filling one's lungs with air that was so cold it felt like water.

Kathy cocooned into the quilt and texted her older brothers to solicit a conference call. She didn't stipulate the urgency, but she never asked to speak to them, certainly not all at once, so the urgency was implied.

Jimmy, the eldest, wore his cell phone in a belt holster, estimating himself the kind of man people needed to reach, and the second born, Frank, jammed his into a cargo pocket so he could have something to dig out and huff at. Paul, the third, was the one Kathy worried wouldn't respond, having

let his device run out of battery or having dropped it between the seats of his car. But three confirmations dinged in
quick succession, so Jimmy set up the conference; his company enlisted the service and he liked to show it off.

Greetings stacked like hands in a team huddle, the more
assertive of their group slamming down a second or third.
Frank was the most persistent. "Hey Jim, is your company
recording this call?"

"Why, you planning on saying something illegal?"

"I just like to know who's listening."

"Can you guys hear me?" Paul still sounded as if he were
calling up to his brothers in the tree house.

"You've got school in the morning. Isn't this past your bed-
time?" Jimmy asked.

Kathy imagined Jimmy's vigorous embrace, Frank's ani-
mated storytelling, and Paul's mulchy eyes. Their voices
rushed her back in time, through the buildup of their complicated adult dynamic—Jimmy cheating on his first wife, a
friend of Frank's; Frank missing his niece's wedding; the older
brothers' impatience over Paul's depression; the younger
brothers' envy of Jimmy's money; Kathy's conviction that
they all mistreated Neil—until she returned to Christmas
mornings, childhood street games, campfire s'mores, and the
bonds of those whose company you were born into. Family
dynamics were geologic. Tender times stacked atop conflict
like shale on limestone, the strata becoming more complex
with each buried layer. The nuances of shared history fossil-
ized but never disappeared.

Kathy wished she didn't have to disrupt this fondness with
bad news. She wanted to shelter her brothers from the truth,

which was that they were entering new territory, in which their mother needed more hands-on care. Or maybe they'd been there for some time, but nobody had been willing to admit that their feet were sinking into its mud.

She brought them up to speed, leaving out, at least for now, the mess in the linen closet, the soup on the burner, Peggy's body odor, and the excruciating statistic about fractures and life expectancy.

"Damn," Jimmy said.

"Shit," Frank said.

"Thanks for being there, Kat," Paul said.

Kathy remembered her mother in the hospital bed, stiff and small, as if she were carved from hollow materials, as if she were a cadaver in a coffin, and Kathy pulled the quilt tighter beneath her chin. "I'm sure she'd love to hear from you three."

Jimmy and Frank grunted their agreement while Paul said, "Of course."

"So what's the game plan?" Jimmy asked.

"The replacement surgery is tomorrow. She'll recuperate for a couple days and then transfer to a rehab facility for—"

Frank interrupted, "Then what?"

"Then sending her home is an option, but—"

"Are you suggesting she live on her own a week after she broke her hip in the very house where she fell? I don't think so," Jimmy said.

That was the second time Kathy's speaking turn had been snatched away, but conversation was flowing in the right direction without her guidance, so she supposed it was just as well for the boys to believe what she was about to propose was actually their idea. She'd shut her mouth, sit back, and let them work it out.

"Her bedroom is on the first floor, so she doesn't have to use the stairs," Paul said.

"Just because she doesn't have to doesn't mean she won't," Jimmy said.

"We'll tell her she isn't allowed," Frank said.

Jimmy laughed. It sounded crinkly, like a popped foil balloon. "Have you ever known Mom to follow rules? The moment she decides she wants something upstairs, or, for that matter, in the basement, she'll go for it."

"Could we install one of those electric lift chairs?" Paul asked.

"Waste of five thousand dollars, if you ask me," Jimmy said. "We just installed one for my mother-in-law. It was top of the line, but even the cheap ones cost a penny. Besides, Mom would climb over the damn thing before she sits in it."

"Why *is* she so defiant?" Kathy asked. She hardly ever got the chance to ruminate on her mother's foibles. Neil was familiar with them, of course, but Kathy didn't like to fire up his resentment. She could vent to other moms from her neighborhood, some who'd assumed caretaking responsibilities of their own, but then she'd have to explain the history. Here were the only other people on the planet who understood them implicitly.

The question set Jimmy off. "Where did she disappear for a weekend every January? When did she really meet Constance, whom she calls a childhood friend, though Constance isn't from Missouri? What did she have against World War II museums? Why did she organize book and wine clubs when they only seemed to bum her out? When it comes to Mom, my questions are endless."

The last of her brother's inquiries caused Kathy the most pause, because she had noticed the same without really considering it. Every couple years, whether they found themselves in a new small town or a big city, stateside or abroad, Peggy attempted to establish herself among the local women. She hosted cocktail hours, holiday soirees, and Mary Kay parties. She attended aerobics classes. She joined the PTA. During each event, she charmed, entertained, and laughed her brassy bark, but after, she'd shrink back down, collecting the dirty hurricane glasses as if cleanup was her mourning ritual. Kathy's father would emerge from where he'd cloistered in their bedroom and extend his wife a questioning look. She'd shake her head and answer, "It's just not the same," leaving Kathy to wonder, *The same as what?*

Paul offered his timid contribution. "And why did she always burst into tears at the same part of the national anthem?"

"'The rocket's red glare'?" Kathy asked.

"And why did she push Kathy so hard when she'd been fine letting the rest of us go to shit?" Jimmy asked, laughing.

Kathy flushed under their metaphoric gaze, but the attention wasn't unpleasant. In fact, it was validating to know they shared her impression of her childhood. Peggy had drilled Kathy, from her schoolwork to her extracurricular activities to her personality, as if training her to be someone else. Kathy occasionally thought of this when she helped her mother navigate to her grandchildren's photos on Facebook, or when she retrieved Peggy's medication from the pharmacy, demonstrating patience and generosity her mother often denied her.

"Mom is a conundrum, but she's also an invalid, so let's focus on what we can actually do something about," Frank said. "We all agree she can't live alone." Kathy bristled at his consensus without having polled the group, though she just so happened to agree. He continued, "Kat, your bedrooms have been vacated, so Mom could just move in with you, right?"

The proposal staled the fondness she'd been enjoying. She imagined Peggy living in her house, her mouth puckering, the fine lines deepening beneath her Estée Lauder Pretty Vain lipstick as she held Kathy's every move under the light: *Do you always eat sandwiches untoasted? Turkey bacon is not bacon at all. This tea is only lukewarm; at least I won't burn my tongue.* Besides, Kathy wasn't the only Mayfield child with spare beds. Jimmy's house was so grand he featured it on his Christmas card each year, and Frank's place in Arizona—a state famous for its senior citizens—had at least one guestroom. Why was Kathy the default, especially after she'd already done her share? But just as her hackles were rising, she remembered her solid defense.

"I start work Monday, so she'd be alone too much of the day," Kathy said, deciding, once again, not to disclose news of Neil's unemployment.

"Wow, a big girl job?" Jimmy asked.

Kathy slid her jaw until she felt that familiar pop. "You could say that," she said, and kept herself from finishing with *if you want to be an ass about it.*

"Congrats," Paul said.

Kathy routed the discussion back on course. "What about an in-home health aide? That way Mom doesn't have to move out of her house."

"I still don't trust her not to attempt stairs when the caretaker isn't looking," Jimmy said. "I'd prefer if she was safe no matter who was or wasn't watching."

"We're all thinking it, so I'll man up and say it," Frank said. "Mom should go into a home."

The hairs on Kathy's arm lifted. "You don't have to phrase it so crassly."

"Were we all thinking it?" Paul asked.

Jimmy said, "What about those places that aren't nursing homes, but have independent units and medical staff on premises? Some are decorated real nice and host activities like poker tournaments and tai chi classes. That could be perfect. Safe and social."

"Actually, I happen to know a guy who runs an assisted living facility up there," Frank said. "It has a clubhouse and a pool—a real country club vibe. These places usually have a waiting list a mile long, but I could talk to my buddy."

"Flex those muscles, Frank. Let's see what you're made of," Jimmy said.

Before Frank could rear back at the provocation, Kathy asked, "And we're sure this is the right thing to do?"

"Absolutely," Frank said.

"It's the only choice," Jimmy said.

"We love Mom and just want her to be safe. Maybe a facility is the best way to accomplish that," Paul said, though it sounded like a question.

This was easy for them to conclude on the phone, but

Kathy would have to be the one to present it. The air around her felt like cold, wet breath. Tomorrow might bring the first snow of the season. There was a screech somewhere in the dark, and it could have been an owl as easily as a hawk. She burrowed deeper inside her patchwork cave.

Chapter 6

November 2009

THE MORNING OF KATHY'S FIRST DAY, THE GARAGE FELT AS good as refrigerated, and she was reminded how meagerly scrubs held up against winter. She maneuvered around artifacts of their parental identities—bicycles, coolers, beach chairs, deflated balls, lacrosse sticks, and sleds—to reach their Subaru, whose leather car seat nipped through her pants fabric that was as thin as a bed sheet. In a different era, Neil might have risen early to warm the car for her. As it was, he was still asleep, or at least pretending to be asleep. He hadn't even wished her luck.

She was glad she'd sprung for the bigger scrub size, this set in a rich cranberry, which would be festive for the upcoming holidays without being garish. She probably could have squeezed herself into a medium, but the waist would have left an angry indent on her belly, and she'd have spent the day worrying the seams would bust around her rear. She'd made the right choice, but it still pained her to know the last time she'd worn scrubs, she hadn't been a large.

That was just one in an infinite list of differences. The last time she wore scrubs, Paula Abdul was on the radio and Reagan was president, there were no HPV vaccines or 3D ultrasounds, and she and her colleagues didn't use electronic medical records or the internet. The last time she wore scrubs, Kathy knew what she was doing as a nurse, as well as in other facets of her life. She knew how to love on her son, who was still in diapers, and how to support her husband, then a young professional. As a daughter, she satisfied at least one parent. Her father was still alive, and he stopped by every afternoon with the intention of relieving Kathy to shower, nap, or read, but she ended up making them a pot of strong coffee and watching *Scooby Doo* cartoons with Noah nestled between them, while Peggy, a sprightly new senior citizen, swam laps at the Y.

Peggy would be transported to ClearView Rehabilitation Center that morning. When Kathy had visited her the previous evening, her hair had been crumpled against her pillow, its bristly roots matted with grease. Without her requisite makeup, her face appeared like an unfilled coloring book, but at least the post-op daze was evaporating.

"I don't see why I should go to a rehab facility. Plenty of people recover from hip replacement in the comfort of their own homes, cared for by loved ones," Peggy had said. "You were a nurse, for Christ's sake. You could finally put your training to use."

Kathy might have felt guilty for all she was withholding—she *was* about to put her training to use, and not only would Peggy be entering a temporary rehab facility, but there would soon be a more permanent placement—had Peggy not taken the opportunity to once again snipe at her choices.

When Kathy first admitted to her mother that she wasn't returning to work, she was in her kitchen, tucking Fiona beneath her breastfeeding cover while Neil and her father assembled a backyard playground to Noah's hopping delight. Kathy felt full, and not just because she was bursting with milk, but because she had everything she wanted right in front of her. She was no longer being schlepped around the country, living out of what she could carry, uncertain what or who the future might bring. She was anchored, and complete. The realization came to her unbidden, and any filter or foresight was worn by sleep deprivation. "I'm staying home this time. For good." Peggy, who was sipping steaming black tea though it was eighty degrees outside, began to blink rapidly. She hadn't even appreciated Kathy becoming a nurse when she could have been a doctor, or at the very least a nurse practitioner. But a housewife, when Kathy had options, when she was *lucky* to have options? Peggy turned away from her. "Sometimes it's hard to believe you came from my body."

In the hospital, Kathy didn't share the reason she couldn't care for Peggy because she didn't want to watch her mother galvanize at the news of her daughter back at work, or draw up smugly. If it was up to Kathy, she'd delay confession until Neil got a job, and then she'd quit and never tell her mother at all.

"I don't know enough about physical therapy," Kathy had said instead.

Her job and the facility's visiting hours meant Kathy wouldn't see her mother until her day off, nearly a week into Peggy's stay, though she failed to warn Peggy about her impending absence, since there'd be no way to explain it.

Kathy had relocated enough to learn that conflict could

be moved away from if one just waited long enough. In the occasional cases that it was necessary to confront a problem, she'd let her mother or her brothers take care of it. They had strong personalities so she didn't have to. Besides, when too many fought for the reins, a family could be steered clear off the road. This was the dynamic that worked for them, or so Kathy had always thought. Kathy's avoidance with Peggy could be called passive, deceitful, even cowardly, but she preferred to think of it as prudent. And this seemed particularly true in the case of her mother. Peggy had a broken hip. They should progress one step at a time.

KATHY'S JOB WAS at a small OB-GYN practice with three doctors—two women who handled the obstetric patients, and one man who covered gynecology. She would be, as she'd put it to Fiona, "working for the man."

Dr. Smith was in his fifties, bald inside a shaggy crown. He was small. It wasn't just that his height was diminished—though he was an inch or two below Kathy's five seven. His nose was just a pull off his face, his eyebrows were fine, and his hands were petite. In fact, it was as if all his bones were slimmer than those of most other people.

What Dr. Smith lacked in stature he made up for in temperament. He spoke just a decibel too loud for comfort. His lips quivered in constant anticipation of a joke. When one finally arrived, his laughter came in spurts.

But he'd also given Kathy a job after two decades working only a few blood drives and health fairs a year, which meant he was more confident in her abilities than she was. (Would her hand tremor when administering a flu vaccine? Could she calm a distressed woman on phone triage? Would she decipher the computer system?)

She worried her skills had oxidized without use, and that she'd be rusted into paralysis. Dr. Smith appeared to believe in her, and maybe that's all she needed to know about him.

DR. SMITH'S DESK might have mistaken itself for a Greek temple with the Corinthian pilasters embedded into the corners. It occupied so much space in his office, it must have been transported in pieces and built from within. Manila folders were stacked neatly, two gold ballpoint pens were stuck like darts in a walnut stand, and a 3D model of the female reproductive system nested inside a pelvic bowl. Everything was in its just right place. Her new boss must have had to adjust his executive chair to its tallest setting. Kathy reprimanded herself for imagining that his feet were swinging off the floor.

Dr. Smith teetered on a grin. "I asked you here early for an orientation, but the truth is you won't need one. I'll always be right in front of you. I just wanted to be the first friendly face to welcome you."

Kathy channeled nervous energy into her foot, which bobbed below his line of sight. "That's so kind. Thank you."

"Hold your thanks until I give you this." A well-oiled drawer glided open and Dr. Smith plucked out a box of Russell Stover Pecan Delights. As he slid it across his desk, his mouth fought against self-satisfaction, but then he saw a receipt clinging to the box's plastic skin. He snatched the thin paper away and crumpled it in his fist. "If twenty-five years of marriage has taught me anything, it's that you can't go wrong giving chocolate to a woman."

An oddness wormed down Kathy's backbone, though she wasn't sure why, as this was, by all accounts, a nice gesture. "I do like chocolate." She balanced the gift on her lap like someone unaccustomed to babies might hold a newborn. "Sorry, but what did you mean when you said you'll always be right in front of me?"

"You're my shadow. That's the purpose of your position. I must have explained that in your interview. You never know what a patient might say these days, you understand. It's better to have a woman in the room during exams, so I hired myself an insurance policy." He smacked his desk because this, apparently, was a very good joke. Kathy was familiar with the use of chaperones of course, but not as a primary job responsibility. She cracked her jaw involuntarily while Dr. Smith rode his hilarity to shore. He weaved his fingers before him and settled. "I'm kidding, of course. Your role is absolutely indispensable. Nurses have the interpersonal skills doctors lack, don't you think? Not to mention prettier handwriting. Teamwork makes the dream work, as they say."

"Wouldn't it be cheaper to hire a medical assistant for this position?" Kathy regretted the question as soon as she asked it. She was on the cusp of her family's first paycheck in half a year—she should just shut her trap and endorse it.

"Don't try talking yourself out of a job. Besides, you aren't only a chaperone. You'll write up and communicate treatment plans. Medical assistants aren't qualified for that. Plus, they have their own responsibilities, or as I call them, the three s's: sterilizing, stocking, and scheduling."

An indistinct prickle wrapped around Kathy's scalp. "Of course."

Dr. Smith made a gesture to stop her right there, although she hadn't gone anywhere. "Medical assistants do critical work too. Don't get me wrong. We all have our lanes. There are administrative tasks and there is patient care. I wouldn't ask the medical assistant to bill an insurance company, just like I wouldn't expect the office managers to perform a pap smear."

The chocolate package crinkled under her grip. "Right."

"Because pap smears are my job," he said.

"I understand."

He leaned back enough to make his chair oscillate, pleased by how he'd handled the situation. That interaction had the potential to unravel had he not been so conversationally dexterous. "Shall we get to it?"

THE FIRST PATIENT was a college student with a soft shape and a nervous habit of adjusting her glasses with her knuckles. When Kathy entered the room, she said, "I didn't shower this morning. That's probably like not brushing your teeth before going to the dentist. I don't want to be rude. Should I just reschedule?"

It rushed back to Kathy—how the forced intimacy of the profession could expedite human connection. It was a marvel and, on that morning, an inadvertent generosity that flattened Kathy's nerves.

"You're fine as you are," she said.

Kathy recorded the patient's medical history before inviting her to change. If a woman had to address questions about menstruation, sexual activity, and discharge, she should be allowed the dignity of doing so in jeans and a sweater. When Kathy exited, she waited exactly four minutes before knocking—long enough for the patient's heart rate to slow to resting before checking her vital signs, but not so long that she'd grow fidgety. Kathy returned but prolonged the girl's privacy by not looking directly at her. She continued this discretion as she invited her onto the scale and maintained a firm nonexpression as she nudged the weight past 180.

"That's actually better than I thought," the girl said.

"Well, good," Kathy replied.

As Kathy took the patient's temperature and pressed her fingers into the soft meat of her wrist, she felt as if she were stepping into a silhouette that fit her. She wasn't pretending. This was her identity. Glitter flurried inside her, and she wondered if everybody could see it.

DR. SMITH BEGAN his exam with a cringey joke. "If athletes get athlete's foot, what do elves get? Mistle-toes." Aside from the self-indulgent pun, which, when Kathy thought about it, didn't even make sense, Dr. Smith was professional. In fact, Kathy was impressed. His hands moved with the grace of a conductor as he readied himself and then looped through the forceps as if he were the one playing the instrument.

After, Kathy followed Dr. Smith to his office, where he received her with the barely contained expression of one teeming with a secret. "Sometimes I wonder if I'm a gynecologist or an agricultural vet."

"I'm sorry?"

"You know, because she's quite the heifer."

Kathy relinquished her jaw to gravity and crossed her arms over her own ample belly.

Dr. Smith laughed more deliberately to emphasize his joke. "I'm kidding, of course. Things can drag around here. We have to find our fun."

Pressure pushed down on Kathy's brain as she returned to relay the doctor's assessment. She no longer felt that she'd stepped back into her own vacated form. Instead, she felt clumsy, as if a foreign force was operating her arms and legs. The patient smiled readily, and Kathy wanted to vaporize.

She assured her that everything looked fine, but if there was one thing to work on, because everybody had something to work on, her blood pressure was slightly elevated. It was nothing to panic about but, if she had time, and Kathy knew kids today lived such busy lives, she had two kids herself who barely had time to call their mother, the patient could benefit from regular walks. Kathy enjoyed a long walk herself. It was nice to get fresh air and free your mind with repetitive motion. Twenty or thirty minutes a day. That's all. No big deal.

The girl's cheeks bloomed pink and quickly deepened to scarlet. Kathy reddened too. She was a hypocrite, doling out advice when she could stand to shed weight herself, as well as a coward, since she'd underplayed the doctor's treatment plan, which was a disservice to the health of the patient. She knew the ineffectiveness of walks; she embarked on multi-mile routes around their town, and that hardly toned her ham-shank thighs. Kathy was saying too much and not enough, when what she really wanted to do was embrace the girl and insist she was perfect just the way she was.

PERIODICALLY THROUGHOUT THE day, Kathy felt a jolt of misplacement, as if arriving in a dream where she'd been tasked to land a plane, and she'd think, *I am not qualified to do this.* She'd steal away to the break room and wait for her heart to come to rest, pretending there was an urgent matter on her phone.

In reality, the screen was blank. She hadn't received one text from any family members. Not her brothers, her husband, her mother (though she had the pass of ignorance), or even her children, which hurt most of all. She wanted to be important enough for them to consider, and if her first day didn't merit outreach, what would?

Maybe if she inserted herself into her kids' atmosphere, she'd trigger congratulations, which would count for something, so she texted Fiona, *Hey honey. Do you need to pop home to do laundry? You know you're always welcome.*

Fiona responded, *There are four Laundromats within walking distance of my apartment. Why would I drive thirty minutes?*

Kathy cracked her jaw and soothed herself with Tetris.

There were many times, though, that the motions of the job came to her naturally, as if she'd picked up with an old friend, the years between conversations shrinking into insignificance.

As for her exchanges with Dr. Smith, the sixteen patients that followed came and left without incident, and those positive experiences were almost enough to smother the memory of his initial deprecation.

Maybe Dr. Smith had just been nervous to train a new employee, or maybe he dispensed enough grim diagnoses that comedy (though inappropriate and not altogether clever) had become a survival mechanism. Besides, he'd given Kathy this opportunity. She had to remember that.

Kathy stopped by his office to say goodbye, and he looked pleased to see her, like they had done good work together, which, she realized, they had. "I know you took a risk hiring a person so out of practice, and I just wanted to thank you for giving me the chance."

"It wasn't charity, Kath," he said, and here she expected him to explain that her performance proved she was worth the risk and every cent he paid her, that she was good at her job, and they needed her as much as she needed them. This was the next step in well-mannered discourse. But Dr. Smith continued, "I actually prefer candidates from your age demographic. If your kids get sick, they're old enough to take care of themselves, so I don't need to arrange for temps."

Kathy mentally scanned the young employees she'd met but realized they all worked for the obstetricians. Everybody on Dr. Smith's roster, from the receptionist to the office manager to the medical assistant, was middle-aged. He had a type.

Being over forty was usually an obstacle. It certainly had been for Neil. Kathy was fortunate to have found an employer who didn't discriminate, and in fact considered her age a perk. She *benefited* from Dr. Smith's particularity, so why had her muscles gone rigid?

"See you tomorrow," Dr. Smith said.

When Kathy stepped outside, the clouds hung like a

dropped ceiling in the sky, so low she nearly stooped as she hurried to her car.

NEIL HAD DINNER waiting when she got home, even if it was only underdone rigatoni and jarred sauce—rigatoni was her preferred pasta variety, so that was notable. They worked through noodles with too much bite and he asked the right questions: How were the patients, your boss, coworkers? Did it all come flooding back? She answered vaguely and tried not to notice that his chin was dimpled, as if inquiring about the bare minimum required a small amount of bravery.

After they ate, though, he split a Miller High Life between two flute glasses. "It *is* the champagne of beers," he said, and lifted his in toast. "To your comeback." He clinked and kissed her. His lips were cool and tasted of grain and tomato.

When was the last time their mouths had merged this way? Kathy wondered. She'd kissed his head to urge him to bed or to wake him from a nap that was bleeding into evening, but she couldn't remember the last time he'd reached and offered his delicate lips, beneath which was an invitation, and the defenselessness of want.

They balanced on leather barstools at the kitchen island, where they ate most of their meals since the kids had left, as if the table, a world away, wasn't worth the trip. Their faces hovered in the space between them. Neil's fingers grazed her jaw, and although she hadn't experienced it in ages, Kathy knew that graze and the persistence of that kiss. A knot of sparks tightened in her groin.

Kathy could see the rest following their prescribed choreography. Neil's lips would remain while his hand searched for hers and he'd guide her upstairs to their bedroom. They would go through the motions of their marriage—good faithful motions that worked almost every time—and she was eager, and relieved to have her husband expressing love again, and to be physically connected after so much emotional distance. It meant that he'd crested a personal hurdle and was feeling able and confident enough in spite of his losses. It also meant he'd forgiven her, though her only crime was competence.

But instead of seeking her hand, he gripped the legs of her stool. Its feet scraped the wood until their seats resisted each other. Then he grasped her thighs, wrapped her legs around his waist, and his fingers reached behind her, digging, drawing her close. For a fleeting moment, she regretted the broadness of her backside. She should have taken better care of herself—for him, for her. But he didn't seem to mind.

His hand weaved through her hair and secured her in place, and his kisses were determined and probing. He wanted her. He needed her in a way that wasn't like him or them, or at least hadn't been that way in a long time. This urgency sent confetti into her head. It had been a while since they'd done anything for the first time. She followed his lead, or perhaps she obeyed—but no, because what he initiated she wanted too.

Soon her scrubs were around her ankles and she was standing in the middle of their outdated kitchen, and he was on his knees, kissing what was suddenly bare so hungrily Kathy worried she'd get caught in his teeth. There was a dull throb as he brushed over an ingrown hair. She dismissed it, laid a hand on his head, and gazed out the window over the sink, whose black mirror reflected two hurt people making each other feel good again. She wondered for a breath who might be on the other side of the night, privy to the scene, but then Neil was on his feet, guiding her across the room and lowering her onto the kitchen table. That day's circulars, awaiting coupon-cutting and recycling, crumpled under her weight. Her shoulder blades pressed into the unyielding surface and Neil shimmied the elastic waist of his pants down. His elbows propped on either side of her, and with a rush and a startle that welled from her belly and out her throat, the two who had been drifting alongside each other were in unison again. But he was setting the rhythm. He was in charge. Maybe that didn't matter as long as it felt good and right for both.

Kathy became cognizant of the onion of his unwashed body. Surely Neil couldn't have known this was the event that would follow dinner, but that didn't excuse skipping so many showers, and how hard was it to apply deodorant?

Kathy concentrated on all that was pleasant, and there was plenty. She became an active participant, rocking in opposition. When she felt her body climbing, she drove harder, and so did he, and they were in collaboration, partners rising to a shared peak. Soon she ascended enough to see her surge ahead. Knowing she'd arrived, and would ride the plateau to the final burst, was a relief almost as satisfying as the climax itself.

They reached the top in a tandem contraction of muscles and nerves, their hearts thrashing against their architecture. When they released, her husband's flushed cheek lowered onto the cranberry polyester over her breastbone, resting atop the symbol of all that she could do.

Chapter 7

September 1943

IT WOULD BE EASY TO FEEL ANONYMOUS INSIDE THE WASP barracks, three rows of squat white dormitories more charmless than a highway motel. Inside were six replicas of everything: twin metal bed frames with rolled-up cots, military blankets and pillows, standing lockers, and plain desks dividing the space in half. Otherwise the room was blank. Their unit was connected to another by a latrine, where twelve women would share a couple toilets, sinks, and showers.

On the bare springs of her assigned bed, Peggy felt herself disappearing. At home, people didn't approve of her, but at least they knew who she was. Her identity was established. Here, she could be anybody, which was a freedom as well as an affliction. Her edges were beginning to fade, which stirred panic, but since she'd already have to sharpen them, she could, if she chose, alter the figure.

Her five roommates—including, to her delight, Georgia, as well as Millie, Pamela, Cheryl, and Connie—were quietly busying themselves, unpacking their few belongings, perhaps staving off their own homesickness. She'd never before been in the company of female flyers. What a phenomenon, to be rounded up with women all bound by the same passion. Who knew what ways they would find to enrich and drive one another through competition, encouragement, and example to betterment? Peggy had been in Texas less than a day, and already Georgia had pushed her to doggedness. Imagine how much they could elevate each other over the course of months. This was Peggy's chance to become the best version of herself, a distinct individual, but woven into the fabric of this singular society.

Peggy wanted to uplift her fellow sky pioneers, likely weathering the same isolation and doubt separately, so she bent over her wooden footlocker and sifted through its contents. There was the dress uniform the women had to purchase themselves, consisting of men's khaki shirts and trousers, a white blouse, and a plain unpiped garrison hat—an outfit famously dubbed the General's Whites—as well as provided flight equipment: a parachute, goggles, helmet, and two pairs of government-issue coveralls.

The WASP had received U.S. Army Air Forces surplus mechanics jumpsuits in sizes large and extra large, as if, because they were performing man-sized jobs, the women should fit into men's clothing sizes. Peggy stepped into the pant legs and slipped her arms through the sleeves. She folded the cuffs over three times. The crotch fell to mid thigh. The fabric billowed.

Her baymates were rousing from their introspection, so she put on a show, sashaying her hips, then lunging to satirize the excess material. The women began to laugh. Georgia even wolf-whistled. It was hot, but Peggy performed anyway, working up a sweat until her nerves had been trampled on the catwalk. Her outfit might have been formless, but she was finding her shape.

Peggy twirled the fabric belt for effect, and then pulled it through the buckle until she met resistance. "We just need to make a few extra holes," she said. "Any of you WASP got a stinger?"

AN HOUR LATER, the new class, dressed in the General's Whites, collected outside. The sun was dropping, releasing its hold on the day, and the easing heat felt like approval.

"Attention!" The officer's olive-green uniform was decorated in badges and pins and topped by a slouched cap. His features were carved with impatience, but Peggy thought she could take a stroll on the ledge of his jaw. She bit the inside of her lips. He barked, "Chin down, shoulders back, heels touched, toes out." The women muddled through the directions, checking themselves against one another to make sure they'd gotten it right. By the officer's resigned tone, they hadn't. "You aren't here for decoration. You will be trained as cadets. Marched, drilled, and put to the test. Prettiness doesn't count in the air, and neither does pouting. Incompetence is dangerous. If you are inadequate, you will wash out."

He marched off, but his warning hovered as heavy as heat.

TO REACH THEIR section in the mess hall, the WASP had to troop by the male cadets, who ogled and whistled as if the parade was for their benefit.

"Careful, today it's horse meat!" one shouted.

Millie, Peggy's baymate with braids the color of apricots, asked, "Is that true? I own horses."

Peggy eyed the gray meat flopped on her dish. She'd offered to eat armadillo, so she figured horse was only an improvement. Still, she said, "We're in Texas, among cowboys. The Lone Ranger wouldn't eat Silver."

When they'd settled around a table, forks reluctantly in hand, Connie, with a face like a drop of cream, asked, "You gals excited to get into the air tomorrow?" Her voice was velvety, as if perpetually confiding.

"More like terrified." Millie's shoulders caved in her chest.

Georgia slapped her back, squashing her slouch, while her other hand shoveled food uninterrupted. She was the only one eating with vigor. Through a mouthful, she said, "What's there to be scared of? Tomorrow is just a show-and-tell with a commanding officer."

Millie upheld her posture but tugged a braid. "What if I get the creep who escorted us in? I don't do well being chewed out."

Peggy revisited that cliff edge of a jaw and said, absently, "Sometimes all bitter coffee needs is a little sweetener."

Millie answered, "Yeah, well, sugar is rationed."

"I might have some to spare," Georgia said. Mischief pranced in her eyes and she plucked a prune from her plate. "In fact, I'm going to squirrel away this here army strawberry until I rustle up some chocolate. Who knows when we'll need to have ourselves some romance."

"What's that grouch's name, anyway?" Peggy asked, doing her best to sound casual.

"Mayfield," Georgia said. She gulped water from her cup and wiped the residue with the back of her hand. "Major Mayfield."

"INSPECTION!"

Their bay was in no state to be inspected. Peggy had yet to make her bed or put away her flight gear. Heck, she was only halfway dressed. But the voice was unequivocal. There would be no rain checks. She yanked her pajama pants on and searched for quick fixes—a tuck, cover, or shove.

"If you're looking for a paddle, it sank farther up shit creek," Georgia said.

"Good evening, major." Pamela's hair was ashy, almost colorless. Loosed from its bun, it cascaded down her chest. Her nose was snubbed and upturned as if constantly sniffing something rank. Her bed was the only one made, its sheets pulled tight enough to play quarters.

"If we'd known we'd be having company, we might have baked a cake," Georgia said.

Major Mayfield's sharp jaw bowed into a chin cleft. His eyes were stern as he walked the length of the bay, his hands gripped behind his back. At the end, he spun neatly. "This is how you present for your first inspection? Clothes strewn, beds in disarray? Three demerits."

"Do the demerits apply to those who passed inspection?" Pamela asked.

"Nobody passed. Haven't you heard? United we stand, divided we fall," the major said. His jaw muscle pulsed like a heartbeat. "There's a can of black paint outside the door. I suggest you apply it to your windows. The cadets are lined up outside, and you haven't disappointed."

A forest fire spread across Peggy's chest. Her temper was another quality condemned back home, such as the time she kicked the shin of a boy who tugged her hair or when she spit at the teacher who called her dense. She wasn't here to be an object for the men to admire. She was here to fly.

She stormed past Major Mayfield into the night. As promised, paint materials had been left at the door. She grabbed a brush by the neck and swung around the building to where four male cadets peeped through their window. Peggy hurled the brush. She missed, but it landed close enough to startle a yelp from a voyeur. They shot to their feet and sprinted across the field.

Inside, Peggy heard muffled cheers.

* * *

The morning reveille blasted Peggy's slumber to shreds. At any other time, in any other place, she would have collected the remnants and stitched them back together, but the sound of warming plane engines grumbled beneath the horn.

The bathroom was instantly crowded with women moving in and out of the toilet stalls like commuters through turnstiles. Peggy fought for a piece of mirror to roll and pin her hair, but was nudged back by others brushing their teeth, washing their faces, and applying makeup.

"Ah aff a spih," a woman said, and Peggy stepped aside.

Just as her exasperation was expanding into something wilder, she spotted Cheryl in their bay, tying up her own pitchy hair in a scarf sling, where it would be stowed away from the wind, sweat, and dust. Sensible, and pretty too.

"Can you show me how to do that?" Peggy asked, and Cheryl went pink with pride.

While Cheryl wrapped, twisted, and tied, Pamela

squirmed into enormous coveralls beneath her bed sheets and Connie did the same stooped in a corner, her back to the group. Georgia, though, didn't seem to notice their discretion. She was sitting cross-legged on her cot, wearing only ruffled underwear and the bra Peggy had borrowed, one knee pulled to her chest, clipping her toenails. Her bosom spilled over the cups, and the pearl flesh of her belly rolled. Peggy had never seen so much of another woman's body. Not even her own mother's. Peggy tried not to stare, though Georgia likely wouldn't have minded if she had. Her thighs dimpled where they met the mattress, and a spate of red blushed down her arms. She was unselfconscious, wholly herself, and beautiful.

Peggy had intended to wait out the bathroom rush and change in the privacy of a stall, but once her waves were secured inside a turban, Cheryl rupturing the knot into a rose, she decided this was no time for reserve. They had work to do. Peggy undid the buttons of her pajama top and let it fall to the floor, revealing to her bay, though, thanks to the painted window, not to the base, her novel bareness.

OVER SEVEN MONTHS of training, ground school subjects would include weather, aerodynamics, principles of flight, military courtesy, engines, navigation, Morse code, first aid, and instruments. As Peggy focused on the sergeant at the front of the classroom, she realized that never before in all her time at school had academics been presented specifically for her. Before, she received an education as a consequence of the boys requiring education, like the chorus of a play brightened by way of the star's spotlight. There were lessons to be taught, and what was the harm including the female students? But now the chorus had been drawn to the forefront. They had been recast.

Each cadet took a turn in a Link Trainer, a flight simulator with tiny wings and the suggestion of a nose and tail. When a pilot climbed in, the hood was pulled over the top, enclosing her in a box, like a coffin with controls. They were assigned a course, and the officer at the panel simulated a variety of weather scenarios and emergency situations. While the pilot worked her instruments, the box shifted, spun, rocked, and swayed.

Then, the hundred members of their group assembled for calisthenics in the quad, a stretch of dust spotted by clumps of grass. Under the glaring eye of the midmorning sun, a new sergeant ordered them to stretch their arms, raise them overhead, and squat and squat and squat. They lunged and marched, dropped to their knees, fell to the ground, and hopped back up again. They jogged and jumped until they were so coated with sweat and tears, the dust on their napes turned to mud.

Peggy's skin radiated and her muscles were weary. She thought of languid walks along the riverbed back home, cruising above Longmeadow in her Model A, a glass of lemonade pressed against her neck, and a breeze sneaking through an open window to whisper secrets across her legs. She couldn't be distracted from her current state of discomfort. Her coveralls were soaked with perspiration. She couldn't find a clean square to blot her running makeup, but she was almost in the air. They were almost in the air.

FIVE PRIMARY TRAINERS perched on the runway. Their blue plywood bodies alighted over fixed landing gear at a forty-degree angle, their propellers trained upward. Yellow wings were spread on either side of tandem open cockpits. These Fairchild PT-19As were more powerful than Peggy's Model A, gulls to her sparrow, and if she proved herself on them, she'd soon fly a hawk.

Major Mayfield marched to the front of their formation, followed by the harried shadow of a male cadet. The major pivoted like a slammed door, and his voice knifed through the humidity. "Attention! The flight line will form at this time every day and will last for five hours. You will be assigned to a civilian or military flight instructor in groups of four. Each group will have an hour with a primary trainer. When you are not in your PT, you will be in formation for the full five hours." Major Mayfield extended his arm toward the male cadet, who responded with a clipboard. "I will recite your assignments. Do not move until all names have been called."

The air was thick, so difficult to breathe that Peggy felt she had to concentrate to sort its properties and keep what she needed, exhaling the rest.

"Lewis, Margaret," Major Mayfield called. "With me."

Peggy clasped her hands behind her back in a congratulatory grip.

The formation fell apart and reorganized before their designated instructors. Peggy was first in her group, with Georgia behind her. She lifted her chin to the major to show attentiveness. He thrust a paper in her direction.

"This is your cockpit procedure. Memorize it forward and

backward. It is your ticket to ride. Know it tomorrow or pack your things."

Peggy read the procedure while Mayfield marched to the administration building. By her sixth repetition, she had it memorized. On her tenth time through, an engine started.

A female cadet was at the helm of the first primary trainer, her instructor in the cockpit behind her. The plane bumped down the runway, as eager and tenacious as its pilot. The rest of the cadets went rapt. This was their revolution. A woman flying for the military. The first trainee of their class was about to take flight. As soon as she returned, the next would have her chance. Cadets already occupied the next PTs, except the plane reserved for Mayfield's group, which sat vacant.

The sun beat down. The grass withered. A bee—or maybe it was a wasp, in a symbol of bitter irony—hovered, dropped, and ascended again in search of pollen. The women in line behind Peggy began to sag, but the circling planes only irritated Peggy. She toyed with her necklace. Her sighs became more unrestrained, until she finally kicked the dirt.

"Cool down, Trigger," Georgia said.

She was indeed behaving like an impatient horse, but there was no reason their group should be grounded, except that their jerk of an officer apparently had more important things to do than teach a bunch of broads how to fly. It wasn't their fault he was sour grapes. They should get to do what they came to do.

When they were dismissed to wash up for mess, the women who'd soared to heaven and back skipped ahead, while Mayfield's group trudged toward their barracks.

"I swear, if we don't get to fly tomorrow . . ." Peggy said, her fists clenched.

"Look at you, madder than a cat getting baptized," Georgia said. "It's adorable, but also impractical. I love a woman's fire, but you need to learn when to show your flame, and when to let it quietly burn. We missed one day. If you flip your wig, you'll lose all the days to come." Georgia patted Peggy's back and then withdrew her hand, which glistened with Peggy's sweat. "Don't take this the wrong way, but you need a shower something awful."

Peggy pinched the damp fabric off her belly. "How are we supposed to wash these monstrosities? They're too big for the sinks."

"I'll wash yours if you'll wash mine," Georgia said, and winked.

They entered the shower stall in their coveralls, each armed with a bar of Lava soap. The women who'd washed before had run through the hot water supply, but Peggy didn't need any more heat. She had this person who seemed to understand her despite barely knowing her, as well as the possibility of flight tomorrow, and all her days to come. If she just managed to listen to her orders, bite her tongue, and stay above one hundred pounds, she'd have more than she ever dreamed. She could do that. Soap and dirt ran off their bodies and puddled around the drain as brown foam, but clean water kept coming, spraying cold absolution. Peggy lifted her face to drink it.

* * *

"Cadet, cockpit procedure," Major Mayfield ordered the following afternoon.

The first cadet in his flight line licked her lips and spurted off the steps. The major turned on his heel and headed toward the planes, but the cadet didn't move.

"Go!" Peggy urged.

Their Fairchild PT-19A awakened from its long slumber. The propeller rotated, and then spun so fast the blades blurred. It rolled, and then accelerated down the field, churning the powdery soil. The back wheel picked up, and the nose tilted back. Then it hopped off its front wheels and floated there, a miracle, unattached. It levitated higher, no longer a creation of man, but a fantastical species. The cadet returned with hair frizzed around her flight helmet, positively beaming.

"Cadet, cockpit procedure," the major said to the next in line.

"Form One checked," the woman began. "Right tank full, left tank full, safety belt fastened, gosports checked . . ." She trailed off, and the major didn't allow time for recollection.

"Next," the major said, dismissing her, and Peggy stepped forward. "Cockpit procedure."

"Backward or forward, sir?" Peggy asked.

"Cadet?"

All her muscles clenched. She had meant to show blind obedience, as if she'd taken his order to know the procedure backward literally. But he thought she was mocking his authority. Mocking the entire system. And maybe she was, just a little bit.

Her gaze fell to the wings pinned to his lapel and she recited the procedure like a prayer she'd known her entire life. When she finished, his stare bore into her, revealing no indication of what would come next. Perhaps he was punishing her with that doubt, or perhaps he hadn't yet decided. Finally he marched toward the PT, and she almost couldn't believe it, her muscles reluctant to unscrew themselves from her bones.

She hurried to keep up, lugging her parachute behind. When they reached the plane, she used the wing to hoist herself into the first cockpit. The tub was deep and narrow, a canoe with wings. Ten dials dotted the dashboard. She straddled the stick and placed her feet over two pedals.

The major tapped Peggy's shoulder, and she flinched. "Gosports, cadet."

Peggy accepted the hoses and stuck them into the flaps of her helmet. The other end was attached to the major's mask so his orders would be sent directly to her.

"Talk me through the procedure, cadet." His mask was strapped on like a muzzle.

"Talk *you* through the procedure, sir?"

"Shall I say it backward?"

She inhaled a measured breath and exhaled her temper. At least she would get into the air. "Form One checked."

A cadet cranked their engine to life and the Fairchild began its taxi. There was the mess hall. There was the barracks. There was the horizon. As they hurtled ahead, scenery smudged into her periphery. The wheels bounced over a divot and dust billowed into her mouth. She clamped her lips and swatted at her face. Then she pulled the goggles down from her forehead. *Pull down your goggles. That should be part of your precious cockpit procedure.*

Then it happened, a moment of indecision, when anything was possible: up or down, earth or sky. They wavered there, and then instead of falling, they rose.

The plane shuddered around her. She'd never been so far above the earth. She simultaneously felt as if they might hurtle into space and as if she could reach down and pluck up the mess hall, or a tiny cadet. She was omnipresent, their world's maker.

Then the nose pulled up, as if climbing onto tiptoes to reach for a top shelf, and the throttle between Peggy's legs shot into her stomach. The engine stuttered and stopped. Silence roared. This was wrong. Terribly wrong. The plane held its position for half a breath. Then the nose dropped. Wind whipped and whistled in her ears. They fell from the sky's arms. She squeezed her eyes shut—she didn't want to see death coming. She didn't think to scream. Then the throttle pitched forward and the engine coughed on. They realigned and flew forward.

Peggy's knuckles had whitened around the steel braces of the cockpit. Her fingers twinged as she unfurled them, and her hands fluttered up to console her heart.

"Stall," the voice in her ears said.

The throttle hurled back into her stomach so fast she didn't have time to protest. Her hands wrapped back around steel.

The nose dipped and Peggy whimpered, anticipating another drop. Instead, they rocked back and forth, the wings waving hello to everybody below. Then the plane jerked, and Peggy's arm crashed against the side. Clouds rotated down while the Texas terrain whirled up. The seatbelt wrenched against her belly. Peggy saw dirt and houses and specks of people above her. They were flying inverted. The belt strained to hold her in. She couldn't feel the seat above her. She hung by a strip of cloth, grateful for every pound she wasn't. The PT rocked as if attempting to loosen Peggy from her seat. Then, with a lurch, it reeled upright and Peggy's bottom bumped down.

She blinked rapidly, but before she could process the events, the plane spiraled, once, twice, three times around, a bottle rolling on its side through the atmosphere. Her surroundings eddied blue, white, and brown and her head marked the degrees of their rotation like a clock hand; she could do nothing but hope time ticked quickly.

When they righted, the voice in her ears said, "Spins."

Rage fogged Peggy's vision. The nerve, the arrogance, all because of a minor slight. It wasn't her fault he wasn't assigned overseas with the action, that he was stuck on the home front with a bunch of sky broads. He'd gone too far. Georgia's warning came to mind, but to hell with it, Peggy thought. Mayfield would see her fire and be scorched.

They landed, and before the Fairchild rolled to a complete stop, she tugged the hoses from her ears, unbuckled the lifesaving belt, and hopped from the cockpit. She hit the ground and stumbled with the acceleration imparted to her by the moving plane. Her fingernails dug into her palms. She seethed.

Major Mayfield unclipped his mask and dismounted the Fairchild in two clean springs. His eyebrow quivered, almost imperceptibly, but Peggy caught it. He was waiting for Peggy to explode. That was his intention—to frazzle her in the air so that, on the ground, she would self-destruct. He wanted Peggy to send herself home.

When Peggy was within arm's reach of the major, his lips parted and his chest rose with breath. But before he spoke, Peggy pivoted around him, pulled herself back up onto the plane's wing, grabbed her parachute, and looped its straps around her shoulders.

"Thanks for the ride, major," she said, and leapt down to the dusty earth.

Peggy wasn't going home.

Chapter 8

November 2009

WHAT STRUCK KATHY FIRST ABOUT CLEARVIEW REHABILI-
tation Center was the stewy smell of baby powder, urine,
and hot TV dinners. It recalled how sensitive she'd been to
odors throughout her pregnancies, when the wrong whiff of
a patient would double her over. She wondered how expecting staff managed in this place.

The décor was sterile, as if a hospital wing had detached
and sailed down the I-95 corridor. The floors gleamed under the fluorescent lights, everything was coated in eggshell
paint, the tables were wood laminate and steel, the doors had
commercial-grade levers and were equipped with handicap-
accessible push buttons, and the only wall art was glass-
encased fire extinguishers and emergency protocols.

What awaited Kathy wouldn't be any warmer: a mother
forsaken to convalesce alone for a week (no, Kathy reminded
herself, five days), without a visit from her only local child.
Worse, Kathy had silenced her phone at her mother's ringtone, as guilt dropped around her like heavy snow.

Instead of groveling, Kathy would break bad news mas-
querading as the opposite. Frank's friend had worked a small
miracle. There was a spot for Peggy at Seaside Assisted Liv-

ing Facility. At the end of her rehab, she would move directly there, without going home.

Kathy passed a man slumped in a wheelchair. She wondered if he'd been waiting for assistance so long he'd fallen asleep or if she should check his pulse. A woman shuffled by on a walker footed with grungy tennis balls. A pair of residents gazed out a window onto the roaring highway below.

Seaside's website featured spirited seniors with shiny silver hair strolling gardens and laughing over games of bocce. Grandchildren spilled across their laps inside their independent apartments. For all Kathy knew, that was deceptive marketing, and Seaside was the hell to this purgatory. Maybe she and her brothers were being hasty—callous, even.

Then Kathy remembered what Frank had said on their most recent conference call. "You have to be firm from the start. If Mom catches a hint of wishy-washiness, it's over. We could lose her spot. My buddy is doing us a huge favor here. Don't be the messenger if you can't handle it."

Kathy clung to her purse like an inadequate life raft and sunk deeper into the building.

IN PEGGY'S ROOM, a coat of fern-green paint, primrose-patterned quilts, and a beige valance over the window were nods toward coziness, but not enough to disguise its distinctly medical property. Kathy thought of one of Peggy's expressions, "You can put lipstick on a pig, but she still stinks," just as an industrial toilet bellowed across the hall.

Though it was still midday, blinds descended the room into evening. The floor-to-ceiling curtain that divided the roommates had been pulled, but not enough to block the view. The woman in the far bed filled the entire mattress. She grinned gummily.

The quilt on the nearest bed, presumably Peggy's, was gathered near the foot, exposing rumpled sheets. Her mother was elsewhere, in physical therapy or, perhaps, Kathy thought hopefully, making a friend. Once Peggy had regularly invited air force wives for mint juleps on the porch, but she'd become solitary in her older age. Many members of her circle had moved in with children, or worse, died. It would be nice for Peggy to have social gatherings again. Kathy made a note to work that into her proposal. Then she gestured an apology to the roommate and stepped out.

"Car trouble?" The wintry gust of her mother's voice whisked around the doorway. Kathy stepped back in and found Peggy in an armchair wedged into the corner, her hands folded primly over the closed paperback in her lap.

"No, why?" Kathy asked. As soon as the words escaped, she saw where this was going. She'd played right into Peggy's trap.

"I can't imagine why else it would take a week for you to visit. Although it doesn't explain your broken phone."

Peggy was still striking, even beautiful, but she appeared to have shrunk, unless it was just the chair, whose cushions were so flat it seemed as if the arms were swallowing her. Her hair fell down her shoulders in straggly curls, dry and frizzy at the ends. The uncharacteristic style made her seem older and younger at once—wild but wearied. Still, she was elegant, even here. Her blouse was stitched with ribbons of lace, and the high, almost Victorian, neck was buttoned to the top, her necklace resting atop the collar. Her makeup was fresh and vibrant, particularly the coral of her lips. Her long fingers were thick and gnarled by age, but coiled around the faded upholstery as if she were a small queen rejecting her diminished circumstances. Kathy became keenly aware of her larger size and frumpiness. She should have put on some mascara, or at least a more fitted top.

Kathy said, feebly, "I've been busy."

Peggy inched taller, as if nourished by her daughter's unease. "Busier than Fiona, who borrowed a friend's car to see me, and everybody who managed a phone call despite jobs and children, some younger than yours?"

"There was—" What, a sick neighbor, a volunteer obligation, the truth? Her jaw edged toward the satisfaction of a crack, but she stopped herself. Her mother hated that habit. "I should have been here. I'm sorry."

Peggy's puffed feathers compressed, almost disappointed, but she composed herself and continued, "Did you see what your brother sent?" Kathy appreciated the change in topic until she realized the question was a different entry into the same conversation: the ways in which Kathy fell short.

A bouquet of lilies the shade of Peggy's lipstick burst from its vase in such gratuity that the whole thing could be toppled over by the draft of vented heat. Each bud was boastful and waxy and of a size that could bite the head off a moderate-sized rodent. It blocked half the television screen and infused the room with the heady stink of mourning. It was Jimmy's work, that much Kathy intuited. His excessive generosity was the certain brand that begged for notice, which Peggy was liberal in providing.

"How could I miss it? How could anyone?" Kathy asked.

"Frank sent chocolates, and Paul a slew of books," Peggy said, motioning to her end table, where the gifts were piled. "They're good boys."

Kathy leafed through the stack. She and her mother shared this pastime, though for different reasons. Kathy read as a means of burrowing into place, while Peggy read to be transported elsewhere. There were seven novels in total, all large-print paperbacks.

Kathy paused over a historical fiction book with a compelling font. "This sounds interesting."

"Take it. There's less of an urge to read about the war when you lived through it."

Kathy anchored herself to keep from rolling her eyes. It was just like her mother to speak for an entire generation, as if she could decree how millions of people felt, as if no one of a certain age watched *Saving Private Ryan* or *Life Is Beautiful*. Besides, what did the heroines of this historical novel have to do with Peggy, who weathered the war on her Missouri farm? Yes, she'd undergone rationing, scrap drives, victory mail, and neighbor boys who were lost in combat, but that was a far cry from being an active contributor. Did Peggy think she'd osmosed the experience of every wartime hero simply by being their contemporary, or had she acquired their exploits by marrying one, inheriting his feats like any other asset? She hadn't even known Kathy's father while he was in combat. They'd met after Japan's surrender, when the troops were sent home.

"I'll leave it here in case you change your mind," Kathy said, and then to punish her mother, added, "I'm busy, re-member?"

After getting their snipes in, they settled into the affable rhythms of a social call. Kathy asked about her mother's hip, the progression of her strength and mobility, and if she was eating. As Peggy answered, sometimes at length, especially about the food, she unfolded her arms and her tone loosened. She called the pancakes flour Frisbees and the beef inadvertent jerky. She was trying to make Kathy laugh, and she did.

As Kathy prepared to merge into a discussion about what came next, she remembered the roommate on the other side of the curtain and felt suddenly self-conscious—so much so that she lowered her voice. "You'll be discharged in a few days."

"Thank the sweet Lord."

Kathy plowed through her mother's rejoicing. "Don't you think it'd be dangerous for a person in your condition to live in a three-story house all by herself?"

"In my condition?" Peggy asked, dryly. She didn't yet see what was coming, so was still trying for humor. "Is there a pregnancy I don't know about?"

"I just mean, what are you rushing home to, exactly?"

"What are you trying to say, exactly?" Peggy mocked, but she'd gone still, a deer in an open field.

Kathy took a breath to calm her nerves, but it only added a flair of melodrama. "We were thinking—"

"We?"

"The boys and I. We were wondering if instead of returning to all those stairs, it might be better to transition you to safer accommodations." Kathy dropped the bomb and rushed to gain distance, dragging her mother before shrapnel riddled them both. "You are too important. We don't want you taking unnecessary risks. You should be surrounded by people who can make sure nothing like this happens again."

"Why don't you just package me in bubble wrap?"

Kathy continued her pitch as if uninterrupted. "But you are in luck. Frank secured you a last-minute spot—"

"I tripped one time and you are ready to institutionalize me?"

"Let's not get carried away."

"You're the one getting carried away." Peggy's fingers interlocked on her lap as if they were the only thing binding her together. "This is no way to treat a person, least of all your mother. You are skipping steps. Entire floors."

"We thought it'd be nice for you to have a built-in social network."

"I have a built-in social network," she said, nearly shouting now. "It's called family."

Kathy felt the ceiling lower. Peggy had four children, but as the nearest, and really, as the daughter, Kathy was the sole buttress of responsibility. Her mother would need critical care. She couldn't be expected to provide that.

"You'll still have your children," Kathy said, though she hardly had three of them as it was. "You'll just gain more people around you."

Peggy's breathing had grown ragged, and she began to frantically pick at lint on her pants. "You're done with me. That's what this is. You and the boys have had enough and are ready for me to die. Well, I'm sorry to break it to you, but you can't discard me like a bag of old clothes. I'm of sound mind and can make my own decisions. If you're too busy, that's your business, but you can't make me someone else's problem. I have free will and legal rights, and as soon as I can manage on my own two feet, I'm walking straight out of this dump and never coming back."

"The other place isn't like this," Kathy said. "It has a pool."

"These crypts are all the same, meant for the feeble or demented—not me." Peggy's voice was rising again, and Kathy worried a staff member would stop by to confirm everything was all right.

"Why don't we table this for now?"

Peggy stared at the blank wall, inches from her face, that divided them from the hallway. Her wistful determination would have looked more natural if her chair was positioned beside a window, as if gazing bleakly into her future. Kathy imagined her mother's internal dialogue: *What does a woman have to do to get a view around here?*

Peggy said, "If I have my way, when I leave my house, I'll be rolled out on a stretcher."

Kathy considered turning some of Peggy's favorite overwrought directives around on her: *Try to mingle. Smile wider. It'll be an adventure; don't you want an adventure?* But just then, an acrid tendril snaked through the scent of lilies, wriggled up her nose, and blossomed into something fetid. Peggy's nostrils flared too.

"Oh, for God's sake," Peggy said in an emphatic whisper, thrusting her head toward the roommate on the other side of the curtain. "She shat herself."

They called for an orderly, who arrived with a bundle of starched linens, as well as the women's lunch. He was rail thin, with acne pockmarks from what were likely difficult teenage years. He dropped the food trays by the door and, without any acknowledgment to Peggy and Kathy, crossed the fog of sick. The woman on the other side murmured a hello or an apology, but Kathy didn't detect any response.

Kathy and Peggy sat vigil while he worked, as if it would be rude to chat while the roommate's humiliation was exposed and sanitized. While they waited, the stirred-up smell only garnered more power. Peggy tucked her nose into her high neckline and Kathy cupped her hand over her face. When the orderly was through with what Kathy knew to be nothing short of a magician's trick—wiping the woman clean, laying a towel down, and remaking the sheets with her body still on the bed—Kathy made a point to search for his eyes, to offer appreciation and admiration, but his attention was locked on the floor, the sheets rolled into a soiled ball at his hip.

Kathy waited for him to wash his hands and return to distribute the meals, though she had no idea how anybody could eat after that. The smell remained tangibly in her mouth and nose, and seemed to have sunk into her hair and clothes. She felt sullied, like Lady Macbeth hallucinating a stain on her hands. *Out, browned spot.* But the orderly never reappeared. He'd left the trays on a stand by the door like a kennel worker leaving a bowl for a dog.

Kathy didn't know much about the roommate beyond that she might benefit from rice and a banana, but Peggy was a woman of good taste, a competitor who refused to call even the longest board game quits until there was a winner, a host who never let a guest's glass go empty, and a mother who annually decorated their houses into Christmas wonderlands.

Her zip and zest may have aged into tartness and tang, but she was a person, and for a staffer to treat her as a stray animal was unacceptable. And Kathy had just been endorsing another facility.

"Hungry?" Kathy asked, but she pushed her tone to ensure the joke wasn't missed.

Peggy expelled a hard laugh from beneath her shirt-mask. "As God as my witness, I may never be hungry again."

"Should we move Jimmy's arrangement closer to get a better look?" Kathy transported the heavy vase to the bedside, hoping one fragrance would overpower the other. They directed their noses to it, repressing giggles so as not to embarrass their neighbor.

Peggy peeled back her mouth covering and directed her face toward the curtain. "How are you doing over there, Trish? Can I get you anything?"

The woman's voice returned meekly, "No thanks, Peg, and sorry for the stink."

"Don't give it another thought. With a nose this old, I can't smell anything anyway."

It was easy for Kathy to overlook her mother's strengths, concentrating instead on the ways Peggy hadn't done right by Kathy. But this grace reminded Kathy that her mother was capable of profound love. She knew how to make a person feel special. Her attention often made Kathy feel special.

Kathy hoisted her purse onto her lap and dug through it until she found a bottle of nail polish, which she shook to incite the satisfying clack. When she was five, Jimmy told her the sound came from teeth pulled from little girls, and Peggy spilled the entire bottle onto a plate to prove to her it was only a metal ball. Then she made Jimmy sing his sister to sleep for the next week, not realizing how attached they'd grow to the routine. Jimmy sang to Kathy most nights until he moved out.

Kathy said, "I know you missed your nail appointment this week, so I figured I could paint yours. You know, if you want."

"I'd like that very much."

The approval sent a tingle down Kathy's spine, and she was brought back to the euphoria of their good times: lying across her mother's lap while she combed her hair; Peggy a cappella bugling while Kathy got ready in the morning; dressing as Lucy Ricardo and Ethel Mertz for an air base Halloween party; dancing to *American Bandstand* in their pajamas; and Peggy bracing Kathy's bicycle seat around a cul-de-sac until she let go, sprinting alongside her shouting, *You're doing it, Katherine. Everybody look at my big girl. She's doing it.*

Kathy's tear ducts burned, so she returned her attention to her purse. "I also picked up your mail."

"Start with the love letters, and never get to the bills."

Kathy set aside anything with a plastic window, and stacked cards with return addresses she recognized—a Mayfield cousin, two air force wives, Peggy's childhood friend Constance—until she came upon creamy stationery that was plush enough to be cloth.

"This one feels expensive," Kathy said.

"You open it. I'm not wearing my glasses."

Kathy slipped her thumb under the corner. The tear was decisive, and she felt a little like she was ruining something valuable. It was an invitation, she could tell by the separate pieces for the ceremony details and the RSVP, but the gold insignia stamp made it seem governmental—a strange direction for a wedding, but military families could prove that brand of patriotic. Even so, the gold tassel was a bit over the top. Then the word "Congress" leapt from the page.

"Holy crap." She read carefully so she didn't misspeak. "You're invited to a Congressional Gold Medal Ceremony."

"You're kidding."

"To recognize the Women Airforce Service Pilots," Kathy said, laughing. Her father had served as a war pilot, though he'd never mentioned anything about the WASP. She felt the familiar rush for the man who had done so much and whose humility kept him from broadcasting it. Her pride was followed by the sharpness of missing him. "Daddy must have done something special, and they're inviting you to honor him. You have to go."

Peggy gripped the arms of her chair, as if electrified. "This has nothing to do with your father or with me. It's a bureaucratic error."

Kathy figured Peggy was being modest on her husband's behalf. "But—"

"It's a mistake. End of discussion."

Chapter 9

September 1943

PEGGY STUDIED THE NAVIGATION CHARTS THAT QUILTED her bed. Her head throbbed, and a blister that contained its own heartbeat bulged beneath her big toe. Her back muscles howled, and her legs dug ditches into her cot. How could she get up and do it all again tomorrow? Then again, how could she not?

She tugged her shirt from the waist of her khakis. The hem was soaked. She never thought she'd miss Missouri winters, with their heaps of snow and winds sharp enough to slice through coats, but here she was, ready to trade inferno for tundra. Here she was, missing ice. Oh, ice. What she wouldn't do to slide a cube across her neck. The idea was nearly erotic.

"Studying is making me a little nuts," she said.

"You need a change of scenery." Georgia tugged a loose cigarette from her shirt pocket and pinched it between her thumb and forefinger, smoking like a man. "Let's go out."

Peggy snorted. "Where, to the mess hall?"

Georgia's lips parted to a glint of teeth. "Downtown."

Millie pulled on her braids. "We're quarantined to base for the first two weeks. If they catch you, they'll dismiss you."

"So we won't get caught," Georgia said.

The same person who reined in Peggy's temper for the sake of her station was now willing to risk it for a fun night out. Georgia either was a tangle of contradictions, was confident she'd evade capture, or simply found another exploit so alluring it made the gamble worthwhile.

The more Peggy got to know her friend, the more it seemed Georgia played by her own rules. She had looked around and found a society that pressured women to keep up with beauty standards that kept changing—flat to ample chest, straight lines to hourglass, bob haircut to wavy tresses—that afforded women the right to vote and encouraged them to work, but only in certain sectors and only until they were married or when dire circumstances necessitated; that paid actresses to exemplify women who gladly gave up careers for domestic happy endings; that provided contraception but also condemned those with reputations. The established customs didn't make sense to Georgia, so she made her own. She decided for herself what was fair, beautiful, and possible. She was the curator of good, the designer of her future, her own pilot. She was a marvel to behold.

Cheryl said, "No way. They might send me home as it is. I'm not volunteering an excuse."

Peggy was thankful not to be the wet towel on Georgia's proposition. She wouldn't want her daring friend to think her a coward. "That's all right, Cheryl. We're clever. We can make our own fun right here."

Connie dropped her paperback onto her footlocker. "Thank goodness. I was going to burrow inside my book until you all returned. What are you thinking?"

Peggy scanned the room. There wasn't much to work with. "You gals like cards?"

"We have too many for bridge," Cheryl said.

Peggy waved her off. "Bridge is a woman's game. Let's play poker."

Mollified, Georgia peeled back her mattress, unveiled a glass bottle, and jostled it so its contents sloshed around its neck. "Georgia's finest."

The women circled on the floor, and Peggy dealt the way she'd heard boys do it back home. "Ladies rule here, so we're playing Follow the Queen. The last card shown after her majesty is wild. Wilds can change, gals. That's the fun of it. No queens, no wilds. Aces are high."

They used tubes of lipstick for bets, but everyone checked the first round. Peggy had a pair of fives as her facedown cards. When she dealt another round of cards up, a queen appeared in front of Cheryl.

"Here we go. Our first wild," Peggy said as she flipped a card in front of Millie. Five of hearts. Peggy was in possession of two wilds. "What do you say? Any bets?" Millie slid a lipstick forward. So did Georgia. Peggy's brick-red Dorothy Gray tube joined theirs.

Peggy continued dealing, her excitement building. She was sitting on a secret, one with potential to grow in power. Would she use her wilds to make three of a kind, complete a flush, or assemble a straight? How surprised the others would be when she turned them over and they realized what all she could do.

Millie dropped out. Georgia added another lipstick to the pot. So did Peggy. Then, in the last round, Peggy overturned a queen, and disappointment dropped in her gut.

"What's the new wild going to be?" Georgia asked, pleasure dancing across her expression, as if she'd known this would happen all along.

Two of clubs. Peggy lost her wilds, leaving her with a pair, and a weak one at that. She had only what she'd been allocated at the start.

She laid the deck down. "All right, Georgia. Let's see what you've got."

"Trip Jacks," she said, handing Peggy the bottle of moonshine before Peggy even conceded her lesser hand. "Something tells me you shoot like a pro."

Peggy threw her head back and gulped hard. At least she made the girls applaud.

They played a few more rounds. Pamela checked or folded, never bet. Connie's cheeks enflamed after her first drop of liquor. "Tastes like gasoline," she said. Cheryl took two swigs and went to bed. Georgia bet strong and never lost, although she took some swigs for fun, while Peggy bet strong and always lost.

Peggy's mother called booze devil's water and never touched the stuff. Her father was gifted one bottle of a neighbor's hooch each Christmas that he nursed all year. Peggy wasn't used to drinking. After an hour, her skin buzzed and her breath huffed hot. She felt capable, hilarious, and impossibly happy. These were her people. This was their time. She'd finally found where she belonged.

She reached for a lipstick and traced its color around her

mouth. "Georgia, my dear, I'm ready for your grand expedition."

Georgia thumbed the mess around Peggy's mouth. "Are you serious?"

She nodded, and the room shifted, so she smacked the floor for balance. "We deserve to blow off some steam, Major Sourpuss be damned. What do you say, gals?"

The skin on Millie's forehead furrowed and seemed thin enough to tear. "You're bonkers."

Peggy swung to her baymate in bed. "Cheryl?"

Perspiration matted pitch-black hair to Cheryl's temples. "I thought we *were* blowing off steam."

"This was just part one," Peggy said.

Cheryl shook her head. "I've got letters to write."

"What do you say, Connie?" Peggy asked.

Connie pulled her knees into her chest and rested her chin atop them. Her face was as shiny and exposed as a clean plate. The blush in her cheeks deepened. "I'm too chicken."

Peggy knew Pam wouldn't go along, but she needed to confirm she wouldn't snitch. She must have revealed this in the lift of an eyebrow, because Pamela twisted her thumb and forefinger at her lips and gestured a key being tossed away. At that, Peggy's fondness expanded enough to accommodate even her.

PEGGY CLUTCHED GEORGIA'S arm as they crept behind the barracks, listening for footsteps or chatter. They'd changed into dresses and heels, their hair was pinned, and their faces painted. If they were spotted, there'd be no denying their intention. Had Peggy's caution not been dulled by liquor, she would have turned back. But the razor edges of her anxiety had been filed down, and she felt sure they could do this, that they *should* do this. They were queens. No, wilds. No, wild queens.

The horizon was striped with lavender, and above it the sky clung to the last remnants of dusky light. The women's silhouettes would be stains against this soft backdrop. They sprinted to the next unit.

"How are we going to get into town?" Peggy was tickled that this only now occurred to her, and a giggle bubbled behind the question.

"Shh," Georgia said. Ahead, two male cadets knelt at the window of a female bay. One cadet's head was adorned with little blond curls, and the other's was buzzed up the side, a gelled wave perched on top. "I was hoping to exit out the front gate, but we can't cross in front of these Peeping Toms, so we'll have to take our chances down that slope and over the chain-link fence."

Peggy kicked off her heels. They'd be in plain sight for the next few minutes. Peggy's feet pounded the sandy earth, her arms worked, and her panting sounded to her ears like wind roaring at high altitude. When she reached the decline, she leaned back against the momentum. Her feet lifted and replanted, lifted and replanted. Then her foot landed on a patch of loose dirt. Stones and sand spilled out from below her. She flapped her arms to regain control or master the fall, but the skating foot ascended before the other was ready to catch her. Peggy crashed on her backside. The impact discharged the breath from her body and sent a jolt up her spine. She tossed and turned down the remainder of the bluff, bashing her shoulder and thigh until she finally rested at its base.

Georgia crouched beside Peggy and searched her eyes. "Not one peep the whole way down. For a pretty little thing, you're as tough as a pine knot."

Peggy patted tears back into place. When she'd gotten a handle on everything that burned—never mind her embarrassment, there was no managing that—she dusted her hands and slapped dirt from her dress. "There better be some killer-diller men in this town," she said, and Georgia's molasses mouth spread.

They tossed their heels over the fence and climbed the diamond slots. At the top, Peggy swung her leg over and took one last glimpse at Avenger Field. Barrack windows glowed with the life within: women writing letters to sweethearts, parents, and friends; washing uniforms for another day's use; setting hair; reading; studying; and dreaming. For an instant, Peggy wanted to return to that place of shared goals and individual ones, to review the triumphs of the day and prepare for the challenges tomorrow was sure to bring, to live in communion. But there would be plenty of time for that, and they'd already come this far.

PEGGY'S BUZZ RECEDED as the two women strolled, arms linked, half-heartedly singing the WASP song: "With the wind and the sand in our eyes and our goal placed up high in the skies, we are the WASP who serve the Air Corps so true. We're coming, just watch us ZOOM down upon you." Once they'd gotten through all the verses, all they were left with was the sound of their shoes on gravel. Overhead, stars pricked through the night's cloak.

"How big of a mistake was this?" Georgia asked.

Peggy laughed. "The biggest."

"At least we tried. No one ever truly regrets having given something a try."

"Tell that to my sore ass," Peggy said.

A rumble rose up from the darkness, and two eyes beamed in the distance. The canvas hood of a Ford Cabriolet was lowered. Inside, the driver's eyes and mouth were small but kind, as if they knew how little they'd been given but were trying to make the most if it. His nose was delicate but long and hooked, and his thin white hair was parted to the side.

"Am I dreaming, or is that the president of the United States?" Georgia asked.

Peggy took this as a sign. Maybe this wasn't the biggest mistake after all.

"Y'all look like you could use a lift," he said.

Georgia opened the door and slid into the row beside the driver. "Take us to your finest watering hole."

A collection of buildings cropped up beyond the plains, four blocks of two-story establishments—a town hall, a movie theater, a candy shop, the Bluebonnet Hotel, and a general store—all built from brick and trimmed with teal.

The driver pointed to the only storefront still illuminated. "White Horse Tavern should suit your needs. If you're look-ing for something a little quieter, Mel's Hardware is around the corner. Mel sells doorknobs and nails during the day and spirits at night. He started carrying liquor under the counter when alcohol was banned, and the practice just stuck."

"Thanks for the ride, Franklin," Georgia said, and patted Peggy's leg to signal their exit.

"It's Bill."

The interior of the White Horse Tavern was wood paneled from head to toe. It could have been the inside of a shipping crate. It was longer than it was wide, with a bar to the right, booths to the left, and an upright piano pushed against the back wall beside a patriotic jukebox. The air had the un-settled feeling of kicked-up dust, as if something significant had just occurred and the patrons weren't sure what to make of it. An older man in a pinch-top cowboy hat sat beside his sturdily built wife at the bar, their forearms tanned. A younger man sat by himself in a booth, half of his face shad-owed under a ridge-top cowboy hat. By his patchy facial hair, Peggy guessed he was in his late teens. A thin woman in a short-sleeved black dress sat at the piano singing Tommy Dorsey's "I'll Never Smile Again." Her voice was resigned, as if she'd accepted her fate of forever being background music.

"Whose funeral have we crashed?" Georgia asked.

The bartender's sleeves were rolled up to the elbow. His mustache lifted in surprise at the sight of them. "All I got is rum," he said, and Peggy noted how meagerly his shelves were stocked. "It's difficult importin' much else these days."

"How do a couple of respectable gals go about drinking rum?" Georgia asked.

The bartender slipped his fingers beneath the base of two glasses curved like women and placed them on the bar. As he mixed brown spirits with vermillion-colored liquid, the female singer began to croon Bing Crosby's "Only Forever."

"They call them hurricanes," he said and eased the glasses toward the women. "On the house."

"What for?" Peggy asked.

"You girls are from Avenger Field, ain't you? For your good work."

Peggy's throat tightened, and she kissed the straw to loosen the lump. The first sip hit her tongue cool and sweet, followed by a chastising bite. When she swallowed, the fruit flavor emerged refreshed. It was sensational.

She went straight to the boy in the booth. "Howdy," she said, trying on the greeting, but he kept his focus trained on his lowball glass. "Howdy," she repeated, more audaciously. The cowboy hat tilted back to reveal closely set eyes. He scowled, as if waiting for Peggy to hurry up and get to her point. "What's a cowboy like you doing avoiding enlistment?" Peggy asked, and Georgia squeezed Peggy's bicep.

The boy's hat pivoted to shield his face. He wrapped one hand around his glass and his elbow stabbed the table as if staking territory. Peggy saw then that one of his pant legs was knotted at the knee, and she pinched her eyes shut. She'd only wanted to be coy. How could she have been so stupid?

She knew the need for an able body in a farm region. How would he irrigate a field, spread manure, haul crops, operate machinery? What would he do now?

"I'm so sorry." Peggy searched for something to say, anything to offer him. "Please, enjoy my drink. It's very good." She knocked the glass against the table and its contents sloshed over the edge.

She spun away, but Georgia caught her wrist. Peggy wheeled to her with an expression that said, *Let's get the hell out of here*, but Georgia dropped into the booth across from the young veteran.

"You're one of the few men around to show us a good

time. This is your window. If you have the good sense God gave a goose, you won't waste it sulking."

Peggy was sure the cowboy would smash his fist on the table and ask what they knew about anything. They were just silly girls breaking sensible rules, searching for frivolity when there was serious work to do, when the lives of the friends he left behind were on the line, when he'd already sacrificed so much. Who cared about a good time when there was so much loss and pain? When evil was real and pervasive?

Instead, he said, his voice a low growl, "All right, but I'm keeping her drink."

Three hurricanes later, the cowboy thanked the women for their company and made his way home. Without a man to blush at their teases, Georgia and Peggy decided it was time they do the same. The horn would sound reveille in just seven hours.

"Perhaps we'll run into a kindly gentleman with an automobile at Mel's Hardware," Georgia said. By now, her vowels had rounded into marbles.

The last drop of light had long since evaporated. Beyond the flicker of street lamps, darkness was heavy and complete. As they made their way down the sidewalk, Peggy's toe caught the back of her heel, and she sailed forward, landing hard on her hands and knees.

Georgia cackled. "Hey lady, act like you've been to town before." She hoisted Peggy to her feet, smelling of cigarette smoke, fruit punch, and sweat. Her eyes were glassy as they fought to focus on Peggy's. "All the gals are aces, but you're my favorite."

Peggy prickled under the voltage of being deemed special

by someone she found so extraordinary. Perhaps a person's first absolute friendship was its own kind of romance, a connection forged between two people who'd been searching for each other before they even knew their counterpart existed. She bit the inside of her lips to keep her smile in check.

"You're mine too, you nutty souse," she said.

The sign for Mel's Hardware was a square plank on a short chain, hand-painted with white letters. Peggy pulled the door handle just enough for its bell to jingle before Georgia encircled her waist and yanked her back.

"What the heck?" she said.

"Didn't you see him?" Georgia's eyes spun like propellers and the corners of her mouth twitched.

"Who?"

"Mayfield. He's at the bar."

Peggy dropped into a squat. "Please tell me this is some kind of twisted southern humor."

"It's the God's honest truth."

Peggy eyed the facade of Mel's Hardware, deciding. Then she waddled back to the window, still in her crouch.

"Are you insane?" Georgia hissed.

There he was, the major, stooped over a jar that once held nuts and bolts but now cradled ice lumps in their own melt. He looked like he couldn't manage the weight of his own head. One of his thumbs consoled the other. His tensed jaw made him seem on the verge of shouting or sobbing.

Peggy was startled by the impulse to stroke the major's cheek, to run her fingers through his hair and pull his head into her chest, to hold him there. Booze was making her bonkers.

"Let's get the hell out of here," Georgia said through her teeth. "The White Horse bartender was about to close up. He'll give us a lift."

They started back the way they'd come. A shaving of moon hooked into the sky, thin enough to shatter but bright enough to demand its own space in the night.

"Cadets!"

Peggy's fingernails dug into her palms so hard they might have come out the other side.

Georgia faced the major full on. "Hell of a night, ain't it, major? We're just here patronizing our gracious hosts and sampling the local culture."

Mayfield was as upright as a flagpole. Peggy cast her attention to his feet. "We are sincerely sorry, sir."

"Apologies do little for your country. If frivolity is important enough that you'd defy your commanding officers, then you aren't deserving of training," Mayfield said. "It's time to free your spot to someone who will take it seriously."

"We screwed up, I know," Peggy said, begging. "But let us stay. Let us prove what we can do."

His Adam's apple dipped. "Why would I do that?"

Her arms opened. "I'm useless at home. I'm useless anywhere but in a cockpit. I can help. Put me to some goddamn use."

Mayfield's eyes seared. "One wrong move, one mention of this night, and I'll send you packing. Do you understand me?"

"Yes sir," Peggy choked out, and Georgia echoed the same behind her.

"You won't leave base for three weeks after you've been

granted permission, and you'll do double time in the Link Trainer. If you stay, I'm going to make you earn your keep."

Peggy didn't dare move until his footsteps faded into silence. Then she turned to her friend and was surprised to find her smirking.

"See? He's a teddy bear," Georgia said.

THE NEXT MORNING, Peggy felt as if all the moisture had been siphoned from her body. She had to unstick her tongue from the roof of her mouth. The memory of their rebuking knocked inside her.

"I was sure we'd never see you again," Millie said, sitting up in bed. "Was it a wild time?"

Connie was brushing her hair, clear-eyed and alert. "Tell us everything."

"It was a hoot," Georgia answered, sounding startlingly, impossibly fresh.

Peggy narrowed her eyes against the brazen morning sun. "How are you so chipper when I feel like I've been run over by a tractor?"

"Because, my pet, I'm a southern lady of substance."

Millie fell against her bed and curled onto her side. "I'm feeling under the weather myself. My monthly curse arrived this morning." She grabbed her pillow from beneath her head and hugged it against her middle. "I might spend the day in the doctor's office."

"Are you serious?" Georgia asked.

Meekly, Millie said, "That's what we do back home during our time of the month."

"If we run to the doctor every time Rosie shows up for her

shift, we'll just prove we are the dainty creatures they take us for. Stick in a tampon and show the world what we can manage."

"I don't use tampons," Millie said, horrified. "I'm a virgin."

"Well bless your pea-picking little heart," Georgia said. "Strap on your sanitary belt then. We've got work to do."

PEGGY BALANCED ON the edge of heaving through breakfast and, during ground school, she willed her fuzzy brain to focus on wind drift and gasoline formulas. The Link Trainer completely undid her.

The officer at the controls sent Peggy through a vortex of maladies only possible at the hands of a vengeful God, a mythical combination of downdrafts, gust fronts, and headwinds; a tornado, blizzard, and hurricane; an engine fire, radio failure, and instrument malfunction. Vomit lurched up her throat. Lights flashed and sirens sounded. Her head was ready to detonate. Peggy crashed into hypothetical burning embers, crawled out, and fled to the bathroom, where she hurled into the sink.

Calisthenics was no treat either. She made her movements small. For the first time in the flight line, she didn't itch for the sky. She yearned for her bed.

"Lewis, you're up," Mayfield said.

Lord have mercy, Peggy thought.

The defeat the major had betrayed the previous night had been patched over. Now he was a beacon of order, so much so Peggy wondered if the man in the hardware store really existed, or if she'd seen a mirage because she'd been searching for it.

"You feeling all right, Lewis?" the major asked and lowered his goggles.

"Swell," Peggy said.

The control tower flashed green, and she shoved her throttle and barreled toward takeoff. The wheels bounced and
sent a sour burn up her esophagus. She swallowed it, rushing
toward the horizon. When they were going fast enough, she
ascended. The fresh air cleansed her like rinsing mud from
boots.

A cloud dazzled in the sun, and their propeller sliced into
its fleece. Peggy reached cautiously toward that misty white.
Her fingertips wisped its surface, and the cotton exhaled
cool breath.

Below, squares of russet, ecru, tan, and taupe patched a
brown coverlet. Two asphalt runways crisscrossed to form an
obtuse X, flanked by a smattering of tiny rectangles—their
barracks. They were flying so high, Avenger Field didn't resemble a toy air base, but a drawing of one.

Peggy took one more loop to allow time to decrease her
altitude and choose the best position for landing. When she
faced the runway head-on, she put on half flaps to increase
drag and ease her descent. She checked the left wing to confirm that the flaps lowered, and when she glanced to her
right, she saw a rattlesnake stretched in a loose spiral, flat
enough that the wind couldn't pick it off.

Its diamond-backed leather crept toward her. It could
crawl into the cockpit, slither up her torso, throw its un-
hinged jaw wide, and sink its needle fangs into her neck. It
could pierce an artery. She could bleed out. This was the
Garden of Eden at ten thousand feet, and the devil was eye-

ing her. The snake's pitchfork tongue flicked from its mouth. The ropy swarm of scales and muscle was steered by an arrowhead and liquid black eyes. She could almost hear its death rattle over the vociferous wind.

"What are you waiting for?" the major said. "Land."

Her breath was shallow and fast, like she was filling a bucket with a teaspoon. She wanted to ask Mayfield what to do, but the gosport microphone worked only one way.

Maybe she should reach over, grab the snake by the head, and whip it off before it got any funny ideas about where to place its venom. She wriggled her bottom; the safety belt was fastened tight. Good for surprise rolls, bad for rattler eviction.

The plane responded to her body. Even a sigh could send the Fairchild in the wrong direction. She clenched her muscles into tight fists.

Peggy felt the snake's attention as she dropped the plane. She tried to concentrate on landing, but couldn't keep out thoughts of *Snake, snake, snake!* The ground rushed up too quickly. The plane would crack upon impact. She'd surely crash. Peggy pulled the nose up to flare the plane. They slowed.

When they rocked to a stop, Peggy released the dam on her fright. She hurled her thirty-pound parachute pack across the wing. It fell to the ground, taking the cowboy Satan with it.

"Not a fan of rattlers?" the major asked, his voice still feeding into her ears.

Peggy ripped out the hoses. "Did you know it was there before we took off?" Her voice rattled as if the snake had made its way inside her throat.

"The question is, why didn't *you* know?" Mayfield said. "Get your parachute and shoot two more landings."

Peggy's fists worked at her hips. "Why didn't you say anything?"

"Why don't I just fly the damn plane myself?"

Peggy had been wondering why he didn't wash them out the night before. Now she knew. He wanted to torture her. No, he wanted a scene, to expel her in public, to hold her up as an example: *This is why women shouldn't be in the air.* She wouldn't allow that. She steadied herself.

In one fluid motion, the major unbuckled his seatbelt and jumped to his feet. "When I say get your parachute and shoot two more landings, I want you out of this plane and on the ground before I finish the order."

She jumped to the ground and skirted the wing. The snake could be anywhere, hiding beneath the parachute, prepared to spring faster than she could react. Missouri had snakes too—copperheads, even a few rattlers—but this Texas variety seemed particularly determined. Its head was the shape of a missile. Could its fangs penetrate her coveralls? If she was bit, how long would she have? Enough time to tell the major she'd seen what he wanted no one to see, or at least she thought she had?

The parachute had landed beside the wheel and was stained by Sweetwater soil. Peggy inched toward it, prepared to retreat at the first sight of scales. Once close enough, she nudged the strap with her toe and recoiled, just in case. When nothing was disturbed, she tugged the parachute toward her. A shadow moved beneath the plane. The snake was behind the wheel, slithering away. Peggy snatched the parachute and scrambled back onto the wing, controlling her breathing so Mayfield wouldn't hear her fright.

"Next time do a snap roll. The snake will sail right off." Mayfield's voice was firm, but there was a flicker of something else inside it. Something hushed.

Peggy stilled, listening, but it was gone.

Chapter 10

November 2009

KATHY RETURNED THE INVITATION TO HER PURSE, WHERE it could mingle with her floss picks and a grubby Chapstick. Later, she'd contact the provided email address and explain that her mother was unaffiliated with the WASP. There must have been a mix-up with her maiden versus married name, or with the pilot license record, or perhaps Peggy was in fact invited on behalf of Colonel Mayfield, despite her insistence to the contrary. As Kathy exited the rehab facility, she wasn't altogether worried about how Congress would accept her mother's regrets. She was far more preoccupied with how she would admit to her husband that she'd accidentally invited her mother to move in with them.

"What will happen when I'm done with rehab on Tuesday?" her mother had demanded as Kathy readied to leave, quaking so much pieces of her seemed to break off and roll to Kathy's feet. "You tell the boys I refuse to go to that place. If you send me there kicking and screaming, I'll call a cab when you leave. I won't stay, I swear."

"I hear you."

"Tell me what will happen. Tell me I'm going home."

"You can't go home." Kathy spoke the words before she'd

thought them. "You'll have to stay with me, at least for a while."

Her release would be two days before Thanksgiving. They shouldn't upheave and dump her into a place she didn't want to go only to pick her up for a holiday dinner. This bridge really made sense, now that Kathy thought about it. Peggy could stay at their house for one week until she warmed to the idea of Seaside. Kathy had most of that stretch off, so she could do the caretaking. Time with Kathy and Neil might be just what Peggy needed to come around to the idea of a permanent facility. Kathy just prayed Frank's connection could hold her mother's room, and that Neil would grin and bear the temporary intrusion—or at least not combust.

Goodwill had ebbed and flowed between her and Neil throughout her first week of work. Sometimes her husband withdrew to his office or wandered the house with headphones though Kathy was willing, even wanting, to talk. But one night, after they brushed their teeth in synchrony and spit into their double sinks, he carried each of her palms to his mouth, and the next morning he woke in time to pat her bum on her way out the door.

By Friday, she'd returned from the office to find him at the kitchen table—which, of late, had been increasingly and inventively put to use—the canvas roll bag of his carving tools unfurled. Neil drew a roughing knife over a block of wood. Strips peeled and dropped to the floor like tiny curls at a beauty salon.

Kathy had always liked to watch Neil whittle, attracted to the way his tongue worked behind closed lips, his intense concentration. Before the kids were born, various projects—a smoking pipe for his father or a birdhouse for his mother—occupied him for hours, and Kathy would pick up her book and read in a seat where she'd have a good view of him. But as the crib and changing table moved in, followed by toy trucks, Legos, and dolls, and as Neil logged more time at the office, the canvas bag relocated from the countertop to the junk drawer to the spare room, until it was tucked away in a locked cabinet in the garage, where the kids couldn't find it—and seemingly, neither could Neil. Aside from smoothing a gauged chair leg or helping Noah with his pinewood derby car, it had been years since Neil had unearthed his tools.

He'd acquired loads of leisure time six months earlier and hadn't occupied himself with his old pastime, but perhaps he couldn't revisit it when Kathy was there to witness him finding pleasure in his predicament. Under her gaze, maybe he felt he had to dedicate himself to clawing his way back to where they'd been. But now that she was out of the house, he had space and freedom to stretch inside the bright spots of where he was.

If that was the case, Neil had been mistaken, because this scene opened a window in Kathy's chest, and relief swept in like a summer breeze. She was afraid to say anything and interrupt the magic, accidentally slamming that window shut, so she waited for Neil. When he'd etched a detail, he looked up, and they exchanged an understanding that was more tender, more dear, than any that week.

Still, their marital harmony was composed by fragile notes. How would it sustain an unappreciative, judgmental, needy houseguest?

Kathy wasn't particularly religious, but she'd gleaned some from her kids' CCD, and she could use assistance from all planes. Inside her car, she paid tribute to the Miraculous Medal hanging from her rearview mirror. The Mother Mary pendant had appeared at the front of their car almost, well, miraculously after Neil's father died. But of course it wasn't a miracle at all, but the materialization of missing someone. Kathy had grown attached to the vague sense of another presence in the car. She was a nervous driver ever since she totaled their minivan against a telephone pole during a snowstorm. The accident was nearly a decade ago, but sometimes that spin still flashed through her.

"We heard a lot about you as Holy Mother, but you were a daughter too, and Jesus's grandma couldn't have been too psyched that you got pregnant before your wedding day. I bet she held it over Joe's head, virgin birth or not. Whatever you did to smooth things over between them, would you mind sending some of that my way?" Kathy tapped a little high five on the golden Mary, the force of which sent her swinging.

NEIL WAS RAKING leaves into papery piles when Kathy pulled into their driveway.

The tree in their front yard was likely a couple centuries old—a common oak, the species was called, though that was a diminishing way to describe something of such distinct beauty. Its branches spanned almost the entire width of their property and its bark was like craggy armor. The base of its trunk had begun to bloat, with gnarly fingers clamping hard into the earth. A neighbor had urged them to take it down and install a porch in its place—for the curb appeal. But Kathy would never tear out anything so stately or firmly rooted. Besides, it was old enough to be considered a veteran tree, which was protected in a town that so valued history. Given the chance, it would develop into an ancient tree. The only thing that could warrant its removal would be disease. Kathy often checked its exterior for signs of decay.

Kathy parked in the garage and met her husband outside. The air was cold and laced with wood smoke. Neil clasped the rake handle with a gloved hand and leaned against it.

"Let me guess. Peggy is thrilled about her move to Seaside, and grateful to her children for arranging it," he said.

All at once, Kathy felt the full weight of the week: the endless hours on her feet, patient interactions, colleague small talk, discussions with her brothers, tango with her husband, and concern for her mother. After so much time in hibernation, her muscles, and her brain too, had been suddenly worked to capacity. She wore the fatigue of that now and wanted to lay it all down, or at least to borrow the support of Neil's rake.

"Not quite," she said, her eyes welling.

At the strain in her voice, his face softened and he tilted his head as if to measure her from a different angle. "She has to come here. You know that, don't you?"

"What?"

"Did you really think you could blindside Peggy and walk out of there alive? She needs to come around to the idea of a facility and get to announce it like she came up with it herself. In the meantime, the bionic woman can't live alone. We are her only choice."

It was nothing short of miraculous. "You'll hate having her here."

"Maybe a little." He sniffed and drew his sleeve across his face; the cold air always made his nose run. "It's the right thing to do."

Her husband was a good man. She knew that already, but here was his grace in action, and here was her breastbone aching to contain her love for him, which often sidled next to gratitude. Her throat knit against her tears.

"It'll just be a week. You won't have to do a thing." During Mr. Begley's illness, Kathy had sat with him three times a week, alternating with Neil's sisters, but it wasn't quite the same, was it?

"If you say so."

"What am I going to tell my brothers? They knew I'd cave."

"Let me deal with Larry, Curly, and Moe." The honeyed light of autumn was almost enough to buff away Neil's pointedness, but they both knew he'd been waiting for the opportunity to retaliate against Peggy's attack dogs. Kathy's brothers had spent decades distancing themselves from their mother, geographically and emotionally, but their distaste for Neil was one of those vestigial instincts to impress her. This included when Jimmy stumbled to Neil the night of their wedding, bow tie hanging around his neck, and said, "Remember, we are military. We know the people with the launch codes." Now, with Neil's propeller blade limbs poised to spin, Kathy was simultaneously touched, maybe even a little aroused, while also infantilized and exasperated by his immaturity. She wanted his protection, and she didn't.

Her brothers—mostly Jimmy and Frank—wouldn't rest

until they'd gotten the entire transcript out of her. Had she posed the plan as a question, like they'd warned her against? Did she lead with their wish for Peggy to gain community? Did she mention the *pool?* They might ask for a demonstration of tone, and she might flounder and then provide it. The prospect made her want to lie with a compress on her forehead.

She sighed like she was singing, as if her own exasperation could be absorbed into her ears and give her strength. "I have to do it, but if they pull my pigtails, I'm tagging you in."

Before going inside, she went to their stoop and gripped the stalk of their Halloween pumpkin, long overdue to be tossed. It tore away from its rotten gourd as easily as wet cardboard.

FOR THIS CONVERSATION, Kathy craved wine that would bite back. While she waited for her brothers to assemble, she upended a heavy pour of a cheap pinot noir into a long-stemmed glass, and then filled her mouth with its tannins and black fruit.

Once they were all tuned in to the same airwaves from their own positions, she said, "Mom won't go."

"You say that like she has a choice. I suppose that's the impression you gave her?" Jimmy's words were issued in a rush between breaths. Kathy imagined him on the treadmill in his renovated basement, speed walking because he was in his sixties, but shucking gel carbohydrates like a marathon runner.

Neil had carried his laptop down and was job hunting on the living room couch. Kathy could see him from her kitchen island perch and suspected he'd left his lair to be close enough to offer support, while remaining far enough not to intrude.

Heartened by his presence, Kathy said, "She *does* have a choice. She isn't a prisoner we can transport from one place to another."

Neil lifted his face from the screen, surprised and perhaps impressed by her uncharacteristic sharpness. Could he know her severity had been for him, a small, strange reward to thank him for emerging? He was pleased by her performance, maybe even proud. She fought against a tug in her lips.

"Seaside isn't a penitentiary," Frank said, snapping back. "It's a luxury facility I went through a lot of trouble to arrange."

Chastened, Kathy reeled her attitude back. "You're right." Neil dropped his attention to his computer, and she angled her body away. "I know you've done a lot already, but is there any chance your friend could save the room while we work on Mom?"

"What do you expect him to do? There's a line of people willing to give an arm and a leg for that spot."

"Come on, Frank. It's one more phone call," Jimmy said.

Frank's sigh crackled at the base of his throat, like static feedback. "I'll see what I can do, but I'm making no promises."

Paul's voice glided through to temper the mood, or at least to help push the discussion over the ditch. "What will we do with Mom in the meantime?"

"She's agreed to stay at my house," Kathy said.

"Lucky you," Frank said. The dry joke was his forgiveness.

Kathy laughed. The release ticked her shoulders an inch lower. She hadn't even realized she'd hoisted them. She pulled in another mouthful of the tangy wine. With her swallow, fondness for her brothers and her peaceful house and that generous pour swept through her veins. "I tried to sell her on our plan. I did."

Paul assured, "We all know Mom isn't exactly the poster child for cooperation."

Kathy wondered if deep down, or somewhere closer to the surface, she knew her mother wouldn't comply with their plan. The boys had made it sound simple, in the way of men for whom the world had often yielded. Where there was a problem, there was a solution. Let's be practical, rational, pragmatic. But Peggy wasn't a problem. She was a person. And not just any person, but one who had been married to an air force officer, which was as good as being espoused to her country, made to surrender decades of choices. For the majority of her adult life, Peggy had no say in where she lived, for how long, or when her husband could come home. She'd been denied autonomy until her husband retired, only to have her children attempt to hijack her sovereignty and ship her off once again. Maybe *they* were the problem.

The siblings drifted into communal silence, and Kathy wondered if the other three chafed against similar guilt, or if that affliction was particular to her. Then another thought struck her with a start: If Kathy suspected their proposal would be rejected, did she go along with it because she'd subconsciously wanted her mother to move in but preferred for it to seem like she'd been forced into the situation?

Finally, Frank said, "This might sound crass, but what the hell. Sometimes I wonder if it'd be better if Dad were the one still around."

Kathy was brought back to their father's burial, when Frank, resolute and hard-nosed, had blubbered like a middle-aged boy. He'd worshipped their father, as well as his identity as a colonel's son. He'd buzzed his hair since he was an adolescent, and still relocated job to job, state to state, as if moving between assignments.

"He was always more content with his lot in life—and with us," Jimmy said.

From Kathy's perspective, her sons gratified Peggy. She assumed her brothers received the fruits of maternal praise. But maybe Peggy projected the infallibility of her boys exclusively to Kathy in another endeavor to prompt her daughter to be better.

"You got the feeling you weren't enough for her?" Kathy ventured, testing the soundness of their solidarity. She intentionally put the question in past tense, so as to place the hurt at a comfortable distance.

Jimmy's voice enlivened, as if papering over vulnerability with jaunty vigor. "I mean, she didn't push us like she did you, and she had flashes of maternal enthusiasm, but let's be honest, not all women are meant to be mothers."

Kathy couldn't decide if the assertion was offensive or empowering, but it didn't seem a man's place to conclude what was fitting or unfitting of a woman. Then again, as Peggy's eldest, he was perhaps the most qualified candidate to critique their mother.

Still, just because Peggy wasn't nurturing in the conventional way, and expressed traits that didn't congeal with the ideal of motherhood—impatience, rage, despair—that didn't necessarily make her any less deserving of children. She didn't spank them more than their peers were. She didn't degrade or berate. Often, Peggy was simply unhappy. Didn't she have a right to her feelings, in all their variations?

Yet Kathy had chosen to be a different sort of mother: uplifting, communicative, and most of all, steady. Maybe that was a more powerful denunciation than Jimmy's comment. The periodic disinterest that had stung Kathy when she was a girl—*Will you stop hanging on me?*—later baffled her as a mother, when she'd clamored for the unabashed sweetness of her children. Why couldn't Peggy cajole her kids without snapping? If her toddler was being indecisive between sandals or sneakers, Peggy would have thrown both pairs against the wall and screamed, "Choose a goddamn pair and stick to it. They're just shoes," while Kathy used breathing exercises or sang funny songs to move him along. Maybe mothering was a skill that came more naturally to some, but not having that predisposition didn't mean you were bad at it. In the same way, some women, including Peggy, knew how to present themselves—applying the right shade of lipstick or choosing clothes with flattering lines—but that didn't mean women like Kathy, whose lipstick caked and whose dresses never fit right, weren't beautiful. They just didn't have the same assembly skills.

The heat rumbled on and hissed through the cast-iron radiators. Kathy filled her mouth with the metallic tang of crushed grape skin and swallowed before her teeth began to ache.

Paul said, "Maybe Dad seemed to enjoy us more because he had to appreciate what little time he had around us. Mom was never gone. She got more than enough."

Kathy thought it may have worked both ways; not only had Peggy gotten enough of her children, but they'd gotten enough of her. Their father worked so much that their awe of him was preserved, while admiration for their mother wore with exposure until she was so stripped of edifice, her children hypothesized swapping her out for their dearly unspoiled departed, esteem for whom was now sealed by the ultimate absence. This was the case for most of them. Paul wasn't so enchanted. He didn't appreciate some of their father's parenting tactics—room inspections, push-ups, and a dress code—which Kathy thought had been a playful way to incorporate his children into his military identity, but that Paul interpreted as imposed toughness.

"You can't blame the guy for working," Jimmy said. Referring to military service as employment was appropriate from the son who'd translated his father's sacrifices to ambition, and ribbons and medals to material possessions.

"Yeah, come on, P-May. Dad loved us. He couldn't get enough of his little soldiers," Frank said.

"I didn't ask to be a little soldier," Paul said, his voice as compact as a walnut. Kathy heard an echo of her mother during a walk to the base commissary, when their father pressed his fingers into Paul's spine and said, *Stand tall, little soldier,* and Peggy swatted her husband's hand. *Let him be a boy.*

Kathy vacillated from one brother's perspective to another's, varied impressions of the same household, all equally right. Each of them possessed their own versions of their mother and father, since their rearing had been modified by their own personalities, where they lived at what age, birth order, gender, and their parents' circumstances in conjunction with their own.

Kathy empathized with Paul, but she wasn't willing to agree with him. There was a reason only the deceased could be sainted. Elevating their memory was a means of honoring them, while dwelling on their flaws felt like mild sacrilege. Kathy meditated on images of her father kneeling to speak to her eye-to-eye, dragging a toboggan of children through the snow, rolling his plane overhead while she stretched out her arms and spun on the ground below, whisking her away for ice cream when her mother was having an episode, and rescuing her from a high school party where she was uncomfortable. He maintained a calming composure when he taught her to drive, even in the face of her fright, assuring her, "You're driving the car. It isn't driving you." He was their family's great equalizer: the two older boys reined in their impulses when he was around; he understood Peggy in a way nobody else could, often anchoring her before she unmoored; and reassuring Kathy with a furtive glance if Peggy was being particularly hard on her. He was tall and powerful, and when he was around, Kathy felt safe, loved, and accepted. Though, she had to admit she felt shy toward him after he returned from each of his deployments, even well into her teenage years.

Despite her allegiance, she could concede to Paul's aim, which was to afford their mother more credit, so she said, "If it was Dad, we wouldn't have ambushed him with the assisted living facility. It would have been too demeaning to do that to a colonel." What she really meant, though, was it would be too demeaning to do that to a man. It was more acceptable to revoke the agency of a woman, a mother.

"Maybe you're right," Frank said, and Kathy was so gratified by the concession, she decided not to take the *maybe* personally.

"There's no sense in speculation. We don't get to choose. We have Mom," Jimmy said, and then added wryly, "Kathy more than the rest of us."

Chapter 11

October 1943

WHEN JACKIE COCHRAN ANGLED HER CHIN FOR TAKEOFF and launched her voice, the WASP half of the mess hall settled in to listen, but the male side chattered and clattered forks unbothered until General Hap Arnold barked, "Attention," and the crowd tamed.

Cochran clasped her hands behind her back and repeated herself. "I am pleased to share that we have received a special delivery of bacon and coffee beans."

There was a downbeat of disbelief as the assembly recalled bacon's salt and smoky fat, and the bitter tang of freshly brewed coffee. Then the room erupted in stomps, cheers, fist-pounding, and clapped backs.

Peggy grabbed Georgia's hand and held it below her chin. "Bacon, from a real, live, roll-in-the-mud pig."

"It isn't live anymore, but it sure as hell died for a good cause."

Now when Cochran raised her hand, the cadets were more willing to yield, restraining their excitement to hear what more there could be. "There is only enough for half of your group. The men or the women. We've decided to let you determine who gets the spoils."

"Men need meat," a male cadet shouted.

"And coffee. Let the ladies sip tea."

Cochran waited for their amusement to subside. "There will be a contest to determine the victors. A battle of the sexes."

Peggy said, "If I have to watch those twerps drool all over our pork, I swear I'll fly a plane straight into Lake Sweetwater."

Georgia said, "We'll just have to win then, won't we?"

"The challenge is this," Cochran continued through the mounting commotion. "You must move a primary trainer from one end of the tarmac to the other—"

"Too easy!" a male cadet shouted.

Cochran's eyes flicked to him. It was a flash of teeth, a growl, a warning of the fierceness she'd harnessed in order to excel in a field that disregarded her. "—without cranking her cowl on. She's a two-thousand-pound bird. How you manage her transfer is up to you. Employ a few representatives or your entire population. Apply brain or brawn. All that matters is crossing the finish line before your opposition. You'll race side by side."

Spoons scraped bowl bottoms. Runny oatmeal was slurped and swallowed. It went down smoother with the prospect of cured meat. They stacked plates and brainstormed, or simply prattled about their good fortune—particularly the men, who figured they might as well be named the winners now and save everybody the trouble and embarrassment.

"They're right. We don't stand a chance," Millie said, jogging with her baymates onto the field.

"That's good. Make them think we are already defeated. That way they won't try too hard," Georgia said.

"We *are* defeated," Millie said. "They're stronger. Cochran set us up to fail."

Most of the men were posturing, jabbing shoulders, tousling hair, and flexing biceps, while their leaders and thinkers deliberated. Occasionally they stole glances at the WASP. Peggy wondered whether they were trying to guess the women's strategy or assess their competition, or if they just hoped they were being admired. To Peggy's dismay, she was admiring them: their childlike charms, their bone structure, and the places their muscles went sinewy. Even their arrogance had a certain appeal.

She shook the attraction away. "They have us beat on muscle, but we have other assets," Peggy said. "Let's bring home the bacon."

They swapped ideas like their mothers swapped recipes. Some were bad, some were worse, and some were halfway decent, but nothing snapped into place as the answer. The sun bore down on their shoulders. Soon they were sweltering and running out of time.

Georgia stomped her foot, rustling up a puff of dust. "If only the Fairchild came with an ignition. Then I could hot-wire her and be done with it." The others turned as if their friend had just revealed herself to be a stranger, maybe a treacherous one, because what respectable lady knew how to hot-wire? "Unclench your hineys. I wish I was Bonnie getting the old yeehaw from Clyde, but it's nothing like that. My daddy runs an auto shop. Engines are the family business."

An idea sparked in Peggy and soon she was primed for

takeoff. Her joy was fuel. She felt uninhibited, like she could do almost anything, even win. She clamped her hands on Georgia's cheeks so hard her friend's lips puckered and her eyes globed.

"You wily minx," she said. "I just fell in love with you a little bit."

TWO FAIRCHILDS WERE poised shoulder to shoulder, thoroughbreds hoofing the tarmac, born for this race, this measure of gender. If the women lost, they'd confirm what everybody thought they already knew. They were the fairer sex, and not the definition that meant just and objective, but pale, by way of comparison. They were delicate, lesser. Losing this contest would be the confirmation so many wanted. Winning, however, wouldn't be as sweeping a victory. This triumph would be an exception to the rule. It wouldn't convince anyone that the women were equal to every task—just this specific challenge in these specific conditions. This anomaly. They had far more to lose than to gain. Still, it was a chance to win something, which wasn't a chance they were often afforded.

The participants were called to the tarmac. The representatives from the WASP—Peggy, Georgia, and Cheryl—broke from the herd and marched to the battleground alongside the ten beefiest men the opposition had to offer. They were Davids against Goliaths. Gazelles demanding respect of lions.

"Are you the cookies sent to surrender? Good for you, escaping with some dignity," a redheaded cadet said. His face was oblong, and his vowels were split open and hurled up into the back of his mouth. Peggy couldn't place the accent.

"You wish," Cheryl said, with contempt. "When I'm scarf-ing down those savory strips, I'll be looking straight at you, cadet."

Peggy laughed like a bugle trill. She didn't know Cheryl had such feistiness in her, and Peggy wondered if Georgia's fire was spreading to the others the same way it had to her.

"Let's let our actions do the talking," Cochran said. She stood between the two planes at the starting line while Gen-eral Arnold was but a blotch at the finish, a mile down the tarmac. At one end the flagless flag girl, at the other end the authority. Figures, Peggy thought.

"The rules are few and simple. When I give the signal, you are free to do anything but crank the cowl or interfere with your opponent. First to the end wins." Cochran backed to the edge of the tarmac and raised her arm over her head. "On your mark, get ready, set . . ."

At go, five of the men sprinted down the runway while the other half bounded to positions around their plane: two on each wing and one at the tail. Surely there was room for more. Their few numbers seemed a statement. They were so confident in their abilities, at least in contrast to the wom-en's, they didn't need to optimize. Five was sufficient. And yet, what did it say that the women dispatched only three?

"On my count, push," the man at the tail yelled.

"No way are there enough of them," Cheryl said, satis-fied. But then they drove against the plane and the wheels creaked. With momentum, the plane rolled steadily. It might take them only fifteen minutes to cover the distance. Cheryl deflated. "Oh, crap."

Georgia was long gone, having shot off at the drop of go,

to the bafflement of their spectators, Peggy was sure. They must be whispering, struggling to sort out where that southern girl was off to. Peggy bit back her amusement, imagining their faces when everyone discovered what she already knew. But it was premature to celebrate. Their plan might fail. There was still much to lose.

Her uniform had absorbed the sun's rays, or perhaps that heat was coming from within. "Come on, Georgia," she whispered. "Time for your grand entrance."

The men were nearing the second crew, who were rocking on their heels, poised to relieve the first. If Georgia didn't show up soon, it wouldn't matter whether their strategy worked. They wouldn't have enough time.

Just as Peggy began to barb, she heard a reverberation, and the cactus inside her sprung up with flowers. Cheryl heard it too. She swung to Peggy, abloom with wonder, and clasped her hand.

Commercial grade wheels churned up sand. Inside the haze, Georgia bumped across the field on an army-green tow tractor, an unlikely knight on a more unlikely steed, the most exquisite cavalry, about as pleased as the shitty pig who might soon feed them. Peggy whooped. The rest of the WASP jumped and cheered on the field.

Georgia swung the tug in front of their plane. Peggy didn't wait for the vehicle to stop before groping for the winch. She and Cheryl yanked two cables around their plane's landing gear and cranked them tight.

"Is this right?" Cheryl asked.

"Hell if I know," Peggy said. "But there's no time to test. Come on." Peggy tore around the tractor and into the seat beside Georgia. The second men's team was already in place up ahead, shoving their candidate forward.

"Leave me behind. Less weight," Cheryl called. They hesitated; if they were going to finish this thing, they should do it as a team. But Cheryl insisted. "Go, go, go."

Georgia gunned the engine. The tractor leapt forward but caught on the weight of its new haul. Peggy feared the cords would snap or the hooks would slip and they'd have come this far to get nothing, but then the plane's wheels revolved and they stuttered ahead. Peggy couldn't help herself; she punched the air and the women on the field roared.

Protests poured from the male sidelines. *No fair. How cheap. They're cheating.* They only provoked Peggy's excitement. Their indignation meant they thought the women might actually win. She held on to the tractor as if to the tail of a firework. A colony of WASP sprinted alongside them, but they pulled ahead, leaving their comrades in their wake.

The group of muscle who'd already finished their shift for the men watched as Peggy and Georgia gained on their plane. They set into motion, hustling around their Fairchild, to double their manpower.

This intensity, this acute aliveness, was almost as good as flying. Peggy could have crowed. They were halfway down the runway, the men still ahead. There might not be enough remaining length to overtake them. Peggy teetered on the edge of their bench and gripped the serving platter of a steering wheel alongside Georgia's hands.

"You gotta go faster," Peggy said.

"If my foot was any lower it'd be on the tarmac."

Their engine rattled something phlegmy. Georgia's hair

whipped against Peggy's cheek and the sun beat down, browning skin exposed by her uniform, which was rolled up to her elbows. Everything smelled hot: engine oil, baked pavement, the green metal of her vehicle, their bodies.

The men were barreling toward the finish-line cones, but the nose of the women's tractor was sniffing the men's tail. Then Georgia and Peggy were cruising alongside their belabored peers, who delivered looks of disdain, outrage, and awe.

General Arnold was coming into focus, clasping his hands at his waist in the center of the tarmac. As the tractor surpassed his men, his countenance remained stolid, but for a corner of his mouth, which ticked up.

"We're doing it. We're doing it," Peggy said as the tractor coasted the line. But theirs wasn't the machine that mattered. She twisted and grasped the backrest to watch the competing planes. Their propellers were abreast. This registered with the men, who clenched and gritted and strained to increase their speed, but they were no match for an engine.

Peggy clamped her friend's arm. Her fingers dug deep. "You're doing it. You're doing it."

They towed the WASP's plane ahead by a margin no wider than a bacon strip.

Chapter 12

November 2009

TUESDAY OF KATHY'S SECOND WEEK AT WORK WAS ONE knot of aggravation strung to another, beginning with a forty-year-old patient who sat on the edge of the exam table swinging her beige-socked feet while Kathy counseled her treatment for a vulvar abscess. "Apply a warm compress three times a day. If it's uncomfortable, you can take—"

"I'd prefer to wait to hear what the doctor says," the patient said, her expression as blank as a frying pan.

Kathy tightened her grip on her clipboard. "This *is* what the doctor said."

She finally relented and left in search of her superior. She expected Dr. Smith to insist she hold strong and remind the patient that she was more than qualified. Then she'd return to the exam room on the good faith that she'd pursued the patient's wishes, but they'd been denied. With Kathy's authority endorsed, she and the patient would have to move forward on their own, with Kathy at the controls. Instead, Dr. Smith chuckled, pleased to be in such demand, and returned like a rock star for his encore. She'd wanted his advocacy, but he'd acted instead like maybe the patient had a point.

Later, a second interaction caused Kathy to cringe. When an obstetrician greeted Dr. Smith in the hallway, saying, "Good morning, Dr. Smith," he replied, "What's shaking?" like she was his teenage niece rather than a respected colleague. It was also worth noting the obstetrician failed to acknowledge Kathy at all. Was it because Dr. Smith hadn't bothered to introduce them, or the obstetrician didn't consider a nurse worth greeting?

The third infraction was at the coffee station. Kathy was making small talk with Susan, the office manager, when Dr. Smith bustled by wearing a smeared-on grin and chirped, "Don't you hens have more important things to do than stand around clucking?"

Kathy thought she caught a pulse by Susan's eyes, a shivering reflex to upend steaming tea over their boss's head. Susan had been in her position for eight years. How many questionable jokes had Dr. Smith cracked in that time? How often had he crossed the line without being aware of his trespasses? Repeated offenses could wear a person's nerves. How long before regular abrading made Kathy's raw?

But Dr. Smith was generally kind. His effusive praise served as proof—*you're so efficient and as sharp as a dog whistle!* And, when Kathy had requested to leave work early to pick up her mother, he'd patted her arm and said, "It's never easy to parent your parent. I can manage the last patients on my own." Dr. Smith meant to be good, and intentions couldn't just be paving stones to hell. There was a difference between those who wished harm and those who ended up there accidentally. Murder versus manslaughter. Though maybe that was a bad example, since both were punishable crimes.

Kathy worked as long a day as she could, and when three thirty rolled around, she shrugged on her coat, wrapped her scarf around her neck, and leaned across Dr. Smith's doorway.

"I'll see you tomorrow," she said with a wave, her bottom half a step down the hall, ready to set off.

"Good luck. My mother lived with me for a time. Of course, her case was different. She descended into dementia." Dr. Smith set sail down the odyssey of his mother's medical history, as well as the not-short story, despite his preface, of his family's dynamic. Kathy opened her mouth at pauses, wanting to derail him, but the gaps were brief, and he was too caught up to notice her cues. Her body began to twinge in its unnatural bend, so she straightened inside his doorway, where the heating vent blew on her neck and sweat prickled beneath her layers.

It was four o'clock by the time she extracted herself. The sky was painted with pastels and golden leaf. The ribbon of her scarf rippled in her haste, and cool air whispered through her unbuttoned coat, whose wool wings flapped at her sides.

Her phone's ringtone crooned, muffled by the walls of her purse. She fumbled for it. It was the rehab center, likely wondering if Kathy's delay meant she'd abandoned her mother. "Mrs. Begley, this is Tina from ClearView. Your mother fell. We don't suspect anything is broken, but she's on her way to the hospital, just in case. You should go straight there."

Kathy cradled her purse against her stomach, as if it too was in danger of falling. "How is that possible? She doesn't have access to stairs."

It was a foolish comment. An elderly person recovering

from surgery didn't need stairs to fall. Peggy could have slipped in the bathroom or in the hallway, believing herself capable without a walker. Or maybe Peggy had made a jail-break through the locked door that led to the stairwell.

"She climbed onto a chair."

"She *what?*"

"Her roommate was complaining about sun in her eyes. Margaret was adjusting the blinds."

Her mother's caprices had—as they often did—made her predicament worse. "Why didn't she use the string?"

"The string was tangled, apparently." A taut wire ran beneath the woman's words, as if she resented having to communicate such absurdity. She sighed—a decision; she was going to go ahead and say it. "Your mother isn't our most compliant patient."

Kathy felt camaraderie with this caller, as well as the reflex to defend her mother. *You don't get to say that.* "I understand."

A web of worry, umbrage, and pity wove so densely that Kathy couldn't see what lay beyond it. Would her mother require another surgery? Was it still safe to care for her in her home, or should admission into the assisted living facility be compulsory? What would they do now?

Her vision went hazy as she rooted for her keys. She couldn't let herself deteriorate. She needed to get to the hospital, and sniveling could cause an accident. Then they'd have another patient on their hands—the last thing they needed. She pressed her eyes against their own sting and forced down the hot clot in her throat.

Just as she was forcibly transitioning into nurse mode, her

phone came alive again. She wouldn't mind if she never heard that chime again. Kathy was about ready to hurl the device across the parking lot, but it could be a doctor from the hospital, calling with an update. Maybe it was good news—that her mother had endured only some light bruising.

"Katherine Begley? I work in Speaker Nancy Pelosi's office. We got your email and have followed up on the matter. I can assure you that your mother did not receive that invitation in error. Margaret Mayfield, formerly Lewis, was indeed a member of the Women Airforce Service Pilots."

Chapter 13

November 1943

PEGGY LEANED AGAINST HER BAY DOORFRAME AND EYED the jet-black sky. She inflated her cheeks and rocked the air from one side to the other before ejecting it in a conclusive huff. "Of course there isn't a moon when Mayfield takes us night flying for the first time."

"I know you're dizzy for that man, but you really think he controls the sky?" Georgia said, distractedly, fixed on letter writing. A cigarette was pinched between her lips and it bobbled as her hand worked across the page.

Peggy scoffed so everybody could hear her objection. "I'm not dizzy for him. It's the opposite, in fact. He's a creep."

"He is not."

"He seems to get an awful lot of joy from making us miserable."

Georgia dropped her pencil, plucked the cigarette from her mouth, and exhaled a mouthful of smoke. "He had every reason to wash us out and he didn't. What does that tell you? He wants us to succeed. So he's a little tough on us—well, good. I'm tired of the world treating me like I'm breakable. If you want a commanding officer who goes gentle on you, that's your business, but I want one who pushes me so hard I surpass the men."

Peggy's baymates awaited her response. Even the grasshoppers paused their chirping chorus. She felt herself grow warm. "I'd rather there was a moon to light our way. That's all."

They marched under the beams of the air traffic control tower. There was a rare chill in the air. The breeze reached under her collar and cooled her neck. Peggy drew her hands into her sleeves.

When Georgia spoke, her voice was suppler than it had been inside the bay. "Do you have trouble finding your way to the bathroom at night?"

"Huh?"

"We know the way. We've done it so many times, it won't make any difference whether it's day or night."

"Except—"

"Hey, there's your man." Georgia jutted her chin at Mayfield's silhouette, the Fairchild at his back. "You think he arranged for God to send us a thunderstorm?" She clasped Peggy's shoulders and maneuvered her to the front of the flight line. "First to fly, first to relax."

At Mayfield's signal, Peggy marched to the runway. They stood side by side and waited as the groups before them inspected their aircraft, checked gas supply, and tested lights.

Peggy's nerves popped beneath her skin. She rocked on her heels, bent and straightened her knees, and whistled the *William Tell* Overture, but quit under Mayfield's silent disapproval. He, apparently, wasn't a fan of the Lone Ranger.

"You have siblings, sir?" Peggy released the question like a firefly into the darkness.

"Yes."

Though she'd posed the question, she hadn't expected any reply. She waited for elaboration, and when none came, she asked, "Are they classified?"

Mayfield's attention floated toward Peggy, but before landing, flitted above her head. "Four brothers."

"I suppose that didn't provide you a lot of time around women."

"I suppose not."

A cadet cranked the cowling of the first plane, and flames shot from the engine in bright bolts, a shocking contrast against the black. Peggy's air pipe tightened against a shriek.

"That's just what exhaust looks like in the dark," Mayfield said. From where she stood, his profile was softer, more forgiving. She wondered if maybe she, too, looked different in the dark.

Peggy smoothed her pant legs as a way to occupy her hands. "They might have mentioned the flames in ground school."

* * *

Nobody warned the WASP that the camera crews were coming. They were just, suddenly, there. By then, two months into their training, hardly anybody in Peggy's class bothered applying makeup. It all washed away in calisthenics or under the enduring sun. Extra sleep was more precious than highlighted cheekbones. This estimation had to be recalculated when a team from *Life* magazine arrived on the premises.

Peggy had stepped outside to greet the morning with a stretch and a yawn when the first flashbulb popped. She blinked at the affront, and her brain worked through the incongruence. When she understood she was being photographed, she sprang back inside and slammed the door behind her. Her baymates must have thought a cockroach had skittered by, as they so often did, or that she'd spotted another rattler.

"Scrounge up your lipstick and roll your shoulders back," Peggy said. "We're about to make our world debut."

The cameras followed the WASP as they marched to mess, assembled engines in ground school, demonstrated their skills in the Link Trainer, managed the altitude chamber, kicked through calisthenics, arranged in flight line, roosted in planes, and flew. They caught everything but their bathroom breaks. The crew seemed particularly taken by Georgia, a queen bee in her flight goggles, and followed her path in the air as she performed spins, stalls, lazy eights, chandelles, and inverted flying. They even snapped what little leisure time the women stole inside their sixteen-hour workdays, as they played cards on the wing of a PT-19 or sunbathed atop GI blankets in an alley between their barracks.

The WASP were doing the impossible and coming through their ordeal exhausted but invigorated too. Tailed by photographers and journalists, they were sharing their accomplishments with the world. Peggy gave herself over to the cameras—chin tipped, lips parted, eyebrow cocked—so that all WASP would be recognized, so that history would remember that they were there too, an integral part of the war effort. The wink, though, was just for her.

A MONTH LATER, a copy of the WASP issue of *Life* was set on each of their pillows when they returned from mess. Peggy lunged for hers and was astounded to find herself on the cover. Though she hadn't yet flown one, she posed on the wing of a B-17 bomber, her legs gathered to one side, her cheek cupped in the palm of her hand, her eyes turned wistfully skyward.

"Look at you, baby doll," Georgia said, whistling through her teeth. "Now what about the rest of us?" She flipped to the article, stuck her finger to the page, and read, "The time-honored belief that army flying is for men only has gone into the ash can. At Avenger Field, girls are flying military planes in a way that army officers a year ago never would have thought possible. These girls joyously scramble into the silver aircraft, fly with skill, precision, and zest. Piloting with unfeminine purpose, they might well be a threat to Hitler."

Peggy crawled up beside Georgia. "A threat to Hitler? How about that?"

The seven-page feature was accompanied by a beautiful spread of photographs, including Georgia in the cockpit of a primary trainer.

"There you are!" Peggy cried, and grabbed her copy to read the caption. "'Goggles secure the hair of one Miss Walden, of Savannah, Georgia.'" At that, Peggy let the magazine drop. "Who gives two hoots about hair? How about, 'Goggles protect Miss Walden from blinding debris'?"

"It's better than my caption," Connie said, mournfully.

"'Short-legged girl stows extra cushion in primary trainer.' No name, no hometown. Just my stubby body type. It's not my fault I need a boost to see over the dash!"

"But you look good," Peggy said, before locating the photo.

"All you see is my rear!" Connie tossed the magazine onto the foot of her bed and collapsed against her pillow.

"For some, that's more than enough," Georgia said. Her index finger landed quietly on Connie's photo in the upper right corner, in which she was doubled over in a Fairchild cockpit, her sweet face out of sight, just an anonymous backside—and that dang flight suit did no shape any favors.

Georgia snuck Peggy a covert look, which communicated their shared responsibility of elevating the room's morale. Being Georgia's confidant, and a leader of this small crew, was almost more than Peggy's heart could bear. She'd wanted to fly planes, that was all she'd ever wanted; she was doing that, while also enjoying the unexpected rewards of this rich fellowship, being half of a dynamite duo whose mission was to seize adventure, take flight, brave new terrain, and most essentially, protect and nurture their kind. Life couldn't possibly be more satisfying than this.

"Prepare yourself for a deluge of fan mail, honey," Peggy said. "A deluge."

Chapter 14

November 2009

WHEN KATHY WAS TEN YEARS OLD, HER MOTHER ORGA-
nized a family picnic at Maxwell Air Force Base in Mont-
gomery, Alabama. Kathy's father wasn't crazy about the
idea. It was 1966. He and many of his colleagues had been
traveling back and forth from Vietnam, some never returning, and there was no end in sight to the fighting.

"Is now really the time for a party?" he asked.

But when Peggy pitched ideas, they were decisions, not
suggestions. "It's a picnic. This war has lasted ten years.
We've got to eat sometime."

There were fried green tomatoes, collard greens, biscuits,
and barbecued pork. Kathy scooped food with her fingers.
When she'd had her fill, she raced off to the egg relay, three-
legged races, and cornhole tournaments, along with other
military daughters who swore they'd be friends forever, but
who also knew a uniformed officer could show up to their
houses with news that would drop their mothers to their
knees, or that their families could be reassigned, never to be
seen again.

That celebration stood out in Kathy's memory because of
an interaction between her mother and a woman from the

WAF (Women of the Air Force), a female branch of the air force tasked with clerical or medical duties. The uniformed woman approached as Peggy spooned banana pudding into bowls for her daughter to distribute.

"My name is Greta, and I just wanted to say that I wouldn't be here if it wasn't for women like you, so thank you for your service." The woman clicked her heels, sending up a current that made her body rigid, ending with a salute.

People thanked Kathy's father for his service on a regular basis, but never once had anyone done the same for her mother. Peggy was thanked for other generous acts—when she dropped off a casserole for a sick family or passed along a bag of hand-me-downs—but not for her service, and she'd certainly never been saluted. That sacred gesture was reserved for fellow military. This officer must know that.

Peggy was adept at flowing through even the most awkward social situations. She prodded Kathy until she lifted a bowl to the woman. "Here, doll. Treat yourself to something sweet."

When Greta was out of hearing range, Kathy asked, "What did *you* do?"

At the sound of her rudeness, Kathy worried she'd trigger one of her mother's tirades. But they were in public, where Peggy wore grace best. She smiled prettily and swept her arm across the airfield made festive with lawn chairs, red-and-white-checkered blankets, and patriotic balloons bobbing in the wind.

"Events like these don't throw themselves, honey. That woman has good manners. Better than yours, I might add. I didn't hear you thank me for my efforts."

"Thanks, Mom."

"That's more like it." Peggy drove the serving spoon into her trifle dish, but her eyes followed the WAF officer to the cluster of women set apart from their male peers. "I know Greta. She played bugle back when there was a WAF band. Those gals were too talented for their own good, traveling all over and broadcasted on television. They got so popular, the colonel of the men's band accepted their invitations and showed up with his players instead. Eventually he got so jealous, he forbade the girls from performing at any civilian functions. That took the toot right out of their horns. They were disbanded. Some left the service entirely. Others, like our Greta, were transferred to admin work. The same gal who played her soul out for presidents now files paperwork. Imagine! I couldn't do it."

Kathy said, "I guess something is better than nothing."

"I'd rather have nothing than be grateful for scraps," Peggy said. "And I'll be damned if I let *you* settle for *something*, little miss."

Kathy always assumed what kept the scene sticky in her brain was the lesson about the futility of talent, which spilled from her mother more naturally than her speeches about ambition. But as Kathy careened toward the hospital, the echo of the researcher from Congress in her mind, it occurred to her that perhaps what made that memory unforgettable were the words passed from one woman to the other: *Thank you for your service.* On some level, her younger self must have known that the officer wasn't in fact expressing appreciation for Peggy's picnic, and Kathy had logged the interaction until she could draw it out under the light of new information.

Her mother had been a WASP all along, all this time.

UNDER A PINK blanket in a hospital room whose floor matched its walls and ceiling, a clinical cube alive in its own right, the bleeps and churns of devices the pulsing ventricles of its heart, Peggy was asleep. Her head was tipped back, providing Kathy a view of black nostril hairs, like spider legs.

When Peggy awoke, it'd be difficult to discern what was authentic and what was an act—she'd always been a skilled performer, the extent to which Kathy was just now beginning to appreciate, so Kathy assessed quickly. She listened for shallow breath or arrhythmia and examined visible skin. The crepe of Peggy's arms gathered against the mattress. Kathy knew these arms capable of hoisting a child on each hip, mixing enough cake batter to feed a base, and yes, flying airplanes. (Could she have flown warplanes too?) Topped by small brown islands, they turned to damaged fruit near her right bicep, where a laceration had been glued, dressed, and taped shut. A white ice pack had slipped onto the tile below.

Kathy placed a hand across her mother's forehead. "Any light-headedness, nausea, or heart palpitations?"

Peggy's eyes fluttered open. Kathy noted the shape of her pupils and their reactivity to light, those hawk eyes that had timed her clarinet practices and backyard sprints, which had also possibly—was it *probably* now?—peered out from the cockpits of bombers and fighter jets.

"I've already endured my evaluation, dear. No need for you to administer a second." Peggy's voice veered into the old-timey cadence she employed to be charming, but that often annoyed or embarrassed her daughter. "I'm afraid I've made quite a spectacle of myself."

"I'm sure the other residents have already forgotten your dramatic exit."

"I suppose that's one upside of humiliating yourself in front of old fogies."

Kathy scraped a chair closer to the bed and sat down. "What were you doing climbing onto furniture, anyway? It's a miracle your injuries aren't more serious."

"It would have gone without a hitch had the floors not been so polished."

"That wasn't the issue."

"It was very slippery."

Getting Peggy to admit fault was like trying to catch a wish in a jar. There had been no mea culpa when Peggy propped the screen door and their family kitten escaped, when she spilled bleach on her husband's uniform, or when she lost track of time flying and missed Kathy's softball tournament. On that occasion, when Peggy, her cheeks chapped and her hair windblown, arrived home to her disappointed daughter, she'd deflected her guilt, saying, *Competitions hardly matter to you. Why should they be important to me?* She wasn't going to start holding herself accountable at the overripe age of eighty-seven.

Peggy's hair spilled down her shoulders in coarse strands of tarnished nickel, save for some dandelion wisps at her temples. She'd grown a fine layer of fuzz along her loose jowls. The skin there was delicate, soft enough to pet.

"So what did he say?" Kathy asked.

"Who?"

"The doctor."

Peggy's eyes flicked up to the dropped ceiling. "I was too overcome to process the prognosis. She promised to return once you'd arrived." She regarded her daughter deliberately. "*She*, Katherine." Then Peggy's gaze traveled to the monitors, medical cart, and workstation with its miniature washbasin and suture tray. Peggy's nostrils flared as she inhaled a long wavering breath. "These places are so sterile, aren't they?"

"Yes, that's the point."

"But do they have to be so decisively unappealing?"

"They're keeping you alive, not running a bed-and-breakfast," Kathy said.

"Where in a place like this is one supposed to scrounge up motivation to live? A beach scene print wouldn't kill them. Any splash of color at all."

"Maybe food service will bake a blackberry scone if you ask nicely."

Peggy's neck strained to get a better look at Kathy. Then her daughter's sarcasm registered and her pillow exhaled as it caught her head. "Oh, Katherine. Derision doesn't become you."

The doctor entered—her coat skimming her hips, her hair in a low chignon, the part sure of itself, like a missile had cleared its path—and Kathy reminded herself she'd never tried to be a woman in a white coat. Medical school, malpractice insurance, wrong or incomplete diagnoses, long shifts across her kids' childhoods . . . it wasn't what she'd wanted for herself or her family. Still, the fact of the doctor's femaleness, her beauty, and Kathy's having to witness it all in front of her mother, caused Kathy to become more cognizant of her oafishness. Her cheeks singed.

"You must be Mrs. Mayfield's daughter. Your mother tells me you are in medicine?"

Peggy, who'd been too overcome to process a prognosis, had still managed to be artfully obtuse about Kathy's career, plugging the field without specifying her daughter's particular role, which she'd deemed unaspiring and unimaginative.

"I'm a nurse, yes," Kathy said, and then, remembering she hadn't yet told Peggy she'd returned to work, added, "Or I was. Anyway, you should still explain everything in layman's terms."

"Katherine is being modest," Peggy said. "She reads medical journals written half in Latin, half in gibberish. She's very bright. She could have been a doctor."

The doctor turned from mother to daughter, finding herself caught in the overgrown weeds of a long, complicated relationship. "We want to admit Mrs. Mayfield overnight. A rib fracture would make her susceptible to pneumonia, so I'd like to order a CT scan and monitor her breathing. Since this is her second fall in a month, I also want to run a few tests to rule out underlying causes."

Kathy ought to save every staff member the care and coding. Peggy had mounted a chair. The cause wasn't Parkinson's. It was pigheadedness. "Thank you."

When they were alone, Kathy drummed her fingers against her knee. A laminated food menu was tucked into the plastic pocket bolted to the wall. She sprung for the distraction.

"Are you hungry?" she asked.

Peggy's upper lip peeled back to expose her teeth, which

appeared as antique parchment, their grooves threaded with tawny stain. "I couldn't stomach a thing, but you go ahead and order."

Kathy flapped the sheet against her palm. It had been hours since her lunch of baby carrots with reduced fat ranch dressing and low-carb bread and hummus. Her stomach was complaining, but to order herself a meal would not just be mild insurance fraud, but classic Kathy, who had exceeded her mother's dress size in middle school. She'd rather get drive-thru on the way home.

She wished she'd brought a magazine or a deck of cards, but of course she'd thought she was collecting Peggy and taking her home, not entertaining them in a hospital room. She turned to her purse for inspiration. Hangman on a scrap of paper? Had Fiona texted a funny photo she could share? Then she saw the congressional medal ceremony invitation and figured this was as good a time as any.

"Listen, Mom—"

Peggy's hand flew up but faltered like a sunflower in the breeze. "I already know what you're going to say, so save your breath."

"You do?"

"You're going to say a second fall isn't an isolated incident, it's a pattern, and you think I shouldn't go to your house anymore but should be sent somewhere right away before I get seriously hurt. But I don't want to hear it. People go to long-term facilities to die." She squeezed her eyelids closed and pressed her lips into a thin stroke, pinching her emotion, which still made its way into her throat. "If I croaked tonight, everybody would say, 'Eighty-seven. She lived a good long life.' Well, I'm not done. I don't want to die yet." Her large knotty hand quavered over her face and beneath it she began to shudder. "I don't, I don't, I don't."

Kathy hadn't been about to broach the topic of Peggy's living situation, but that didn't matter. She reached for her mother, though her hand dropped short, landing feebly on the rumpled blanket. "You can live with me until you get your strength back, or for forever. You can stay as long as you like."

Peggy batted the air. "Promises given under duress are like piecrusts, made to be broken."

"I swear," Kathy said, sincerely, and then added, "on my mother's life."

Peggy coughed a laugh into her palm. "I hate having to depend on you, or anyone else for that matter. You must know that."

"We're happy to have you."

"You lie," Peggy said, sniveling. "But I thank you for it."

Then, to Kathy's surprised pleasure, her wizened hand swung down, grasped her daughter's fingers, and carried them to her lips, which were hard and damp with tears.

NIGHT DRIVING RANKED as high on Kathy's anxiety chart as navigating through downpours and blizzards—as for stormy nights, forget it, she'd rather sleep on the shoulder and wait for dawn or emergency evacuation. Ever since she'd entered her fifties, it was as if invisible sunglasses were hooked over her ears around sunset. Nobody warned you about that. It had to do with shrinking pupil size, fewer rods, and cloudier lenses, but it couldn't help that Kathy's eyelids had fattened and drooped. Now she lifted them like stubborn blinds, hoping extra light exposure would clarify her vision. She must have resembled a character from *A Clockwork Orange* as she steered from the hospital lot, her spine a rod angled forward, and still the streetlights wore fuzzy halos and oncoming cars blurred and flared.

"Come on, Mare," she whispered to the Miraculous Medal dangling inches from her face. "Do your thing."

The notion of confessing to Neil that the temporary circumstance with Peggy might have kinda sorta become indefinite made colliding with the highway barrier a touch more appealing. But, really, what was she supposed to do? Let the woman wallow? If Kathy found herself in the same position thirty years down the line, she hoped Fiona—or Noah, it didn't have to be the daughter—would be as gracious. But she'd never do that to her children. She'd never want to transition from mother to responsibility and crying her way out of a plan that made good sense would be emotional manipulation.

That wasn't how she'd describe Peggy's behavior, though. What transpired at the hospital was an honest opening up between two people who often protected themselves from each other. It was one woman admitting to another that she was afraid. To suspect anything else would be to depart completely from the assumption that people in your life were decent and true, and once you stepped off that ledge, what on earth would catch you?

Indeed, that was how Kathy felt—like the ground had shifted below her feet—even before arriving at the hospital, even before her mother became overcome. Because if it was true that before Peggy was Kathy's mother, she'd been a WASP, then everything Kathy had been shown about the world had been founded over hollow bedrock. Kathy had to seek surer ground. She had to confirm what now seemed clear.

Her mother hadn't been in any state for confrontation, and anyway, Kathy didn't trust her to confess. She'd spent her life hiding behind this secret and had already denied the legitimacy of the invitation. A discussion would yield more of the same. If Kathy wanted the truth, she had to present her mother incontrovertible proof.

PEGGY'S FRONT DOOR stuck. As Kathy pushed it open, there was a sucking release, followed by a small crack that sounded loud only in the silence. In the ten days since Peggy's first fall, the scorched stench of the soup had dissipated, leaving behind the default of pepper and powdery perfume.

Just as with every other aspect of her life, Peggy's house didn't have an open-door policy. She invited visitors but expected them to arrive on her terms so she could welcome them with a drink and prepared saga. Kathy felt through the empty dark without having been granted permission, intruding on what her mother kept private. But Kathy was desperate to drag her mother's past into the light, to see it fully, and gain understanding as to why so much of her childhood had felt tumultuous, to know what had often haunted her mother, and by consequence, the rest of them. Kathy was nearing a revelation, and the closer she got to it, the more she felt its pull—a force that was strong enough to overpower her mother's right to secrecy.

Kathy switched on every light, including the stove hood, to burn out the sense of the illicit, this violation of confidence. Even when illuminated, the house retained a spooky quality, like being caught in a museum after hours.

By the time her parents moved there in the 1970s, only Kathy, the youngest of their children, lived with them in this modest three-bedroom Cape. Kathy was thankful it wasn't one of their more sprawling houses down South, with rooms spilling into one another and countless dressers and storage nooks to search. Still, there were fifteen hundred square feet, and she was glad to be fueled by a full stomach; her hunger had compelled her to McDonald's, where she'd splurged on starch, fat, and sugary dipping sauces.

Kathy flipped through antique editions of classic novels on her mother's bookshelf, self-conscious in her amateur sleuthing. Her fingers skimmed beneath hutch drawers. She considered the door to the basement—a brick-lined pit big enough for the boiler, water heater, electric panel, and, back when her parents hosted parties, cases of beer—and decided against it. Whatever was down with the mouse pellets could stay there.

She came upon saved birthday and Christmas cards, wedding invitations, and thank-you notes; school photos of her nephews and grandnieces; deli receipts; grocery store coupons; and her father's memorial prayer card as well as, unsettlingly, a photo of him at his wake, laid out in the coffin. There were chipped serving dishes, commemorative air force coins, and DVDs of black-and-white movies. There were canned goods years past their expiration, barbecue sauce Peggy ordered from a restaurant in Kansas City, and enough Grape-Nuts to get a person through winter. There was a box of musty handkerchiefs in lace, silk, and linen, including the Hermès square Jimmy had gifted Peggy for her eightieth birthday, rumpled alongside the rest like she didn't realize its value. Kathy sniffed a laugh despite herself, but was quickly served her own medicine when she found the wooden statue of three generations of women she'd given her mother after Fiona was born, on its side, tucked in the back corner of the linen closet, in a plastic bin of candlesticks and outdoor glassware, where it had likely been hibernating for twenty years.

In the master bedroom, Kathy sorted through cloth hat-boxes stuffed with clutches, dress gloves, and costume jew-elry. She groped the sleeves of the cardigans her mother draped around her shoulders, and then paused fondly at the lineup of her father's dress shirts. Kathy eased out the flat storage box on the floor below them and lifted its lid to see his air force blues. Most people, particularly his colleagues, had been shocked that he wasn't buried in his service dress, but Peggy had balked at the convention. She wouldn't ship her husband to Arlington, and she kept his uniform where she could visit it.

The coat was the deep indigo that hovered at the height of twilight. Woolly, its fibers were soft but with a hint of scratch, and contained a stale smell, but also that of jet fuel and orange peel—her dad. It caught as a sweet memory in Kathy's throat, and suddenly there he was, buttoning his jacket while Kathy watched cross-legged on his bed. There he was, bending to touch the tip of his nose to hers, rising be-neath a dogpile of his three sons, slow dancing with Peggy to

"Sunday, Monday or Always" while crescent rolls burned in the oven. There he was, answering Peggy's perpetual question of *What am I supposed to do down here?* by saying, *Can't you find a way for this to be enough?*

His silver nametag was pinned to the right lapel, *Mayfield* engraved in blue letters. Ribbons, wings, a Bronze Star, and other medals decorated the left. "More hardware than a Home Depot," as Peggy had liked to say. The service cap, with its leather chinstrap and silver grommet, was wedged in the corner of the box. The visor was embroidered with aluminum wire in the lightning-and-dart design that marked colonels.

Kathy considered having the uniform properly preserved. They were lucky the moths hadn't gotten to it already. But she imagined her mother sitting with it, her fingers tracing the stiff seams and pleats. Some things were more precious than posterity.

Peggy had remained dignified through her husband's funeral—chin up, lipstick fresh, eyes respectfully watered without making a show of her tears. She hosted the repast in her home and regaled mourners who'd traveled from across the country with tales of the colonel's escapades, inside and outside of service: the time he flew an entire mission with cramped feet, not realizing she'd stuffed his dress socks into the front of his shoes; how he'd visited a deployed colleague's newborn so the baby would know the feel of a man's arms; how he was so confident he could drive his family from the base in Aurora to the one in Colorado Springs on half a tank, and when the car coughed three miles out, he lugged his daughter on his shoulders and a son in each arm the rest of the way, never admitting defeat. The guests laughed gamely and admired Peggy's resilience, especially when held up against her grieving children, who ranged from sullen to bereft. "Your mother is a special kind of lady," they said. "One of a kind." It was only after everybody left, when it was just Kathy and Peggy collecting cups and used napkins, clearing the dining room table of serving platters, that Peggy picked up a blue Italian porcelain tureen still half full of beef stew and drove it into the floor, like a bomb dropped from a plane.

That was one outburst Kathy didn't need explained. She felt the gutting grief herself, as well as the concurrent disorientation. What would their family do without their emotional mainstay? Fifteen years later, Kathy had learned the answer. They'd drifted. Frank refused to celebrate Christmas in the family home, staring at their father's empty chair. Jimmy didn't call the house as much without the prospect of speaking to Dad. Paul was struggling enough before taking on counseling his mourning mother. The Mayfield dynamic had shifted, and it became easier to opt out than to traverse something painful and new.

In Peggy's dresser, Kathy pushed aside compression socks, hosiery, and panties padded for incontinence. Her fingers brushed against something sharp in the back of the drawer, and she extracted a faded pack of cigarettes—Chesterfields. Its open top revealed a few degraded cigarettes. Kathy pulled out one and sniffed it. It was faintly stale, but almost odorless. How strange that Peggy had saved this memento. Kathy hadn't even known her mother had been a smoker, but that should come as no surprise; Kathy could fill a book with all she didn't know about Peggy Mayfield.

When Kathy bent to replace the cigarettes, her eye caught on a glint of white. An envelope. Its open mouth bulged around paper baked with age. Kathy loosed the bundle and unfolded it, but instead of finding historical documents of—what, the government commending her mother for her secret service?—there was only the lopsided scrawl of her younger self: *Dear Mom, thank you for the pancakes; Dear Mom, please wake me up when you get home from your party; Dear Mom, you are the prettiest.* Kathy knew the fierce devotion of young children, as well as the grief sustained when they aged out of it. It was easy to forget that she too had been a girl who worshipped her mother, and that Peggy had to watch that girl grow up to resist her. And what of the boys, who went from hanging on Peggy's every word to dodging her phone calls? Only a mother was demoted the longer she remained in the position.

Upstairs, Kathy collected her nerve in front of the attic. A person was more likely to stow clues to a sixty-year-old family secret in the rafters than with the pots and pans, but Kathy had hoped she could avoid this climb into cobwebs and obscurities. At least it was a walk-up, and she wouldn't have to bother with hatches and hinge ladders. She knocked on the door and listened for skittering paws. When was the last time anybody had been up there? It'd be a miracle if it hadn't become the neighborhood's rat cooperative. She flicked on the light and braced herself.

The staircase's unfinished pine was kept fresh by the chill of the alcove. The temperature continued to drop as she ascended, and Kathy was grateful she'd never removed her coat.

Kathy made fast work of her hunt; God forbid she was up there long enough that the rodents grew comfortable in her presence. She dug through bags of costumes. There were princess dresses and astronaut suits, and even a bomber jacket, but not one sized for a petite woman. There were boxes of paperback books that should be donated to a library before they were spoiled by mildew. Hundreds of GI Joe figures were zipped into bedding storage bags. There were bins of baby shoes and blankets, family albums, china sets, punch bowls, a bassinet whose wicker had grown brittle and snapped, and half-finished crafts from Peggy's jaunts into needlepoint and watercolor. There was a Mr. Potato Head, his Mrs. presumably broken and thrown away; folders keeping Kathy's old paper dolls flat; and the Easy-Bake Oven she'd begged for and was so disappointed not to receive on Christmas morning that her father went out and bought one the next day. *Childhood is for dreaming and playing make believe, and what do we give girls?* Peggy had lamented. *Toy ovens.*

Kathy began to accept there was no evidence to unearth, and she'd have to confront her mother on the basis of hearsay.

Then, in the far reaches of the garret, lodged against the sloped ceiling, was a box marked with Peggy's pitched capital letters, a crooked mountain range that spelled *Memories* in black permanent marker—a redundant category, in Kathy's view. What was this entire storage space crammed with if not memories?

Up until now, box flaps had been carelessly dropped and secured with a second box, or manipulated shut with interlocking tabs. This was the first box sealed by a length of tape. Kathy wiggled her fingernail beneath a corner. With enough purchase, she shucked the adhesive off, its tear shrill.

The top layer was a thin parcel wrapped in parchment paper, pulled as taut and neat as a present. Kathy's fingers were stiff with cold, but she was warmed by the sense of nearing something vital. She fumbled over the tape and then, impatient, tore the paper open.

It was an old issue of *Life* magazine, black and white except for a bright red stripe along the bottom and a matching block around the title. The issue year was 1943, and the cover photo featured a woman, thoughtful in her repose.

Kathy gasped, the intake as sudden and sharp as if she'd surfaced from fifty-three years of submergence. This was what she knew deep down she would find, the crucial detail hacked from her family's story, the missing piece that explained so much. Those high cheekbones, the slender fingers, that carved-out beauty—this was her mother, but with an expression that made her wistful and unfamiliar. Strangest of all, young Peggy was wearing a flight suit and was posed, quite comfortably, on the wing of a bomber.

Chapter 15

December 1943

THE BOEING B-17 FLYING FORTRESS WAS THREE TIMES larger than any aircraft Peggy had ever flown and could travel faster, higher, and farther. This wasn't just a plane. It was a weapon equipped with eight machine gun posts and destined to drop explosives. The Fairchild, which more closely resembled her crop-dusting plane, was for training purposes only. It never saw battle, just aerobatics, and its appearance reflected such innocence, painted in primary yellow and blue that could as easily be found on a child's toy. The B-17, however, was the full-fledged war machine featured in newsreels. It was the plane of Americans coming to the rescue against deranged evils. This vessel was olive-green with the U.S. Army Air Forces insignia painted on its body and wings. A PT-19 could hold a mere two passengers whereas the B-17 held ten, as well as plenty of cargo. Unlike the Fairchild's, this cockpit was closed; the B-17 flew too fast and high for the pilot to be exposed to the elements. Called the Flying Fortress because it was designed to withstand attack, the bomber could inflict damage and survive it. It was the eastern diamondback rattler of planes: enormous, swift, poisonous, and resilient.

The WASP cadets beheld the lineup in silence. These were true military aircraft, the real vehicles of war. The B-17s were why the women were here. There was reverence in having arrived at their purpose, as well as fear. A bomber provoked devastation. The cause was noble, but it didn't lessen the cost of human lives, which Peggy would now contribute to in small part, and if a bird of this magnitude fell from the sky, survival was unlikely. A flush burned up Peggy's neck and smoldered at her hairline. She turned down the collar of her leather flight jacket.

Peggy was relieved to be third in her line. She could steel herself by watching Georgia and Pamela take the B-17 up and down before climbing into the cockpit herself. But when Major Mayfield reached them, he said, "Lewis, you're first," a targeted attack that seemed excessive, even for him.

An invisible string tugged behind Pamela's eyebrows and knit her features into a scowl. Peggy widened her expression as if to say, *This wasn't what I ordered either. Take it up with the honcho.* Georgia, though, smacked her backside as she passed.

As she and the major neared the bomber, his assistant placed a crate beneath the cockpit hatch. Peggy was used to hopping onto the wing and dropping into her seat from above. Now she'd have to lift herself into the nose from below, and the crate was in anticipation of an upper-body-strength deficit. The precautionary measure was deserved—her biceps were about as impressive as a pair of turnips plucked too early. Yet she was insulted.

The major braced either side of the opening and swung himself up and in. Peggy considered kicking the crate away and attempting to be equal in all tasks, but she was confident she'd lose that gamble, and without seeing that she'd done away with the crate, the major would assume she was incompetent even *with* the handicap. For now, she stepped onto the box, but vowed to do pull-ups so that when it came time to solo, and Mayfield watched her from afar, he would see that she was capable of all things.

The cockpit was a cave of steel and glass, its dashboard riddled with gadgets, gauges, and dials. "Hot damn," Peggy said. Then she realized that the major sat in the copilot seat. This wouldn't be a trial ride. She would shoot the first flight herself. "Hot damn."

She lowered into the pilot's seat and straddled the throttle. There were more instruments than she could count, an array of peculiar switches and buttons. She braved a glance out the windshield. The runway seemed a distant galaxy that had nothing to do with her or here.

The major's eyes skated over her. "You all right, cadet?"

Peggy wouldn't reveal weakness. She stretched the headphones over her ears. "Sure. This right here is every gal's dream."

The BT cockpit procedure was extensive, six lists each with twelve items to satisfy before takeoff. The process was too elaborate to memorize, so pilots were allowed to carry the lists with them. Peggy pulled the papers from her jacket pocket and rested them against the dashboard to stifle their crinkling. It took ten minutes to make their way through the first five lists. The sixth was a call-and-response. She felt sheepish launching into engagement with the major.

"Cowl flaps."

"Up," the major answered, clear and calm. It was as if the thought of Peggy flying the B-17 didn't scare him.

"Wing flaps."

"Down."

"Oil cooler shutters." This was officially the most sustained interaction Peggy had ever had with the major, free of raised voices and admonishment. It was an even exchange, a partnership. For him to sit where he was sitting, and for her to do the same—they had to trust each other with their lives.

"Up."

"Crew." A sunray pierced the glass panel above their heads. Mayfield reached into his jacket pocket for a pair of aviator sunglasses and unfolded their silver arms with care. The brown lenses created a barrier between himself and the outside world, but from his periphery, Peggy could still see his eyes, narrowed but also at ease, as if here, in this cockpit, was the place he was meant to be.

"In position."

"All right." Peggy narrowed her eyes against the glare. She was so used to wearing goggles, she hadn't thought to bring sunglasses. She was still learning what could cross her path, and all the ways she must be prepared. "Say your prayers."

The plane snorted and Peggy guided the throttle forward. They began to roll, and all the confidence she'd accumulated during the checklist vanished. The bomber had too much power. She was a speck attempting to tame a tempest. Somebody more competent, fierce, and wise should be in control of such an unwieldy beast. Not her. She was too small. Barely one hundred pounds. Couldn't the people in charge see that? Where was her second weigh-in? Now her life was in danger, and she'd take the major down with her. Heck, she could barrel right through her entire class.

"Lord almighty," she said.

She angled herself toward the windshield, as if a closer look was all she needed. But the outside world, so far away, felt disconnected from what she was trying to do in the cockpit. Maybe she was dead already, recounting her last moments from above. She gripped the throttle so tightly it might have burst into dust.

The B-17 was galloping, a mustang free of its jockey, bolting for the fence. She had no idea what it would do next. It could race down the runway exactly as she wanted or it could rear back, thrash its head, and toss them out.

The engines made her seat vibrate. They roared in her ears. "Lord almighty."

They were tearing down the runway. It was now or never. Peggy pulled back on the reins. The plane tossed its mane. She was too deep into the takeoff to back down. Surrender would be more perilous than forging ahead. She pulled resolutely, as if to say this was not a negotiation, and prayed the plane would believe her. It relented, kicking itself up off the ground, but half-heartedly, to show this didn't mean it was broken. The plane was flying not because it was trained, but because it wanted to fly, and was likely to change its mind. That's why cadets called bombers flying coffins. They were stubborn and liable to defy orders, even if it meant destroying themselves in the process.

Peggy was alert, all synapses firing, her vigilance an enduring intensity.

She and the major were high enough that the base below could be swept into a bin and stored in a toy closet. How Peggy wished for some all-powerful entity to go ahead and whisk those dear girls off, to clear them from this soaring dragon they mistakenly assumed Peggy could command. She couldn't operate a creature of this magnitude. She could barely breathe.

All at once she realized that was true. The air was too thin. She snatched at it, but inhaling was as productive as trying to capture oxygen between her fingers.

"You're flying the plane. It isn't flying you," the major said, steadily.

Peggy was choking now. Tears stirred in her eyes and nose. "You only see what it's doing, not what I'm *trying* to make it do."

Mayfield exhaled a puff of air through his nose, and Peggy's eyes flicked to see the corner of his mouth edge into a smirk. It was a porthole into who he was, or maybe who he had been: a boy sprinting around his backyard with a model plane he'd glued and painted, a young man kissing his mother's cheek on his way to heroically combat the most formidable evil the world had ever known, then a veteran pilot reassigned to a women's air base.

"Did I just make you laugh, sir?" Peggy asked, straining against her panic. She switched the cowl flaps to neutral and then rushed back to the yoke, as though clutching it until her knuckles burned was the only way to maintain a lick of control. "And here I thought flying this bomber would be today's greatest achievement."

The plane dropped, faltered, and jounced. Peggy was too

busy reading meters, flipping levers, and generally keeping them and everybody below alive to worry about providing a smooth ride.

They careened toward their landing much too fast. Peggy had miscalculated their weight and speed. She hadn't cut the engine in time. A moment away from death, she yanked back on the yoke, lifting the bomber's nose. She had just enough time for her brain to issue a single-word prayer—*please*— before they leveled out and glided past the runway.

Her heart punched up into her throat. "I'll circle back around. I'll get her next time."

"Come at it shy like that and you'll kill us," Mayfield said. He spoke squarely, but the color in his cheeks had faded, and he pasted himself against his chair back. "She's big but you're in charge."

Peggy approached the runway a second time and plunged their nose too low, as if from a high dive. She recognized her mistake, and Mayfield confirmed it with a faint groan. She wrenched back in reflex, but it was an overcorrection, and they dropped, smashing down on all wheels. Peggy's neck snapped forward and her teeth clamped her tongue. She hadn't handled a plane like such a greenhorn since she wore white collars and Mary Janes. Too humiliated to raise her head, she moved through the remaining checklists.

"It sure as hell wasn't anything to write home about," Major Mayfield said as the engines purred to a quiet. "But we're alive."

Peggy's hand trembled uncontrollably. It had been made sepia with dust and sweat. She flipped it over to her palm, with its topography of calluses and cuts. It was a different hand than she used to know, but it was hers. "I suppose we are."

She still had two more flights to shoot.

The next time she drifted in for a landing, she hit an air pocket and the plane picked back up, a child refusing to be set down. The bomber might be mighty, but gravity was the stronger force. They bounced on the runway until finally rooting.

Peggy hadn't gotten airsick since she first learned to fly, but the B-17 was like learning everything fresh. All those old feelings were reincarnated. Queasiness seeped its way through her limbs, making her entire body stale. This was better, however, than Pamela, who flew next, and upon landing promptly vomited into her lap.

It was only a matter of getting to know this warbird. The first impression was bristly, but once Peggy spent enough time exploring its inner workings, she discovered something she recognized. The B-17 was just another gal tired of being told what to do. So, when it was possible for her to roam free, Peggy sat back and watched her. And when it wasn't, Peggy directed her with respect and appreciation.

When it was time to solo a week later, any sense of poise she'd mustered uncapped back to raw nerves. She wasn't ready to ditch the supervision of an instructor. What if she panicked? What if the plane was feeling particularly prickly? There'd be no extra set of hands, no sage advice, no one to catch her before they crashed.

Uncertainty rose up from the thirsty Texas dirt as Peggy marched from the flight line. She could feel its grip circling her ankles, threatening to pull her so far under her mouth would fill with dust.

Yet somehow she arrived at the plane. The cockpit gaped open above her and Major Mayfield's stare reached through the winter to lay heat on her back. She considered the crate briefly and then kicked it aside, grasped the bars on either side of the opening, and oscillated up and in.

Her body shivered as if with fever. She drew in a few purposeful breaths and then settled into the pilot's seat. She averted her attention from the empty space beside her, but its presence loomed large. There was no instructor, no backup. It was just her and the plane. But that was okay. She didn't need an expert. She *was* the expert.

Peggy patted the dashboard. "Finally, some girl time."

* * *

Before they moved on to the B-26, nicknamed the widow-maker for the steep rate of accidents sustained during take-off and landing, Peggy's class had to pass a flight check on the B-17. They would get one shot. No second chances or redos. For those who failed, this was the end of training. They'd say goodbye to Avenger Field, their barracks, flight school, and working toward the impossible. They would go home.

The latrines were occupied by nervous stomachs, and plates of uneaten lunch were emptied in the garbage before being stacked for washing.

Class 44-2 retrieved their flight gear and dragged thirty-pound parachutes and their trepidation to the flight line. That subdued procession was downright celebratory in comparison to the gloom of their recession after twenty-five girls, a third of their population, were dismissed.

"It's no reflection on you as pilots," Lieutenant Colonel Walker, a silver-haired father figure, reminded them. "Some of the best pilots never get the knack for the bombers, men included. You might be a damn fine flyer in a different vessel, but we need bomber pilots, and that's a fact."

Georgia, Connie, and Peggy encircled Cheryl on her bed. "I knew it was going to happen. I just knew it," Cheryl said, bowing to hide her face, her frame as small and fragile as if it were made of wire.

"They're just a bunch of bullies," Peggy said. Her fingers wove through Cheryl's shiny black hair to rest between her shoulder blades.

Cheryl shook her head. "No, they are right to wash me out. Those B-17s aren't like other planes. I can't operate them." Peggy opened her mouth to insist that that's how they all felt, that everybody was just faking until their confidence turned real, and such pretending was how men made it in the world so women should get used to pretending too, but Cheryl rushed on. "I'm not saying that so you'll disagree. I'm saying it because it's true. I gave it a shot, but I should go home before I hurt myself or somebody else."

"I don't see the utility in all these tears," Georgia said, knuckling a stream from Cheryl's cheek. "You get to see your family, sleep in, eat decent food, take a shit in private, and do whatever you want whenever the hell you want to do it. You ought to be grinning like a possum eating fire ants."

Georgia had set her tone to upbeat, but her words were flimsy, and Peggy was sure they all knew it. There were inconveniences on base, but they were shallow in the face of being challenged, stimulated, and held to higher standards. Their country needed them, and they were rising to that need. They were accomplishing the remarkable and working toward a cause that mattered. When had they been offered such a chance? When would they again?

"I'm going home too," Millie said.

Peggy spun toward her baymate. "What are you talking about? You passed the check."

The way Millie hunched her shoulders and stroked the ends of her braids made her appear like a girl. "This just isn't for me."

"What about it, exactly?" Peggy asked, as if Millie had insulted her personally.

"The pressure, the testing, the drills, the bombers. It's all too much."

Cheryl's sobs had slowed into sporadic intakes of breath. "What are you going to do?"

"Go back to my ranch. Help my daddy with the horses. Maybe meet somebody."

"And that's enough for you? After everything?" Peggy asked.

Millie shrugged. "It's always been enough."

"You're lucky, then," Pamela whispered from across the room.

They retreated into their private worlds, six hearts beating on their own separate planets, orbiting one another, together but apart, in quiet solidarity for one last night, just a little longer.

Chapter 16

November 2009

AS MUCH AS KATHY WOULD HAVE LIKED TO GO STRAIGHT home after a long shift on her feet, it was Thanksgiving Eve, and somebody had to do the grocery shopping.

She could have given Neil a list. Since she was taking on what was formerly his role, it was only fair that he cover hers, at least in part. Yet it seemed she was now responsible for both, earning an income *and* managing the household. She had to keep patient records in her head alongside what produce needed to be eaten before it turned, when laundry needed doing, and if they were low on toilet paper. Last week, Neil had checked the open dishwasher and asked, "Is this clean?" and she'd wanted to scream. The state of their dishes was her responsibility even when his head was inches from crusty plates? She took umbrage that such insignificance was ever presumed to be her purview; however, Thanksgiving was not the occasion to pass the food foraging torch. She imagined Neil wandering aimless for hours, carts bumping around him, aggravated wives wondering who'd sent the newb on a day reserved for pros. He'd come home with canned corn instead of frozen, pumpkin pie filling rather than puree, and one type of orange juice instead of the multiple brands preferred by each member of the family. It was easier to just do it herself.

Besides, since Kathy couldn't take more time off work, Neil had been the one to pick Peggy up from the hospital—that alone was enough to secure him a spot in heaven. He'd texted updates throughout the day: *We're home and I apparently could give Indy 500 drivers a run for their money. Peggy ate half a sandwich and wonders why we buy wheat bread when it tastes like cardboard; she's eaten white all her life and is still ticking. She's either sleeping or quietly plotting my death.*

Kathy staggered into the house with a platoon of plastic bags digging into her forearms. The kitchen smelled rich and garlicky. A pan of sausage and peppers hissed on the stove, a package of hot dog buns beside it. She'd written out the cooking instructions, but still, after eight hours of patients and the chaos of last-minute holiday shopping, her mother was safely home, dinner was waiting, and she was grateful.

Neil was carving at the kitchen table, perhaps, Kathy conjectured, releasing Peggy-related frustration on a block of wood. Spending time with her mother sometimes made Kathy herself daydream of small blades. But no, he was working toward his goal of transmuting Noah's childhood toy blocks into a football-themed chess set. It was a time-consuming project, but what did he have if not time? Neil didn't expect to have it done by Christmas but hoped by then he could at least show his son what he'd been working on. That seemed important to Neil.

A shape was emerging from his first piece, the mound of a helmet sloping into wide-set shoulders. When his wife entered, schlepping what felt like half the grocery store, he returned it to the table beside his tools, dusted his hands, and came to her. She wanted to tell him he should keep working, if he liked. He should pour himself into joy wherever he found it.

He took the bags and set them on the island. She knew he'd go to the car next, but the frigid garage would keep everything cool, so the rest could wait. Neil had driven to the hospital, listened to Peggy's discharge report, and chauffeured her home. He'd helped her upstairs, taken her lunch order, and delivered it. He'd checked on her. He'd kept her hydrated. He'd stomached what was likely a murder of disapprovals and side comments. Kathy knew how taxing providing care could be.

She gripped his shoulders, but then thought she could do better, so she cupped his face, lifted onto her tiptoes, and kept her lips soft as she placed them over his in the kind of movie-moment kiss that was sultry and sweet. Neil didn't pull away, but he didn't melt into it either, or wrap his hands around her backside, as he often did. He just stood there waiting for it to end.

Kathy lowered onto her heels but remained close. "I know she's a buzzkill, but we can do better than that."

Neil's lips worked against their seal. His hand rose up to her arm, rubbed swiftly, and then squeezed hard to communicate consolation.

Kathy stepped back from the harbinger. "What's wrong?"

"I didn't want to tell you over text." His hand wriggled into his jeans pocket and he pulled out a scrap of paper. "The doctor found what is causing the falls. A—" He checked the paper to make sure he got it right. "Aortic stenosis. A severe case of it, apparently. The valve isn't opening enough, so her heart has to work really hard to pump the blood through."

"I know what aortic stenosis is." Kathy's mind stretched to encompass everything she remembered about the condition. "Does the doctor recommend valve replacement?"

The faint flames of Neil's eyebrows flickered. "Yes."

Kathy's jaw began to itch. She didn't want to expose her worry, so instead of cracking it, she massaged the urge with her thumb. "Was she open to the idea?"

"I believe her exact words were, 'Over my dead body.'"

Without surgical intervention, the prognosis was bleak. For Peggy's age and circumstances, there was a good chance she'd die suddenly within the year.

Neil said, "Maybe she'll change her mind."

"Have you known her to be adaptive and open to suggestion?"

"I'm sorry."

Her mother's heart was straining blood through too small a space. She was upstairs dying beat by beat. She could have millions left, or the next could be her last. How would it feel when Kathy was, for the first time, without either of the people who'd raised her? Her eyes began to burn and heat spread across her chest. She turned before her husband could see. "Thanks for getting dinner together. I'm just going to check on her."

Peggy was staying in Fiona's bedroom. Kathy thought her mother would be happy among her granddaughter's things, those typical of teenage girls—lilac walls, body sprays, lip balms, and bangles—as well as those that made Fiona distinct: *A Field Guide to American Houses* on her nightstand, eight hundred pages long; an architectural drawing of the Empire State Building; the Megaminx, a Rubik's Cube on steroids; and a Marie Curie Bobblehead.

A lamp shed buttery light on Peggy's profile—those defiant cheekbones, her suede-soft skin—as she peered out the window into the neighbor's yard, where a Yorkie bucked against its lead and yapped into the dark.

"If we're lucky, it'll break its neck," Peggy said. She was atop the quilt, fully dressed in loose black slacks and a blouse with a beaded neckline, the arms of a red cardigan hugging her from behind. The only marks of her compromised state were the nonskid hospital socks and walker set against the wall. She was nonplussed, unless, actually, her breath intake was a little sharp, and perhaps it had been for some time now, and Kathy, supposedly a medical professional, hadn't noticed.

"How are you feeling?"

Peggy swept her hand from her shoulders to her knees, as if she were Vanna White presenting herself. "Like a very old lady."

"No surprise after two falls," Kathy said, and because tears were tingling behind her eyes, she added, "and for anyone alive during the Dust Bowl."

"Do you insult all of your houseguests, or is that a special honor reserved for your mother?"

Kathy considered the edge of the bed, but to sit so close to Peggy, like a mother tending to a child, would be more intimate than they were accustomed. The only other chair in the room was an oversized beanbag. If she managed herself into it, she worried about getting back up, but her feet ached, and this conversation called for sitting down. Kathy thought she caught amusement around Peggy's eyes before she dropped. The bag puffed and wheezed as it caught her weight.

When the stuffing stopped complaining, Kathy said, "I heard about your heart."

"No body lasts forever. I've put a lot of miles on mine." Peggy's feet, uncharacteristically free of shoes, flexed back in an arc. "Maybe I can see the Wizard and ask for a new ticker."

"You can, Tin Man. They're called doctors, and it's called surgery."

Peggy stiffened. She didn't like being outwitted. "I don't remember offering you a penny, but thanks for your thoughts just the same."

Kathy shimmied herself up a couple inches, as if her mother might take her more seriously if only she had higher altitude. "Fifty percent of those who forgo treatment die of heart failure within the year."

"At my age, I should be grateful for that much."

"It could be less." The yipping ended abruptly as the neighbor called the dog inside. Kathy almost missed the noise, the clamorous urgency that had accompanied their discussion.

"When God takes me is up to Him."

Her mother didn't usually reference a higher power but racing toward an afterlife could sharpen a person's values. Only Peggy didn't have to be traveling toward her end at such velocity. The very woman who just twenty-four hours before had wept with the desire to live should be eager to accept reasonable risk. Peggy, as always, was an enigma wrapped in a Chico's tunic, and Kathy, as always, was struggling to make sense of her, even after fifty years. "You're the one who said you weren't ready to die."

"That's precisely why I won't volunteer for a risky surgery," Peggy said, her emotions building behind her protest. "This isn't my first day at the poker table. I'm not going to gamble for the big pot and lose it all, or stroke out and end up a warm vegetable, so here's my answer in five different languages: no, no, no, no, *nein*."

Peggy's obstinate display reminded Kathy of another topic that had made her mother dig in her heels, and the evidence Kathy had obtained that would knock her off her feet. Maybe now, in the throes of this heart discussion, wasn't the ideal moment, but time wasn't infinite, and Kathy wouldn't waste any more. She buried her hands in the sack and launched off without explaining where she was going.

Kathy had brought home her mother's box of memories—letters, a flight manual, goggles, silver wings, pressed rose petals, and the goddamn World War II Victory Medal—and stored them under her bed, but the WASP issue of *Life* magazine she'd placed on her vanity table between two framed photos: one from her wedding and one from her parents'. The two contemporary Peggys gazed at each other—a contemplative war pilot eyeing a joyful bride. The Mayfields had married in 1945, the year the war ended. Peggy had recited the story of their meeting enough times, and in precisely the same way, it had spun into family legend: she and Kathy's father had attended a scavenger hunt–themed party and each—Kathy heard the punch line in her mother's voice— "satisfied the other's list."

Only then did it occur to Kathy that perhaps Peggy had

leaned so heavily on the script of this tale because it was rehearsed. It couldn't have been a coincidence that two war-time pilots met. Was the party actually at an air base? Or was it a complete fabrication? The entire story of how Kathy's family came to be could be false. Her identity was without any sturdy underpinning. Peggy was lucky Kathy couldn't yell at a dying woman, at least not so soon after learning she was in fact that.

When Kathy returned, it was to her mother's bedside, and she spoke with the gentleness of breaking bad news. "I stopped by your house and came upon this."

She watched carefully as Peggy's eyes fell to the image she likely hadn't seen in decades, drenched in the light filtered through her granddaughter's ruffled lampshade. There was a pull between her eyebrows, a tug that might have been connected to a heartstring, and then a quick release and retreat as she sank into her pillow.

"You just happened to come upon that in the recesses of my attic?"

"I'm sorry for snooping but—"

"A key to the front door isn't free license to rifle through a person's private belongings."

"This is you," Kathy said, stabbing the glossy page. "You're this pretty young miss with something to prove."

Peggy's lips puckered with angry lines. "This isn't any of your business."

"You're my mother."

"Even mothers have a right to their own inner lives."

"This should make you proud. Why haven't you been shouting it from the rooftops?"

Peggy toyed with her sleeves until her fumbling hands found comfort in each other. She held herself tight and returned her attention to the neighbor's backyard, where the dog lead was slack but illuminated. "It's ancient history."

"That didn't stop you from bragging about your Pie Baker of 1967 title through the Ford presidency."

"That meringue put prissy Sheila Johnson's apple crumble in its place."

"This isn't history anymore. They want to give you a medal in four months."

"Would you accept a wedding ring on your deathbed from the very man who left you at the altar?"

"Better late than never."

"Most of us are six feet under. For them, fifty years late *is* never."

Since her mother was immovable, at least in that moment, Kathy approached the topic from a different angle. "Where did Daddy figure into all of this?"

At that, Peggy softened. "He was my commanding officer."

"But you met at a party. You said so a million times."

Peggy flicked her untruth away as easily as a speck of lint. "That was the plot to *Christopher Strong*, which was not only a damn good romance, but written and directed by women, in 1933, no less. Katharine Hepburn played a female pilot, for goodness' sake. I dropped all the bread crumbs. You just weren't willing to follow them."

"I shouldn't have to follow bread crumbs to find out who my mother is," Kathy said, her fingers tingling. "I don't understand why you kept this all a secret."

"You're one to talk about secrets." Peggy cocked an eyebrow and appraised her daughter. "The apple hasn't rolled far."

Kathy physically withdrew from the comparison. "What's that supposed to mean?"

"My heart may be defective but my brain works fine," Peggy said, tapping her temple. "I noticed Neil was home on a Wednesday while you were out past six."

"Fine, you got me. Neil was laid off and I'm back to work. I didn't tell you because I knew you'd be judgmental."

"Then our secrets have much in common," Peggy said, knowingly. "We kept them both to protect you."

* * *

The kids arrived Thanksgiving morning like a sonic boom, grabbing drinks from the fridge, jamming chargers into outlets, slamming doors, abandoning shoes by the entryway, and chatting, mostly about themselves, which distracted the adults from all that needed saying. They spoke of Fiona's classes and Noah's work, the best burritos in Cambridge, annoying roommates, and whether *Parks and Recreation* had potential to be as good as *The Office*. Kathy felt as if they'd commissioned actors to perform for them. This was how it had always been since the kids were born. The grown-ups receded into the background to bask in the glory of new life, invigorated by proximity. She could see this at work in Peggy, who angled herself toward Fiona on the living room couch, their bodies coming together at their knees to create a heart. She clasped Fiona's hands within the clamshell of hers and prompted her granddaughter for information. *Tell me about this Ecological*

Urbanism class. Do you raise your hand? Does your professor give you the right attention? And Fiona went on about using nature as a medium, and the partnership between habitat and design, while Peggy drank her in as if she were the medicine that would unblock her calcified valve.

Neil set up camp with Noah, a beer wrapped in a Patriots koozie for each, to hear about the product his son's employer was developing: a wearable device for arthritis patients to collect behavioral patterns and develop personalized treatments. Noah described the technology and Neil shook his head in wonder, occasionally punctuating his marvel by smacking the granite countertop with a stiff palm, saying, "That's wild."

Kathy visited both conversations but couldn't fully enter either. She was too busy snapping the ends off asparagus, basting the turkey with white wine and butter, roasting carrots, dicing celery for stuffing, and blanketing the sweet potato casserole with mini marshmallows. Would she have liked to catch up with the children she hadn't seen in a month? Would she have appreciated some help, or even an offer to suggest the other four capable humans didn't presume an entire Thanksgiving meal, including appetizers and three varieties of pie, was entirely Kathy's responsibility? Yes, and yes.

Maybe it wasn't fair to resent their happy absentmindedness when it was Kathy who'd trained them to assume it was her job. She'd single-handedly cooked every dinner, packed every lunch, and ensured breakfast was served by the time they made it downstairs. She'd dusted and swept and scrubbed bathrooms. She'd prepared elaborate holiday meals. It wasn't their fault things were suddenly different because Kathy was working—and for other reasons too.

She surfaced from plucking rosemary sprigs and caramelizing onions to eavesdrop on the lives of her son and daughter. Certainly they didn't always go on about themselves to such an extent, but they had the attention of their adoring family, so this was their time to preen. This was the natural order of things. But Kathy felt herself resist the tide of how things had always been. Things weren't the same. Fiona and Noah knew about her job. Wasn't it common courtesy to ask about the patients, the pressure, the transition, and her boss? Wasn't it decent to take a breath from complacent conceit to wash a dirty pan, squeeze the cook's shoulder, or pour her a drink? Her children were good people and her most beloved gifts, but surely there were matters of greater importance than how many Starbucks they passed on their morning commute.

Kathy's vexation snagged when she overheard a discussion she did find of great importance. Fiona was describing a study abroad program in Barcelona that would begin the following fall. She'd already applied. Kathy's reaction wheeled from feeling hurt that she was hearing the news secondhand, to worrying about accommodating additional expenses into their already constrained budget, to preemptively missing her daughter, to calculating all new foreign worries. Maybe this wasn't such a good idea. She wouldn't want Fiona to overextend herself because she thought a semester abroad was what she was supposed to do.

From the edge of their conversation, Kathy asked, "Are you sure you'll be able to manage all your requirements?"

Fiona cupped her wineglass like she was protecting it from everybody else in the room. "It's a program designed for architecture students. Ever heard of Antoni Gaudí? The requirements are built right in." She rolled her eyes at Peggy conspiratorially, as if Kathy couldn't plainly see them. The elaborateness of the gesture indicated she'd already had too much to drink. "Mom doesn't think I can handle anything."

Kathy stiffened against the sharp-edged conclusion. "I do so. Why would you say that?"

Peggy looked from one half of the duo to the other. Then she placed her hand over Fiona's and soundlessly lowered her from hostility. "You know, your mother was an asset back when we lived in Spain. She was the only Mayfield who actually learned the language."

"You lived in Spain? You speak Spanish?" Fiona swung to her mother, wide-eyed. The contempt she'd so recently wielded was replaced with something like wonder. "How did I not know this?"

As always, Peggy was overselling her daughter's talents, and now Kathy would have to reset expectations before others were disappointed. "Because it isn't true. I mean, the Spain part is, but not the Spanish," she said, although it was at least *parcialmente verdad*. While she'd lost fluency, she still understood much of what was said, so much so she'd been able to redirect a Spanish-speaking family who'd gotten turned around on the Minuteman Bikeway, each communicating in their own tongue. "You lose a language when you don't practice it."

Fiona's admiration passed like a drifting cloud. "Noted. I'll be sure to use my Spanish when I get back."

Kathy didn't bother telling her they speak Catalan in Barcelona. If she was so sure of herself, let her figure it out.

Kathy brought the turkey to temperature, broiled the marshmallows into a sugary crust, dusted the asparagus with Parmesan cheese, and tossed sliced almonds with the string beans. She warmed maple syrup, simmered savory herb juices, and sprayed dishes with a lemon wedge.

Her shirt was damp beneath the armpits, and she pulled her hair up off her neck. She was more than the chef and dishwasher. Neil and Peggy were more than rapt audiences. They all had things to say—some with limited time in which to say them. Their grandmother was a resource they were squandering.

It had been only a couple days since Kathy had learned her mother was a former war pilot, and less than twenty-four hours since Peggy had confirmed it. Kathy still needed to page through her childhood and translate her memories through this new cipher. This could be the reason that explained so much. But she hadn't had time to process. Everything felt jumbled and obscure—unbelievable—though she knew it was true.

The most prominent puzzle was the secrecy itself. Why squirrel this history away? Peggy claimed it was for Kathy's benefit, but this rationale felt flimsy even without synthesis. What detriment could there be? Already she felt her pride swelling. All this time, when her mother baffled or hurt her, she could have been cushioned by that respect. She could have been inspired. The hollow justification seemed a deflection, a way to blind Kathy with guilt so she stopped searching for the real reason.

Peggy was insistent that the truth remain between the two of them, at least until she was ready to share. The fact of Peggy's heart condition and her noble history pulsed in Kathy's throat. It bothered Kathy to perpetuate the legacy of secret-keeping. She wanted to unleash the bombshells and watch them shudder across the expressions of her children, to recognize the complexity of her own emotions reflected back to her, and to hear the echo of her questions: *How can you not do everything possible to stay with us longer? Why did you withhold such an essential part of yourself all this time?*

Yet the news was not hers, so she held it inside, along with her crossness that her family, equally capable, was letting her do so much. Of course they were tuned in enough that they pushed to their feet and followed the serving dishes that Kathy carried to the dining room, even transporting platters with them, a too small gesture arriving too late.

Chairs scratched floorboards, forks clinked china, and her children chirped their praise: Everything looked so delicious. How did she juggle so much at once? Kathy uncorked the bottle of pinot noir Fiona had already started and overturned it so that liquid garnet glugged into her glass. She filled her mouth with the salve of rich, velvet berries.

She whirled her wine and beheld what she'd laid out in gold-trimmed dishware: dinner rolls drizzled with garlic butter; cornbread stuffing; greens glistening with oil; mashed potatoes with steam swiveling to the ceiling; two types of cranberry sauce, a quivering ruby geode topped with sugared orange peel and walnuts as well as the gelatinous log suctioned from the can to retain its impression; and the star of the show, the twenty-five-pound perfectly browned bird.

Her guests murmured praise, but there was a performative quality to it, as if expressing appreciation was their role in response to hers. She served and they received. That was the way it was meant to be, and it had been enough for her in the past, but a quake had been sent through their convention, yet only Kathy appeared aware of it. This wasn't the sum of her parts, to be scooped and passed and consumed until bellies were full, and then scraped into the trash and forgotten. She was more than a fleeting feast. She was bedside manner, an assessing eye, vaccines, blood pressure cuffs, and heartbeats. She was a daughter, exasperated by her mother and terrified of losing her. She was a sister who missed her brothers yet savored her martyrdom. She was a mother who loved her children but didn't like everything about them, and a similarly asymmetrical wife. More than anything, she was tired.

Neil sawed the serrated blade with great ceremony. Kathy wanted to fight back against their tacit family positions, and in doing so, humble her children. Since she couldn't use Peggy's past, and she couldn't rightly elevate herself, Kathy raised her glass to Neil, as if to toast him. "This is hardly your father's first carving this week, now that he's whittling again."

The silver of the knife disappeared into the breast meat but materialized as a glint in Neil's eye.

Fiona's wineglass hovered short of her lips. "Oh yeah?"

The first slice of meat fell away to expose the textured grain. Neil said, "A little."

Noah bobbed his head, waiting for the rest. When he realized there was no more to come, he said, "It's nice to keep busy. Good for you, Dad."

As a boy, Noah shuffled around in Neil's enormous dress shoes. As a teen, he memorized the Red Sox starting lineup to impress his father, though he didn't personally care about sports. Now, he spoke to Neil as if commending a child for not spilling his juice.

Kathy realized her mistake. The children weren't privy to their father's interior life, just as Kathy hadn't been privy to Peggy's. They didn't know he'd spent the last six months mourning and self-flagellating, and that carving was a hint of forgiving himself and returning to life—his reawakening. They didn't know how much this keeping busy meant.

Maybe it wasn't their job to appreciate their father's psyche, or to analyze his behavior for deeper context, but they could have put on a better show, or at least bit down on their condescension. How many years had Kathy and Neil oohed and aahed over their drawings and test grades, clapping and celebrating every small victory? They didn't have to be so transparently unimpressed.

A rashy blush spilled down Neil's neck. His fair complexion was incapable of bluffing, and this embarrassment ran deep. Kathy scrambled for something to direct attention away from him, but her good intentions had already imploded on her. She'd only wanted to lift her husband up, to make him feel adored and admired, but it had come off as false amplification, as if she were reaching for something he could be proud of to hide the fact that he had nothing.

"I had no idea you were a craftsman." Peggy's hands were folded in her lap and her gaze extended across the table as a branch. She'd struck the right note of serious without overselling, and most importantly, without a trace of pity. "I'd like to see your work sometime."

"Sure thing, Peg." Neil drew his knife through the next slice, and when he looked up, he appeared relieved and genuinely happy to have her at their table. They'd exchanged one kindness for another. "We'll be spending enough time together. Maybe the two of us should set up shop."

The air loosened and everyone filled their plates. Kathy tried to catch her mother's attention to communicate her thanks, but Peggy passed dishes and moved on without recognition. This woman—so obdurate and critical in one moment, so generous and thoughtful in the next—might never stop surprising her.

Chapter 17

December 1943

JACKIE COCHRAN APPEARED BEHIND GEORGIA AND PEGGY at breakfast and laid the gavels of her hands on their shoulders. "I need to see you both in my office," she said, and didn't wait for a response before marching out of mess.

"What was that about?" Connie asked.

The weigh-in. Cochran had promised to put Peggy back on the scale before letting her near a bomber. Peggy had assumed she'd forgotten, and maybe she had—until now. Was Peggy over one hundred pounds? She had no clue. With new workouts and a change in diet, she was lean but brawny and had lost sense of her size. Her time might be up. Her bite of oatmeal lay like a dollop of plaster on her tongue. She wanted to swallow it but feared it would trigger her gag reflex and she'd lose her breakfast when she needed every spare ounce. She brought a napkin to her mouth and spit out the oatmeal.

Once they were under the sun's watchful gaze, Georgia swatted her arm. "Let's hear it. What did you do?"

They traveled through mini–dust tornadoes whose flying pins pricked Peggy's eyes. She blocked them with her arm, though she'd been at Avenger Field long enough to know it was no use. By the time they reached Cochran's office, her mouth would be chalky and her skin unnaturally tanned.

"Last I checked there were two of us on this funeral march," she said.

"I've kept my nose clean since our sojourn into town. I can only assume you've been naughty, and Cochran lumped me in by association. If I'm going down, I at least deserve to know why, and the telling better be titillating."

"There's nothing to tell." Peggy's thumb thrummed against the hard notch of her hipbone. If this was about her weight, why would Georgia be called too? "What do you imagine I've done?"

"Off the top of my head, I'd say you finally canoodled Major Handsome."

Peggy's laugh propelled from her stomach, too loud, she thought, too showy. She tried to counter it with nonchalance. "How could Cochran lump you in with that?"

"As Bill Shakespeare put it, 'Let me count the ways.'"

Peggy raised her hand. "Please don't."

Georgia knocked against Peggy as they walked. "You didn't object to the idea of canoodling Major Handsome."

"I did so."

A flagpole struck the sky above their heads and whipped the stars and stripes like it couldn't believe its good fortune to be given the responsibility. Georgia raised her voice to be heard over the thrashing. "Your hackles only went up at the suggestion of me joining. You don't despise the man. You want him to yourself."

They'd reached headquarters, a one-story, plain-faced building that made Peggy feel like a Texas Ranger entering a police station. Peggy brought a finger to her lips, glad she didn't have to defend herself, and pulled the door open. The air inside hit them still and sober. It urged them to be professional, even supplicating. Peggy slipped that persona over her head, but not before fitting in the last word. Straddling two worlds, inside and out, she turned to Georgia and mouthed, *You're sick.*

Two other WASP were seated before Cochran's desk, as rigid as employees about to be canned. This wasn't about weight or canoodling officers. Were there just too many women around and they needed to cull back? Were they getting too big for even their oversized britches? The oatmeal sat high in Peggy's stomach.

Cochran folded her hands on the desk and began in her signature motivational manner. "As you've all learned by now, the B-26s are finicky ships. If you don't abide their particularities, they betray you. The final runway approach must be precisely 150 miles per hour, which is too fast for some pilots, especially those accustomed to a short runway. But if you dither in the air, the engine quits. This has made the male cadets in Dodge City a little skittish. B-26s are called widowmakers for a reason, and those boys would prefer to die in combat than in an airfield accident at home. I've been asked to round up a few WASP to show them how it's done. Based on your records, you're the four for the job."

Peggy would have bet Mayfield made her out to be dizzy in her records, but maybe her performance had been so good, even he wasn't able to tarnish the reports.

Georgia assumed the pose of a proper lady—legs pressed at the knees and sloping in a gentle diagonal to the floor—but her voice was waggish. "I know an esteemed woman in your position has to be diplomatic but, just to be clear, you want us to humiliate a bunch of cadets into strapping on a pair?"

Peggy couldn't believe her friend. They were at Avenger Field by Jackie Cochran's good graces. The postures of the other WASP tautened with Peggy's as they waited to find out how Georgia's brashness would be received. But Georgia didn't betray a whisper of regret, like it never occurred to her that she might have misfired.

Cochran worked to flat-line her mouth. "That more or less sums it up."

Georgia slapped her knees. "Show me the way."

Cochran and her pilots drove seven hours to Kansas. It had been nearly three months since Peggy had been outside Sweetwater. Grass cropped up in northern Oklahoma, so lush and green she wanted to grab fistfuls and stuff it into her mouth.

Georgia cranked down her window and rested her arm on its ledge. Her hair rippled like a flag and her fingers surfed the air currents, self-assured, as if she'd been made a promise and was finally on her way to cash it in.

When Georgia began to sing the WASP song, she took her time. Her voice was husky and a little flat, but arresting in its conviction. "They built the barracks six cots to a room."

Cindy, a cadet with hair cropped around her chin, joined Georgia on the second line. "Filled 'em with cadets, but they found out soon."

Peggy couldn't believe this place, these people, this job. She joined in along with the last cadet, "Those boys couldn't take it, too hot, no air."

Then, to their delight, there were five voices, not in harmony, and not quite on key, but now Jackie Cochran was singing too, "So they moved 'em out and put the gals in there."

THE MALE CADETS lined up before their officers to greet the arrivals. As the WASP stepped from their car into the radiance of the evening, their formation constricted in unison, spines straightening, feet shifting. They hadn't been told the pilots coming to teach them were women.

Peggy went first. She took the plane up and circled five times, even rocking gently to make the wings wag. When she landed and jumped from the cockpit, she flashed the boys sweetness that likely made them want to marry and kill her at once. After Georgia returned to earth, she sprang from the cockpit, yawned big and showy with her arms stretched over her head, and patted her open mouth. It was cheeky, but in the very next moment, she shot the cadets a wink that let them know she understood just how scary those bombers could be.

They said women couldn't fly military planes, that their nature—too gentle, too fair—made them incapable and hazardous. Now they needed women to show the men how. They needed them.

* * *

Peggy wasn't sure how she'd muster any holiday cheer without heaps of snow, the smell and crackle of wood fire, her mother's sticky molasses loaf, and her father unwittingly humming along to radio carols, but her baymates pieced their spirit together. They made little gifts from folded paper or yarn repurposed from old sweaters, or they traded items they'd brought from home. For dinner, Georgia carved and served a soft wedge of Christmas Spam. They gathered around the radio in the rec room and swayed to their favorite festive songs, except Bing Crosby's recent hit, "I'll Be Home for Christmas," whose tender, almost tragic, words made them sit very still and remember all they were trying to forget.

The real magic arrived in the following days, when a rare cold front dropped temperatures below freezing and snow twirled in the sky, light and hopeful, wishes pirouetting in the wind. Then the flakes fattened and fell with purpose, drawing a curtain of silence with them. Planes were grounded and the soft white blanket muffled all other noise. It seemed to Peggy that Avenger Field had never known such peace.

Peggy marveled at the hush from her doorway, and then swiftly shattered it, throwing out her arms, parting her lips, and hollering so her throat ached. The dark sky was an unwavering contrast against the expanse of white, and she sprinted toward the place where one color met its opposite, the snow crunching under her boots, the chill nipping her cheeks in toothless bites.

"Look at you, happy as a pig, not seeming to realize that snow is so miserable the devil won't allow it in hell." Georgia stood in the bay doorway, barefooted, one arm wrapped around her front, the other holding a cigarette. She pulled in a drag and let the smoke wander from her mouth.

The waltzing flecks were a fleeting joy. It wouldn't be long before they blackened with filth or melted altogether. Peggy bent, scooped a handful, and patted it into a ball to make it last.

"Don't you dare." But Georgia knew enough to step back and swing the door closed to catch the snowball. Her face appeared in the window and she stuck out her tongue. Connie's head popped up above Georgia's and she waved gleefully.

On her own, Peggy tilted her chin up toward the night and the flakes dropped damp kisses on her face. She blinked away bits from her eyelashes and took in the great chalky surface that rippled as if a current ran beneath it.

She plopped into the snow and lay back. The sheepskin of her flying suit sheathed her so she didn't feel the chill. She spread out her arms and dragged them through the snow, up and down, invincible. When she'd finished, she turned over very carefully and climbed to her feet.

Would you look at that? she thought, admiring her angel. *There are my wings.*

Chapter 18

December 2009

ON THE FIRST WEEKEND OF THE NEW MONTH, KATHY SET-
tled her mother on the loveseat with a wool blanket and a
mug of black tea while she and Neil hauled musty boxes of
decorations from the attic, strung lights, positioned candles
in the windows, hung stockings, and shook out the artificial
tree. Kathy felt the preciousness of festivity more acutely
than ever before. They'd have only this month to enjoy poin-
settias, greenery, and sparkling ornaments before Christmas
gave way to New Year's, and who knew what 2010 would
bring, and who would still be there by its end?

The boys wouldn't be visiting for Christmas. They had
their own nuclear families with whom to celebrate, and
while they knew of Peggy's falls, they hadn't been told about
her heart. Peggy didn't want to burden them with the news,
which made Kathy want to tally her own burdens. But Kathy
suspected there was more to her mother's withholding. Peggy
wanted her sons to return for her love and company, not out
of obligation, guilt, or anticipatory mourning.

They were, however, coming for New Year's Eve, which
Kathy considered a win for Peggy. She couldn't remember
the last time the boys had come to Massachusetts at all,

let alone for a major holiday. Paul's family would drive up and stay at the house for two nights while Frank and Jimmy would fly on their own and do an overnight at a hotel. They treated their homecomings with the efficiency of business trips—in and out so fast they didn't have to check baggage. Still, it would be something to have the Mayfields together again.

Kathy catalogued the image of her mother in the living room. It had been an unexpected gift to have Peggy in the house the last ten days. She goaded Neil, of course, but she also gave him something to do. It wasn't the purpose he would have chosen, but he was needed again, which energized him. Kathy was glad for that, and also grateful to be collecting memories, especially ones in which she appreciated her mother more fully, in abundance. She was creating and storing them away where she could return to them after the season of her mother had passed. She'd taken to delivering Peggy a tray each morning: a mug of coffee, a separate carafe of cream, and a continental breakfast. It was one less chore for Neil, but it was also an act of love, a way to communicate to her mother what she couldn't express in words, which was *I haven't had my fill of you yet.*

The ornaments shed glitter onto the rug around the tree. It would need to be vacuumed but, for now, its fleeting nature only made it more enchanting.

Peggy sipped the tea and smacked her lips. "Could your faucet be leaching, Katherine? I detect a distinctly metallic taste."

* * *

The holiday party was Dr. Smith's doing; that was clear. While the doctors, nurses, and staff mingled in the break room, he fizzed like the sparkling cider he refilled in their cups, reminding "his girls" that there were three varieties of dip; a vegetable platter he mistakenly called charcuterie; and, in a pink bakery box, gourmet donuts crusted in Oreos, glistening with fruit syrup, or studded by candied pistachio.

"And if you're worried about your waistline, you can tell your husband it was Dr. Smith's fault," he said.

Kathy recalled a trip to New Hampshire, one of their rare expeditions, when Neil had concluded, "Family vacations would be a hell of a lot nicer if it wasn't for the kids." Likewise, this party would have been a hell of a lot nicer if it wasn't for the host, but maybe Kathy was just feeling particularly sensitive to Dr. Smith's antics. That very morning, he'd joked about the number of positive HPV tests, saying, "I suspect there will be some frustrated frat boys next semester." She should have verbally objected, but she hadn't, so now she was punishing him by reserving her approval.

Neil and the kids called this treatment the Ice Wall. Noah and Fiona swore they'd rather be publicly upbraided than have to endure prolonged emotional freezer burn. But Kathy herself had a volcanic parent, and she wasn't so sure her kids knew what they were talking about.

As Kathy socialized, she was astonished by the breadth of interests pursued by her coworkers: ceramics, bouldering, Zumba, improv, and triathlons. She began to feel self-conscious of her own limited dimensions, offering, feebly, "Well, there's my children, but they're out of the house now. . . . I used to canoe with my son but . . . I don't know. . . .

Reading? Walking?" aware that these weren't points of pride so much as skills mastered in elementary school.

It would have been lame, and not a small amount of nerdy, to answer, *Here, my job, this is my hobby,* since her coworkers did similar work. But nursing was, in fact, her rediscovered passion. She liked meeting people and tending to their concerns with a clinical mind and a compassionate heart. She liked the puzzle of diagnosing on the fringe of accountability. She liked the hubbub, leading patients around the office, examining them, processing referrals, inputting records, and transmitting prescriptions. She liked how others marveled at her proficiency, swiftness, and general productivity. She'd awakened a hibernating identity and was exhilarated by her own functionality. It was similar to the challenge and satisfaction of those early years of motherhood, when she realized just how much she could handle, just how much she could do—even wrangle a toddler and an infant to the beach on her own, while Neil, on the other hand, was reluctant to stay home and mind only one. She was still a mother, wife, and daughter, but this job reminded her that she was more than that. She had many meanings.

"All right, ladies. Let's get a picture for the holiday card," Dr. Smith said, and shepherded the women against a wall. He'd already set up a minitripod on the opposite counter. Kathy imagined he'd posed for practice shots to ensure he'd capture the group in frame.

As they amassed, Dr. Smith was suddenly wearing a Santa hat. Kathy had no idea where it came from. He inserted himself at the center between the two other doctors, who looked to him, and then to each other, with what Kathy would describe as patience. They cared for the man, but he irritated them. Maybe Kathy needed to settle into a similar dichotomy.

"On three, say Santa and the Rockettes!" he said.

Surely the comment was rattled off the cuff (though the hat was premeditated), and so he hadn't considered the sexualizing of long-legged dancers, or their uniformity in contrast to a patriarchal figure. He was only pointing out that he was the one man in a room full of women. He didn't mean any harm, and if Kathy had gone rigid, that was on her—wasn't it? There was unenthusiastic mumbling with the right number of syllables, but Kathy pressed her lips tight.

They disassembled. Most left to pack up for the day and head home, but Kathy stayed back with a couple of the admins to collect trash and wipe surfaces. She found herself beside Angela, the receptionist whose bottle blond hair began an inch after dark roots, and whose speedy keyboard clacks could be heard from down the hall. Kathy estimated Angela to be the perfect confidant. The female doctors would feel obligated to respond to anything resembling a complaint, and Kathy wasn't ready to instigate action. Angela was the type to answer a question directly without making a big deal of it.

Just above a whisper, Kathy asked, "Do you ever find Dr. Smith to be—I don't know—a teeny bit inappropriate?"

"You mean all his little comments?" Angela's vowels squatted into the accent of a northern Boston suburb. In the next second, her smirk dropped, and her eyes flicked down the length of Kathy. "Or do you mean something else?"

Kathy flushed at the implication. "Just the comments."

"Oh yeah." Angela's posture thawed. She stacked used paper plates and the tower curved around crumpled napkins. "Definitely inappropriate."

"Have you ever wanted to say something?"

"I've thought about it, but it'd turn into a whole big thing, and who's got time for whole big things? This is a good job, and he's a good boss, all in all. It's easier to laugh and let it go, you know?" She dropped her pile into the trash and dusted off her hands. The matter was settled, in her view, although Kathy wasn't so sure. "So, any exciting holiday plans?"

"My kids are coming home," Kathy said, and she felt a stir of joy saying that out loud. "What about you?"

"Just the regular family stuff for Christmas, but I do the Polar Plunge every New Year's. It sounds crazy, but it's actually pretty rejuvenating, and loads of fun. You should join me."

"Yeah right."

"Why not?"

Kathy laughed. Which completely justifiable reason should she choose? There was the unseasonal exposure, the silly spectacle, the shocking plunge, and the equally painful retreat, just to name a few. But when hesitations were so obvious, they were hardly worth saying out loud.

"I'll think about it," she said.

PEGGY WAS LYING on the couch in the living room, perhaps admiring the novel twinkles. Theirs was probably the only house on the street that still strung multicolor lights, but Kathy wouldn't give them up, those little fireworks sustained in time, despite social pressure. Most of her neighbors didn't even deck their own halls, so to speak; they paid professionals. But Kathy could handle being different in small ways. Her kids had eaten sugary generic granola bars rather than organic, she had no clear answer to the question "Where are you from?," and she would be damned if someone else trimmed her Christmas tree.

A pillow was propped beneath her mother's feet. Kathy was curious if Peggy had wrestled it there or if Neil had arranged it for her, but it felt too intimate a question to ask. The two had been building a strange partnership over the course of recent weeks. Kathy was now, in some ways, the outsider.

Peggy gave a brisk wave to Kathy, who was slipping out of her coat, and said, "It just occurred to me that Fiona shouldn't be exiled from her things all Christmas break. Shall I relocate across the hall into Neil's office?"

"That's all right." Kathy stepped on the heel of her shoe, freeing one foot and then the other. The sudden liberation after hours of containment felt nearly delicious. "Actually, Fiona keeps her apartment over break, so she'll only be home a couple nights." She pitched it as if the arrangement made sense, which she supposed it did, but she wished viscerally that her daughter was moving home again, even if only for a month. If she didn't return now, would she ever again?

"I see," Peggy said, as if attuned to Kathy's fragile composure, and tiptoeing across it. "How lovely for her. And Noah? How is he?"

Kathy traced her memory for the last time she'd heard from her son. Certainly they hadn't gone without speaking since Thanksgiving. She'd called and left a voice mail the previous week but, now that she thought about it, he'd never called back. The same boy who once joined Kathy in the bathroom because he couldn't stand for them to be apart, who had to be picked up early from sleepaway camp, who called her every morning on his way to class his freshman year of college, had now gone over three weeks without reaching out to her, not even by text.

Perhaps Peggy already knew this, and her question was a rhetorical means of pointing out that Kathy's children were drifting and everybody saw it. Maybe she was opening a conversational door, inviting Kathy to admit the growing distance and thus share her fears and grief with someone who had feared and grieved, or maybe her motivation was smugger. She'd likely perceived Kathy's parenting style to be a critique of her own, yet now their divergent approaches were heading for the same result. Just as Peggy's sons had moved away from her, physically and emotionally, so might Fiona and Noah from Kathy. This could be Peggy's acquittal; no matter her strategy, it was impossible for a mother to love her children well enough.

"Noah is fine," Kathy said, flatly. On any other evening, she would have plopped onto the loveseat and shared a funny anecdote about a coworker or an interesting patient case, drinking in this one-on-one time with her mother, newly revealed to her and ephemeral. But this interaction had introduced an acrid flavor to the room, and it felt less like Peggy's existence was precious and threatened, and more like she might expand into the corners of Kathy's house and persist there forever. "I'm going to lie down for a while. Are you okay getting to bed yourself?"

Chapter 19

December 2009

THEY SPENT CHRISTMAS MORNING SIPPING COFFEE AND nibbling cinnamon buns while holiday pop music played through their outdated sound system. Nothing felt better, safer, and more right, Kathy thought, than waking up in the same house as her children and spending the day in pajamas, knowing nobody had anywhere else to go. Fiona teased Noah for his bedhead and he poked fun at her clown feet. Peggy took turns holding her grandchildren's hands. Kathy leaned against Neil and his arm dropped heavily around her shoulders.

She dwelled on the American flag ornament, which commemorated a family joke from when Fiona was having a tantrum one summer afternoon, and Noah, weary beyond his five years, shook his head and said, earnestly, "Come on, Fi. Not on Flag Day."

Kathy's family had been knit so intrinsically back then. Her children had depended on her, and in a different but equally powerful way, she'd depended on them. And then there was Neil, like the knitting needles themselves, bobbing back and forth, attached to as well as binding them, even when Neil was unseen. Their weave had since loosened in the natural course of families when children were grown, but when the separate parts rejoined under one roof, they eased back into place, just as they always had. They remembered where one stitch fit into another, having held the memory of their shared shape, the time between their reunion simply a waiting period until they could find one another once again.

Christmas gifts had never been extravagant in the Begley household, their most thrilling being a ride-on Jeep Wrangler Kathy had accepted from a friend whose kids had grown out of it, but now that their budget was even more inhibited, they'd agreed to exchange simple pleasures.

Kathy normally presented her mother something generic, books or a bottle of wine that could be given to just about anybody, figuring it wasn't worthwhile to invest in an inventive gift her mother would likely toss aside, never to be used. But this year was distinctive: Peggy was living with them; Peggy was dying; Peggy had a secret and impressive past that likely informed so much of the mothering her daughter had resented. Kathy wanted to honor that in some way, while also coaxing more out of Peggy, prolonging her.

She gave her mother a *Family History* journal, with legacy prompts followed by plenty of blank pages. She'd selected the most unsentimental option she could find. Other brands featured pink covers patterned with roses and titles like *Mom, I Want to Hear Your Story*. Still, this was a more cloying and invasive gesture than Kathy was used to, while also being more honest.

"Thank you, dear," Peggy said. Then she nodded to a present still under the tree. "I'll do yours if you'll do mine."

The package, stamped with her name in Peggy's increasingly toothed squiggles, was clearly a book. Perhaps the apple didn't fall far after all. She unwrapped *Midlife Crisis: Designing Your Next Great Adventure*. She had to laugh, and Peggy joined her, capturing a raspy chuckle in her fist, while the others watched, confused, from the outskirts of their joke. They were remarkably in tune, buying books that pushed their own agendas while being disparately motivated. Kathy was interested in the life Peggy had already lived while Peggy was intent on what Kathy hadn't yet attempted.

The next unearthed gift was a sizable square box, wrapped in newspaper comics and tied with red shoestring.

"That's for you and Dad," Fiona said. "Savor it. That is your birthday gift too."

"You can't even afford wrapping paper. I don't think they're banking on second gifts," Noah said.

He'd meant it as a joke, but it grated against Kathy's good mood. He was the highest earner in the room now, so the remark contained an underpinning of arrogance and disdain, qualities Kathy didn't attribute to her son and didn't wish to. But Noah was new to his rank and perhaps hadn't learned that he shouldn't deride those below him—or perhaps it hadn't yet occurred to him that he'd ascended.

She pushed the irritation aside and shimmied the lid off the box. Inside was an architectural model of their house— white clapboard siding, black shutters, twin chimneys, and the grand portico around the front door—strung with miniature Christmas lights. Kathy's jaw slackened while everything inside her tightened. She couldn't summon any words, so she dipped the package this way and that to show the others what was inside.

"Fiona, that is magnificent," Peggy said.

"Way to make the rest of us look bad," Noah said.

"It looks more impressive than it is," Fiona said. "It was a class project. Everybody made one. The 3D printer did most of the work."

Kathy almost told her daughter that she shouldn't diminish her creation, which was not just a meaningful work of art but downright professional. It was okay for her to accept praise. But Kathy stopped herself. She didn't want to embarrass Fiona or make Noah self-conscious about his own gift to his mother—bath beads, which produced a slick whose cleanup wasn't worth their clout, but he couldn't know that. Besides, Fiona's humility had its own value.

"Humility doesn't serve you, my dear," Peggy said. "If you don't tout your talents, nobody will."

"You're right, Gammy." Fiona tossed her hair over a shoulder—thin like her mother's, but red like her father's. "I crushed it."

The two women, generations apart, were nearly soppy with affection for each other, and Kathy felt on the periphery, observing a tribe to which she didn't belong.

"You didn't inherit artistic impulses from me, but it might be a Begley trait," Kathy said, unsure if she was severing the connection between Peggy and her daughter out of indignation, or if this was an innocuous natural sequitur. Some intentions were too obscure to dissect, or too ugly to uncover. "Neil, you should show Noah your progress."

As Neil reached for the box, Fiona rounded her eyes at Noah in the purposeful know-it-all way she did when he mispronounced an SAT word back in high school. He nod-

ded in return, as if to say, *Message received*, but with a be-
grudging eye roll that was tossed up and finished before Neil
rotated back. Kathy caught it, though. She recognized that
the siblings had spoken about their father's hobby when they
were out of their parents' hearing range, comparing misgiv-
ings and perhaps their new kind of pity.

Neil passed the parcel to his son. Its snowman paper
puffed in bulky folds at the seams that were sealed by too
many strips of tape.

Noah had inherited his grandmother's long, slender fingers. *Maybe he'll be a concert pianist*, Peggy had said when he
was born. *Or a basketball player*, Neil had replied. *Or just a
nice guy with big hands*, Kathy had thought. The same adept
fingers that had dug moats in the sand and flitted through
robot kits faster than Kathy could buy them fumbled over
his Christmas present. He itched the top of his head, and
his dark Mayfield hair, as rich and shiny as an espresso bean,
retained the muss. His cheeks flushed.

Towering over his son, Neil wasn't sure what to do with
his body. He didn't appear to want to stay close but also
didn't want to commit to returning to his chair. He folded
his arms, opened them, and then refolded one and cupped
his chin in his other hand.

Please like it, please like it, Kathy silently begged her son.
And then, as her confidence eroded, her prayer changed.
Fake it, Noah, and fake it well.

The paper dropped away to a shoebox. "Sneakers? Nice,"
Noah joked, thinly.

Sixteen chess pieces huddled inside individual tissue paper nests: four wooden helmets engraved with the patriot

in the tricorn hat, four footballs with carved laces, two line-backers in a defensive stance, two running backs cradling the ball, two wide receivers reaching for a catch, one quarter-back prepared to throw, and a Vince Lombardi trophy.

"I still have to make the other team, obviously," Neil said. "I was thinking the Eagles, so it could be a Super Bowl XXXIX commemorative set, but I figured I'd let you choose."

"Holy shit, Dad." Noah lifted each piece and turned it over as if inspecting an artifact. "These are actually really good."

Kathy hated her son for the *actually*, and also loved him for it.

Neil colored and stood a bit taller. "The wood is from your old building blocks."

"You're kidding," Noah said, his wonder augmented.

"So this is what you've been toiling away at," Peggy said. "I was sure you were making voodoo dolls of me."

"I was, but those are upstairs," Neil said.

Noah closed his long fingers around a piece and shook it in his father's direction. "You know, crafting isn't just for bored housewives anymore. You could sell these."

"Hey, I resemble that comment," Kathy said. She'd always been hurt by the derogatory phrase, which diminished all she'd done as a nonworking mother. Still, she hoped her jest was strong enough to mask her insult. She wouldn't want to detract from Neil's triumph, no matter how patronizing her son had sounded, as if all stay-at-home mothers were just lost souls searching for meaning in macramé.

"I'm serious," Noah said, oblivious to his offense. "There's a global online marketplace for this kind of stuff. Take advantage of the digital era. Launch a business."

Neil laughed, and it was as if he'd expelled the air directly into Kathy's lungs, inflating her. She didn't think it was a half-bad idea. Her husband might have pursued a career in woodworking had he not been so set on securing a certain kind of life for himself and his family. Maybe now was his chance to take his passion full-time. But a hitch inside told her he wouldn't. Men were meant to work and earn until retirement, not occupy themselves with premature fancies. Women were given more room to be frivolous—though permission for little else.

Kathy felt sorry for Neil. While she pumped blood pressure cuffs and listened to heartbeats, he studied videos, practiced, and submitted follow-up questions to online forums. They were both occupied with vocations, but more value was placed on Kathy's—literally, by way of a paycheck, and culturally. Kathy doubted Neil would take his son's suggestion seriously, but at least there was this moment, when Neil was augmented by his family, who considered his art worthwhile.

"Make Noah your business manager," Fiona said. "Then you can call your company Chip Off the Old Block."

Chapter 20

December 1943

THE NIGHT OF THE AVENGER FIELD NEW YEAR'S DANCE, stars were strung like twinkle lights, and a crisp breeze swept through their barracks. Peggy separated a section of Connie's damp hair, combed a plastic curler through the hair from her scalp to the tip, rolled it up, pinned the loop, and did it all again.

"I'm so grateful you're doing this. I'm helpless when it comes to beauty," Connie said. She'd been asked to the dance by a shy cadet named Freddy, and when Peggy spotted her pawing at her locks, her eyes watering, Peggy capped her lipstick and took over. Now Connie sat cross-legged in the center of her bed and fiddled with her shirt hem. She wasn't wearing pants, and her creamy thighs spread like spilt milk.

"You don't need any help. You're a natural dish," Peggy said.

"I've never even been on a date before," Connie said, with a quiver. "I'm a nice girl, I know, but I'm chubby in all the wrong places, and most guys don't take the time to learn any more than what they see before them. I'm surprised he asked me."

"I'm not. Not one bit. Besides, your silhouette is all the rage. Check the magazines. You're a regular sweater girl."

The baymates collected their dresses, which they'd stored beneath their cots to keep from wrinkling. Pam, in a long-sleeved, belted, plaid dress, looked like she was meeting her mother's friends for lunch, her hat brim wide enough to block a sun that had already set. Georgia's neckline scooped down each shoulder, her full skirt bloomed when she twirled, and she had pinned a veiled cap into place. Connie, all done up in coils, zipped into a dress borrowed from Georgia whose halter top divulged her full chest. Peggy drew eyeliner up their calves, what they called liquid stockings, to provide the illusion of seams from rationed nylons.

Once she was done, she stepped into a dress from home, but it didn't fit as she'd remembered. She'd always had a small shape, but with gentle womanly contours; that feminine suppleness had calcified, and her formerly favorite dress draped where it once hugged.

THE MUSIC DRIFTED into the quad and roped around Peggy's waist, drawing her toward the mess hall. Inside, horns bleated and drums thumped in her chest.

The room was packed. Cadets bounced in pairs, or chatted in groups, raising their voices to be heard and gesturing emphatically. Everyone, it appeared, had emerged from their dorms to seek respite from training, studying, letter writing, and the persistent worries of war. The only reminder of the state of the world was the American flag hanging behind the band, and the uniformed men, many barely eighteen years old, with smooth cheeks that had never known the edge of a razor blade. Peggy, only a few years older, felt like their mother. They were going to war as boys, and there they would age.

The band closed their first number and picked up the pace with Glenn Miller's "In the Mood." The music seemed to originate at Peggy's center. By the time the brass joined the clarinets, she couldn't keep the bounce from her shoulders.

A cadet with close-set eyes touched her hip and gestured to the dance floor. Peggy let herself be guided but regretted it when he ground her knuckles together and tugged her gracelessly through the steps. As soon as she located his rhythm, he varied it and threw in extra surprises, spinning and yanking so she fell onto his chest.

The drums struck a tantalizing beat to introduce Benny Goodman's "Sing, Sing, Sing," an energetic swing. The cadet pulled Peggy tight before she could resist. Peggy was being heaved and hawed like a filly refusing to be broken. By the midsong drum solo, she shook herself free.

She found Pam reclining from her dance partner as if he had rancid breath. Connie swayed with Freddy, both seemingly unaware of the swift beat. She giggled, and he beamed as if making her laugh had been his one goal for the evening and he couldn't believe he'd accomplished it so soon. And Georgia, where was she? Peggy searched pair to pair until she spotted her friend. A lanky cadet stood like a post while Georgia spun herself around him. She went and returned, a self-operating yo-yo, her face open and bright, her lips encircling a guffaw.

Peggy laughed, and wondered what her former roommates were doing at that moment. Cheryl, who wasn't allowed to stay, was probably beside her fireplace, knitting, reading, or dreaming of chances she couldn't get back. Millie, who chose to leave, was brushing her horse or visiting a neighborhood soldier returned from war, her arms heaped with blankets and cookies and hope for her future. Peggy missed them, her war women. But now was not the time or place for melancholy, and though she was reluctant to interrupt their timid romance, she weaved her way to Connie.

"You're going to want to see this," Peggy said, and pointed at Georgia, who held her man's shoulders and dropped herself back into a dip.

"She doesn't need a partner, does she?" Connie asked.

"No, Georgia is enough all on her own."

Peggy waited out the rest of the song beside the restroom so as not to appear stranded, but she kept her eyes on the dance floor, looking for someone and no one in particular.

The men's door opened and a cadet tripped out, his collar parted, his tie hanging loose. Peggy recognized him. He was the one with the oblong face his peers called Boston, part of the team who towed the men's plane across the runway in their battle of the sexes. Now he looked a little worse for wear. His copper hair was dark and slick with perspiration. Reeking of liquor, he studied her beneath hooded eyelids.

"Hiya, honey."

She couldn't tell if he'd recognized her; maybe his vision and memory were too flooded by booze to place her in the tractor beside Georgia. "Hi."

"I'm willing to let bygones be bygones, even though you and your friend cheated, because hey, it's a party. So what do you say? Let's dance." His speech was slurred, but he had the accent of Jack Haley as the Tin Man.

"No thanks. I've got a fella," she lied.

He made a show of surveying the mess hall, as if playing a dopey game of charades. "Is he here?"

"Well, no."

"Then you ain't rationed. Come on, sugar."

He grabbed her forearm but she took it back. "I'm not interested."

"Just one dance. That's all I'm asking."

She wanted to say, *You're drunk and a jerk, and you stink*, but she didn't want to egg him on, or hurt his ego, which would be the same as egging him on. She could unleash her temper, but this soldier was going to battle soon; maybe she shouldn't be too rude. "I'm sure there are plenty of gals out there who would be lucky to have a dance with you, but I'm waiting for the bathroom."

His face darkened. "You got what you wanted. Your team won. Now it's my turn. Don't be a cold fish."

He grabbed her waist and forced her to move with him. She pressed her hands against his chest but he responded with the bulk of his body, knocking her into the wall. He buried his face into her collarbone, his red hair damp against her cheek, his breath hot and sour. His tongue lapped her neck and his hands slid around her hips to her backside.

"Hey," she said, and tried to shove him off, but he was a solid force. She protested louder, but her voice couldn't compete with the brass. Then he straightened so the wool of his uniform muffled and suffocated her.

"Be a nice girl, or have you forgotten how?"

She felt him drive against her. A black rose budded in her stomach. She closed her eyes and waited for the petals to drop. His hand reached up her skirt.

Then he was wrenched away. When she braved her eyes open, she saw that Major Mayfield held him up by a fistful of uniform. Her commanding officer's face was etched into jagged pieces.

"We were only having some fun," the cadet said, hitching his thumb in her direction.

Mayfield shook the cadet and added a punctuation Peggy couldn't hear. Then he cast him off. Chastised, the cadet scurried away.

Peggy felt as if her lungs had been slashed, or that she'd been catapulted to a too-high altitude. She was dizzy, but didn't want to reveal weakness, so she gasped for air as imperceptibly as she could manage. Major Mayfield appraised her. Could he see what was going on inside—that her heart was pattering, her head pounded, and she was sick with shame? She was supposed to be courageous, defying the odds of her gender, defying gravity. Yet when she'd been cornered, when her instincts were challenged with fight or flight, all she'd done was freeze. She was a WASP. Flight was what she *did*. It was her identity. Yet she couldn't summon the reflex when she'd needed it. She'd just stood there and accepted her fate.

Mayfield lifted his chin in question. She lowered hers to answer that yes, she was all right. And she was, wasn't she? She'd felt the black rage of the cadet's impulse, his power, but it could have been worse. He might have forced her into the bathroom, where nobody would have seen. She could shiver at what could have been, or she could shake off the violation, terrifying as it was, absorb the impact, swallow it down, and make nice. She was a woman, after all, and that's what women did.

Mayfield stepped forward, as if to do or say something more, but then he thought better of it, turned, and was abruptly gone.

Peggy's heart still thrashed as if to escape an attacker. She moved on wobbly legs into the bathroom, shut the door behind her, and slid to the tile floor. Enclosed, she was safe and alone—she just needed to convince her body of that. She crawled to the sink, pulled herself up by the porcelain edge, and splashed water on her face. The mirror reflected cheekbones dripping with black tears.

You are fine, you are fine, you are fine.

As she reentered the hall, the music almost embodied a physical presence. The singer warbled with one hand tucked into his front pocket while the other rested at the crest of his throat. His expression balanced on the edge of emotion, as if he might break down and cry at any moment. He was middle-aged and had seen so much already. Two centuries, one Great Depression, two world wars. There was plenty to cry about.

"Where have you been?" Georgia asked. She held a cigarette in one hand and a drink in the other, and alternated which she administered to her lips. Judging from her loose posture, this cup of punch, now nearly empty, hadn't been her first.

"Just window-shopping for my next dance partner."

Georgia pointed her cigarette across the hall to where Mayfield chatted stiffly with another officer. "No sense trying budget versions when we know what uniform you really want."

Peggy drew Georgia's arm down to her side. "Don't be absurd."

"Enough already. Everybody knows you're nuts for him." Her words were heavy, as if spoken with a swollen tongue. Ash expanded on the end of her cigarette until it bowed as a tree branch laden with snow. She moved, and the lump dropped into her drink. She carried the cup to her lips and her eyes widened at the sight of the pollution, but then she sipped anyway, debris be damned.

"Georgia, you're drunk. Here I thought you were equipped with a hollow leg." Peggy whisked the drink from her friend, unwrapped the napkin from its circumference, and skimmed out the detritus.

"Don't insult my southern disposition. I'm merely buzzed."

As Peggy returned the punch, Georgia caught her hand with unyielding pressure. The assertiveness felt too familiar too soon, and Peggy's heart rate rose. But then Georgia's grip slackened. She flipped Peggy's hand and stroked her forearm, caressing where Peggy's skin was most tender, wan and thin enough to reveal her veins before they disappeared on their private course to her heart. Georgia's face was set, as if asking for an answer, but Peggy didn't know the question. Something about that probing look, or how soon this small invasion followed the severe one, ran a clammy finger up Peggy's spine. She had something she wasn't willing, or at least not ready, to give. She retracted her arm and held it against her body.

Georgia softened and her eyes tapered. "Did that hurt?"

Peggy clutched her arm as if it had indeed been injured and laughed nervously. "You just gave me the chills."

"Well, go on," Georgia said, gesturing toward the major. "Ask Prince Charming to dance."

Peggy wanted to paper over these interactions. She wanted to be with someone safe. "You know what? I will. Why the heck not?"

"That's my girl," Georgia said, and raised her cup.

Peggy took in the major's angles—the square of his shoulders, the ridge of his jaw, his strong nose—all contrasted against the softness of his lips. Caterpillars wormed inside her abdomen and, as Peggy approached, they cocooned and sprung out as butterflies.

She weaved through dancers, issuing an "excuse me" here and there. When she was just a few feet away, Mayfield shook the hand of his colleague and turned for the door. She stopped short because she was too late—he was leaving. She dug her fingernails into the meat of her palms. No, she wouldn't freeze again, not twice in a row. She would thank him, at least. That was the decent thing to do.

The door hadn't fully closed behind him. She caught its edge, slipped out, and let it shut on the festivity at her back. The still of the night was so different from the base's daytime bustle of churning engines, barked orders, and marching feet.

"Mayfield," she said.

She hated the sound of her voice carving through the quiet, and the need she heard in it, the way she made his name sound like a plea. She hated that she hadn't called him major, and that she hadn't used his first name. What *was* his first name? She hated that she had to think about it. *William.*

He looked over his shoulder, and when he recognized it was Peggy, he squinted into the distance, and then pivoted his body, reluctantly, to her.

It took all her concentration to hold up her smile. "I just wanted to thank you for, you know, stepping in before, and I was hoping you'd do me the honor of a dance."

"I don't think that would be appropriate," he said.

"Don't think so hard, then. It'd be good for the gals to see your human side." Her voice was high-pitched, a girl's. She clenched her teeth. She would not allow herself to speak again.

"I'm not much of a dancer," he said, but then his shoulders rounded, making him look more like a man than a soldier.

Hope sparked in Peggy because now she knew he would accept, even if only out of courtesy. "Any dead hoofer can dance to a slow number."

She waited for him, longing to feel his hand on her upper back as he guided her into the hall. When he did indeed reach, she took in a breath, but he was moving beyond her for the door.

On the floor, she opened herself to him, but he couldn't see because he stared at a place over her head. His Adam's apple slid with his swallow, and his arms moved stiffly. He glanced down quickly. She was waiting to receive his attention. One hand found her hip while the other slipped through her fingers.

"If you're satisfied I'll be at your side Sunday, Monday, or always."

She felt the heat of him through his uniform, this man with four brothers and aviator sunglasses. William. He smelled of smoke, soap, and cloud cover. Peggy allowed herself to consider what Georgia had been insisting all this time; second only to flying, this was what Peggy had wanted since the day she'd arrived. Was it possible he wanted it too? She wanted to say something, to put a name to what was happening, but what if she shattered what had taken so long to manifest, or worse, what if she was wrong? She bore witness to every feeling, pressing the flavors against the roof of her mouth and letting them spread across her tongue. She willed the seconds to last, but they ticked by anyway. Soon the final note played and faded, and the music was replaced by applause.

"Good night, cadet," Mayfield said.

"Good night, major." Peggy licked her lips, searching for the remnants of their moment, any residual taste, but it was over. She looked up at him, silently begging for him to change his mind, ask her for another dance, reveal any hint of affection. But he only nodded curtly, spun on his heel, and marched toward the door.

Warm fingers wrapped around Peggy's upper arm and tugged her from her pining. "That was short-lived," Georgia said.

Peggy didn't just want Mayfield to reappear. She wanted to press her hand against his chest, to feel his heart beat in her palm. She wanted to smell his hair, his skin. She wanted to learn him until she understood him. And she wanted Mayfield to continue pushing and challenging her, to expect excellence and not come out disappointed. But he had left, and she brooded on the threshold of his absence.

"But not so short it didn't mean anything," Georgia said. Then she tilted her head back, emptied the pink punch into her mouth, and forced the cup into Peggy's hand. "Now if you'll excuse me, I'm taking one of our Peeping Toms for a walk around base."

Peggy followed her gaze to a cadet with tiny ringlets. "Are you sure you're in any state to be alone with a man?"

Georgia's lips spread like warm honey and she pinched Peggy's cheek. "I'd wallop that infant into next week if he got fresh in a way I wasn't keen on. Though I'm pretty much keen on everything."

Peggy felt the way she did when she dropped suddenly in elevation, like gravity didn't have the same pull on her organs and they'd been left overhead. Georgia couldn't have known about Peggy's recent paralysis, but she might have interpreted her body language had she not been so soused. Peggy pulled away from her friend's sting, physical and otherwise, but Georgia only followed her. Her pinch flattened into a firm pat against Peggy's cheekbone.

"Don't wait up," she said, and tottered off to her cadet. As she crossed the floor, she tripped and bounded ahead, roaring with laughter even before the cadet caught her. He set her back on her feet, and she hooked her arm around his shoulder and guided him to the door.

Mayfield's assistant, Richard, was smoking at a table, and Peggy hurried to him. There were plenty of empty seats, but Richard still surrendered his chair. Peggy waved away the chivalry. She didn't have time for it.

"What do you know about the cadet leaving with my gal?"

"I know taking your gal for a walk was the only way he could return her to her barracks. That dolly belongs in bed—on her own. Don't worry, if he isn't back in ten, I'll hunt him down with you."

"Rescue him is more like it. Georgia has more than a walk on her mind."

They shared amusement, which buckled under the expanding silence, so they scanned bopping dancers, instruments, and patriotic decorations for their next topic. Connie and Freddy stood almost motionless on the dance floor, still unaware of the song's rhythm. Her wrists rested on the back of his neck and he hugged her lower back. They'd found each other in this shifting uncertain world and created a dreamland of their own.

Richard said, "I saw that you corralled the major onto the dance floor. That must have been quite the feat. He doesn't seem the type."

"I don't know him well enough to say."

"I stand beside him most of the day and don't know him from Adam. He's stoic. Not that I blame him, after all he's been through."

Peggy watched Richard's eyes under his cliff-edge forehead, much like the blunt brink she teetered on, eager for more about Mayfield's history. But nothing came, and Peggy didn't want to admit she knew even less about her major than this man claiming to know nothing, so she crossed her arms over her chest. "Yes, I can't imagine."

"It's a wonder he isn't spooked from flying altogether."

"A wonder." Peggy tucked a strand of hair behind her ear. There was no sense in being coy. This was her opportunity to gain a window through Mayfield's opaque facade. She shouldn't misuse it for the sake of self-consciousness or vanity. She didn't need to impress Richard. She decided to ask what he meant directly, when Richard's mouth cracked open.

"Hot diggity dog! Get a load of this."

Georgia's escort staggered toward them, his cheeks and neck smudged red. "That dame is khaki-whacky. I barely made it out of there alive."

Chapter 21

December 2009

ON NEW YEAR'S EVE, THE MAYFIELD BOYS TOOK THE BEGLEY house by storm. They arrived simultaneously, or perhaps the bustle compressed and blurred the hours between their entrances, but it seemed to Kathy that Jimmy's hard gut rammed open the front door and the rest poured in behind him.

Frank still wore the same buzz cut, now glinted like silver moss. He made cynical jokes about narrow airline seats, the inanity of flying somewhere colder, and the observation that drivers in their state put the "ass" in "Massachusetts."

Though Paul was the tallest of the Mayfield children, he dipped his head as if stooping beneath a low ceiling and looked perpetually bashful. He'd dropped his wife, whom he'd met at a dog park when he was in his early forties, at a friend's house in Connecticut, but had brought along his twin ten-year-old sons, who kissed their adult family members dutifully before finding a place away from the commotion to lose themselves on their devices.

Jimmy slung a heavy arm around Paul's shoulders while Frank paced a tiny perimeter. He'd never been able to stay still but, for the first time, Kathy noticed a bucking stagger from pain in his left knee.

Neil seemed to shrink into the margins, while Peggy swelled at the center. Her children circled where she sat primly on a kitchen chair, her hands folded in her lap. She gazed up at them as they passed stories, teased, and asked after the adult children not present. Peggy was the guest of honor, the matriarch. She used to be the master of ceremonies too, regaling them with theatrical tales of their father, or reminding them of their own mischief, but she'd grown too tired to perform. Now, she was still the sun to which they gravitated, but instead of shining, she drank in their light.

"What an act of love for you boys to make the trip up here, and with all those gifts." Peggy waved vaguely toward the living room, where the Christmas tree had been replenished with presents.

Kathy ground her teeth against the comment. She'd taken her mother into her home this past month and a half, and had acted as her closest companion in the fifteen years since their father's death, while her brothers had lived their own lives free of responsibility. But as soon as they pranced up at their convenience and lavished their mother with twenty-four hours of attention and store-bought fealty, theirs was the love worth saluting.

Kathy wanted to yell, *What about me? And what about you?*

The Mayfield children were running out of time to hear firsthand what it was like for Peggy to leave her farm, live in barracks, and do things no women had done before. Had she been afraid? Why did she return to homemaking after such adventure? They should get to watch their mother accept the medal and accolades she long deserved. Instead, they were chattering about the sports car Frank was restoring.

Peggy would soon be gone from this earth without warning, and her history would spill out unexplained, uncelebrated around her children's feet.

"Who's ready for a drink?" Kathy asked.

KATHY WAS REFILLING mugs of spiked cider that she'd mulled with cinnamon sticks and cloves when there was a knock at the front door. They weren't expecting anybody. Kathy's kids had claimed plans with friends, though it meant missing their uncles. Could they be surprising her? Neil shot up, and she wondered if he was in on the plan, or if he was just desperate to be anywhere but in a room with Mayfields, including Frank, who'd asked, "How's living the cushy life of a stay-at-home husband?"

When Neil returned, he signaled to Kathy. "A delivery man wants us to sign for a pretty big package. Did you order something?"

Jimmy raised his hand, tickled conceit at his lips. "That one's on me." Then he clamped Frank's shoulder. "Our Bostonian brother will need a hand. Think those bum knees can take it?"

A moment later, Frank's voice traveled to them from the front stoop. "Mom's name is on the label. That figures. You always were a suck-up."

Peggy wriggled taller in her seat. "What on earth?" she said, which was exactly what Kathy was thinking, but without any of the glee.

The box was large enough for a forty-pound bag of dog food and its matching Great Dane. The three men shimmied it down the hall until they reached the tree.

"The rest of you should exchange first," Jimmy said, puffing his chest for effect. "I wouldn't want to cast a shadow over the other gifts."

"Aren't you sweet," Paul said, wryly.

Frank said, "As sweet as shit pie."

For Kathy, there was a memory foam pillow Frank swore by; for Peggy, slippers with heavy tread; for Jimmy, a fly-tying kit; and for Paul, a history trivia game. Only Paul gifted something to Neil—a whiskey glass etched with the Boston subway map. Kathy tried not to take the others' oversight personally. After all, she didn't get anything for her absent sisters-in-law—though they hadn't been tasked with the indefinite care of her mother.

When Peggy opened homeopathic health tablets from Paul, Kathy wondered if her brother knew about Peggy's heart after all. The two spoke on the phone regularly and, of the Mayfield boys, he established the safest space for expressing vulnerability. If Peggy had confessed to him her reluctance for surgery, Kathy wished she would have shared that their circle had expanded, because Kathy would have appreciated the chance to commune with a sibling. She didn't want to be alone with the knowledge anymore.

Peggy thanked Paul but shoved the tablets out of sight. Kathy suspected they were as good as trash, and for once she agreed with her mother.

Jimmy's gift to Kathy came in an oversized satiny envelope, which brought to mind the Congressional Medal invitation, and the secret squirmed inside her. She thumbed open a full-day treatment at a luxury spa, including a massage, pedicure, manicure, microdermabrasion, facial, and haircut. It must have cost him hundreds.

"Oh, Jimmy. This is too much."

"You do a lot for us. You deserve a day for yourself."

She was touched, not just by his unexpected generosity, but by the acknowledgment that caring for others came at the cost to oneself, and that the giver needed to be replenished. She was warmed by the sense of being seen at last—though Neil, who'd shouldered much of the caregiving, remained invisible. Something slid up behind that stirring, and it had spikes and snap. Here was just another instance of a brother riding in on a gallant white steed, brandishing a grand gesture, and then riding off into the distance. A day of self-care was nice, but it was a flicker inside so many other days—years, decades. In that way, it wasn't nearly enough.

"Thank you," Kathy said.

Then it was time for the star of the show. Although Jimmy had joked he didn't want to dwarf the other presents, his enormous box had hulked on the wings of their exchange, waiting out the opening acts.

Neil retrieved a box cutter but, as he sliced the tape, Peggy wheeled over her walker. "It's my name on the label, isn't it?"

He passed it to her along with an admiring smirk. Such affection caught Kathy by surprise. She had little idea what transpired between them in the hours spent together the last month and a half, the camaraderie that had inadvertently developed like unit cohesion between soldiers. Kathy recounted the interactions she'd witnessed between them of late, and she realized that Peggy had been gentler to her husband, more appreciative. She'd complimented his haircut. When he brought her a glass of water, she'd thanked him without commenting on the metallic taste. She'd enlisted

Fiona's help in her Christmas shopping and gifted Neil a workshop apron embroidered with his name, as well as carving blocks of exotic wood from around the world.

Peggy aimed the blade like a riveter with her gun. She gutted the box and yanked the panels open. "Oh, Jimmy! You didn't."

"I did," Jimmy said, self-satisfied.

"What did he do?" Neil asked.

"It's the Japanese toilet he installed at his house, the one with the heated seat. I've told him how frigid your toilet gets, what with your house set to arctic temperatures."

Kathy served her words in measured portions. "We keep it at sixty-eight."

"Exactly. I understand you are on a budget, but understanding doesn't warm the porcelain."

Kathy's jaw glided into a crack. She faced her brother and tried to sound upbeat, though it came out testy. "So you bought us a toilet. Unsolicited."

"I requested it, in a way," Peggy said, defending him. "And it's not for you. It's for me."

"Does it come with a plumber?" Kathy asked.

"I already shelled out a grand for this bad boy, which is going to increase the value of your house, by the way. I think you can take it from here," Jimmy said.

Kathy's contours were smudging. Her voice was going in and out. Soon she'd disappear altogether, while Peggy's heart flickered and the tree ornaments winked like artificial medals.

"There's no need for a plumber. Neil is quite handy, as it turns out. And he has the tools," Peggy said.

Neil's frustration was sealed taut, but the wrapping was thin. "So it's a gift for you, but a job for me."

"Haven't you been looking for one of those?" Peggy asked, demurely.

Time skidded to a stop. Kathy's eyes smeared the Christmas lights into a colorful haze and her ears began to ring. This excruciating unease was a callback. In the company of her sons, Peggy had regressed to the way she used to treat Neil before he counted her pills, helped her down the stairs, and toasted her bread the exact shade of brown she preferred. This was a disregard of all he'd done for her and a betrayal of their new relationship. Kathy watched as a curtain lowered over Neil's expression, but her mother didn't appear to register the change. Somewhere, beneath the crackling static of their tension, Louis Armstrong croaked, "What a wonderful world."

"Mom," Paul said.

Peggy waved the censure away with her long, gnarled fingers, so much like tree roots. "Neil knows I'm joking. Don't you, Boston?"

Neil's face went dark. Kathy couldn't risk his answer. This short visit with her brothers, the congeniality between her mother and her husband, the caregiving situation that had worked so well—it was all about to erupt.

"I'm doing a polar plunge tomorrow," Kathy blurted.

Her family stilled into individual ice floes and rotated toward her.

"A polar plunge," Peggy repeated, as if she'd never heard of such a thing and was trying to correctly pronounce it. "You, Katherine?"

"Yes. With my coworker."

"Our Scaredy Kat," Frank said, equally disbelieving, "is going to leap into freezing water in the middle of winter for absolutely no reason?"

"I'll probably ease in, and everybody has their reasons, but yes."

The Mayfields looked to one another, and then they broke into unbridled merriment. Kathy laughed herself, at the absurdity of her declaration and her spontaneity. But it had worked. The room had relaxed. Even Neil's features had opened. He'd released his hold on the cloud covering his expression.

Caught up in mirth, Peggy lost track of her breathing. She began to wheeze and coughed to regain control. Neil braced her arm instinctively and Peggy clasped his hand right back. There was a flash between the Mayfield brothers, a silent remark on the revealed intimacy between their brother-in-law and mother—his holding her up, her clinging to him—as well as a small revelation as they registered Peggy's compromised health.

"That plunge," Peggy said, clutching her chest, "is something I must see."

THERE WAS A time when having sex in the nascent hours of the new year was as faithful a custom as the countdown. The tradition broke with the arrival of their kids. Kathy was enamored with her needy little creatures, but so very exhausted. Neil took it personally the first time she asked to be excused from their private holiday celebration. He harbored a complicated envy for having to share his wife. The following year, though, he was the one to fall asleep.

Now, so many new years were stacked behind them, Kathy doubted if sex was on either of their minds as they pulled back the sheets. They were already up past midnight, a small phenomenon, and the house was brimming with Mayfields. Her head fizzed with too much champagne and her feet ached from the motions of hosting: setting out appetizers, clearing plates, making beds. She just wanted to hold her husband, press his warmth against her body, and inhale the salty silt of his skin. He'd endured her brothers—there was no other way to put it—and nothing was more desirable than that brand of devotion. Her arm circled his ribs and he palmed her hand against his chest.

"What's this about a polar plunge?" he asked.

Kathy laughed; she'd almost forgotten. "I had to say something. You looked like you were about to punch an old lady."

"If anything it would have been Jimmy, the toilet elf."

"That might have been worse. He's litigious."

"How are you going to get out of it?"

"I don't know." She'd made the proclamation in a panic, but now she was smiling into the back of Neil's neck. It was easier to be brazen in the dark, so she admitted, "I kind of want to do it."

"You do?"

Maybe it was the bubbly, but she found it was true—she wanted to do something bold. Peggy had flown airplanes during a war. Fiona could soon build skyscrapers. Kathy's coworkers found their ventures. In light of her mother's past, and with the rest of her life yawning before her, Kathy was reconsidering the merit in Peggy's values. Returning to work had served Kathy a taste of bravery. It richened her days with honey and spice, and she craved more. Her son had recently described the category to which Kathy had belonged as "bored housewives." She didn't want her children to see her that way. She didn't want her mother to see her that way. Heck, she didn't want to see herself that way. After a lifetime playing it safe, following the rules, and staying grounded, Kathy was ready to transcend.

As Angela had phrased it, why not?

THE DRIVE TO the ocean was forty minutes, which gave Kathy plenty of time to deliberate her mistake. Maybe she could have weaseled her way out of it, claiming congestion or a scratchy throat—everyone got sick over the holidays. But she had doubled down to Neil the previous night and would appear twice as cowardly or capricious if she buckled now. Why had she had that fourth glass of champagne? Well, she was sober now, and feeling ridiculous in her bathing suit, sandals, and pink terry cloth robe while the other passengers wore puffy winter coats. Heat cranked from the car vents and fat flakes of snow dropped from the sky. What on earth was she doing?

The parking lot wasn't full, but it wasn't empty either. Several groups unloaded, fully dressed spectators among those in cover-ups and swimming caps. Angela had warned Kathy to arrive promptly. Plungers didn't loiter. There was no time for small talk in the cold. They got out, and they got in.

Kathy drew her robe tighter at her neck. When a car door slammed, she jumped.

"You sure you want to do this?" Neil asked. He seemed to see something that concerned him.

"Yeah." Frank made a big show of bouncing his bum knees to generate heat, cupping his hands around his mouth, and exhaling into the pocket. "It's pretty brisk out here."

"She's sure." Jimmy was behind her, massaging her neck and doing his best impersonation of Mickey from *Rocky*. "You're gonna eat lightnin' and crap thunder, kid."

Neil dipped his chin to emphasize his message: *Ignore your brothers. They're idiots. Do what you want to do.* But her family had trekked to the beach in four separate cars. Even Noah and Fiona had made it, dragging themselves through hangovers to see their mother do an audacious thing. Kathy's own mother was walking haltingly, supported by Paul, surveying the scene, her lips ticked up at the corners.

Kathy forced a smile though she felt sick. "No turning back."

It was the first day of a new year, of a new decade, in fact, and the horizon was licked violet and fuchsia. A half mile of smooth tawny sand was nestled inside a crescent of grassy headland. The secluded cove might have been mistaken for a tropical paradise were it not for the stinging wind. The air temperature hovered just below freezing, only a few degrees colder than the ocean—Kathy's destination. Dread eclipsed the picturesque view.

Her children nursed Dunkin' Donuts cups. They hugged her first and then greeted their uncles, who prodded them to divulge their escapades from the previous night. Kathy couldn't pay attention. She was forcing her legs toward the teasing ocean, its foam skidding up and sucking back, its surf as white as ice.

Angela waved from a cluster of plungers broken off from

their families. Kathy offered hers a fleeting goodbye and the sand squeaked under her weight. One man wore a plastic Viking helmet while another wore a shower cap. A woman had on what appeared to be an Ariel mermaid wig; another, a feather boa. The others were more standard issue in Hawaiian board shorts, diving suits (Was that cheating? Why hadn't Kathy cheated?), and fleece jackets over bikinis. Their eyes were bright and shining, their mouths stretched wide. They were abuzz, and their energy seemed to lasso Kathy and draw her in.

She'd arrived just in time because, before she knew it, voices were rising in a rousing "Ready, set," and her heart began to batter in her chest. On "Go," arms looped overhead to twist off shirts, and pants wriggled to the ground. Kathy trembled and her pulse knocked against the walls of her veins. She kicked off her sandals and her toes tunneled into sand as soft and cold as snow. Clothing littered like foliage released from trees. In her hesitancy, Kathy was falling behind. She yanked the knot of her belt and shook her robe off her shoulders and there she stood, on a beach on the first of January, in a one-piece bathing suit she hadn't worn in years. But she didn't have the capacity to worry about her sagging belly or to pose her upper arms so her bicep mush didn't jiggle. There was only the gnashing chill and all the cold to come.

Angela grabbed her hand. Her coworker's face was plump and undefended. Her sparkling eyes peered into Kathy's like they were about to do something thrilling and she couldn't believe their luck. Then they were running, and for a moment, Kathy felt like a girl again, sprinting with a friend she'd just met toward the end of the earth. Up ahead, the Viking hollered and the lady in the feather boa yodeled a battle cry. Kathy chased this peculiar throng of strangers, all seeking glacial proof that they were alive.

She heard Fiona first. "You're doing it, Mom!"

Then came Frank. "Show that ocean what you're made of."

"You got this, Kit Kat!" This was from Jimmy, but it could have been her father's voice, and suddenly she was back on a softball field. For Kathy, those games had never been about winning or being named the most valuable player or earning a college scholarship, as they had been for Peggy. They had been about team dinners, huddles, and this, the sound of her family cheering her from the sidelines.

Her brothers would be gone that evening, leaving everything to her and Neil once again, but they were there now, watching her, backing her, and she loved them.

Warm tears fell down her cheeks just as her toes struck sleet. She might have stopped there had it not been for Angela pulling her forward. Kathy shrieked. She was scared, but also exuberant, because she was the daughter of two war pilots, and she'd resisted the spirit she'd been bequeathed, the bravery modeled by nature and nurture, to choose a conventional anchored life, which had fulfilled her enormously until she'd outgrown it, and now here she was, supporting her family, uncovering secrets, and reinventing herself. Here she was, middle-aged and wild.

The water smacked her legs as if with shards of glass, then pierced through her bathing suit, but she persisted. It was punishing but exhilarating, to find what she was capable of withstanding.

Angela let go; Kathy's hands came together and she dove. The immersion froze her heart and held here there, shocked and paralyzed under the water. For an eternal moment she was stuck in that cutting quiet place, a plane between death and life, and then she was on her feet, systems reeling, staggering to shore, gasping for air, burning and numb, baptized by fiery ice.

As she made her way up the beach, she thought her legs might give out. Her heart thrashed and her lungs were clenched and achy. Her body screeched, but her family hooted and applauded. Neil wrapped her in towels and fit a travel mug of hot chocolate between her hands. Her teeth chattered and she shivered uncontrollably as she upended its sweet warmth into her mouth.

"Wow, Mom," Noah said. "I didn't think you had it in you."

"We may have to change your nickname to Hell-Kat," Frank said.

Paul generated heat along her arms while standing far enough back to avoid her frosty runoff. "I can't wait until next year."

"I see you took my Christmas gift seriously." Peggy's jaw jutted toward the sky, where seagulls cawed and circled, and she cast a sidelong look down at her daughter, as if judging her anew.

"I guess I did," Kathy said, convulsing. "Now you have to make good on yours."

Chapter 22

January 1944

SO MUCH RESTED ON THE B-26 FLIGHT CHECK: TRAINING on the AT-6 planes, the smoothest birds on the market; graduating and applying all Peggy had learned to wartime duties; and even more exhilarating, the simmering rumor that every graduated WASP would be commissioned into the army air forces and assigned an official rank. Not only was that a tremendous honor, it was an opportunity. They'd be veterans of the war, given all the benefits bestowed upon men, as well as the offer to become career pilots. If Peggy passed this check, she was one step closer to a life previously thought impossible. If she failed, as most did, she'd pack her belongings and board a bus back to her family's farm, where her neighbors didn't consider her competent enough to fly a crop duster.

No wonder she felt fit to puke, freezing in the flight line. How could she produce so much sweat while chills ran down her arms? It couldn't be nerves alone. She must be ill. It would be just her luck to have contracted pneumonia, today of all days. Shuddering, she dried her hands on her flight suit, but a new coating surfaced. At this rate, she'd be slipping all over the dash.

She felt Georgia's breath on her neck before her friend

spoke. "Why did the farmer's wife breed an owl with a rooster? To finally get a cock that stayed up all night."

Peggy snorted and leaned back on her heels to hear Georgia deliver more dirty jokes. The first part of the check would be a buddy ride, performed with a peer pilot. Then she'd fly solo. But at least, for a while, she'd have her friend.

When it was Peggy and Georgia's turn, Major Mayfield walked the pair across the swathe of burnt grass to the runway.

"A private escort. To what do we owe the pleasure?" Georgia asked. Peggy widened her eyes in warning, but Georgia only bustled ahead.

Georgia had also trained to board without the aid of a box step, but before she swung into the cockpit, she winked at Peggy, pursed her lips, and wolf-whistled at Mayfield. Then she was inside the plane, out of sight. By the time Mayfield turned, there was Peggy on her own, her mouth hanging open. She stammered the beginnings of an explanation, but then gave up and climbed into the cockpit.

"You are unbelievable," Peggy said.

"Relax, pit stains," Georgia said, buckling herself into the pilot's seat. "He knew it was me."

Peggy slid into the copilot bucket. "Did you rush up here for that prank or so you could pilot first?"

"A pinch of this, a dash of that." Georgia pulled out the cockpit procedures. The papers ruffled noticeably.

"You okay?" Peggy asked.

"Of course. Never better," she simpered, but perhaps only to make up for her trembling hands. She was, apparently, as nervous as every other gal, but if it made her feel better to pretend otherwise, Peggy was game to play along.

"Then let's fire up this rocket."

After the call and answer of the checklists, Georgia's fingers gripped her half wheel. She leaned forward in her seat and challenged the runway. The bomber climbed above Avenger Field, and when Georgia reached the desired altitude, she cranked her flaps up and turned her propellers to high pitch. Only then did she sit back in her seat.

Georgia asked, "After the whistle, did Mayfield reprimand you? Give you a demerit?"

"You said he knew it was you," Peggy said.

"Just answer the question."

"No."

"What does that tell you?"

"That he was as confused as I was?"

"If brains were leather, you wouldn't have enough to saddle a June bug," Georgia said. "He didn't punish you, plus he hasn't made a move though you've been all but begging for it. He cares for you. He hasn't gotten fresh because, if anyone found out, nothing would happen to him, but they'd wash you out faster than you could say Eleanor Roosevelt. He's protecting you. He *likes* you."

Peggy chewed her lower lip. "I don't know."

"You're a mule," Georgia said and threw one hand in the air while the other kept hold of the wheel. "I'm flying with a mule!"

They switched seats for Peggy's turn to pilot. Up they went and down they came with the familiar jolt of landing, the last word spoken by a stalwart ship that didn't want to be flown in the first place. When they came to a stop, Georgia unbuckled and reached for the cockpit latch. Peggy was in the pilot's seat.

It made sense for her to stay there, to do her solo check first. But at the idea of Georgia leaving her in the cockpit, with all those women watching, with Mayfield watching, with everything at stake, her heart began to beat so hard she thought it might ricochet up her throat and choke her.

"I can't do this."

"Sure you can."

"I can't. Something is happening to me." Peggy's heart hammered. She looked down, half expecting to see it banging through her breastbone. "I can't breathe."

"You're just caught up in your pretty head. If my gal can't do it, nobody can."

Peggy gasped and clutched her throat. "I'm dying."

Levity cleared from Georgia's expression. She was resolved now, zeroed in, her eyes flickering with something like fear. She released Peggy's belt and hoisted her to her feet. "Hold on, baby doll. I'm getting you to a doctor."

"You can't. Then he'll know."

"He?"

"Everybody. If you come out with me, they'll know I needed help." Just the prospect of escaping the cockpit was already untying Peggy's airway. Her dizzy was slowing. "I'm all right. I just need to stand on solid ground and catch my breath."

"Are you sure?"

"I'm sure."

The cockpit door pitched open and they peered down at the world from the beast's belly.

"Don't you die on me, Lewis. I can't lose my brightest thing," Georgia said.

The women exchanged concern for gratitude. Then Peggy dropped to the hard dust, washed by the desperate relief of having emerged from being underwater longer than her lungs could manage.

She returned to the flight line on shaky legs. She had to pull herself together. This wasn't how a wartime pilot behaved, an officer of the army air forces, a veteran. It was bad enough Georgia had seen her like that. Her friend bought her time, but when she landed, that time would be up.

Georgia's engines thundered. When the bomber reached its maximum ground speed, Peggy imagined she saw it lift off almost before it had. The back wheel floated up, and the nose tilted back as if in joy—like plane like pilot. Just off the runway, the B-26 continued to levitate, a beautiful assistant at the mercy of her magician. It rose and rose and rose, and then, suddenly, seemed to take control of its own destiny.

When the plane was at 750 feet, the right wing wagged, and Peggy sniffed a laugh. Even in the air, Georgia was trying to put Peggy at ease. She was going to get chewed out for trying aerobatics without permission but, knowing her, she'd joke her way out of trouble.

But the wing didn't pick back up. It drooped farther, rotating thirty, forty, fifty, sixty degrees, like a clock's second hand. But time wasn't passing. It was frozen, forcing Peggy to drink in this sickening image before the plane corrected itself. *Correct! What are you waiting for?* Peggy stepped forward, a single step.

Now the bomber wasn't just turning, it was losing altitude. The plane was completely sideways, its nose pointed down. There was no stopping it.

The ringing in Peggy's ears overlaid the sounds around her: a woman's scream, a man's shouts, the moan that rolled up from her own belly and spilled out. The world spun.

The right wing hit first, collapsing as easily as if it were made of sugar, as if steel were inconsequential. Then the body collided with the earth and ignited into gray smoke and flame. The explosion happened on Peggy's skin. Within her chest. Inside her ears. It filled them to the brim. She stumbled into the cadet behind her. The woman's fingers dug into her shoulders. They woke her up.

Peggy pushed the hands off and bolted toward the crash. The column of smoke was black now. Georgia was trapped inside that dense, swampy darkness. Soon the ground would open up and her beautiful friend would be inhaled by the ravenous earth. Peggy sprinted harder and faster. She had to pull Georgia from the wreckage.

An arm encircled Peggy's waist. She tried to pull free but it was a thick rope. She couldn't form the words to say *Let me go! Let me save her!* so she shrieked. She slapped the arm with one hand and then with both. She writhed and thrashed. She threw all her weight against it. She swung her arms behind her and elbowed her captive in his ribs.

"Peggy, Peggy," Mayfield said in her ear. Then he shouted behind him, "Richard, hold her!"

Mayfield's arm was replaced by another. This was her moment. She pitched forward. Her knees hit the ground and her fingers drove into warm sand. She crawled forward, every breath a gasp, every exhale a whimper. From there, on all fours, she gaped at the inferno.

Mayfield raced toward it and disappeared into the smog.

He reappeared seconds later, coughing and sputtering, and then he reentered the smoke and emerged again, just as quickly, hacking and groping his eyes. Peggy could smell the fumes from where she was. They were smoldering and toxic. They burned her nostrils.

"I'm sorry," Richard said. "I'm so sorry."

Peggy stopped crawling. Her fingers burrowed into the earth so hard it grated against the tender skin beneath her nails. She dropped onto her elbows and took one last look at the wreckage, a burning phoenix's final plumage before disappearing into a pile of its own ash. It hurt her eyes. She lowered her forehead to the ground. Her necklace—Georgia's necklace—was a swinging pendulum before her.

GEORGIA'S EMPTY COT seemed to throb as a damaged muscle, like Peggy's heart had been ripped from her chest and placed across the bay. There were Georgia's rumpled blanket, the slack sheets, and a pack of Chesterfields at the foot, its lid open from that morning when Georgia had loosed cigarettes to store in her front pocket. Peggy lifted the pack to her nose and inhaled. Stale, smoky, and sweet.

On the windowsill was a photo of Georgia's family standing on their front porch, her parents bookending their three children. Mr. Walden wore a short-sleeved undershirt and suspenders, and a bandana tied her mother's hair into a knot at the top of her head. Her two older brothers were tall and thin, each in army uniforms. Georgia was in the middle, her mouth wide and open, as if caught mid-laugh. She stood on her tiptoes and hooked her arms around her brothers' shoulders. Everybody's head tilted toward her. She drew them in.

Peggy's legs shook. She dropped onto Georgia's bed and covered her face with quivering hands. Lieutenant Colonel Walker had directed her to locate a suitable container for a collection. "A collection for what?" she'd asked. He'd taken off his cap and skimmed his hand over his head. "For money to send her home."

The pain in Peggy's chest was sharp and palpitating. She grabbed a handful of Georgia's pillow and pulled it into her body, pressing it to the invisible wound, breathing in the perfume of sweat, cigarettes, and cinnamon until she couldn't sense it anymore.

When she replaced the pillow, she saw the December issue of *Life* magazine with Peggy posed on the wing of a B-17. Georgia had kept the issue under her head while she dreamed. Peggy's heart filled her chest to capacity, weighing on the organs below it. Then it burst, and her torso was completely, achingly, empty.

Women outside the barracks slung arms around one another, paced, and whispered. Cindy, who'd traveled with them to Dodge City, sat with her back against an exterior wall, hugging her knees to her chest, her eyes swollen and her cheeks splotched red.

Peggy wanted to scream until her vocal cords were raw. To pound the ground with her feet and fists. To run. To vomit. Her breath came in short huffs. She held out her empty suitcase.

"Collecting money to send Georgia home."

"But Georgia—"

"Her body."

"The army air forces sends its people home?" The woman's voice was a question whose answer she thought she knew.

"We aren't the army air forces' people," Cindy said between sniffs.

"Not yet," Peggy said, gruffly.

Frown lines creased Cindy's mouth. She considered Peggy like she had something more to say, some awful news to break, but then she only pushed herself to her feet. "I'll find some cash."

* * *

Peggy, Connie, and Pamela rounded up enough black dresses and nylons from the other women on base so that, on the eve of Georgia's funeral two days later, they were properly dressed for mourning.

When they filed from their barracks, the three were met by a formation of WASP hundreds strong standing at attention in the quad, their government-issue coveralls meant for men rolled up to their ankles and wrists. The assembly was reverent and resolute, frightened but trying to be brave, a solemn platoon of female revolutionaries. They'd dedicated themselves to a noble but potentially perilous cause, and one of them had just paid that terrible price. This was what they could do, offer an unofficial memorial to honor the fallen who could have been any one of them. The three baymates marched before the legion of their peers, and the women's hands flew to their foreheads, one after the other, in salute.

Mayfield, the sole officer allocated for the trip, waited beside the hearse. The escort car followed the hearse to a civilian airport, where men loaded the coffin into a commercial airplane. Peggy, Connie, and Pamela boarded alongside the other paying passengers. Although the WASP received army orders, although they had to be granted leave to attend their friend's funeral, although they died supporting their country, they were not soldiers.

The engines purred and, as they raced toward the first flight since the one that ended in embers, a howl lodged at the base of Peggy's throat.

Chapter 23

February 2010

DR. SMITH HAD BEEN RIGHT ABOUT ONE THING: IT WAS UN-nerving to parent one's own parent.

Kathy had been tending to Peggy prior to the falls, but with Peggy's compromised health, the role reversal had in-tensified. Now that Peggy was living under Kathy's roof, in what was once Kathy's daughter's bedroom, Peggy's heart whipping woozily on the other side of the wall, Kathy found herself half listening for her mother in the middle of the night the way she had when her children were young, worried her mother might forget to take her walker to the bathroom, or that she'd wake confused and frightened, wondering how she ended up in a dark bedroom that wasn't her own. Just as she'd prompted her children to finish their homework, Kathy reminded her mother to complete physical therapy. Just as she'd urged her children to drive carefully, Kathy ad-vised her mother not to attempt the stairs alone. Weekends that were once for sports sidelines and Neil's family time were now for watching classic movies and providing Neil some family time *off*. It was a throwback to a previous time but warped and made bizarre.

Sometimes it was depressing. Rearing children, though

tiresome, reaped great rewards: marveling at acquired skills, receiving uninhibited adoration, tracking growth, and witnessing as unique personhoods developed. Nursing the elderly was implicitly more hopeless. There wasn't a future before them but rather a dead end, and the caretaker was tasked with stewarding them toward it with at least a semblance of grace.

Sometimes it was frustrating. At least with kids, there was recourse for disobedience. What was Kathy to do when Peggy refused her dinner, neglected treaded socks, or behaved rudely? She couldn't discipline her mother. When Kathy responded patiently, offering another meal choice, fetching the right kind of socks, or biting back retaliations to impoliteness, she couldn't help but think that Peggy had never cared for her so well.

Sometimes it was painful. She once watched Peggy get breathless climbing to her feet, wince as she shuffled to the bathroom, and then freeze, awash in horror, as a dark stain ran down her pant leg. Peggy squeezed her eyes closed against the warm shock, and the humiliation of having her daughter see, and Kathy's eyes stung. Consolation would only strengthen the throb, so Kathy guided her mother upstairs and cleaned her without a word.

But sometimes it was rewarding to ride on the wings of this fleeting moment, and know she was making herself present, doing all she could to soften her mother's landing. And sometimes it was sweet. On mild winter afternoons, the two women bundled up on the back deck with mugs of tea or sat on the couch with photo albums between them and flipped through old times. Kathy was grateful for the bonus tenderness she'd been granted at the tail end of her mother's life.

Those intimacies were enough to bolster Kathy's empathy during the trying times. It couldn't have been easy for Peggy, once so capable, to be at somebody's mercy, to go from flying bombers to making lunches to not being able to hold her bladder. It was a large-scale version of the uselessness Kathy felt when the kids left for college, and the futility she imagined Neil experienced when he was let go. Kathy, however, was being put to work once again, and Neil, too, had discovered new utility. It was only Peggy who was on a downward trajectory, weathering the absence of possibility.

Unless, of course, Peggy agreed to attend the Congressional Gold Medal Ceremony the following month, which, as far as Kathy could tell, was an honor rousing enough to send her skyward. She couldn't understand why her mother, of all people, was so reluctant to fly.

AS KATHY CAME in from work one February evening, Neil met her in the mudroom, tucking the corners of his lips into his cheeks like he was a boy showing off his rock collection. She slid her coat off and hung it on the wall hook, all while waiting for her husband to divulge, until she finally demanded, "All right already. Spill the big fat lima beans."

"I got a job offer," he said.

She smacked his arm. "That's amazing." It had been months, maybe years, since she'd seen this shade of pride on him. She wanted to pile on the kindling and keep his fire burning so their connection as it was now would never end.

"What's the company? What's the position?" She sensed a startling cadence of disappointment but managed to keep it from her voice. She'd enjoyed knowing she was the bread-winner and had been pleased by Neil's reinvention, his surprising satisfaction in his new roles as artist and caretaker. Plus, there was the matter of who would look after Peggy. The situation, which had been working so well, was about to change. "I'm so happy for you."

"I'm excited too," he said, but his expression had dimmed. It was barely distinguishable, but enough that she noticed. "There is a downside. The job is in Nashville."

They held each other at a loose arm's length, fingers grazing elbows. Kathy adjusted her grasp. "Like the capital of Tennessee?"

"Yeah, that one."

Kathy stepped back. "That's some downside."

Neil reached but didn't touch her. "I know you never wanted to move again, and you don't have to. Flights are only a couple hundred bucks. I can go in for the week, stay at a rental, and come home every weekend, or at least every other. And you can visit. It could be fun." His river of reassurances rushed over her but sloughed down her arms. "The best part is we won't have to give up the house."

She might have said, *What good is the house without you in it?* but her skin had gone clammy, her legs were weakening, and her pulse was quickening—the trademarks of physical shock manifesting after an emotional collision.

"And you can quit your job," he said.

That comment activated her. Her shoulders hitched, and she said, "I *like* working."

"So keep it. Do whatever you want. Now you have the choice."

Why did her job have to be elective recreation rather than the sustenance of their family? Why couldn't she and her husband maintain the rhythm of the new roles they'd discovered?

"Is this because of what my mother said on New Year's Eve?" she asked.

"What?"

"The dig about your job hunt. What she said in front of my brothers. Are you trying to prove something?"

Neil shook his head too hard. "I hardly remember that."

She dropped her eyes to the raw almond of the wood planking, with its sporadic black knots, soft enough to have been scarred by the ins and outs of their lives—the wheels of Noah's speedster toy, chairs dragged to make room at the table, two hundred years of wear that could be buffed and refinished but never erased. Kathy had slipped her work sneakers off, and now her socked feet, innocent and childlike beside Neil's giant moccasins, straddled planks of varying widths, set at slightly different heights. She was off-balance, but barely.

In another time, even just the previous year, Kathy probably would have offered to move to Tennessee with him, despite how rooted she was in Massachusetts, the nearness to her children, and how she'd disavowed nomadism, because that was what wives did. They followed their husbands. But she wasn't willing to deny herself for this—Neil chasing an identity he didn't even like. Maybe Neil knew that, which was why he didn't ask it of her, or maybe he loved her enough to leave her behind, just not enough to neglect his ego.

"Flying back and forth, being apart all week . . ." She trailed off, hoping her words would trigger something in him. She wanted Neil to hear the scenario for the mistake it was, to complete her sentence with *would be intolerable*. Instead, he waited for her to finish. "What kind of a life is that?"

"What kind of a life is this, me stuck in the house all day, cleaning, cooking, shopping, and now, with your mother, acting like I'm some kind of nurse?"

He might as well have boxed her ears, describing her thirty-year contribution to the family, the world, with disdain. A storm brewed behind her forehead. She could rain down on him with tears. Or better yet, fling bolts of lightning.

"Some kind of nurse?" she repeated.

His hands swiveled into a position of surrender. "That came out wrong. It's fine to be a nurse. For you. Okay, I'm digging myself a hole. I just don't want to nurse my mother-in-law. You can understand that. It isn't who I am."

"But a long-distance husband. That's who you are?"

"You're making me sound like a jerk. It's money. We can't turn down money."

But it wasn't their only source. She was earning. Their bank account wasn't overflowing but they had health insurance, they were getting by, and it could be enough if they made other changes—big ones, yes, but less drastic than boarding a plane every Sunday night and flying a thousand miles away.

"Have you really been miserable?" she asked. He'd been

despondent in the months following the layoff, as well as when she'd first returned to work, but Kathy actually thought, since then, he'd risen into a new form. With his carving, and even with Peggy moving in, he appeared to have uncovered a fresh sense of purpose, another way to be satisfied. It had seemed as if he was flourishing as a nurse, even that he *liked* the work.

But perhaps it was more complicated than simple enjoyment. Kathy transitioning into the breadwinner was a move to applaud—a societal promotion. Women had made progress and could play parts once assigned to men. Their culture didn't yet value what was traditionally seen as women's work, so the inverse was still stigmatized. Neil acting as a caregiver at home, doing so-called feminine work, was perceived as a demotion, and it would take a special kind of man to accept a reduced reputation for the sake of his happiness. In order to stay near his wife, could Neil be that special kind of man?

Kathy asked, "What about Noah's carving business idea?"

"That wasn't serious."

"So you can just be done with your art now?" she asked, but what she really meant was *So you can just be done being with me?*

"It's a decent offer."

She felt dizzy and clamped her hand over her forehead so her thumb and middle finger pressed into her temples. "How much time do we have to decide?"

Neil's Adam's apple buoyed over his discomfort. "I already accepted the offer."

Neil had made their biggest life decision since—when, moving to Lexington?—without even consulting her. Rain unleashed behind Kathy's forehead and lightning cracked through her jaw. Was this some misguided attempt to reclaim his masculinity? *I am man. I am in charge.* Or was he just so afraid she would object that he curtailed her opposition by making it a done deal? Either way, she didn't understand their marriage as she thought, and that was as discombobulating as it was devastating. Her heart had been ambushed. She'd been funneling her energy into averting a calamity they'd already sustained. She thought she could keep her husband, not knowing she'd already lost him.

"I'm going to check on my mother," she said. She jostled into him as she pushed by, and he let her go.

Kathy was so distraught she forgot about the still-boxed Japanese toilet outside the upstairs bathroom and jammed her toe against its corner. "Shit."

"If you don't want to keep knocking into that thing, you could consider installing it," Peggy called from her room.

Pain flared Kathy's sorrow into indignation. It wasn't her fault the box was still in the hallway. It was Jimmy's, for introducing that uninvited leviathan to their household in the first place. It was Neil's, for neglecting it, too busy applying, interviewing, and negotiating a position he wasn't telling her about. It was Peggy's, for angling for her son's pity and, therefore, attention, by way of a cold toilet seat. Kathy's resentment mounted even as the pulsing quieted.

Peggy had all but vanquished the vitality in Fiona's bedroom. Even the air felt stiller, like the molecules had slowed to Peggy's pace. The scent of peach body spray was replaced by a heady perfume and a lightly sour mustiness. Peggy's cardigans filled the closet, dusty cosmetics cluttered the dresser, and four romance novels were arranged on the end table to camouflage the WASP issue of *Life*.

Peggy herself was posed on the bed buttressed by a pillow throne with a TV dinner tray table bridging her narrow thighs. She was in the midst of letter writing, perhaps to Constance, a longtime pal in all things, including pen. A reading light was clipped to the bed frame and illumed Peggy in a spotlight.

Peggy continued, "I could die any day and Jimmy's generosity is out there rotting on the vine. At this rate, I'll croak before the first flush."

"That would be the true tragedy," Kathy said, tightly.

"I'll shell out for a plumber if that's the issue, though I don't see why Neil can't do it himself."

Kathy didn't want to flatter Neil with loyalty so soon after their fight, so she kept her voice low. "There aren't many sons-in-law who would do for you what my husband has done, especially after the way you've treated him."

Peggy tipped her chin defiantly and her elbows cocked like drawn pistols. "I'm not going to apologize for wanting the best for my daughter."

"That's your excuse for everything."

"It's true."

"Of course it's true. You're a mother. That's what mothers want. But it's also a total cop-out," Kathy said, her volume rising. She wasn't used to yelling. It was a rush to be blunt and brave, a relief to shed the protective gear of compounded years and sprint barely, wildly, into the cold. "Maybe I can buy it as the reason you made yourself my enemy. I wish things could have been better between us, but maybe you thought I needed the pressure. I can even accept it as the reason you were cruel to Neil, though I resent that. But I refuse to believe it was in my best interest to keep secret the fact that you were a WASP. Jimmy was around for ten years before I came along, and you never told him either. Besides, how could withholding that information benefit me? There has to be more to it."

Peggy turned to the window. Her mouth buckled and her eyebrows drew together so that her features concentrated into the center of her face. The glass was liquid black, and a reflection of herself.

Kathy had her own theories as to why Peggy had been so abstruse. Maybe Peggy hadn't wanted to serve as an example of a woman who lived a dream and then fell into step with the convention of the age. Or perhaps the end hadn't been voluntary, and Peggy didn't speak of the WASP out of bitterness. How must it have been, then, for Peggy to support her husband's air force career, knowing she should have had one too? But why had she sat quietly with self-perceived injustice? Why hadn't she raised hell, petitioning the way she had when Kathy's softball team didn't have the budget to travel to the state playoffs? Unless the time and circumstances had rendered her powerless, or the size of the loss was so unwieldy even a war pilot couldn't get it off the ground.

Kathy continued softer. She had the courage to venture this scenario only into a small existence. "Did you not want to talk about it because you loved it, and it was taken away?"

Peggy's eyes flickered to her in sharp recognition. She swallowed hard. "In more ways than you know."

"Tell me," Kathy said. "Then I'll know."

"I didn't tell you about the WASP because then I'd have to tell you about Katherine, and that was too painful a prospect."

Kathy sensed danger and prickled alert. Was this a mental break? Her mother had been stressed: two falls, the heart diagnosis, moving into a new house, and history forcibly uncovered. Add to that Kathy's maternal indictments, and maybe Kathy had fractured an already strained mind. Or maybe this was a harbinger of dementia—more deterioration, more loss to come.

Kathy moved to her mother's bedside and touched her shin. "Mom, it's me. *I'm* Katherine."

Peggy studied her daughter's hand as if it didn't belong there. Then she dismissed it with a wag of her fingers. "For goodness' sake. Not you. The original Katherine."

Chapter 24

January 1944

THE WALDENS WERE WAITING ON THE TARMAC WHEN the cadets and the major arrived in Savannah. Their bodies might have weighed the same, but with far different distributions. Where Mr. Walden's form was stretched, Mrs. Walden was set wider and lower to the ground. Their arms met in the middle as they clung to each other. Mrs. Walden's wails were a siren carried on the wind. She seemed to approach death the same way her daughter approached life: loud and unapologetic. Peggy didn't blame her. She'd only known Georgia six months, and still her grief was gutting. How must Mrs. Walden feel having produced such a treasure from her own body, and loved and admired her all this time?

Peggy extended her hand to Mrs. Walden, who climbed it like a rope.

"Oh Peggy," she said, addressing her as if they'd known each other their whole lives. Mrs. Walden lay her damp face on Peggy's chest. "What are we going to do now?"

Behind her, Mayfield cleared his throat. "Mr. and Mrs. Walden, your daughter was a dedicated cadet, a courageous woman, and as skilled a pilot as I've ever had the pleasure of

flying beside. It was an honor to be her commanding officer.
I am sorry for your loss."

Mr. Walden opened his mouth, but then shut it, and
something elongated his expression. His mouth sagged, his
forehead rippled, and he swept his hand over his bald scalp
as Georgia's coffin was wheeled toward them.

"I want to see her," Mrs. Walden said, but what lay inside
that coffin was nothing a mother should see. Mr. Walden
grasped his wife's shoulder and she swatted him away. "I
want to see my baby."

He wrapped his arm more insistently and whispered in
her ear. She resisted, but then that whisper unlatched something inside her and she relented, leaned against him, and
rested her hand on the coffin.

"Katherine," she cried into her husband's ribs. "Our Katherine."

It should have been Peggy soloing that B-26. It should have
been her gripping the yoke as the plane tilted. It should have
been her father beside that coffin in his worn suit, her mother's soft body wracked with grief. If she hadn't panicked, if
she hadn't begged Georgia to be the one, it would have been
her, like it was supposed to be.

> All the gals are aces, but you're my favorite.
> If my gal can't do it, nobody can.
> Don't you die on me, Lewis. I can't lose my brightest thing.

Peggy spun inside memories of Georgia's wide smile, her
eyes elongated into mischief, her contagious audacity that
convinced Peggy they could do anything. All that was locked

inside that box, about to be buried. Peggy thought she would be sick.

Connie's cold fingers slipped through Peggy's, and Mayfield edged closer on her other side. He didn't lower his head from the horizon, he didn't lift his arms, he didn't reach for her, but he stood close enough that she could feel the warmth of his body. Close enough that, if she fell, he could catch her.

SAVANNAH WAS FERTILE and ripe, not just in the lush green of grass, palm fronds, and saw palmetto leaves, fuchsia azaleas, and reds of winterberry, but in the creamy pollen of the Spanish Renaissance Union Station and the camellia blossom of the Olde Pink House. Every square was manicured, flowered or prepped to flower. It made perfect sense this was where Georgia had been raised, but no sense at all that this was where she'd be laid to rest, and on the kind of blue-sky day that spoke of spring, making promises of warmer days to come.

Among the thirty surrounding her open grave, there was an apparent lack of young men, with so many shipped to various corners of the world. Her brothers were still in Europe and would remain there without any hint of the loss they'd sustained. The Waldens wouldn't share the news while their sons were out there, fighting for their lives. Besides, it would be impossible to put such torments into ink.

"'Fear not,'" the preacher said, as he massaged the Bible's bookmark ribbon between his thumb and forefinger, "'for I have redeemed you; I have called you by name: you are Mine. When you pass through the waters, I will be with you. And through the rivers, they shall not overflow you.'"

His reading was interrupted by a sonorous trumpet peal,

which repeated and then climbed one note higher. This was taps, the anthem of mourning, a sorrow song that put sound to Peggy's pain. Only, its resonance was diluted by distance.

Another group gathered across the cemetery, accompanied by a full blue-uniformed military escort that hoisted the flag-draped coffin of their fallen sailor. The contrast to their single representative was painful, and Georgia's coffin palpably bare.

If she were there, Georgia would have said something funny and poignant about the contrast. She would have put a fine point to the injustice while also sanding down the sting. But Georgia wasn't there.

The preacher read, "'When you walk through the fire, you shall not be burned, nor shall the flame scorch you.'"

Peggy relived the revolting spiral, the too easy impact, the smoke, and the flames. The WASP were training, doing without, doing their part. They were dying. Where was their nation's grief for them, their due gratitude and respect? She pinched her eyes closed and rolled her fingers into fists.

Across the burial ground, rifles fired the three-volley salute, which was once a signal for opposing sides to cease fire, collect their dead, and resume the fight. In a way, it still was, because when their ceremony was through, the navy soldiers would go home, wipe their tears, and pick up the cause where they'd left it.

The salute hadn't been for the WASP, yet they'd do the very same.

THE WALDENS INSISTED the mourners from Sweetwater stay at the house, a quaint three-bedroom with a green tin roof and a wraparound porch Peggy recognized from the family photograph.

Mrs. Walden set Mayfield up in the basement, two floors from the ladies for propriety's sake, and arranged Connie, Pamela, and Peggy on the top floor, same as the Waldens, in the boys' bedroom. Georgia's bedroom remained conspicuously unoccupied.

"Be as loud as possible, y'all. Noise beats the heck out of the sound of my own thoughts," Mrs. Walden said. She tried to look welcoming, but her face was swollen and heavy. Then she was gone.

"I wish I could call my mother," Connie said.

Peggy struggled to settle the dissonance of being in Georgia's house with her parents, among her brothers' baseball cards, fishing rods, and cowboy figurines, without her there to revel in it, enjoy her people all in one place, and joke in Peggy's ear.

There were no new memories to be made with her friend— her first, and perhaps last, truly kindred spirit. All she had was Georgia's past, and now was her chance to access it.

"Write your mom. It'll make you feel better," Peggy told Connie. "I'll be right back. I need to freshen up." Then she eased into Georgia's bedroom and shut the door gently behind her.

"Peggy," Mrs. Walden said, sitting upright on the bed.

"I'm so sorry." Mrs. Walden couldn't know how profoundly, and how multifariously, Peggy meant those words. "I didn't know you were here." She reached for the knob.

"Stay. Please."

The room was cluttered with all things Georgia. The walls

were pasted with movie posters and sports team flags, her bedside table was crowded with a radio, cigarettes, and two issues of *Cosmopolitan*, and clothing and shoes were strewn across the floor. It smelled of smoke and cinnamon and a person who had too little time on this earth to waste any of it cleaning.

"I know I should have picked the place up, but with Arthur and me here alone, I liked it looking like Katherine was still around. Now I'm glad. I'll keep it as is, like a museum."

Peggy felt inadequate, as if Mrs. Walden required the precision of tweezers but all she'd brought from Sweetwater were bludgeons and bats. Every word that came to mind felt cumbersome and ill fitting. But it turned out Mrs. Walden didn't need her to say anything at all.

Mrs. Walden's eyes welled and she wiped them with the butts of her palms. "My Katherine sure was fond of you. Now I see why, bless your heart."

Peggy flushed, remembering the strangeness the night of the dance, and Georgia's lingering touch on her arm. What had Georgia told her mother? What had Georgia felt? "I was fond of her too. We were very close."

Mrs. Walden's chin textured with emotional strain. "I see you've got on my mother's necklace."

Peggy's stomach flipped and her hand flew to her chest to thumb the cool silver. "But—" She stopped herself. She couldn't admit that Georgia had pawned off this family heirloom as a trinket her ex had purchased at a junk sale, so she reached around her neck to unclasp it.

"Keep it," Mrs. Walden said.

"It's your mother's."

"If Katherine wanted you to have it, as far as I'm concerned, it's yours."

It wasn't Peggy's place to insist. Mrs. Walden held rank in the grief hierarchy. "I'll cherish it."

Mrs. Walden leaned back against the headboard and blinked at the ceiling. "I have to trust the Lord that Katherine died for good reason. I may never know what that reason is, but the only way I can survive this is to believe it wasn't for nothing. Maybe that plane was a bomb my daughter threw her body on, and she died so another wouldn't. Katherine died for the sake of someone destined to make this world a better place. That's what I have to remind myself."

"But who could do better than your daughter?" Peggy asked.

Mrs. Walden's face fixed like she was thinking the very same thing. Her voice had the edge of an accusation. "Heck if I know. I lay my questions at the foot of the cross."

Peggy's tongue seemed to expand, leaving no room to swallow, or to breathe. She was drowning and suffocating simultaneously. She rushed from the room. Her steps thudded down the stairs with the hollowness of drums and then she was outside, where the air wasn't so thick with Mrs. Walden's grief and stifling credence.

A breeze stroked her cheek—a consolation and a tenderness. She thought again of Georgia caressing her arm at the dance, but maybe it had just been Georgia's way of showing alliance, a gesture as distinct and fleeting as the person behind it. Now, because of Peggy's cowardice, that person was buried, and Georgia's parents, Peggy—the whole world—were denied her vibrancy, and Georgia had been deprived of the life she deserved. Peggy found herself on her hands and knees, heaving sobs into the porch floor planks, begging forgiveness.

Peggy felt him first: a hand on her shoulder, picking her up and into him. His arms encircled her. She sank into his sturdiness. His fingers combed the hair at her temple.

"You're all right," he said.

If events had unfolded as they were meant to, Georgia would be preparing to return to Avenger Field. She'd fly planes, contribute, and be commissioned into the army air forces. She'd change the world for the better. Georgia could do that. She could do anything, everything. Peggy only pretended at valiance. Her friend had been the real thing.

"It should have been me," Peggy said.

Mayfield tucked his finger beneath Peggy's chin and raised her face to his. His hair was wet from a shower and slicked to the side, rippling and carrying the moon's reflection like a night sea. His irises were circled in brown ebony and filled with mahogany. A single stress line creased between his eyebrows and, together with the groove above his lip and the cleft of his chin, marked him in perfect halves.

To behold him from this angle and in this place fragmented Peggy into loss and longing, jagged and ill defined, a mosaic both broken and new.

She needed someone. She needed Mayfield, and he was there, just as he'd been there in the town of Sweetwater, just as he'd been in the sky, just as he'd been at the dance. He was here now, again, and always—the final punctuation of a love letter that had taken months to write.

Anybody could vanish at any moment. To delay sweetness

in a world as cruel and arbitrary as theirs was a more perilous risk than any other, a disrespect to all who couldn't be
there to live and savor. The pair of them had waited too long
already.

Shadow clouds drifted across his forehead, cheeks, and
mouth. Peggy bent forward to press her lips against his, taste
his warmth and salt. But she brushed against bristle, and her
eyes shot open to find Mayfield had turned his head, offering
the stubble of his jaw line.

"Peggy—"

She'd given herself over to him, presented him her unpro-
tected heart. His rejection was a lash against bare flesh. "You
don't have to explain."

"It wouldn't be right," Mayfield said.

"I'd appreciate if you didn't mention this to Jackie Cochran
or anybody else." She pushed herself to her feet, smoothed
her dress, and wiped the dampness from her face. "Good
night." Peggy stuck out her hand, but before Mayfield could
accept, she let it drop, shook her head at her own foolishness,
and fled, letting the screen door smack behind her.

The girls were already asleep, and Peggy was relieved not
to have to make conversation. She changed into a night-
gown, crawled into bed beside Connie, and concentrated
on her friend's even breath. Outside the window, the live
oak glowed in a pool of moonlight. Its branches were draped
with strands of Spanish moss, as if they'd plunged into a pile
and come out with its phantasmal shroud.

Peggy licked away the roughness of Mayfield's turned
cheek and squeezed her eyelids against the pity in his eyes.
But in the dark, too much remained. She heard the echo of

Mrs. Walden: *Katherine died for the sake of someone destined to make this world a better place.*

* * *

Back at Avenger Field, a single rose rested on Georgia's pillow, and a bar of rationed chocolate lay on each of the three returning cadets'. Their bay had been straightened and their latrine scrubbed to spare them chores before their next inspection. These were small comforts, but by the week anniversary of the crash, things had to return to normal. Training couldn't wait on grief or terror. If Peggy wanted to continue in the program, she'd have to climb into the plane that had fallen from the sky. She had panicked even before the crash. How would she fare knowing all she now knew? Maybe the men had been right all along. She was weak. Emotional. She couldn't handle the pressure. Perhaps it would be better, safer, if she stepped aside.

Peggy ferried her breakfast past the men to her section, though she doubted she could eat it; sickness hovered at the top of her stomach, where it had been poised for seven days.

"The engines quit. Mechanical issues. That's what I heard," a cadet told his table, unaware she was near.

Peggy stopped. Before she could ask if they'd determined the cause of the accident, another cadet snorted. "I heard she was on the rag. Insufficient blood in her brain."

Peggy's tray slipped from her fingers and clattered to the floor. Her oatmeal upended and her coffee mug shattered, spewing a tawny puddle across the linoleum.

The cadet rotated slowly on his bench, but Peggy didn't

wait to see his expression before she drew her hand back and released it across his face. The slap cut through the cafeteria noise, dropping it to silence.

Her words were small furies. "Our lives are a joke to you?"

He clutched his cheek, which was already turning rose. "It wasn't a joke. That was what I heard. Honest. They conducted a menstruation study."

"Miss Lewis." Jackie Cochran was behind her, stern and stiff. "Let's take a walk."

Peggy began her apology as soon as they were outside, but Jackie lifted her palm to intercept. "Miss Walden was a hell of an aviator, and that crash was not her fault. People die flying. Men and women both. I don't expect that makes her loss any easier."

"No, but they don't have the right to blame her when she's not here to defend herself. They know how good she was."

Jackie Cochran said, "What people know and what they'll admit are two entirely different things. Our only recourse is to establish the truth until it's undeniable."

Peggy scuffed her feet against the dry earth. "That sounds tiresome."

"Yes, and it makes smashing your breakfast particularly foolish, seeing as you'll need the fuel."

"I'm not sure—"

"Several WASP have approached me with resignation papers. We can't lose faith when we are close to gaining so much. I need you to set an example. Get back in the air. Show these women that you are not afraid, or that you are at least willing and able to fight through your fear. They'll follow. We're asking a lot of you, Miss Lewis. I realize that.

But we've asked a lot of you all along, and you've risen to the challenge, so why should now be any different?"

Peggy wished she could begin with a primary trainer and ease her way skyward, but the army air forces didn't have use for Fairchild pilots. They needed girls who weren't afraid, even after seeing the worst befall the very best of them.

If Peggy dropped out, she'd reinforce the perception that female pilots were emotional liabilities, and Georgia's death would result in a ripple of failure, when she'd been charged with establishing the very opposite. Peggy had no choice but to fly.

AVENGER FIELD UNFOLDED its barren landscape to the horizon. A smattering of sparrows and chickadees hopped along the tufts of dried grass, while the silhouette of a bird of prey circled between Peggy and the sun. It might have been a hawk, but it also could have been a vulture.

Mayfield marched past his group to the center of the WASP formation and pivoted, the bombers at his back. "We lost a trainee a week ago. Katherine Walden. She was an expert flyer and a tenacious woman. Take a moment to offer your prayers and honor her memory." They bowed their heads and murmured. Then Mayfield discharged them with an amen, turned on his heel, and approached Peggy's line. His attention rested on her for a moment, but he lifted it before she could be sure. "I'll be copiloting with you all today. Consider it an unofficial officer flight check."

Whether it was to reassure the female pilots or himself, Mayfield would be on board. He'd be there. He was making a habit of that.

Peggy studied takeoffs with new a focus. Her toes curled and her fingers worked her pant seams. The bombers ascended, ignorant to their sister's tumble seven days prior. Peggy tracked their progress fastidiously, as if the next accident was waiting for the moment she stopped expecting it, so she remained in a constant state of expecting it. Georgia likely aimed her crash safely away from the flight line to protect the other WASP. She had the skill for that, and the presence of mind. The next unlucky pilot might not. Each successful landing felt like a granted favor that laid its hand on Peggy's hitched shoulders, inviting her to relax, but she wouldn't dare.

Peggy remembered Mabel Stark, a circus performer she saw once in Kansas City. Mabel wrestled big cats. In one act, a tiger reared up on his hind legs and wrapped his paws around her neck. They tumbled once, twice, three times before Mabel pinned the tiger. He opened his great big jaw, and she stuck her entire face inside, daring him to gnash his teeth—or proving her certainty that he wouldn't. In the next act, eighteen tigers, panthers, and lions circled her. They all had their chance to attack, to snatch her up in their maws, and chose not to—at least not that time. But Mabel had been mauled before, dragged from the ring unconscious, her arms broken. She got back in the ring because she was sure the animals were inherently good. She was never afraid to begin a new conversation with them. Peggy's daddy called Mabel a yuck. Peggy wasn't so sure.

Maybe the plane was like any other domesticated beast. It would always possess savage potential. It could never truly be tamed. But the U.S. Army Air Forces needed girls who'd confront them anyway.

"I am that girl," Peggy whispered, her stomach oscillating on itself. "I am that girl." She gripped the cockpit braces and pitched her body inside.

Mayfield swung up behind her. "How do you feel, cadet?"

They were back in their natural habitat of dashboard dials, steel, and rivets. This was familiar. Petrifying, but familiar. She'd lost her orientation in Savannah, with its palm tree silhouettes and Spanish moss. She'd soon feel herself again, and she'd realize she was just looking for comfort and distraction, and Mayfield had saved her the trouble of having to undo an ill-advised liaison.

Oh, but that slate jaw. Those loam eyes.

"It doesn't matter what I'm feeling. I'm ignoring it," Peggy said.

"You graduate in a month and a half, cadet." Mayfield picked up his headphones and clamped them over his ears. "It'd be a shame to throw it all away."

Peggy's nerves were frayed and her muscles knotty. Her body was an oracle portending disaster, flinching a beat before destruction. The engines rattled and roared, and she locked a scream at the base of her throat. If Georgia had spiraled out of control, Peggy couldn't possibly emerge from this unharmed. Her friend had earned a safe landing, yet she'd been incinerated. Peggy didn't warrant a different ending, but she also couldn't just walk away from the danger.

They took off. If her commanding officer could have seen the storm cloud of her fear, he would have grounded the plane. It was pulpy and black, and filled her top to bottom. She may as well have been flying blind.

Then it loosened. It didn't disappear, but she could see

around fear's edges. There was the road to town. A flock of crows. The thud of her heart. Patches of sky. She was rigid, angled toward the glass and panting—but she was alive.

Soon the panic receded enough to reveal the varied landscape of pain. Peggy wasn't just petrified and mourning. She ached from the burden of two formidable loves without a landing place. Their flow was not something she could control with dials or switches, so it emanated from her unfettered as the plane cut through the atmosphere, searching the altitudes for the severed connection to Georgia, and extending unrequited across the cockpit to Mayfield, Peggy's parallel sorrows, the spread wings of grief and heartache, fated to forever circle.

Chapter 25

INSIDE CEILING SHADOWS THAT CIRCLED TOWARD MID-night, Kathy saw the bomber plunging before the field of female flyers, her mother moving forward as the friend who lived, bearing and birthing three boys before finally fitting a daughter in the crook of her elbow, a girl she called Katherine. How strange to find in middle age that she, as a namesake, had been unknowingly carrying the legacy of somebody she never knew existed. All this time she'd been haunted by a ghost. Georgia's memory had sat at their dinner table. She'd moved with them from house to house. When Peggy called for Kathy up the stairs, when she cheered for her on the sidelines, when she clapped at graduations, it was her daughter's name she used, but her lost friend's too. Was it any wonder, then, that Peggy had often looked at Kathy as if she saw somebody else and spoke to her as if she hoped a different voice might respond?

Kathy had resisted her mother. She'd bucked, opposed, and ignored. Most significantly, she'd resented. It never occurred to her that Peggy's teachings had been hard earned, as well as a means of honoring a loss and reconciling searing regret.

If Peggy felt responsible for the death of a beloved, it was no wonder she had never spoken of the WASP. Who would want to admit such a heartbreak?

Kathy thought back to a county fair when Peggy joined her boys and a few of the neighborhood kids on the most rickety roller coaster on the grounds. Another mother remarked, "Peg, you are brave." Peggy dismissed the comment, but when the other mother insisted, Peggy responded with too much snap, "This isn't bravery. It's a child's thrill ride. Don't you know the difference?"

Neil was asleep, comfortably heading toward eight hours of rest, but unconsciousness felt well beyond Kathy's grasp. She swung her legs out from under the blankets. Since she couldn't quiet her thoughts, she could at least keep busy while her brain sorted and sieved. She could perform a kindness, perhaps one that was long overdue.

KATHY PLACED TOOLS around her as if for a hardware séance—plunger, adjustable wrench, putty knife, heavy-duty lubricant, and rag—and her fingers, clumsy inside yellow rubber dishwashing gloves, flipped the owner's manual to a page not written in Japanese characters.

A list of the company's other products revealed that her brother didn't have to puff his chest so gratuitously; he could have sent a warming-seat attachment rather than the whole hundred-pound appliance. But then, Kathy supposed, Peggy wouldn't have benefited from the other features, like an electronic lid that opened and closed on its own, an automatic flush, a built-in air purifier, and a bidet with spray positions at the front and rear as well as three wash modes: hard, soft, and oscillating. Good grief.

Kathy sensed the stillness of the house beyond the bathroom. How silly to be working like this, in the dead of night. Yet there was also a mystical quality about it, as if she were the last woman on earth, inside her own little pocket, alone with this one task.

She watched a few online instructional videos, the volume at its lowest setting, her ear cocked an inch from the speaker in order to hear. When she felt ready, she cranked off the water supply to the toilet, flushed and plunged it dry, and began the process of removing the too-cold porcelain.

People were never more self-centered than they were in relation to their mothers, Kathy thought. Children rarely considered who she was before, as if the life up until their birth was erased with their arrival. But of course, everything that transpired informed how they were raised. A mother's past cast anonymous reverberations into her daughter's future. A girl inherited joys and sorrows, blessings and traumas. She was filled by her mother's good fortune. She felt the chasm of her slights. She paid for her talents and for her mistakes.

The wrench slipped and clanked against the toilet tank. Kathy waited for the echo to pass. Then she fit the steel teeth around the bolt and tugged it loose.

This newest disclosure burned more haze off her mother's squalls, every dark mood that blasted their house or sent Peggy to her bedroom to lie in the dark, their father diverting the needs of the children: "Let's not bother your mother." Her tempests could have been the battering of furtive grief. Now Kathy was sifting through the wreckage, inspecting the memories under the light of this revelation and the nickel-brushed wall fixtures of her second-floor bathroom.

Kathy grunted and shimmied the tank onto the tile floor. It was only thirty pounds, but she didn't often bear such heft. She sensed a pull in her muscles and knew that the exertion would leave an impression over the next couple days.

With the old toilet set aside, exposing the flange and brighter tile in the shape of what had been removed, Kathy was feeling pretty pleased, if a bit breathless. She didn't have to rely on Neil's whim or hire a plumber (likely another male). She could rummage for tools, follow the diagrams, and roll up her sleeves. Then came the matter of dragging the new toilet in, and with a drop of disappointment, she reached the limit of her independence.

She glared at the box in the hallway as if a solution might present itself given enough time, like perhaps the toilet surrendering, unloading, and installing itself. Forget adjustable spray nozzles—*that* would be a feature worth paying for. When speculating didn't yield results, she returned with the putty knife and sawed through the packing tape, hoping she might transport it in parts.

"What the heck are you doing?" Neil asked. He stood in their bedroom doorway, gray sweats slung low on his hips and a stretched Red Sox T-shirt hanging lopsided, his eyes pinched against the light.

Kathy put her finger to her lips. "What does it look like?"

He moved closer and made a big show of whispering back. "Like you're a couple nights away from starting your own fight club."

"I'm installing my mother's luxury crapper."

"Now?"

"It's not like I have a lot of free time." She said this as if she were drawing a weapon and regretted it immediately. Her mouth pulled into contrition, and she corrected her tone. "I was wide awake. I had to do something."

He accepted her explanation, or apology, with a nod. Then he shochorned his arms in the box alongside hers. When they gripped either side of the upper compartment, he counted off and they hoisted the piece out together.

Unbeknownst to her, Neil had purchased a wax ring in preparation. Kathy was glad he'd awakened in time to put it to use. He laid it atop the flange and they maneuvered the toilet into place, pressing down to create the seal. Then they knelt opposite each other to tighten the bolts.

"This feels like Christmas Eve, staying up late to assemble the kids' toys," Neil said.

"Except now the kid likes large-print books and prune juice."

"I'm not changing diapers this time."

"Did you change many back then?" Kathy asked, but she made sure to add a wink to her voice.

"Some," he said, with mock defensiveness. "I worked so much. Probably too much."

As they guided the tank onto the base and tugged the nuts snug, Kathy's wristwatch clicked against the porcelain. It was a gift from Neil on their fifteenth anniversary—the year for watches. Neil relied on those circumscribed gift programs for inspiration. Who invented these lists, Kathy had no idea, but she had them to thank for an iron paperweight, linen napkins, and a tin mug. While those were all stowed away, the watch got regular use. Its leather band, broad face, and bold numerical indices resembled a timepiece meant for a man, but its sleek gold-brushed dial made it lightly but distinctly feminine. She liked the design, but also the reminder that Neil, like every-body, didn't always know what to do. While many years she threw her arms up, saying, "I didn't know what to get so I went with nothing," he had looked for guidance. He tried.

"I don't want to be without you," she said.

"We're having a good time," Neil said, a mild plea. "Let's not talk about Nashville."

"We have to sometime. It may as well be in the bathroom at three in the morning."

Neil didn't look at her. Maybe he couldn't. "Would you come with me?"

She thought about beginning again among country music, biscuits, a reproduction of the Parthenon, and the Cumberland River. She'd recently reinvented herself. What was one more adaptation? "I would if this job will make you happy, but not if you are taking it just to maintain a lifestyle or to prove yourself." She felt new and brave, alone with him in the night. "You're more than a suit. You are a father and an artist and my love. You could work at Home Depot, or sell your carvings, like Noah said. That could be serious, if you let it. Don't move to Nashville because you think that's the only way to be who you are. You can do anything."

Neil's mouth strained as he reattached the water supply line, twisted the valve, and flushed. The bowl filled. They'd done it. *She'd* done it—mostly. Pride must have opened her expression, because Neil regarded her like he had back when they were first dating, when everything she did he perceived as adorable and endearing.

She was flattered by the attention and laughed. "What?"

"Nothing," he said, his mouth lopsided. "You're glowing."

KATHY LEFT FOR work before her mother awoke, before she reacted to the tangible condolence—was it contrition?—her daughter installed decades late.

Winter's white had blanched the scenery. Snow was no longer a novelty, as it had been at the start of the season, fluffy, pure, and revitalizing. By February, it had crystallized and stretched mercilessly over meadows and parks, down playground slides, over rooftops, along sidewalks, on either side of the highway—everywhere. Its blinding blankness, its utter absence of anything else, had become tiresome. Ice spilled a glistening black over driveways, poured a thick frozen carpet down front steps, and suspended menacing spikes from gutters, as if just waiting for enough melt to unhook and drop shattering daggers into the ground.

And yet, despite the relentless cold, despite the snowflake icons lined up on the forecast like foot soldiers, despite the treacherous walkways and the wind that whistled through a set of invisible teeth, a promise hummed below the surface. It rose up through the frozen earth and packed snow to drift through the air as vapor. One had to strain to hear it, and grasp tightly to keep it, but to know there was a climate beyond this bleached state, one with buds and green and dew, was to believe that winter wasn't a suffocation, but a temporary erasure. There would be a second chance, a fresh canvas prepared for a new world.

NO MATTER HOW vigorously the patients and staff members kicked their boots against the brick exterior or scuffed them on the welcome mat, they tracked sidewalk salt and slush through the waiting room. Wet boot prints receded into the carpet fibers, and salt was ground up into the low pile, but the mess didn't seem to bother anybody in the doctor's office—except for one.

Dr. Smith was persnickety in his workplace housekeeping. He kept a duster in his desk drawer for routine maintenance despite the thorough attention of a nightly cleaning crew. He went over his wool coat with a lint brush before draping it on a coat rack hook, curling his lip at a neighboring trench spangled with dog hair. He asked the office manager to rinse the coffeemaker midday so that its lines were clear for his afternoon jolt.

Kathy could see the effort it took Dr. Smith to avert his eyes from the entrance. The sight of it, drenched in melt, visibly pained him. By lunchtime, he couldn't take it anymore. He brought a fat roll of paper towels to the front, laid pieces down in a careful, layered, white carpet, and tapped the toe of his buffed loafers until the water soaked through.

His attention drifted to Angela behind her desk, and he presented her a leading smile, as if to say, *Perhaps you should be doing this?* But no, the coffeemaker was one thing. This chore wasn't in her job description, so she just manufactured obliviousness and returned to keyboard clacking.

Kathy entered the waiting room to call their next patient in time to watch this discreet interaction and tried to conceal her amusement. "Annie?"

The woman's pink paisley shirt was buttoned to her collar. She ducked her head as she passed Kathy, nervous or incredibly shy. She was in her midthirties with a snub nose that looked as if it had been nipped off before it could fully develop. According to her file, she was in for a breast irregularity she'd found during a self-exam. That, Kathy supposed, could explain her skittishness.

Kathy proceeded gently through her vitals and prepared her face during the patient history for reference to cancer in the family, though none was mentioned. Then she left the woman to change.

"This one's a bit anxious," she told Dr. Smith, and he jutted his head meaningfully, as if he knew exactly what to do.

"Good afternoon, I'm Dr. Smith, and I'll be taking a look at you today," he said. Annie wore a silent greeting that came off a little grim. Dr. Smith swung his thumb back at his nurse. "Kathy here will be acting as a chaperone to make sure you and I behave ourselves."

The patient jerked her head so her neck absorbed her chin all but for a roll of skin beneath her jaw. Then she twitched, shaking off the remark. It wasn't the first tasteless joke she'd heard, nor would it be the last. Annie was going to let it go. That was easiest. Kathy recognized the utility of tolerance. She'd applied it herself. She too rolled with the punches, took a beating, if necessary. She wouldn't spearhead a movement or start a revolution. She wouldn't defy the odds or break barriers. She kept her head below the glass ceiling, barely standing up for herself. She wouldn't change the world, not the way her mother would have liked, or how the first Katherine might have, had she been given the chance. But Kathy had just finished telling her husband that he could be different. She could be too, if that's what she wanted. She was in the midst of evolution. She'd returned to work. She'd romped into the wintry ocean. She'd installed a techy toilet. She was reimagining her mother. She didn't have to be the person who stood quietly by while a doctor said inappropriate things to a patient who was naked beneath the paper dress he'd given her, a woman only hoping to hear that the mass in her breast was benign.

Dr. Smith reached for the clipboard in Kathy's hands. She gave it up. He flipped a page, ready to move on, and she was about to let him.

"He makes jokes with every patient. It's how he breaks the ice," Kathy blurted. "Usually it's harmless, but that wasn't. I don't think he meant what he insinuated. He probably just wanted to make you laugh, but it was highly inappropriate, and if you want to report him to the medical board, I will serve as your witness."

The patient parted her lips and blinked rapidly. Maybe it had been unfair to force her into the middle of Kathy's insurgence. Maybe it would have been unfair not to. It was difficult to know what was good and right. But Kathy could try. She had the power to do that.

Dr. Smith was stunned. He'd been double-crossed. The assault had come from inside his own bunker.

"Should we talk in your office?" Kathy suggested, and then she strode out of the room and down the hall, her backside clenched like that of a student on her way to the principal's office, though she was in the lead. She waited until his door clicked shut and then she crossed her arms over her chest to project authority as well as to protect herself. "You probably want to fire me but are worried about a lawsuit. I don't want to work where I'm not wanted, so maybe I should just leave."

The repercussions began to crystallize. Her household would be without any income, and Neil would have to take that job in Tennessee. Unless her little speech had made an impact, and he'd already declined the offer. Would it be too terrible to ask for the job back?

"I'm not going to fire you," Dr. Smith said. His hands rested awkwardly against his lab coat, as if covering a bullet wound.

"You aren't?"

"I . . ." He searched for the right words. "I am not interested in that patient."

He said it as if that mattered, as if, because the patient was comely, the premise was so absurd as to be safe. As though, if anything, the patient should be flattered to be an object of desire, even inside the confines of a joke.

Kathy's fury was revived. "That is beside the point."

"You're right. I . . ." He scrambled for an explanation and then surrendered. His shoulders sank and his arms dropped against his sides. "I just try to make people smile."

Kathy was struck, for a moment, by this unifying trait of the human condition: everybody's heart pumped to the beat of what they could or couldn't do, and who they might or might not be.

She felt the urge to reassure her discouraged boss that what he said, the things he'd always said, hadn't been so bad. She wanted to raise him up, nurture his ego, secure him in his position and she in hers, to put everything and everyone in their right place. Maybe consoling him was the decent thing to do. It certainly was what she would have done last year, even last week. But Kathy had spent a large part of her life taking care of people. She'd run out of space to accommodate even one more person's needs—especially not at the expense of her own. She clasped her hands at her waist and held on to herself for dear life.

Dr. Smith fidgeted inside the barbed silence. Finally, he cleared his throat. "I think it best you consult with the patient and see what she wants to do from here."

"Understood." The aisle between his desk and the door was so narrow he had to press against the wall to make room for her to pass. She opened the door slowly so as not to squish him, and then returned to the hall, relieved to have this confrontation over with, and with so little resulting damage, at least for now. But there was one more thing. Well, there were hundreds of things, but she could at least address one more while he was paying attention. She turned and added, "By the way, your employees are educated, licensed, and middle-aged, for goodness' sake. You can't go around referring to us as 'your girls.'"

Chapter 26

March 1944

INSIDE THE LATRINE, THE SOON-TO-BE GRADUATES FLATtened flyaway hairs, sharpened eyebrow pencils, and swapped lipstick shades. They wore their official Santiago Blues—the first uniforms that properly fit since they'd been made specifically for them and, unlike their General's Whites, these regimentals had been paid for by their government. With their blazers tailored at the waist and their knee-length skirts, they were pilots in the shape of women. The following day, they'd be dispatched to cockpits around the country, as civilian flyers with the promise to be folded into the military.

Peggy twirled before the mirror. In her periphery, she caught Georgia's bed through the doorway, the sheets pulled tighter than they ever were during her friend's time in them, that rose still lying on the pillow, as stiff as a corpse. Her fingers trembled as she tightened the knot of her necktie.

You look as fine as frog's hair, she could hear Georgia say.

It should have been you here, Peggy thought.

Her lips were painted cherry red and a clean black line swept across her eyelids. The WASP letters were pinned to her lapel alongside the prop and wings, a military insignia given to all aviation units. Her shoulders were stamped with the army air forces patches and, during the ceremony, General Hap Arnold or Jackie Cochran would secure the WASP wings over her heart. For now, that space was empty. She looked like a woman to take seriously—one who could serve and leave her mark on the world. Her fingers traced the thick stitching of the uniform. A real army gal.

She followed Connie and Pamela into their bay. Before she went out the front door, she brushed her hand along the foot of Georgia's bed.

FORTY-EIGHT GRADUATES, WHITTLED from a class of 102, paraded in as the band performed. They filed into chairs before WASP trainees, all facing a stage occupied by some of the most important people in military aviation, as well as their commanding officers, including Major Mayfield—not that he mattered.

The previous month, Peggy had flown the AT-6 on a five-hundred-mile tandem cross-country to Austin and back, with Mayfield in the bucket seat behind her. Compared to the bomber, this plane was smooth, a bird winning over the wind.

On the way out, the clouds had been a snowy plain below them, but on their return, the clouds had concentrated into a black column. They couldn't fly through the storm, so when a field opened, Mayfield directed her to land. She touched the wheels down like setting a teacup into its saucer, and the sky unleashed what it had been holding inside.

Rain hammered the glass-encased cockpit. The noise was unbearable. Mayfield tapped her shoulder, pointed to a tool shed across the field, and shouted, "We'll go deaf in here."

They unlatched the ceiling and were besieged by a thousand cold pinpricks. They hopped down to the grass and raced toward the shed, but the door was padlocked. A crack of lightning ripped overhead.

Peggy was panting from the sprint, and her drenched flight suit clung to her ribs and hips. They burrowed beneath the shed's roof. Rivulets ran down Mayfield's temples and dripped from his jaw. Peggy wondered what he'd taste like mingled with rain. If there was ever going to be a moment, this was it.

He stepped farther away. "This storm won't last long," he said. They stood apart, as stiff and cold as the wet cabin logs.

Now, at graduation, Peggy knew Mayfield's coldness was a blessing. She'd soon be towing targets, conducting strafing missions, or ferrying or testing planes. It would be easier to contribute without having to consider him. Then, after the war was over, she'd be free to pursue the many opportunities that awaited her.

The band belted its final note, and Jackie Cochran approached the podium. "Greetings, officers and WASP trainees. To the graduating class of 44-2, congratulations, and thank you for your service to your country. You have suffered great personal sacrifice to be here today. You've uprooted yourselves, some leaving children to be cared for by friends or family. There was, too, the loss of your classmate, Katherine Walden. I never for a day forget the women who courageously accepted the potential risks and faced them in their final flights. Their bravery was fueled not by the promise of glory that combat provides, but by a fervent belief in the importance of their cause.

"In flight, speed is determined by thrust versus drag. It is the same with people. You've overpowered the drag of adversity to speed along the path of progress. You are making way for future generations of women, not just in aviation, but in all disciplines previously deemed the pursuits of men alone. You've proven that planes can't discern between genders. I admire you, I thank you, and I beseech you to continue pitching forward against the opposing forces you are bound to encounter."

Peggy's gaze fell to a patch of green in a desert of parched earth, life thriving alongside that which had withered, and she thought of Georgia. She always thought of Georgia.

General Hap Arnold, his white hair matted between his ears and his cap, shook Cochran's hand and took his place, stalklike, behind the podium. "As graduating members of the Women Airforce Service Pilots, you will go on to serve a variety of invaluable charges in the army air forces organization. Domestic flight duties are now almost entirely conducted by women, allowing us to deploy as many fighters overseas as possible. The army air forces are proud of you and indebted to you. We welcome you as service pilots in our organization, and it won't be long before we pass bill H.R. 4219 and can salute you as commissioned officers of the United States military." At this, the WASP sprang up and cheered wildly. General Arnold smirked despite himself and waved for them to settle down. "When I call your name, report to the stage to receive your diploma and wings."

Without the perpetual revving of airplane engines, Peggy heard birdsong, as well as the American flag beating on its pole as if it were a winged creature. The temperature was mild, but the liquid gold sun poured onto the shoulders of the women, and the light turned the dust to copper.

Peggy felt as if she were flying when she climbed the stage steps. She shook Jackie Cochran's hand and accepted her diploma. She was a working pilot. While General Arnold fastened her pin, Peggy took in the crowd behind him, hundreds of uniformed women on their feet.

Once every graduate was decorated with WASP hardware, General Arnold asked the assembly to rise and sing the national anthem. The brass blasted each note, but the altos and sopranos floated above their bold foundation, each telling her own story, with pasts Peggy knew and didn't, a future none of them could: the thirty-year-old widow; the mother separated from her baby so long he wouldn't recognize her when she came home; the sister whose brother was missing in action; the fiancée whose future husband was now disabled. The voices of women in war were strung on all sides, holding Peggy up.

Present though absent were those who had been dismissed, who chose to leave, and who had been taken. The rocket's red glare was Georgia's plane on fire, the terrible bursting in air that would be imprinted on Peggy forever. The anthem itself was charged with new meaning. Their flag was still there. This was the land of the free, and the women who were brave.

THE PROCESSION DROPPED the new graduates before their barracks. They were fizzy with what was to come, chatting about hoped-for assignments and who planned to remain with the army air forces after the war. But below their exhilaration, an invisible weave tightened around them. This community had learned, loved, and lost together. They'd been challenged and had taken risks. They'd inspired, sacrificed, and comforted. They were pioneers, bound by a shared experience that was expiring. This was the last time they'd be with one another in this way—in fact, they'd likely never be part of anything quite like it again.

Peggy's eyes grew misty thinking of it. Just as the bitter was overtaking the sweet, an army-green beacon sifted through the sea of blue.

"Cadet," Mayfield began, and then corrected himself. "Lewis, may I speak to you privately?"

Beside her, Connie waggled her eyebrows, but she didn't know about Mayfield's turned cheek on the front porch in Savannah, or how he'd stepped away from her in the rainstorm. Their commanding officer had been presented opportunities for romance, and he'd unequivocally squashed them, so that was not what this was about. Afraid she was in trouble, Peggy dug her toes into the soles of her shoes. Had they only just remembered to check in on her weight again? Was it possible they could rescind her diploma because she'd never belonged here in the first place?

The interior of the administrative building was dark, but light streamed through the windowpanes in solid, geometric pieces. Their footsteps accented the quiet as they headed down the hall to a door stamped with Mayfield's name.

His office was devoid of personal features, furnished only with a plain desk, a lamp with a green glass shade, three neat stacks of papers, and a black rotary-dial telephone. A framed photograph of a World War I Breguet 14 biplane bomber plane hung on the wall beside a map of the Pacific theater.

"You've graduated," Mayfield said. His eyes were walnut, but the midnight at their center held her reflection. She saw the way she looked at him. She felt their breath meet at the middle.

Was his a statement of the obvious, or a precursor to a heartbreaking *but*? Peggy felt as if she were finding her way without navigation lights. "I have."

His hand rose from his side cautiously, unsure of itself. She watched with similar uncertainty as it traveled the space between them, holding very still while his fingers grazed her cheek. She might have rested against his touch, but for the Walden porch, the rainstorm, the countless times they were in a cockpit alone. He didn't want her. If she let herself believe anything else only to be denied again, the next blow could break her.

Peggy stepped back. "Sir?"

Mayfield retracted his arm and carried his attention over her head, as if he'd lost something and was searching for it on the horizon. "I thought we shared an understanding."

She zeroed in on Mayfield's lapel pin, wishing to lose herself in the dark lines beneath each feather. "When it comes to you, major, there isn't much I understand at all."

"Then let me be clear." He wouldn't look at her, and his voice was thicker than it ever had been coming through her gosports. "Since you landed before me, shaking with so much rage and readiness that you jumped from a moving plane, Peggy, I've loved you since then."

She remembered the reckoning after that turbulent flight

when she'd swallowed her fury as Georgia had advised. Yet Mayfield had caught the flash of Peggy behind the artifice. He'd loved what was purely hers.

Peggy took his face in hands that were calloused from computation, dry air, and flight, and guided him as if he were an aircraft. He allowed her to show him the way. At first their kiss was hard, fueled by a hunger that had been eating her insides, but it quickly tapered into tenderness. It lasted only a few seconds but held an entire narrative of beauty, suffering, and relief. The end was even sweeter than the beginning.

"I do too," she said, and shook her head. "Love you, I mean." And of course she did. He didn't let her settle. He kept her safe. He provoked her. Mayfield and airplanes were the rare subjects that never dulled. She'd loved him all along.

He cupped the back of her head and pulled her against him. Their bodies met, and her nerve endings were hyper-aware, radiating pleasure. He pressed against her enough that she gripped the desk edge behind her for support. Then she let go, and Mayfield laid her down, his chest against her chest, his hips against her hips, his mouth tasting her mouth, and then her jaw, neck, and ear.

He retraced his steps, kissing more unhurriedly. He propped himself on an elbow, tucked her hair behind her ear, and studied her eyes, as if he'd be asked to re-create them later and was memorizing while he had the chance. Peggy looked away and laughed, at the attention and herself and all those months of doubt and longing, only to end up right here. She'd graduated from the program. She'd get a career in flight. And now, Mayfield. If only she had Georgia, then she'd have everything.

"I have a graduation present for you." He shifted beside her and pulled an envelope from his coat pocket. "Your assignment." She snatched the envelope, topped with the army air forces insignia, and tore it open. He said, "I put in a request for you to be assigned to Fort Worth, only three hours away. I hope you don't mind."

"It took seven months to get close to you. I'd hate to go far now."

"I also took the liberty of procuring this," Mayfield said, and retrieved a bottle of sparkling wine from his desk drawer.

They propped themselves against the front of his desk and passed the bottle between them, their lips bracing the thick glass, the sweet bubbles prickling their tongues like the rain in that storm. They sipped and talked and kissed, sometimes gentle or teasing, sometimes greedy and aching, while the sun sank and the sky blushed until what was once blue turned to black.

Flecks of light emerged against the backdrop as Peggy traced Mayfield's chin, his neck. She touched his earlobe, the rounding of his chest, the indents of his rib cage. He held her hand and lifted it to his mouth, kissing her wrist first and then each finger one by one. It was like cranking a cowl.

She turned her back on the sky and shifted on top of Mayfield so she saw only him. Her lips orbited his mouth, jaw, and neck. She was in control. Then he overturned her, taking the power back, just for now, and unbuttoned her shirt, removing the uniform he'd worked so hard, resisted so much, so that she could earn.

The thought flitted across her mind that she should stop him, put on the coy airs of a lady, show that she was a prize worth his wait. But if Peggy had learned anything during her time at Avenger Field, it was that nobody knew how much time they had left, what their next flight might bring. All they knew was now.

There was a shooting puncture as she allowed Mayfield, once again, to bring her where she'd never before been. She gasped at the shock of it. Peggy thought of the millions of women who had come before and those who would follow as she bore through until the pain yielded. There was blood and birthright, but there was also Mayfield above her, gripped by desire yet restrained. She longed to please him. She was Atlas bracing the heavens, and her task had never been so easy.

Peggy fell asleep in disarray, her jacket tossed across the room, her pants unclasped. But her head was resting on Mayfield's chest, and his arm draped around her shoulder, everything where it was meant to be.

She woke to the pink luster of morning and squeezed her eyelids closed, begging the universe for more sleep, more time, just a minute more, before she had to pack up, board a bus, and leave him behind.

* * *

In Fort Worth, Peggy was the only woman on base. She slept in the men's quarters. She ate alone at a table reserved just for her. The only other women she saw were the defense workers at the factory across the street. When they stepped into the sunlight for their lunch break, she reached high in greeting.

She missed her hive, and the fellowship of women united

by passion and purpose. She missed the laughter, the com-
miseration, going to sleep among them, and the bustling
waking up of their morning routines. She missed powder,
headscarves, cinched waists, and soft curls. She missed celebrating their victories and knowing her own had been witnessed.

Her only companionship was in letters. Connie's arrived
on a weekly basis, and Peggy dwelled in the curved shape
of her words, like so many women lounging atop cots in the
golden light of evening, smoking, bowed with laughter. She
read them multiple times through to prolong their pleasure.
Then her pen met paper, and she reached beyond her bedroom walls, clear across the country, to share loneliness with
her friend, brag about new adventures, and remember.

Mayfield's letters delivered daily intimacy. Peggy took her
time with them, carefully undoing his seals, allowing gravity
to drop them open. She brought each letter to her nose and
searched for his trace scent. Then she kept it close, imagining she was inhaling the words directly from his mouth.
She would have much preferred to inhabit the heat of his
skin, for her lips to collapse beneath his, for their fingers to
intertwine, and to bear the weight of his body, but there
was value to this entry into his mind. She glimpsed what he
otherwise kept buttoned, including learning some of what
he'd endured in the Pacific under the command of Lieutenant Colonel Jimmy Doolittle before being reassigned to
Avenger Field. He told her about his childhood, and the kind
of life he wanted for himself—for them. After seven months
of furtively loving each other, they'd had one night to test
the longing of their hearts, finding it more charged and acute

than their daydreams, only to be severed and catapulted apart. Given the chance, Peggy would shrink the distance between them, but she had to admit there was sensuality in this forced patience, this conscious discovery, as they took turns swimming through the other's introspections, one posted exposure at a time.

MOST OF THE men on base did what they could to welcome Peggy. They tipped their hats, listened respectfully to her reports, and stood when she passed on her way to her private dinner table. Bob, the tower radio operator, was particularly congenial. When she called in, "Radio, radio, how do you read me?" his voice crackled back through the speaker, "As sweet as honey, Lewis."

Others weren't so hospitable.

Her first morning on duty, Peggy asked Donald, the base mechanic, if the plane was ready for testing. He didn't bother looking up from his work when he said, "It's ready, all right. I'm just waiting for the pilot."

"Wait no further. I'm the pilot," Peggy said brightly, though she suspected he already knew this.

He assessed her up and down, repulsed. As she endured the physical slick of his slow, measuring gaze, she manufactured contentment, because she had work to do and needed his cooperation to do it.

Peggy would test the Consolidated B-24 Liberator bombers repaired at the factory before they were returned to combat. After the mechanic approved them on the ground, Peggy took them up and put them through all the motions so they wouldn't fail the men overseas. Every takeoff required faith that the repairs had been comprehensive, or that she'd be adept enough to escape an unaddressed defect. Georgia was at the forefront of her mind as she sped down the runway and urged a wounded bird into the sky. Her heart lived pressed up against her breastbone.

Three weeks into her assignment, Peggy was fifty feet off the ground when both of her right engines coughed. She'd never heard such a dry wheeze. She gripped the yoke and searched her dashboard, but before she could locate an issue, anything she could fix, the engines hissed and died, and her plane drooped. She fought to straighten it, but that was like catching Jack's giant as it tumbled down the beanstalk. The wheels crashed against the pavement and Peggy's head snapped forward.

But she was alive. She proved that fact by taking inventory of her breath, her beating heart, the jagged edge of a thumbnail. Still, she'd tasted what Georgia had before the world ended.

Peggy made her way to the hangar on shaky legs. Donald balanced on a ladder against another bomber.

"That bomber gave out from under me," she said.

His eyes were cartoonish in size and watery, and he had the floppy mouth of a bass. "I'll look at it in a minute."

He should have run to meet her, tripping over himself to ensure she was all right. If she'd been hurt, it would have been because he'd approved a faulty plane. He should be horrified. But he wasn't. Because he'd expected it. He *knew* the plane was going to die. He'd been the one to kill it.

Peggy palmed her hips to hide how she trembled. "You'll take a look right now."

He wiped his nose with the back of a wrench-wielding hand. "I don't take orders from you, dolly." But then he descended, tossed the wrench on his worktable, and picked up a screwdriver. "This is why women shouldn't fly. Too emotional."

Donald hauled the ladder under his arm and set it down before the plane. At the top, he began to unscrew the engine door, but then stopped and turned to Peggy below. "Do you mind?"

"I most certainly do," Peggy said.

He repositioned his body but couldn't block her view, so when he removed the door, she saw the oily rag caught in the mechanism.

"Gee, I must have forgotten that in there," he said.

"Donald." Peggy's chest was tightening. She strained for oxygen. "You had no way of knowing how far I would have climbed before the engines gave out."

"It's not like I did it on purpose."

"And the second engine? I suppose you forgot a rag in there too?"

"You wouldn't have gotten past sixty feet."

So much could go wrong without a pilot being sabotaged. It was his job and moral obligation to protect her, but because she was a woman, she would have to earn what she should have automatically been given if she wanted to survive.

The next time Donald declared a plane fit for flight, Peggy waved him along. "You're coming with me. That way I'll know there's no funny business."

"What did I say about not taking orders from you?"

Many mechanics were former pilots who'd been injured in

combat or washed out of their training. Peggy was banking on the perpetual yearning of flyers to get back into the sky. "When was the last time you went on a ride?"

"You expect me to climb into a plane flown by a dame?" Donald said.

If the U.S Army Air Forces could admit she was an expert flyer, who was he to know better? But it was her duty to get the work done, and that would be impossible with an ogre in her way, so she'd have to win him over, for the sake of the cause and for her safety.

"Why don't *you* fly it, then?" she said.

Donald's entire body seemed to lighten, as if already drawn toward the sky. But he quickly hid his eagerness by gathering his fat lips together. "Swell. Now I'm doing both our jobs."

If Donald had washed out of his program, there might have been a reason, and Peggy could have been better off flying with rags in her engines. But she'd have access to her own controls, and if Donald failed or froze, that lesson would have its own merits.

Donald thrashed into the bomber and she followed easily behind. "The checklist is there," she said, pointing to the gap between his seat and the plane wall.

"Nerves are normal," he said, studying the sheets.

"No matter how many times I fly, I'm always a little nervous."

He gripped the half wheel, and then his hands fell into his lap. "Maybe you ought to pilot first, until I'm reacquainted."

"One ride and it'll all come back to you. I'm sure of it."

Major aerobatics were reserved for the escort fighter planes, but there were certain maneuvers the hulking bomber could manage. Peggy performed medium, climbing, and descending turns. All the while, Donald beamed at the view below. She recognized that delight, the pining satisfied only at a certain elevation. What torture it would be to have your days devoted to planes without ever reaping the rewards, to be near flight without getting to feel it for yourself. Worse, to watch another person do the job you wanted, while your own wings were clipped. To be grounded that way would be like watching the love of your life go on to marry another.

"And you're just a slip of a thing," Donald whispered.

Peggy could get used to that feeling of pride, like her vital organs were tingling. "You're welcome to join me any time you'd like."

"I have my own job to do." He slumped in his seat. "This plane is in good condition, like I said. Now you're wasting the army air forces' time. This isn't your playground, dolly. It'd serve you well to remember that."

Chapter 27

February 2010

IT BECAME KATHY'S NIGHTLY RITUAL TO CHECK HER mother's vitals. The days were stretching longer now, so when she sat on the edge of Peggy's bed, the sun burned in the bottom corner of the window, and her mother glowed almost ethereal in its fiery light.

Peggy's large hand looked wind-whipped, a desert in aerial view. Kathy cradled the glass of Peggy's wrist and palpated her artery through the bundle of veins. Kathy counted the beats inside a minute and penciled the results into the notebook she reserved for her numbers, though they didn't tell her much. She couldn't sense if the rise of the pulse was slow or the peak plateaued. This was just an entry, a place for her to begin.

Now Kathy shifted farther up the bed. She dipped the tips of her stethoscope into her ears and slipped the bell through the open collar of Peggy's blouse. Her mother shuddered at the cold, and Kathy waited for her to adjust before tuning in.

There was the high-pitched murmur of the telltale heart, the song that wasn't quite right. The organ was just inside the cage of Peggy's breast, inches away, calcified and struggling through an abnormal rhythm. Kathy wanted to break through blood and bone and clear it herself, but there was nothing she could do but stand by and listen.

Peggy watched her daughter work, but differently than how she'd once watched Kathy practice piano or go through her multiplication tables. There wasn't any hint of impatience or anticipation. It was more reminiscent of the way she'd observed Kathy brush her dolls' hair or sort pieces before beginning a puzzle. She was beholding her daughter without agenda in a type of meditation.

Kathy worked slowly to monitor Peggy's breathing—was it more labored than the day before?—but also to linger in a realm where nearness didn't embarrass them. She slid the blood pressure cuff over Peggy's arm, whose skin felt like dough dried by too much flour, and pumped the bulb until it was fully inflated. 110/70—better than the previous night. Not at risk of syncope. Maybe the small measures she insisted her mother take were having at least some effect. She hoped so. They'd accumulated many years in which Peggy had been a mystery. Kathy wanted to know her mother longer inside her new truth. She wanted to believe there was time for that.

Kathy peeled Peggy's compression socks over skin that had slackened around the kneecaps and flaked and scaled down the shin. She considered applying lotion, but that would be crossing a line, so she just followed the route of tentacle veins, checking for swelling and lacerations. Skin at that age was delicate and prone to tear, and infection could be deadly for someone with Peggy's defect. Kathy replaced the compression socks with fuzzy purple ones, a gift from Fiona, that made her mother's old feet look achingly dear.

Peggy accepted the next ritual—a bowl of pretzels and a glass of water. She munched and nursed while Kathy relocated to the beanbag chair, which was at a comfortable distance when she was not acting in a medical capacity. There, she compared that day's stats against the preceding day's.

"How are we looking, doc?" Peggy asked.

A previous version of Kathy might have interpreted this quippy promotion as a minimization of her actual job, but not now. "You'll make it another month."

"Is that supposed to be reassuring?"

"It is to me." Kathy laid her notebook on her lap and folded her hands atop it. "Because I, for one, am going to your medal ceremony."

Peggy was taken aback but recovered quickly. "Send me a postcard."

"We could make a family trip out of it. We'll get the boys—" Kathy stopped. If it wasn't right for Dr. Smith, it wasn't right for her. "Your sons to meet us with their families, and all spend a few days in D.C. together."

"If it's a family vacation you want, I'd prefer to sip piña coladas under a palm tree."

"Don't you want some closure?"

Peggy scoffed, and her attention traveled out the window, where the sun was a drop of apricot preserve on the horizon. "I'm not sure my poor old heart could handle it. They took enough from me. They don't get my dying breath too."

"If you say so," Kathy said, and though it had the smack of sarcasm, she meant it. Kathy didn't know what it was like to do what no other women had done before, train and sacrifice, beg your friend to take your seat only to watch that seat go to ash, cling to the hollow promises of your country in the hopes that your loss would be vindicated, and then have that solace be wrenched away too. Kathy could only speak from her own experience, which was the desire to see her mother honored in a way Kathy herself hadn't known to honor her.

Kathy wiggled off the beanbag and resisted the urge to squeeze the plush chenille that encased her mother's foot. Before Kathy left, she extracted a floss pick from her pocket and passed it over as a parting gift.

"Here," Kathy said. "Oral hygiene is good for that poor old heart."

THE ATMOSPHERE AT work had turned steely, with Dr. Smith moving around Kathy in the straight lines of a robot vacuum, bumping against furniture, inexpressive. Kathy almost missed his perpetual smirk and eagerness to humor, but only so much as it had filled the space between them, which now gaped emptily. At least she still had a job, and so did he, since their patient wasn't interested in pressing charges. Annie hadn't understood why this nurse had made such a big deal of a single comment and was more peeved her exam had been derailed, since Kathy had had to locate another doctor, which added an extra fifteen minutes to Annie's wait, and she'd hoped to complete an errand before her lunch hour ended. She hadn't asked to be a pawn in Kathy's insurrection.

According to Angela, this was the first Valentine's Day in all her years that Dr. Smith didn't distribute heart-shaped boxes of chocolate. She looked over her glasses at Kathy when she said this, assigning onus.

Kathy didn't need her boss's chocolate, and not just because her hours at work followed by hours with her mother left little time for once habitual walks, which meant her pants had grown tighter these months, but because Neil had carved a tree from a block of cedar, with boughs that stretched and bent into the shape of a heart, its trunk etched with their initials. It may have been the first gift whose inspiration was born by him alone.

Kathy had reciprocated with a take-out bag of the thickest, greasiest hamburgers and onion rings Lexington had to offer, which meant Neil didn't have to cook. Kathy remembered the gift of such a relief.

After dinner, Neil pushed himself from the table, his fingers glossy, a dab of ketchup caught in the corner of his mouth. "That was good, but you know what a lot of wives give their husbands for Valentine's Day?"

"Custom golf clubs?"

Neil grazed his thumb along her knuckles. He watched their fingers as he spoke. "It's been over a month."

It always embarrassed Kathy to speak openly about their sex life. She wanted to pull her hand into her lap but made the effort to leave it beneath his. "It's not easy with my mother in the house."

"She's asleep."

"She could wake up."

"We could do like we did with the kids and send her out for ice cream."

"Think she could take Fiona's old bike?"

Neil sat back with control she couldn't quite read. The tick of the oversized farmhouse wall clock was the only sound between them.

"How's this for an aphrodisiac?" he asked, finally. "I turned down that job in Nashville."

"You did?" A spark of relief shot from her feet, sending her upright. "What made you change your mind?"

His smile was a horizon, so pleased was he by her pleasure. "You were right. I should pursue my passion."

"Woodworking?"

"No, you."

The remark picked Kathy up and sent her flitting down the channel of their marriage: strolls around the Lexington Green, their fingers loosely laced; salty snacks and Sunday football; Neil's arms folding their family together under fireworks; their bodies dropping onto the couch after long days, his work shirt rumpled, her hair in need of washing, exhausted but fulfilled, all in all; Neil rubbing her feet. Disagreements and tedium were part of the landscape too, but their presence had been lightened by retrospect, and by the overwhelming fondness of that moment.

"Those might be the most romantic words you've ever uttered," Kathy said, and then, to dilute the potency, emphasized, "Admitting I was right, I mean."

"Of course."

"What will you do now?" she asked.

"Maybe I'll see about this 'global online marketplace' for woodworkers," he said, casting his voice to Noah's conceit as he moved across the unfamiliar buzzwords. Kathy laughed. It felt good to share an interpretation of the world, to be in on the same joke, even if it was at their son's expense. Neil continued slowly, testing the temperature of the next topic. "And maybe we should start looking for smaller places?"

She lifted his hand and carried his rough knuckles to her lips. "When it comes to real estate, never say 'smaller.' It's 'cozier.'"

Neil scraped his chair toward Kathy. "Speaking of cozier . . ."

But before he could land his kiss, their landline trilled. The phone was posted at the kitchen desk, where Kathy used to sit and pay bills before they became automated, and before her work was what paid the bills.

She grazed her lips against her husband's. "Hold that thought."

The caller ID read Alfred Ford, though Kathy knew it was his wife, Constance, who was calling, since Alfred had been dead for three years and, even when he was alive, he'd never been the one to phone. Constance, however, called Peggy weekly. The Fords had been family friends of the Mayfields since time immemorial. Constance lived in Florida now, and in fact had never once resided in the same state as Peggy, but they'd visited each other every summer or met for vacations at various national parks around the country and, once, Virginia Beach. Constance was Peggy's childhood friend, her maid of honor, and godmother to each of her children. She was the only woman Peggy took seriously despite being demure, a quality Peggy normally rebuffed. Perhaps their friendship endured because their energies balanced each other's. Constance was the grounded to Peggy's flighty, the sweet to her spice, and the traditional to her resistant.

It didn't feel right to desert Neil's gesture toward intimacy, but Constance didn't call Kathy's house line enough for this to be standard procedure. It would be reckless to screen what could be an emergency in favor of a marital romp.

Constance's voice had the softness of worn suede. "I'm sorry for calling when you are probably celebrating V-Day with your honey. I just wanted to say hello to my funny Valentine, but her cell went straight to voice mail. I'm guessing she forgot to charge it again."

"I think she's napping, though her phone could be dead too. Should I wake her?"

"Heavens no. You know what they say. Never wake a sleeping biddy."

Kathy scanned her memory for the last time she'd talked to Constance. Could it have been September, after Fiona returned to school and Constance checked to see how Kathy was bearing the quiet? No, it was months later, because Kathy had delivered the news of Peggy's first fall. Then Constance left a message after Peggy moved in, asking if the "old bird" was making Kathy crazy, but with her job and the holidays, Kathy had plain forgotten to call back. She kicked herself for this now, because with everything she'd uncovered about her mother, how could she have not considered hashing it all out with Constance? She was another untapped resource.

"I'm glad you called, actually. I've been meaning to ask you about some things. I was wondering, well, I was wondering if you know. If you've *known*, all this time."

"Have I known what, exactly?" There was an upward lilt to her tone, and a leading quality to her pacing, like she'd been waiting for Kathy to ask and just needed to hear the magic words.

"That my mother was a Women Airforce Service Pilot."

"Yes, dear. I've known."

Kathy exhaled her relief. "You have?"

"Of course," Constance said. "I was right there with her."

"You were *what*?" Kathy's world tilted again. "I didn't even know you knew how to fly."

"I guess you never asked."

Kathy felt as if every neuron were burning bright in her brain, working to process this new revelation. She whirled to Neil, agape, shaking her head in disbelief. He searched her face for answers. She pointed to the phone receiver and mouthed, *Constance*, and then extended her arm and mimicked a plane. His forehead tightened, deciphering, and then his expression opened. He mouthed back, *No way*. Kathy was glad to have him to share in her awe.

"And the ceremony?" Kathy asked Constance, her eagerness mounting. "Are you going?"

"You're darn tootin'."

"You aren't bitter or—" Kathy thought about Georgia, her mother's departed friend, who was perhaps Constance's friend too. She was reluctant to bring up that loss, so she finished, "Or anything?"

"Our country needed us and we showed up. Most of us understood it wouldn't be forever."

"Do your kids know?"

"Oh yes. I told them first chance I got. I wanted them to know their frumpy old mother had been daring once. I suppose your mother let you know that in her own way."

"You could say that."

"I had to prep Caroline and Timmy every time we saw you so they didn't blow the lid off the whole charade. It wasn't easy, especially after they read Peggy's letters from her assignment in Fort Worth. They wanted so badly to interview her for school projects."

At that reference, the bulbs in Kathy's brain popped and settled into a sort of understanding. "I have to go, Constance. I'll tell my mother to call you back."

Kathy signaled a nonexplanation in Neil's direction, abandoned him in the kitchen with their dinner detritus and sexual frustration, and bounded up the stairs as nimbly as her fifty-year-old knees would allow. She checked her mother's room to confirm she was still asleep, and then continued into her own bedroom, where she removed the WASP box from beneath her bed and combed through for the letter.

May 20, 1944

Dear Peggy,

My helmet is made by David Clark. Can you believe it? The same company that produces girdles and brassieres has made its way into aviation equipment. I suppose it makes sense. Bras and planes—it's all defying gravity.

You'll never believe the escapade I got myself into this week. I'm almost too embarrassed to share, but I think you'll get a kick out of it. For the sake of your entertainment, here goes my pride:

I was ferrying a Boeing Peashooter from Seattle to Oroville, California. Have you flown one before? It's a darling monoplane with an adorable bulbous propeller nose.

About three hundred miles into the trip, my instruments failed and I lost radio contact. I flicked every switch I had, but it was no use. I had to navigate by map alone, and you know what a pain that is in an open cockpit.

As if flying without radio wasn't enough, I hit a patch of air pockets that tossed my fighter around like it wasn't three thousand pounds. I was sure I was done for.

I prayed, "Dear Lord, I know your attention is demanded in all corners of the globe. I know you have more important people to attend to than a chubby young lady in a Peashooter. But if you could spare a moment to guide me to safety, I'd be most appreciative. If I live through this day, I'll devote the rest of my life to spreading your word. I truly will. That's all for now, Lord. Thank you and amen."

Just then, a clearing opened, like God was handing me a field. I took the plane down. But the field wasn't empty. In an instant, people who looked Japanese surrounded me. I thought, "I made it clear across the Pacific Ocean. I'm one woman facing the enemy."

Then someone spoke in crystal-clear English, "Ma'am, are you all right?"

It was an internment camp. And oh, those poor people. They were so kind to me, despite their circumstances, despite that I worked for a country that had stripped them of their dignity and freedom and locked them out of sight. They made sure I was all right and had all the information I needed to continue on my way.

The camp was in Tulelake, California. From there it was a straight shot south to Oroville. I made it safely, as

you can tell from the writing of this letter. If I'm to keep
my promise, now I'll have to spend my days spreading the
good word!

Your friend,
Connie

P.S. Did you read Jackie Cochran's recent editorial? Slews
of people are writing letters to the Capitol in our support,
but I still suspect our commission may be on the line. I
know you have your heart set on a military career, but
maybe you should prepare yourself for things to go south.
If we're discharged, maybe they'll at least grant us mili-
tary status for a day so at least we can be recognized as
veterans. It wouldn't be all you dreamed, but it'd still be
something special!

Kathy had read this letter back in November, and the voice
had felt familiar and dear in its warmth, but she'd never put
together that the author was their cheery Constance, despite
the signoff. How had she missed that? Perhaps it was easier
to see things as she'd always understood them than to reset
and perceive them as they were—as they'd been all along.

A floorboard creaked in the hallway, so Kathy slipped the
letter into its film folder and shoved the box under the bed,
and just in time, too, because Peggy shuffled into her bedroom. She wore a cornflower-blue housecoat and her coarse
hair was tied into a bun, but frayed where it had been crushed
against her pillow. It was late in the day to have taken a nap.
Kathy worried fatigue was a symptom of her heart failure.

Exhaustion, of course, could indicate a different sort of heart issue altogether, as evidenced by Neil's malaise the previous year. Maybe, after disclosing the truth about Georgia, her mother was grieving anew. None of this explained what she was doing scuffling through Kathy and Neil's bedroom without acknowledging her daughter's presence.

"Hi, Mom."

"Katherine." Peggy revolved toward her stiffly, her hands up as if feeling for something in the dark. Her features roused and she clutched her chest. "What on earth? You scared me half to death."

"I'm sorry," Kathy said, though her crime began and ended at sitting atop her own bed.

"It's all right. You were just so surreptitious." Peggy made no effort to justify why she was there, an island in Neil and Kathy's one remaining private place. She didn't appear embarrassed or driven by purpose. She was just idle, paused. Was it possible she didn't realize where she was, and that she'd breached an unspoken rule?

"Are you all right?" Kathy asked.

"Perfectly. Why?" Frail but upright, her head held high and topped by that mess of sterling, Peggy resembled a heron taking in her surroundings.

"Were you looking for help with something?"

"No."

"It's just that—"

Peggy's posture collapsed as she discarded whatever she'd been trying to don. "Forget it. I can't hold my bladder at my age so I don't have time for games. I need to use your bathroom."

"What's wrong with *your* bathroom?"

"The new toilet." Peggy shook her head, as if she'd done all she could to avoid this admission, but now had no choice. "It's too damn hot."

Kathy kept herself from laughing outright, but there wasn't much she could do about the tickle at her mouth. "I'm sure you can adjust the temperature."

"I tried, but they make the words so small. I only made it hotter."

"Go on," Kathy said, laughing freely now. "Relieve yourself on my cold commode."

By the time the toilet in the master bathroom flushed and the faucet ran and shut, Kathy still hadn't decided if she was going to bring up what she'd learned about Constance or let this new disclosure, yet another in their recent whirl, rest. They'd traveled back in time through the turbulence of resentment, grief, and shame. How much more unsettled dust could they blink from their eyes, clean from their nostrils, or hold in their mouths before it turned to mud they had to spit or swallow? It must cost Peggy something each time she was transported, draining something vital, deducting life force of which she had little to spare. Her heart was already struggling to do the bare minimum. Maybe what Peggy had confronted was enough, and any more would just be a way for Kathy to rebuke her mother for keeping it to herself all this time.

But then there was the ceremony, a celebration and an honoring Kathy desperately wanted for her mother. Constance would be in attendance, and Kathy thought she could use this fact as a dangled carrot—one last chance for Peggy to be and do with her friend, for old times' sake.

Kathy escorted her mother across the hall to her bathroom. The remote control for the electric panel was mounted to the wall above the toilet paper holder. Kathy unsheathed it. There were buttons on either face and along three sides—one could get lost in all the features—and indeed, marked by letters so small as to be indecipherable.

"What did I tell you? This contraption is idiotic," Peggy said.

Peggy was expunging history once again, this time acting as if she hadn't been the one to advocate for this gadget. Kathy resented her attempt to warp their realities so much that her previous restraint began to unravel.

She said, "Your wartime pilot pal called."

"Who?"

"Constance."

Peggy sniffed so hard her nostrils contracted. "That old blabbermouth."

Kathy pressed what must have been the power button because the display on top of the toilet flashed awake. "Keeping a secret for sixty years is the opposite of being a blabbermouth."

Kathy's reading glasses would help with the legibility, and a pair was tucked inside the book on her end table. She could retrieve them and be back in under a minute, but that would release Peggy from the tension of another exposed mystery. Besides, it was just as easy to stab buttons until the toilet responded appropriately. She tried an embedded square. The lid levitated. Kathy kept her eyes from widening to fool her mother into believing she knew what she was doing.

The next switch beckoned a current of air through a vent

inside the bowl—the bum dryer, she figured. Kathy thumbed it off and touched the toilet seat, as if her random selections might have magically made the difference. It singed even her fingertips, never mind a delicate backside.

To distract from her bumbling, Kathy asked, "Meeting Constance in D.C. doesn't pique your interest in attending the ceremony?"

"Not in the slightest."

Kathy smelled something citrus, like grapefruit or blood orange. Had she provoked some kind of deodorizer from the toilet, or had Peggy been experimenting with Fiona's body sprays? What else, Kathy supposed, was there to do all day? She accidentally sent the lid back down, and opened it manually since she doubted she'd find the right button again.

"Come on, two old friends collecting the medals they long deserved—that doesn't sound appealing to you?"

Peggy crossed her arms over her chest and held herself as if out in the cold. "Why is this medal so appealing to *you*? That's what I want to know. You never chased this kind of thing before. You just wanted to be. And fine. 'So be it' is what I had to accept. Why are you so keen on recognition for me?"

"Because you always wanted it, and now here it is, and you're turning your nose up."

Flustered, Kathy mashed the remote in the frantic way Fiona used to work video game controllers to keep up with her brother. Water began to glug at the back of the bowl. Kathy tapped again, but instead of shutting it down, she intensified the steam. She clicked the rectangle beside it and the jet began to oscillate.

"They want to congratulate me for the crumb I scavenged after promising me a three-tier cake. Attending that ceremony would imply I forgive them, which I don't. My grudges are like Cutco steak knives. They slice deep and come with a lifetime guarantee."

"Any official responsible for your dismissal is long dead. Protesting the ceremony punishes you and you alone. Your grudge is slicing off your nose to spite your face." Kathy heard pressure building behind her voice. "Is it possible *you* are the person you can't forgive?" Kathy's throat grew thick and she spoke directly to the remote. "It's time you let yourself off the hook. You never would have sent Georgia up if you knew that plane was going down. It wasn't your fault."

Peggy held herself tighter. "You don't know anything about it."

"Don't I, though? I've watched you take your guilt out on yourself and everybody around you all my life."

Peggy ruptured, her arms bursting open, her hands flinging free. "I'm sorry the worst thing that ever happened to *me* has been so hard on *you*."

"That isn't what I—"

"Maybe I'm *not* ready to forgive myself. I'm in good company, because it seems you aren't either."

"You're right, but we both better get our acts together, because you're running out of time." Inside a fist of frustration, Kathy strangled the remote. The water fountain rocketed out of the bowl and axed its wet blade into Kathy's chest. Peggy shrieked and slammed the toilet closed. The water pummeled the lid with the *pt pt pt* of a machine gun.

Kathy held the remote close to her face, squinting for the off switch. She groped until the appliance quieted.

The women caught their breath, waiting for their bodies to reabsorb the adrenaline they'd released and for their hearts to catch up to the safety their brains already knew. Peggy unspooled a wad of toilet paper and handed it to her daughter. Kathy looked down at her scrubs. They were soaked. When she began to laugh, her mother followed. No amount of squares could dry that damage, so Kathy dabbed her eyes instead. The two women steadied in the only way they could, after absurdity had stripped them of pretense.

Kathy took in her mother, as unkempt as she ever caught her: lipstick faded, braless breasts slumped, hair matted, and her velvet housecoat bald where her bones had pressed against her mattress. It looked as if she was molting and brought to mind Jet, the Major Mitchell's cockatoo that had been gifted to Frank on his thirteenth birthday by their father's superior officer, motivated by the aptness of the species name. Jet was affectionate and energetic, with a rosy chest and a brilliant sherbet crest that bobbed like an elaborate headdress. Frank cared for the bird in spurts, in the way of a gruff, active, easily distracted adolescent—which wasn't nearly enough. She was separated from her flockmates, caged in a too-small enclosure, and neglected for most of the day. Jet let her displeasure be known. She cawed wildly and paced. When Frank returned to her in the evening, she nipped or ignored him completely. When he left again, she pecked at her bars as well as herself, biting her claws bloody and plucking her feathers. Then one day, Jet was gone. Her cage was empty, the door open, and their house was blatantly without her squawks, shrieks, and song. Peggy explained to her weeping son that Jet was so clever and determined, she'd returned herself to the wild, so they should be happy for her. Jet was back where she belonged: her wings stretched, testing lift and thrust on a rising air current, among the other birds.

It occurred to Kathy only then, half a century later, that Jet hadn't escaped. Peggy did for that bird what nobody had been able to do for her. She'd set her free.

"That medal is yours," Kathy said to her mother. "Take it."

Chapter 28

June 1944

SUMMER DESCENDED ON TEXAS. AS THE TEMPERATURE ticked well over ninety degrees, sweat seeped through Peggy's shirt and dampened her Eisenhower jacket, with the occasional trickle snaking between her breasts. She longed to trade her flying uniform for a bathing suit, and her cockpit for a swimming hole, or at least to return to Mayfield and her community at Avenger Field. But work was her duty and isolation her penance. This was the price she paid for being the one who survived, so she bent her head to her tasks and let herself cry for Georgia, her truncated romance, her sudden unbelonging, and the soldiers abroad only when she was in the privacy of her bedroom.

One evening after dinner, an officer placed a wooden radio in the middle of the table and adjusted the dials until the sound focused. They gathered around and conjectured about what was happening across the Atlantic. Peggy listened like a girl among her father's friends.

Then the slotted speakers crackled and hissed, and they all fell silent. "Ladies and gentlemen, the president of the United States."

Peggy smoothed that morning's edition of the *New York*

Times on the table. The newspaper had printed the prayer Roosevelt was about to recite so their readers could follow along with him. She felt the heat of officers peering over her shoulder.

"Last night, when I spoke with you about the fall of Rome, I knew at that moment that troops of the United States and our allies were crossing the Channel in another and greater operation. It has come to pass with success thus far. . . ." His voice was simultaneously tinny and booming, and purposefully paced. "They will be sore tried, by night and by day, without rest until the victory is won. The darkness will be rent by noise and flame. Men's souls will be shaken with the violences of war. . . ."

In Peggy's imagination, she heard grinding tank wheels, bullets clinking through weapon belts, soldiers shouting to one another. She saw Ally boots plunging into wet sand, flames, a silhouette sinking into an explosion, a beach made rusty with blood. She saw the vacant eyes of the amputee soldier in the Sweetwater bar, and her own reflection the night of Georgia's crash. She knew that when the Allies returned from this invasion, they'd bring this day with them.

"They fight not for the lust of conquest. They fight to end conquest. They fight to liberate. They fight to let justice arise, and tolerance and goodwill among all Thy people. They yearn but for the end of battle, for their return to the haven of home.

"Some will never return. Embrace these, Father, and receive them, Thy heroic servants, into Thy kingdom. . . .

"Give us strength, too—strength in our daily tasks, to redouble the contributions we make in the physical and the material support of our armed forces."

This odyssey would release them changed, or it wouldn't release them at all. But the cause was worthy. It was for democracy, for humanity, for goodness itself. And Peggy's part was as critical as anybody else's. Her country counted on her to take damaged planes into her arms and send them to the sky reborn. That was how she could better the world, so she would dedicate herself to that task—for the soldiers overseas, for those who had died, and for Georgia, who couldn't do it herself.

Their president finished: "Thy will be done, Almighty God. Amen."

And everyone in the mess hall replied, "Amen."

* * *

The WASP militarization bill was defeated in Congress by nineteen votes. The country hadn't sustained as many pilot deaths as anticipated. New male pilots were being trained every day, and the war was coming to a head. They no longer needed women in cockpits; they certainly weren't going to accept them into their military.

On June 26, General Hap Arnold discontinued the WASP training program and ordered the new class at Avenger Field to turn around and go home at their own expenses.

These were blows, but they weren't necessarily the end. Graduated WASP were still operational, they were still of use, so Peggy felt more activated than ever. It was up to her to prove their worth, to give officials reason to fight for them through appeals, new legislation—anything. She pushed hard, remembering Jackie Cochran's words: *I beseech you to continue pitching forward against the opposing forces you are bound to encounter.* The discontinuation was just the drag of the plane, and Peggy and the other graduated WASP had to speed forward against it. Though their country had paused new training, WASP who'd already qualified would be grandfathered in—or grand*mothered*, as the case was. To dismiss them would be a waste of their own resources, as well as an insult to the women's contributions and sacrifices. Georgia and twenty-two other women hadn't died so the rest could be tossed aside and forgotten. No, the United States of America, which maintained justice and tolerance in foreign lands, wouldn't abandon its own citizens.

Peggy toiled through July, August, and September, uncertainty more oppressive than the heat. The sun scorched her nose and striped her neck. Her tongue stuck to the ridged roof of her mouth. It had been a year since she'd seen her parents, and she was only able to steal away to see Mayfield for a day every four weeks, all for her country's cause and Georgia's legacy. In those months, Peggy sent 320 planes back into combat.

Their end was lit by portents. Most of the WASP likely accepted it as predestination from the start, because any other outcome would be such a drastic departure from their appointed courses as to be considered an impossibility. Their deviation had been born by dire circumstances, but the crisis was passing, and they couldn't be permitted to remain at elevated heights in ordinary conditions.

Sheer will so tunneled Peggy's vision that when she

dropped onto her cot and tore open a letter from the army air forces, she didn't see the heartache as it was careening toward her. She only felt the collision.

October 1, 1944

To Each Member of the WASP:

I am very proud of you young women and the outstanding job you have done as members of the air forces team. When we needed you, you came through and have served most commendably under very difficult circumstances.

The WASP became part of the air forces because we had to explore the nation's total manpower resources and in order to release male pilots for other duties. Their very successful record of accomplishment has proved that in any future total effort the nation can count on thousands of its young women to fly any of its aircraft. You have freed male pilots for other work, but now the war situation has changed and the time has come when your volunteered services are no longer needed. The situation is that if you continue in service, you will be replacing instead of releasing our young men. I know that the WASP wouldn't want that.

So, I have directed that the WASP program be inactivated and all WASP be released on 20 December 1944. I want you to know that I appreciate your war service and that the AAF will miss you. I also know that you join us in being thankful that our combat losses have proved to be much lower than anticipated, even though it means inactivation of the WASP.

*I am sorry that it is impossible to send a personal letter
to each of you.*

My sincerest thanks and Happy Landings always.

H.H. Arnold
General, U.S. Army
Commanding General, Army Air Force

Peggy's stomach hardened. Everything else unraveled. It
was as if a screw had been wrenched loose on the back of
her reality and the world—her arms, her bare bedroom, the
base, gravity itself—revolved into amorphous ribbons that
blurred and whirled around her.

No more heart-pounding takeoffs, no more navigating
uncharted terrain, no more exhilaration, no more flying
for good. It didn't matter what they had demonstrated.
Who they had lost. Who they *were*. Their promise, potential, and permanence had been snatched away and, in just
two months, they'd be discarded as easily as torn nylons
and lipstick stubs. America had needed them, but now the
country was through with the WASP—until their next
total effort.

An additional insert instructed WASP in good standing to
inquire about flying to the vicinity of their respective home-
towns as passengers in military planes, provided space was
available. Otherwise, they'd have to arrange transport at
their own expense.

*We thank you for excelling at what was considered impossi-
ble, for flying planes men were too afraid to fly, for facing death,
and for dying. But that's all over now, so go home to your sewing*

and your cosmetic counter, to your husband and your domestic duties, and don't cost us anything on your way out.

The letter slid off Peggy's knees. She looked around at her stark room, everything in it army issued: the end table, a lamp, the narrow bed, a footlocker, the chair, the uniform draped over it, a ceramic mug she'd pilfered from the mess hall for her evening tea. She only had what she needed to do what was needed. Now she herself had become superfluous.

She wondered how hard General Arnold had fought for the WASP, and how painful it must have been for their supporter to compose this letter and authorize its mailing. But he was still a general. He still had that.

Peggy and her peers weren't Women Airforce Service Pilots anymore. They were civilian castoffs, chewed up and spit out. They were just women.

Peggy's reeling slowed and her future came suddenly, sharply, into focus. She saw down the narrowed corridor of her life all that she was allowed to be and all she wasn't. Her finger hooked the mug handle. With a howl, she hurled it to the linoleum, where it ruptured into shards she wouldn't soon pick up. The pieces would slice the tender arches of her feet and lodge into her heels, but it was a comfort to manifest what was otherwise invisible, to see brokenness she recognized.

IN THE DAYS that followed, Peggy continued her good work. Soldiers would suffer by her carelessness, or heck, she'd hurt herself, and neither were the parties responsible. But her heart was absent from the cockpit. It was out in the ether, searching for others who hurt.

All she found on base were piteous looks—asymmetric smiles, helpless shrugs, and clichéd head tilts. Donald even offered his apologies, along with a qualifier: "One day you'll see it's for the best."

Peggy snapped back, "Do you see *your* washing out as for the best?"

A week after the notice from General Arnold, she returned to her room to find another envelope had been slipped beneath her door. This time, in the upper left corner was stamped *Stinson Aircraft Company*—a commercial airline.

Laughter bubbled out of her mouth. This was it: sweet retribution. The work of the WASP had been noticed and would be remembered after all. They'd proven their value, and people would be wise enough not to let them go to waste—a piloting life could still be lived. *Take that, America,* Peggy thought. *We're being whisked up and put to use elsewhere.*

October 7, 1944

Dear Miss Lewis,

We at Stinson Aircraft Company would like to enthusiastically invite you to join our talented team of stewardesses.

Peggy's mouth fell open. A commercial airline with far more manageable planes than military aircraft estimated that seven months of military training followed by seven months of practical duties translated, postwar, to female pilots serving cocktails.

The window was locked and the door was closed, but rain pelted her hair and winds swept through her veins. There was a storm coming, and she'd contain it. It would rattle the panes of her rib cage.

What happened next nobody but Peggy could see, and she'd spend the rest of her life both concealing it and demanding the world know. Bone split skin at her shoulder blades. It radiated out and knuckled at the joints, dense but pneumatic so her lungs would inflate them. Feathers sprouted, contoured and downy. Their spines were delicate but their edges were barbed to bind them against the air. That was the anatomy of wings. Her talons sprung next, then fangs, until her transformation was nearly complete. Her hair was undone, full, and wild, her pretty face warped. She was enraged and rapacious, equal parts human, bird, and tempest. Her country had taken a woman and made her a harpy.

Peggy shrieked. She ripped the letter in half, but it wasn't enough. She shredded it until disregard fluttered to the ground like unswept confetti long after a celebration was through. Then she threw herself on her bed and pounded the mattress with her fists.

Her bedroom door creaked, likely an officer checking on the commotion. She knew what he'd be thinking. *This is exactly why women don't belong.* Only those enjoying placid conditions could judge a pitch through turbulence. Peggy palmed her tears. She'd greet him and insist she was just fine. She'd tuck back her wings and curl her claws into her palms to make him comfortable.

But it wasn't a Fort Worth officer. It was Mayfield.

She'd needed love and he'd come. He was there for more,

for the worst. She wouldn't have to hide her beast from him. That in itself was enough to tame it—at least temporarily.

She went to him. "It didn't mean anything to anyone."

He cupped her face and his thumb grazed the high ridge of her cheekbone. "It meant something to every girl who saw your picture in that magazine." He stroked her hair and kissed her, as if dabbing ointment, as if his lips might sting her. "It meant something to you. It meant something to me."

Peggy wanted to kick her feet, to scream: *Don't they understand what we did, what we can still do if they just give us the chance?* The words would grow so loud and large they'd scrape her esophagus. But nobody would hear her. Nobody would listen.

And Mayfield was right: she would remember, and he would remember. His arms were around her now, his hands found the small of her back, a place of equilibrium, and she wanted to believe that could be enough.

Chapter 29

February 2010

WITH PEGGY'S PERMISSION, BUT NOT HER PRESENCE, Kathy requested another phone conference with her brothers.

As she illuminated all she knew about their mother's contributions to the war, how she really met their father, Georgia's accident, the dissolution of the WASP, the upcoming medal ceremony, and her heart condition, excitement expanded Kathy's chest, lifting her. She no longer had to be the sole archaeologist digging through their shared history. She hadn't realized how alone she'd felt these last months, the only child inside refashioned memories, until now, when she was on the brink of emotional company. She finished, eager for partners in thorny enlightenment. The four dwelled in silence for so long she began to think they'd gotten disconnected and she'd have to recount it all again. But her brothers were only absorbing the truth. It took time to catch up on sixty years of not knowing.

Paul was the first to respond. "It's sort of a relief, isn't it?"

"How do you figure?" Jimmy asked.

"We knew something was weighing Mom down, didn't we? Now we can finally see her baggage."

"Terrific. Now we know Mom sometimes treated us like shit because she wanted to do something other than raise us. That feels freaking fantastic." Frank's words strained from his throat, like a child trying not to cry.

Kathy's anticipation crested and crashed. She'd harbored her own complicated perspective of Peggy, who had certainly made mistakes—being human was a mother's most inexcusable offense. But Kathy didn't realize the extent to which the parasite of resentment persisted inside her brothers. Was this why they'd set themselves apart, as if in quarantine—so as not to contaminate the others? Or perhaps they'd grown attached to their resentment. They wanted to protect what they'd memorized about their mother, the way they understood their upbringing, resulting relationships, and themselves. Facing updated versions of loved ones might threaten their narratives and serve as the antidote. There was something delicious about battening down, sequestering, and holding on to pain. It was snug and appealing—far simpler than forgiving and moving forward. But it was no way to live. How many opportunities for healing had they wasted to feed their toxins?

Of course, she was just as culpable. It had been comforting for Kathy to cast people in their defined roles: mother as shrew and daughter as sufferer, or brothers as bullies and sister as burdened caregiver. It helped her better comprehend her story, in which she was the martyr. But with the unveiling of Peggy's past, she learned it wasn't so simple. Kathy had been her own unreliable narrator. She didn't have all the facts. Outside her story there existed an infinite number of others, each with its personal hero.

She too had participated in the thinning out of her family. Her brothers may have drifted, but she'd let them go because their absence reinforced her self-righteousness. She condemned them for not visiting, but had she invited them? Had she boarded a plane to witness their lives? Had she initiated phone calls? Or had she grown just as complacent? These men had once galloped down streets with her on their shoulders, built her a dollhouse from nails and scrap wood, pitched her curveballs long after the sun went down and the bugs came out. In a childhood without locational permanence, they were one another's familiar. They were home. Now they were islands floating apart. The many disagreements battled across the decades had acted as shoves toward their separate objectives. When Peggy eventually passed, there would be even less holding them together. They could end up on the opposite ends of the earth. The idea of losing them and, in the same way, losing her own children one day was enough to send Kathy into a panic.

"Yes, Mom wasn't perfect, maybe far from it. But neither am I, and neither are you. You can choose to forgive and love her well while she's still here, or you can wish you'd forgiven her once she's gone. The same goes for every single one of us." Kathy's voice rattled, but took off through the airwaves, flying faster than the speed of sound.

"Look who suddenly sounds like the matriarch," Jimmy said. "Bravado suits you."

* * *

Kathy wasn't sure she'd ever before seen her mother nervous. Incensed, afraid, despondent, playful—yes—but never nervous, not like she was the afternoon of their flight, as Peggy examined herself in her bathroom mirror. Her hair was piled high in her signature style, at once windswept and intentionally arranged. Blush highlighted the reaching cheekbones that were set on her face like a shelf. Her everyday pendant sat as armor, a miniature breastplate. Her mouth was painted the exact shade of garnet as the cardigan looped over her shoulders. Otherwise, she was dressed in black, simple but fashionable, and perhaps a salute to all she was mourning.

A pin had been secured to her ribbed turtleneck just above her heart, and Peggy adjusted it a degree to the left and then two to the right, until it returned to its original position, which was perfectly straight.

"It's a bee, not a wasp, but still apropos," she said, meeting her daughter's gaze in the mirror.

"It's lovely," Kathy said. What she really meant, though, was that Peggy was lovely.

Neil and the kids had flown to D.C. on a cheaper flight earlier that morning, but Peggy had had a cardiologist appointment that Kathy wasn't willing to miss. They would arrive later, but in plenty of time for dinner with the Begleys, Mayfields, and Fords. Together they'd attend the ceremony the next day, and then, at Peggy's request, spend the rest of the day in the hotel pool.

Although Peggy wouldn't admit it, because that would make her daughter right, Kathy suspected her mother was looking forward to the trip, if not for the emotional significance, at least for having all her children, grandchildren, and great-grandchildren in one place—her lifework, for better or worse—jesting and loving and being with one another. At her age and in her condition, with her harvest scattered across the country, this would likely be the last of that particular pleasure.

"We better go," Peggy said. She snapped her blush clamshell shut and dropped it into her purse. "We wouldn't want to be late."

THE ATRIUM OF Logan airport was a glass-paneled hive. There were spring breakers in yoga pants and sheepskin boots, children in matching Dora the Explorer pajamas clutching ZhuZhu Pets beneath their chins, rolling suitcases and messenger bags, automated ticket machines, agents in bold blazers and neckerchiefs, earbuds and neck pillows, puffy jackets and fleeces. Travelers zigzagged through black-belted stanchions, crossing lily pads of light in the thick resin of the floor. Activity clicked and hummed and chattered in white noise, laced by a loudspeaker. The energy was immersive. It seeped into Kathy and agitated her own healthy heart.

"Let's get you wheelchair assistance," Kathy said, scanning the crowd.

Peggy tipped her chin up, as if beckoned by invisible fingertips. "I can walk."

This was debatable, but imprudent to debate. "A wheelchair will get us through faster."

"At the cost of my dignity," Peggy said, ruffling further.

"You're nearly ninety, and a veteran of World War II. Take a load off." This was the first time Kathy had referenced her mother's service in those words. It sent a shimmer beneath Peggy's acerbity.

The wheelchair attendant shamelessly cut off passengers and jumped to the front of lines, darting through the airport current while maintaining an expression of mild astonishment, as if the wheelchair was in control and he was doing his best to ride its fin. Kathy jogged to keep up and issued half-hearted apologies to jostled passengers.

Peggy, though, had no remorse. She was a figurehead at the bow of a ship, regal and defiant. Wisps of her hair fluttered in the generated breeze and she palmed her purse, pleased by the special privileges she'd been afforded, and the speed. Kathy had only flown once with her mother as pilot. She had trembled and sobbed from takeoff to landing, a petrified state that had repulsed her mother so much she never took her to the sky again. Besides, planes were her mother's solitary, childless space. But this, careening through the airport on the edge of a wheelchair, tickled and proud, was how Kathy imagined her mother must have looked in cockpits.

The attendant deposited them at their gate with more than enough time for boarding—so much time, in fact, Kathy wasn't sure what they would do with themselves. As Kathy went for her wallet, Peggy patted her arm. Kathy reddened, sure her mother was about to say something rude, like, *You don't need to tip him. This is his job.* Instead, Peggy fetched her own wallet and plucked out a ten-dollar bill, twice what Kathy had intended to give. She handed it to the man and said, almost flirtatiously, "That's the most fun I've had in a very long time."

Kathy texted Neil, who responded with a photo of him

and the kids in front of the White House. Noah stuck out his tongue and crossed his eyes, Neil's hand lay flat over his heart, and Fiona's arm extended out of frame. She would have been the one to suggest the selfie, and to arrange it with the right angles. The sight of them stirred up longing in Kathy, and envy that Neil got to enjoy special time with their children.

But this could be a special time for Kathy and her mother, she reminded herself. Peggy must be feeling vulnerable as she prepared to reunite with other WASP; to accept gratitude from a government that, in her view, spurned her; to confront long-protected grief; and to be open with her family about an identity she'd kept hidden. She was about to move back in time, travel through painful and joyous memories, and bring them to her present. If Kathy had the courage and attunement to join her mother at such a sensitive time, Peggy wouldn't have to do it alone. This was an opportunity for them to coauthor new history.

A businessman plugged a laptop into the outlet beneath their seat. A young woman in a beanie pulled back the foil of a homemade sandwich. Twin girls hurtled across the dingy carpet. The boarding area was filling. Peggy and Kathy were in far too public a place to expose themselves, so they retreated inside books about the emotional lives of domesticated women.

After Kathy reread the same passage the fourth time through, she abandoned the effort and put her nervousness in motion. "I'm going to find something to eat. Any requests?"

"Airport food is extortion—and repellent, to boot," Peggy said.

"My treat."

"Don't waste your money on a twelve-dollar muffin."

"A sixteen-dollar turkey club, then."

Designer bag displays butted against a pyramid of Red Sox pint glasses. Kathy perused paperbacks and considered souvenir teddy bears for her grandnieces. She stopped in the bathroom though she didn't need to go and tried three sinks before a motion detector responded to her hand. In the food court, she reviewed every menu before deciding on her first instinct.

She returned to her mother with minestrone soup, a caprese baguette, and a brownie to share. Though she'd burned at least thirty minutes, the flight display indicated more time until departure than when she'd left.

"Delay," her mother explained, and flipped to her next page.

Kathy beseeched the blazing blue sky on the other side of the floor-to-ceiling windows. "It can't be bad weather."

"There are all kinds of reasons planes get held up. You know that." Peggy flapped her book closed and exhaled through the caverns of her nostrils. "I should have cancelled that doctor's appointment. We left his office with the same information as when we'd arrived. I'm diseased and resisting the cure. Blah, blah, blah. Now we may not make it for dinner."

They couldn't both fret, and this was Peggy's occasion, so she had more of a right to it. Kathy's anxiety shrank back and allowed for her other reflexes to emerge. She lowered into the beam seat beside her mother and applied her bedside manner.

"We will make it," she said, and traded Peggy's novel—still glossy and firm with newness—for the plastic-wrapped chocolate brick. "We might as well eat lunch before we worry about our next meal. Here, this was six dollars. Enjoy every last crumb."

AFTER TWO HOURS and several more delays, the gate agent announced, too perfunctory to be contrite, that Flight 371 from Boston to D.C was officially cancelled. The designated pilot had been grounded by a storm in the Midwest, and they hadn't been able to enlist a replacement.

Indignation had been simmering among the gathered passengers, and now it boiled over. They threw up their arms and pitched to their feet, prepped to protest, or at least to exercise their upset. Kathy watched as something sharp flickered across her mother's face. Something like fear.

"I bet you could handle a Boeing," Kathy said. "Should I tell them you're available?"

"This whole thing was a bad idea. I said so from the start." Peggy clung to her purse and huffed despair. "What are we going to do now?"

"We'll get on another flight." Kathy made it sound simple and obvious, though hundreds of people were at that moment scrambling to make that very arrangement. Travelers were charging the gate agents, making phone calls, uncapping laptops, and scrolling furiously. All available seats on later flights would be snatched up by the more technologically proficient, or by the more demanding, who were sticking their fingers into the faces of airline personnel, while Kathy sat beside her mother, her hands idle, trying to pretend her stasis wasn't a symptom of the hopelessness into which she wasn't sinking.

Normally she'd be with Neil, and he'd be the one to act. Or she'd oversee her children, who were more savvy at summoning travel options, their thumbs ticking phone screens until a final flourish magically accomplished what Kathy would go cross-eyed double-checking. But they were all in D.C., along with Kathy's brothers and their wives and children. Everyone was ready to assemble around the guest of honor, only Peggy was stuck with the daughter who'd insisted this happen, but whose determination to also keep an appointment had stranded them away from it all.

"And if our next flight gets delayed or cancelled? What then?" Peggy asked.

Even if they somehow claimed two seats on a later flight, there was the possibility that another issue would bump them so far down their schedule that they'd miss the ceremony altogether. Peggy's seat in the rows of WASP would remain empty, and all of Kathy's family, who'd flown and rented cars, who'd made reservations, paid money, and taken time off from work, who'd made an effort to forge new bonds with one another, would be futilely in hotel rooms, or in the Capitol Building watching a ceremony honoring mothers that weren't theirs.

"We should drive," Kathy said. As she articulated the idea, she became more certain of it, and was grateful she'd insisted they restrict their luggage to carry-ons. Now they could move quickly.

"All the way to D.C?"

"It's seven hours. That's not so bad. We'll miss dinner but

will make it in time to go to bed at a reasonable hour and wake up bright eyed for your big day."

Peggy's mouth crumpled as she considered this work-around. "You can drive all that way?" It was a question led by hope, with only one answer that wouldn't disappoint.

Kathy barely tolerated driving in the most ideal conditions—on back roads she knew, guided by the sun, for stints that were less than fifteen minutes—never mind highway driving through multiple states well into the night without reviewing the route or mentally preparing for such an expedition. But her mother had served in a war and lost her best friend. She'd wanted more for her daughter than her country had afforded her, and her daughter had rejected her for it. Bitterness had bruised her, and in turn, those around her. It had driven her sons away.

"You flew bombers," Kathy said, bracing her mother to her feet. "I think I can handle my Subaru."

Kathy supported her mother's elbow and Peggy clasped her daughter's arm right back. They held on to each other as they pushed through the airport door and into the starkness of the waning winter afternoon, giddy as schoolgirls cutting class, as if turning their backs on flight was an illicit act, and they expected somebody might be on their heels to stop them.

They laughed at a raven pecking spilled French fries, the veer of a city bus around a bend, and the incessant honking of their car as Kathy fumbled for the key fob in the parking garage. The spontaneous redirect of their adventure instilled them with the audacity and precociousness of the young, and they rode this spirit south through the undersea tunnel to Boston that normally palpitated Kathy's heart. They could do this. *She* could do this. This was ability in motion.

By the time the channel walls dropped into highway and the glass and steel columns of downtown towered at their backs, jauntiness slouched, and they were reminded that they still had seven hours of driving ahead.

Kathy thrummed her fingers against the steering wheel. "Music?"

She scanned the radio to an oldies station playing "Dancing Queen," whose bright disco seemed just the vibe to restore and prolong their good mood. The crooners and the synthetic keyboard propelled them over the lull and got them both humming. Then the whimsical notes of ABBA transitioned brusquely into the hard drums and brass of Creedence Clearwater Revival, as well as a throaty voice rasping, "737 coming out of the sky . . ."

"Oh, I love this song," Peggy said, and touched the volume knob more as a gesture of approval than a discernable adjustment.

Around the third iteration of "flying across the land, trying to get a hand," Peggy chuckled to herself. Kathy looked to her, beckoning for explanation.

"You remember Jimmy's engagement party, when the band played this song and Paul started dancing. What did they call that move? The lawnmower? I didn't know he had such showmanship in him."

Kathy called back the more than thirty-year-old scene of her brother, only twenty then, his shaggy bangs slick with perspiration, hopping around by the yank of his elbow. "He was drunk."

346   Alena Dillon

"Still." Peggy leaned back in her chair, mirth spreading into pride. "That was a good party."

"It was." Kathy was only seventeen at the time, but she still remembered it: colorful paper lantern lights strung across their patio, a bowl of beaded necklaces for guests, an outdoor chandelier, martinis, and mosquitos. The event commemorated the first engagement in their family, Jimmy to Lydia, who would turn out to be his first wife of three, but it also marked the Mayfields' departure from South Carolina to Massachusetts, which they knew would be the last stop in the colonel's career. It was the final going-away soiree. Peggy always relished the chance to host, and this party was awarded particular pomp, with a live band and high schoolers hired to pass food.

"What'd we do for your engagement?" Peggy asked.

The question cleaved between Kathy's ribs. At first she thought Peggy asked it to be cruel, but there wasn't any meanness in her voice. In fact, the sun peaked through the passenger window over Peggy's shoulder, highlighting her serenity. Peggy, too, had been enjoying their candor, the shared nostalgia, and was trying to extend it.

For that reason, and because she'd so recently preached forgiveness to her brothers, Kathy spared her the bald truth. "I don't remember."

"We always made a big deal of engagements," Peggy said, insistent. "Even when Paul was middle-aged. Even for Jimmy's second marriage. We must have done something big for you."

Kathy's grip tightened on the steering wheel. "We didn't."

"You're mistaken."

Kathy had made a good faith effort to stave off this particular reminiscence, but if Peggy was determined to steer them down a rutted road, so be it. Here could be another opportunity for excavation. It could be the healing Kathy was after. Or perhaps she couldn't resist the sick satisfaction of picking an old scab.

Kathy said, "I suggested a party, but you said, 'What's there to celebrate? This isn't the start of a love story. It's the sad finale to a series of missed prospects.'"

Peggy's face slid into waxy blankness as her bad behavior hissed in the space between them. Kathy wished she could take the reminder back, but was also glad for it, and the way it must be prickling the soft underbelly of her mother's regret. Kathy cracked her jaw and then zeroed in on the lane ahead until her mother blurred into her periphery.

Finally, Peggy cleared her throat. "You were always prettier than you gave yourself credit for." There was assurance in her voice, as if this sideways compliment might justify fifty years of not quite seeing Kathy for who she was, or seeing her and wishing she were someone else.

SNOW BEGAN TO fall as they crossed the George Washington Bridge. They'd spent the previous four hours in the posture of those sitting on thumbtacks, without any vestige of their previous camaraderie. Aside from sighs as they crawled through rush-hour traffic and a tight exchange at a Connecticut rest stop, they'd been bound by tense quiet.

As they vaulted across the Hudson River, with the Manhattan skyline embedded into the horizon on their left, and the last traces of tangerine daylight draining from the sky, flakes began to whirl around them. Kathy thought, *Just what we need*, as Peggy said, "Isn't that lovely?"

It wasn't unusual for snow to hit the Northeast in March; why hadn't the possibility occurred to Kathy? She'd considered the length of the drive and the dark, but overlooked the fickle whims of Mother Nature. It was just as well. Foresight would only have afforded hours of anticipation and worry, all to get her to this place, in the midst of a blizzard. But that was dramatic. The flurries were barely sticking.

By the time they passed through the gut of New Jersey, the world fully descended into night and thickened with white. Snow collected in a slippery paste on the sides of the highway. Kathy kept painstakingly to the tire tracks before her and halved her speed, but the flakes pummeled her windshield. Their velocity and sheer number demanded attention. They were difficult to see beyond. An itch slinked up her spine and bit into the back of her neck.

It was only snow. People had driven through more dangerous conditions. But they had three hours to go, and it could get worse. They could slide like the time Kathy had crashed into a telephone pole—the weightlessness of a car lifted out of the universe, followed by feeling the very opposite: a crush of metal, the jolt she felt in her fillings. This medal ceremony seemed suddenly far less important than it had in the months leading up to this day. It was not worth a fatal accident. Maybe they should curtail this drive while they could, find a hotel to spend the night, and head out in the morning, or not even risk a detour and ride out the blizzard on the side of the road.

Kathy looked to her own medal, the swinging pendulum of a miraculous mother. *Help us.*

"I never should have said what I did," Peggy said.

It took Kathy a beat to realize her mother was picking up the conversation where they'd left it three states back. She angled forward, concentrating on the road, but allocated her mother a fraction of her attention. "So why did you?"

"I associated Neil with some unpleasantness that I won't go into. A person has the right to some secrets; I still believe that. But I'm afraid I may have penalized Neil for being someone he wasn't, in the same way, I suppose, that I did for you. Perhaps that was a habit of mine. A troublesome one, I'll admit. Searching for ghosts in the living."

There was much Kathy could have said, but the blur, her heart rocking up her throat, the sunbursts from the streetlights, and maybe she should test her brakes—all this locked her jaw in place. It would take great effort to unfreeze, and she feared any deviation from her task would send them spinning.

"I behaved unfairly. Is that what you want me to say? I thought a mother shouldn't admit to her daughter the battles she'd lost, but now I'm not so sure that's true anymore. I didn't tell you how I'd been cheated, or why I was sad. I just tried to create in you all I didn't have. I tried to make you her, and neglected to see you as you were, which was more than enough. You and your brothers filled the mother part of me to the top. That version of myself was overflowing, and I love you for it. It was the other parts of me that were neglected. There was nothing you could have done to change that, and I should have done a better job hiding my emptiness from you."

Kathy's heart was pounding and, in the seat beside her, so was Peggy's, as it always did now, working too hard to pump through constriction. Her mother's most vital muscle was scarred and would continue to weaken until its last beat, which could be, as far as anybody knew, in the next moment. But that was true of even the most robust. Cars could skid or truck brakes could fail just as easily as a heart. What good was it to spend a life gripping grudges against mothers and country, punishing others when life and love were fleeting, and when those who most suffered the consequences were the grudge holders themselves?

Kathy had felt her mother's mortality more acutely the last few months, and yet she'd still given in to petty impulses, been cruel when she could have been kind, fired bullets when the shot was clear. She would likely surrender to temptation again, act spitefully in the name of retribution, because she was a human who had been hurt, which was to say, a human, spending time with the source of her hurt. But here the source was, baring her overworked heart. Here they were, sliding on perilous roads. Here Kathy could be, offering her what they both needed.

And Kathy hoped when she found herself in her mother's seat, the passenger all her children were driving, they'd turn to her with understanding and mercy, they'd see their mother for her exquisite humanity, and instead of sentencing her for being too sheltering, too prosaic, too underestimating, they'd see her as an evolving culmination, a compilation of places she'd lived and people who'd loved her, dread and passion, damaged but trying, a mother who erred because there was no other way, but who prized them above all else, and who now laid herself at her children's feet.

"Katherine, please. Don't leave your mother out on a limb all by herself. Say something."

Kathy's heart had jostled up into her throat, but she elbowed it aside. "I forgive you, Mom, and I love you very much. Now please shut up before I accidentally kill you."

Chapter 30

March 2010

PEGGY SAT BEFORE A REFLECTION UNLIKE HER LAST IN those uniform blues. Her skin, once elastic and taut around high cheekbones, hung loose from her jaw. Her hair, once auburn with glowing undertones, was a pewter nest beneath her beret. Her hands, once nimble as they whizzed across a dashboard, were bloated and knotted and trembling around her jacket's brass buttons.

"Let me," Katherine said, and she knelt beside her mother and took over the task.

If time insisted on bowing Peggy's spine, sapping her vitality, and calcifying her heart, she was grateful, at least, for her daughter, whom she was appreciating more each day.

Peggy had always judged her daughter as too careful, which was a nicer way of saying she took her for a coward. As a girl, when Katherine refused to fly with her mother after that first disastrous jaunt (perhaps Peggy shouldn't have taken her through so many stalls and spins), Peggy called her Scaredy-Kat. It was under her breath, but Jimmy heard, and when he recovered from heaving laughter, the name stuck. Peggy regretted conceiving the cruelty, though she considered it accurate. Katherine was a wary, timid homebody.

Even the way she entered rooms was like an apology. While Georgia had declared her own terms of beauty, cavorting so confidently she converted onlookers into seeing what she saw, Katherine was self-conscious and uncertain, as if she didn't know who was right or what to believe.

Not all bravery looked the same, and the quiet variety wasn't any less real. Katherine's courage more resembled herself: unobtrusive, practical, and benevolent. There was wisdom and value in both. Georgia chased outward exploits while Katherine exercised her daring inwardly, peeling back layers to better know herself and doing the same for others. Georgia was assertive while Katherine made space for other viewpoints. Georgia was rash while Katherine found her fun where she was. Georgia was willing to endanger her physical self while Katherine was willing to expose her heart.

Memories of Georgia were buried beneath accumulated experiences, but whenever Peggy called for them, they shot up through the stratum, razor-sharp. She often unearthed her tenderness the night of the base dance. Peggy never spoke of it to Constance or Will, and certainly not to the therapist Will forced her to see after she set that bald bird free, but Peggy assessed it privately, rotating its meaning so the sun glinted off its altered angles. She couldn't decide if it was a peculiar gesture born of booze and festivity or if those factors had loosed Georgia's defenses, shifting open a window into what Georgia otherwise kept closed.

Maybe her friend wasn't as bluntly herself as Peggy had once thought. Her impulsivity could have been fear that someone might stop her if she didn't move quickly. Her recklessness could have been because she figured she had nothing to lose in a world she scorned. Her audacity could have been a distraction from vulnerability. If this was true, Peggy might have struggled to bequeath the facade of fearlessness, yet her daughter had somehow walked away with the real thing.

By now, Peggy was more acquainted with Georgia's ghost than the living being. While Peggy had aged, Georgia was preserved in the amber of time. If their friendship had progressed beyond Avenger Field, what would have become of them? Maybe Georgia would have become her children's beloved aunt; maybe Peggy's family would have occupied so much of her life, there wouldn't have been room for her wild friend; or maybe domestic Peggy would have disappointed Georgia, compelling her to move on to her next fancy, abandoning Peggy like a toy she'd outgrown. Their dynamic might have been tinged by animosity or diluted by disconnection in an infinite number of ways. Had Georgia lived, Peggy could be sitting before this vanity the morning of the medal ceremony dreading the prospect of their reunion, or Georgia might have eroded into the sort of forgettable person who slipped from her mind, and when they met again after so many decades, Peggy might have strained to surface the appropriate greeting: *It was Katherine, wasn't it?*

As it was, Georgia had been snatched in the honeymoon of their friendship, which was Peggy's first, a singular romance. Maybe that sweet graze was Georgia's way of expressing the same: *You are something to me.*

Peggy never learned how to fold her grief for her friend, the WASP hive, and her revoked purpose into her life. With the wrong movement, it needled and pierced through to those around her. She'd refused to be placated. She wanted all there was. As a result, she'd become so consumed by the dark of what wasn't that she'd failed to open her eyes to her splendors: the husband who admired her along with her unpleasantness, a friend who'd witnessed her many selves, three sons who were each flawed and magnificent, and Katherine. Even if Katherine had complied with her mother's will, Peggy had wanted a reincarnation, and no amount of muscled child-rearing would have brought her friend back. If Peggy hadn't been so stubborn, so desperately distraught, she'd have understood that her daughter wasn't a replacement but enrichment in her own right.

As Katherine fastened the jacket, Peggy stared at the top of her head. Her pale part jagged once at the crown and sprigs of white leapt defiantly from her auburn waves. Peggy felt dissociated, as if she were seeing her younger self from above. One day Katherine's mane would tarnish, just as Peggy's had, but for now, it was rich and smelled of hotel shampoo. More remarkably, Katherine could still squat. She was always more robust than Peggy ever gave her credit for. She was also so emotionally attuned, she'd perceived what was at the heart of her mother's lifelong concealment. If anybody in Peggy's inner circle had sensed it, they'd never named or reassigned it, and so Peggy had cradled her blame to her chest as truth, nursing it in solitude until Katherine excavated her shame, drawing it into the open and denouncing it. *You never would have sent Georgia up if you knew that plane was going down. It wasn't your fault.* It hadn't been enough to purge seventy years of remorse, but it was indeed an undoing. Katherine's exoneration was as close as Peggy would come to forgiving herself.

Because of her mother or despite her, Katherine had become a fierce mother, devoted wife, and professional committed to good work. Peggy thought of a lyric from an old WASP song: "If you have a daughter, teach her how to fly." Katherine wasn't a pilot, but Peggy suspected she'd done just that.

Katherine secured the last button and lifted her face to her mother's. "Ready?"

The drive from Boston had taken over nine hours, but that was a blip against what had been required to get Peggy to this place. Still, had they known the extent of the trip, Peggy wondered if they would have attempted it at all. Good thing people weren't prophets.

They'd arrived at the hotel just after midnight. She and Katherine had pushed through the gold-plated door to find the entire family in the lobby: three sons and one son-in-law, three daughters-in-law, ten grandchildren, and two great-grandchildren. An entire crew was draped over low-slung couches, rubbing their eyes, chatting in the unnatural glow of the late hour, and throwing back the ice melt of old cocktails, all of them hers, by birth or by choice. She'd been searching for community without wholly appreciating the one for which she was a founding member—*they* were a place she'd always belonged. They were what she'd done, a glory each and every one.

When her children had hung from her limbs, she'd wanted to wrench herself free, but then they were gone, and though she marveled at her creations operating as sovereign entities—Jimmy an endearing braggart, Frank a hard-nosed softie, Paul a sensitive thinker, Katherine a cultivator—she felt unmoored without them. She'd been dulled and harried by bath times, roasted turkeys, muffin tins, drapery fabric, and shirt mending, and then gutted when she wasn't needed in those departments anymore. She'd spent her kids' childhoods desperate for them to grow up so she didn't have to blot away every stain and answer every cry, only to realize her children made her important.

Peggy didn't celebrate Kathy's engagement because her daughter marrying and moving out left Peggy with nothing. Neil stripped Peggy of purpose, just as her country had. She couldn't confess that part in the car ride, or that her son-in-law recalled the nasty cadet, which was the rotten cherry on top.

Now, in her hotel room, decked in thick Santiago fabric and adorned with WASP pins and patches, Peggy gazed into the bright face of her daughter, gently worn at the edges, and wanted to kiss her forehead. She could live a thousand lifetimes and never get it right, never be the mother this woman deserved. Peggy's eyes went hot. She hadn't yet gotten enough. She didn't want to leave her yet.

"Ready," she said.

THE MAYFIELD FAMILY'S three-car fleet joined the military caravan of black sedans delivering three hundred WASP and their families to the domed symbol of democracy on the hilltop.

Seven hundred women were missing from the parade, thirty-eight killed in the line of duty, the rest perishing in the six decades since their discharge. Peggy didn't know how to manage the grief of hundreds. She held on to the knees of her grandchildren.

At least some of those women had lived to be distinguished as veterans. In 1975, the U.S. Air Force announced women would fly military aircraft for the first time in the United States' history—thirty years after the WASP had been those very trailblazers. Not only had they been dismissed, they'd been expunged. That afternoon, Will stopped home, presumably to check if Peggy had heard the news. She was waiting for him on the front porch. "Hey colonel, they say women will pilot air force planes for the first time. What did you take me up in all those years ago? Stage props?"

The WASP raised hell with supporters and politicians. They petitioned signatures from moviegoers waiting in line to see *Star Wars*. Their classified records were unsealed, and they found an ally in Senator Barry Goldwater, who presented a bill amendment to the House, which was voted down, so he took a separate bill to Congress.

General Hap Arnold's son, Colonel Bruce Arnold, testified that their military training, discipline, uniforms, and top-secret missions meant the WASP didn't function as a civilian organization and were always intended for militarization. His claim was supported by other witnesses, including a former commanding officer, Byrd Howell Granger, who compiled over a hundred pages of documentary evidence, as well as testimony from Colonel William Mayfield.

Peggy didn't make a single phone call or write one editorial. She didn't even sign the petition herself. Her husband couldn't fathom it, just as their daughter wouldn't understand thirty years later—before she did. Mayfield took his bewilderment to his grave. The great injustice of Peggy's life was facing a reckoning, and his wife, who simmered with passion, wasn't raising a fist. Who was this woman of surrender?

Peggy tried to explain that this was a battle she'd already fought. They were middle-aged. It was too late for change to make a difference. Recognition thirty years late wouldn't undo all the casseroles she'd baked and put her back in military uniform, so why should she rise to her knees just to receive another kick to the ribs?

She said this, but when her baffled husband traveled to Washington to speak on behalf of the WASP, she paced their living room like a caged cougar. Katherine, who was in nursing school, asked why her mother was so wired, and Peggy blamed it on menopause.

President Jimmy Carter signed the bill he originally opposed, granting the WASP military status, but it didn't encompass every benefit. Peggy still could only be buried in Arlington because she was the spouse of an air force colonel, *not* because of her own service, which meant neither she nor Will would set a stiff foot in that cemetery.

The following Veteran's Day, though, Peggy visited Mrs. Walden, a widow then, and together they placed a wreath on Georgia's grave. That was something.

Peggy quietly became a war veteran at fifty-five years old. There was no pomp and circumstance. In fact, nobody appeared to know at all. Despite the G.I. Bill Improvements Act of 1977, very few people ever heard of the Women Airforce Service Pilots.

Until now.

THEY WERE CREEPING up the Capitol Building driveway. Two vehicles ahead, a young airman reached through an open car door to brace a uniformed woman with the hairpin shape of the elderly. Peggy glanced at her own arthritic hand—claw, was more like it. They were old now. It was hard to believe they'd once done the impossible.

"You okay, Gammy?" Fiona asked.

Her granddaughter, who dreamed of building cities, would carry Peggy's DNA long after she'd left this earth. Composed of all that had come before and all that hadn't, she would ferry those impacts and absences onto the next generation, and the next. She would be distinctly herself as well as what her predecessors had made and would produce someones who were as unique as they were propagations.

Peggy patted Fiona's knee and said, "This is about as good as it gets."

Emancipation Hall was sprawling, with vaulted ceilings, a gleaming floor, giant sandstone columns, and two skylights the size of house foundations that afforded views of the dome above. This was the most well attended event in Capitol history, but even filled with visitors, the room commanded a cathedral's reverence.

Behind the main stage and bunting of American flags stood the formidable twenty-foot plaster cast of the *Statue of Freedom*, a female warrior wearing a military helmet topped by an eagle's head and feathers. Thick robes flowed from her body and gathered in folds. She grasped the hilt of a sword and balanced a shield on its point. Twenty-four other statues lined the perimeter of the hall, acting as her bronze-and-marble sentry. Staircases leading to the Capitol flanked her back.

The WASP were shown to seats at the front of the audience while their families were relegated to the rear. The commotion was an overload for Peggy's senses. She'd grown used to a slower existence. She searched for something tangible to focus on in the faces around her, women from her ranks who were now strangers and, she thought, the human equivalent of dried fruit. *You are what you eat.* It was hard to imagine any of them handling a bomber, but they must have thought the same of her.

"Marie Fitzgerald, class of 44-3." Thick lenses magnified the hazel eyes of a WASP whose lips were stained cotton-candy pink.

Peggy shook the woman's bony hand. "Class of 44-2. We must have overlapped in Sweetwater. I'm Peggy Mayfield."

Marie's pink lips parted to reveal ivory veneers. "You married him, did you? Is he here? I'd love to see him after all these years."

Peggy heard Mayfield's voice in her ears over Avenger Field. *Climb, cadet. Climb!* Then shouting with similar gusto at Katherine's softball tournaments. *Show them what you're made of, Kit Kat!*

Peggy faltered, but only for a moment. "In spirit. He wouldn't miss it."

Marie's smile shrank and her eyes clouded with the sympathy that became reflexive to those their age. "How long?"

"Almost fifteen years."

"That's a shame," Marie said, and shook her head. "He changed us, you know."

Whenever Mayfield had found Peggy in the midst of a tirade or depleted by too many loads of laundry and peanut butter sandwiches, banality driving her to madness, he stole her to his air base where he put her in a cockpit, and together they launched into the sky, soaring as they once had toward the firmament. When they landed, hair mussed, as flushed and exhilarated as if they'd had sex, he kissed her cheek and whispered, "Back where you belong," and she knew he meant their visit to heaven rather than their return to earth. Her husband was her home, someone who appreciated her talents, somewhere she didn't have to pretend. In turn, she was his vibrancy and his conviction.

Peggy clenched her teeth against a burn in her throat. "He'd tell you it worked both ways."

Marie looked at Peggy over the rims of her glasses. "I've never forgotten."

"Forgotten what, dear?"

"That terrible day. That kind of thing never leaves you. It can't have left any of us."

Georgia, Peggy realized, and she wanted to agree, to elaborate and lament for as long as Marie would allow. She felt she'd been carrying that day all by herself, but of course a version of that burden had been shared by each of these women. Tragedy stayed with a person and evolved over a lifetime. Hers had begun spiny, prone to impaling and shattering off, but waned into plates she wore like armor. Before Peggy could ask how Marie's had altered, and how it had altered her, a cool knuckle grazed her neck.

"After all your bellyaching, you beat me here." Constance pressed her downy cheek against Peggy's and lingered there, smelling of lily and the chemical breakdown of time. Her hair was a pure white puff, as if she'd taken a bit of cumulus cloud and fit it as a cap around her ears. Her reserve had been razed by the decades, leaving only kindheartedness behind. She beamed, and the sight of her in uniform submerged Peggy into stinging nostalgia.

Peggy strummed a brass button on Constance's jacket. "Look at you."

Constance had worried her body would inflate until she became, in her words, a bloated old toad. Instead, she'd filled out into a compact cylinder and stayed that way, a form as steady and solid as she was.

"Look at *us*," Constance said.

The loudspeaker crackled and a voice encouraged the attendees to their seats. Constance carried her friend's hand into her lap. Peggy was reluctant to spend the entire ceremony without ownership of an appendage, but she knew Constance enough not to resist. It was a small sacrifice. The conclusion of it all was about to begin.

Speaker of the House Nancy Pelosi was the first to the podium, and twelve people followed her: senators, congresspeople, Tom Brokaw, and a former WASP. They spoke of moxie, patriotism, and patience. They called the women pioneers who had piloted all manner of military aircraft for a total of sixty million miles. They were heroines, an elite fraternity of aviators, and perhaps that was true because, out of 25,000 applicants, only 1,830 were accepted and, of those, 1,074 graduated. In nearly every speech, they were heralded for serving without desire for recognition, which ruffled Peggy, because that wasn't the case for her, nor was it for the many in uproar after the air force announcement in the 1970s—and so what? Deference wasn't a noble act. There wasn't anything wrong with women wanting what they deserved. But there was no use getting caught on the splinter of a comment or two. They were being formally recognized, finally, and by the highest honor Congress could bestow. That was the important thing. That was the point.

The light snore of a distant engine rumbled beside her, and Peggy turned to find Marie's jaw hanging slack. She'd fallen asleep, poor old girl. Peggy poked her thigh until she snorted awake. Then Lieutenant Colonel Nicole Malachowski wheeled to the podium, her leg casted in plaster, and her belly round with pregnancy.

Inside menial moments, when rinsing a cloth diaper or waiting at a bus stop, Peggy regretted having failed Georgia and Mrs. Walden. She was supposed to justify her friend taking her fatal seat by contributing something great to this world, yet there she would be, her hands wrist deep in filthy water, or idle on a street corner: a mother, nothing more. She ceded the responsibility to her daughter just as she'd passed on Georgia's name. Her daughter became something special, just not what Peggy had in mind, and Peggy had to admit there was no better way to honor Georgia's legacy than with a woman not doing as she was told. Still, all this time, Peggy had assumed she'd misspent her friend's life, but here was Lieutenant Colonel Malachowski, a decorated officer of the air force, a direct descendent of the WASP.

Being dismissed didn't negate what the WASP had accomplished. They'd flown every bird in the USAAF inventory, amounting to seventy-eight different types, delivering over twelve thousand planes. They towed, transported, tested, and taught. They broke barriers. Yes, the walls were rebuilt at the end of the war, and advocates would spend decades pummeling its stone with antidiscrimination laws, civil rights movements, and equal opportunity policies just to access what the WASP had earned back then. But they had been the ones to demonstrate possibility. When Peggy had witnessed with wonder, and no small amount of envy, women climb the ranks, with 156 entering the U.S. Air Force Academy at their first opportunity, she should have felt more pride for having cleared their way. Ten years later, a female was the top graduate, and six women served on tankers to refuel FB-111s during a raid on Libya. In 1993, Sheila Widnall became the secretary of the air force, and female pilots were no longer restricted to noncombat aircraft, though they still weren't assigned to units based on proximity to combat. Yes, the work was ongoing, and required more advancement since sexual harassment and assault were often ignored or covered up by military leadership. There were still obstructions to clear, but the WASP had illuminated the course. They'd proven that the path existed, demonstrating what women could do. *That* was Georgia's legacy, and Peggy's too.

The WASP weren't mobile enough to make their way onstage, so distributors descended to issue their medals. An airwoman moved down Peggy's row. As she approached, her mouth was soft and serious, but, like Georgia's, her eyes narrowed at the sides, as if the two women shared a secret. She delivered a thin forest green box into Peggy's hands.

"Thank you for your service," she said.

Even when Will wore civilian clothing, strangers at pizza parlors or playgrounds intuited his service and thanked him for it. Even after Peggy had been made a veteran, no one ever intuited hers. She could count on one hand with fingers to spare the times her contributions had been acknowledged in sixty years. Now there was also today.

She spoke through mist. "Honey, thank you for yours."

Peggy pried open the leather square to reveal an oversized coin embossed with the profile of a WASP in a flying cap and goggles. Three figures strode beside the bust decked in full flying gear, lugging parachutes. They stepped over the border of the coin while an advanced trainer soared overhead. Peggy's head clouded and her heart began to work harder. She wasn't sure she could take any more, but she had to try. She flipped the gold medal. The backside depicted their three aircraft—a trainer, a bomber, and a fighter—and its edge was etched with a proclamation that could never be erased: *The first women in history to fly American military aircraft.*

Peggy's complicated history had collected atop her shoulders, within her joints, and in her valves. It was the lens through which she witnessed, rejoiced, and raged. It was the ghost that haunted her children. It was the bequest she left them. To be seen after decades of invisibility, and to be appreciated at long last, belayed an equal but opposite phenomenon.

She'd created four people, which was no consolation prize, but now there was this too. Peggy had made mistakes, done things she could never forgive, but here were her two great things: family and flight. This was Peggy's miracle, to have lived long enough to look down and see a pilot reflected back, and to have her family, somewhere in the room behind her, finally know what she'd done, and to understand who she was, who she'd been all this time.

The medal weighted her palm, but her head felt suddenly light, like her tethers had been cut, like she'd spun herself dizzy, like she no longer answered to the forces of gravity, like her heart pumped fast and free. Her future was at her back and her past was before her, and she felt as frail and fleeting as she was, but also—yes, it was as real as anything—like she could stand up and fly.

Acknowledgments

FROM INITIAL CONCEPTION TO LANDING ON THE SHELF, each book takes a village of readers, writers, editors, literary pros, and supporters, which just might be the best kind of village. This, a project that spanned over a decade, was no exception.

I'd like to thank Nicki Richesin, my agent, who helped me develop the premise for the contemporary plot line, and my editor, Lucia Macro, who continues to advocate for my stories as well as bolsters them, including this, the first I submitted on proposal.

I am grateful for every speck of feedback from these talents: Ioanna Opidee, Jennifer Cinguina, and Jillian Ross (if I'm forgetting someone, which I likely am, thank you and forgive me). Thank you Mark Berry and Chip Shanie for their aviator's insight, Amy North for her wisdom about growing up in a military family, and Andrea Krasnowiecki, whom I hounded with medical questions even while she was managing a newborn.

Thank you to the copyeditor, Hope Breeman, the designer of this compelling cover, Elsie Lyons, and the whole team at HarperCollins/William Morrow, including Asanté Simons, Holly Rice, Kerry Rubenstein, Jessica Rozler, Lainey Mays, Jennifer Hart, Iris McElroy, and Amelia Wood.

Thank you to my media rights manager, Katrina Escudero, who so adeptly navigates a fascinating but, to me, baffling landscape.

Finally, a million thank-yous to my husband, who has developed a keen editorial eye over the years, and thus enriches my work as well as my life.

About the author

About the book

Insights,
Interviews
& More . . .

Meet Alena Dillon

Debasmit Banerjee

ALENA DILLON is the author of *Mercy House*, a *Library Journal* Best Book of the year; *The Happiest Girl in the World*; and *My Body Is a Big Fat Temple*, a memoir of pregnancy and early parenting. Her work has appeared in publications including The Daily Beast, Lit Hub, *River Teeth*, *Slice* magazine, The Rumpus, and Bustle. She teaches creative writing and lives on the North Shore of Boston with her husband, children, and black Lab. ❧

Reading Group Guide

1. Had you heard about the WASP before reading this novel? If so, was there anything about their characterization that surprised you?

2. Even though the WASP didn't work out the way Peggy had dreamed of, was her experience in Sweetwater still worthwhile? How might her life have turned out had she not seized such an opportunity?

3. Why was Peggy drawn so powerfully to Georgia?

4. In what ways was Mayfield a supportive husband? In what ways could he have done more to nurture Peggy's neglected identities? Do you think this would have been feasible in that era?

5. Did the migratory nature of Kathy's military upbringing affect her adult life? Did it affect her brothers in the same way?

6. Was Peggy's tempestuous nature understandable, given her secrets? Did learning about her mothering stir more compassion in you for Peggy, her children, or both? ▶

7. Would it have been helpful to Kathy if Peggy had been more transparent about her experiences?

8. How did Kathy's and Peggy's contrasting parenting styles influence their children?

9. Was it reasonable that the elder care fell almost entirely to Kathy and her household?

10. When Kathy became the sole family earner, she still managed much of the domestic duties. Was this fair considering the care Neil was providing her mother? Would it have been different had Peggy not moved in with them?

11. What did holding the World War II timeline up against 2009/2010 demonstrate about the ways in which the patriarchy has or hasn't evolved?

12. Dr. Smith's scenes are set between 2009 and 2010. Has enough changed that his character couldn't exist in the present day?

13. In the Thanksgiving scene, which character did you hold most accountable for Kathy's frustration as she juggled all the food preparation?

14. Ultimately, was Neil's layoff beneficial to his marriage? Can long-term relationships ever transform similarly without a drastic catalyst? ⮑

Two Letters from Peggy's Time in Fort Worth

May 14, 1944

Dear Momma and Daddy,

I took on new responsibilities—target towing and strafing missions!

The men on base needed antiaircraft artillery practice, so I pulled a banner behind me and men on the ground tore into it with live ammunition. It sounds dangerous, and I suppose it is, but I have faith in our men. Plus, one bullet alone isn't enough to ground an American bomber—they don't call them Flying Fortresses for nothing—so they'd all have to be dead set on taking me down, and I'd hope by now they're a little warmer to me than that! Of course I felt a bit uneasy with a row of guns pointed in my direction, especially when the bullets began to pop one after the other, but I concentrated on breathing and made it through just fine. I wasn't nearly as uncomfortable towing targets as I was on the strafing mission.

The boys also needed to experience the burn of tear gas and to test their oxygen masks, so my job was to fly above them and press the button to release the poisonous gas—as if they weren't anything more than cutworms on a corn crop. First they walked with protection, and then they removed their masks and breathed the gas full on. Oh, seeing those poor boys convulse before replacing their masks nearly broke my heart! I know it was my assignment and that the boys needed to undergo the discomfort so they'd be prepared, but I felt so guilty— I was the evildoer who inflicted them with that pain, after all. I wonder how soldiers carry the weight of their actions no matter how justified they may be.

Donald, the mechanic, finally felt ready for his first flight yesterday. It was a clunky ride, but not bad for his first in quite some time. He was over the moon. Hopefully that will buy me twenty-four hours without a sneer. Fat chance!

Thanks for sending letters to the Capitol in support of the WASP program, but it isn't necessary! People who claim we're stealing men's jobs and that women have no business piloting military planes are just a bunch of fatheads. Washington won't listen. They've seen the facts. They know how invaluable we've been, and they'll give us the commissions we deserve. It's just like Jacqueline Cochran's editorial said: "It's time to give these young women their due recognition." They either have ▶

**Two Letters from Peggy's Time in
Fort Worth** *(continued)*

*to make us part of the army or give us
our discharge. And if we're to be discharged,
the least they can do is give us military
status for a day so we can be recognized
as veterans. But it won't come to that.
We're running all domestic flight duties!
They'd be fools to let us go.*

*Daddy, I pray for your health every
morning and every night. You'd tell me
if it was getting worse, wouldn't you?*

Your Peggy

June 1, 1944

Peggy,

I've been debating whether to share with you the story of the accident that brought me to Avenger Field. While I don't want to burden you with this pain of mine, I worry keeping the fact of it hidden is as good as hiding from you myself, which I don't care to do. A pilot should know her copilot. Here is how I was pulled from active duty in the army air forces.

Our mission was to bomb military targets in Japan and land safely in China. B-25s had never been used in combat before, and the mission commanders worried we wouldn't have the fuel to make the trip, so they lightened our load. They stripped us of machine guns and replaced them with wooden dowels. We had fewer guns, but we each carried four five-hundred-pound bombs. One of my bombs was wired with a Japanese friendship medal their government had gifted an American serviceman right before bombing Pearl Harbor.

Even with the lighter load, there wasn't enough fuel to get us to our target in China. As soon as we passed the border, my crew and I had to ditch the plane and parachute into rice paddies carved ▶

Two Letters from Peggy's Time in Fort Worth *(continued)*

into the side of a mountain. The ground was uneven and my ankle snapped at impact.

We weren't alone in that field. A group of farmers in straw hats hurried toward me. With my ankle, I couldn't run, but I didn't have to. Those farmers carried me and my crew for miles to their nearest military base, where we found other B-25 crews waiting, also rescued by Chinese civilians.

Their soldiers welcomed us like heroes. They wrapped my ankle and served us food, cigarettes, tea, and rice wine.

The next morning, Japanese planes flew overhead, and the Chinese snuck us out of their country by boat. They were so kind, and they would pay for that kindness.

The Japanese searched for us and killed hundreds of thousands of Chinese civilians in their hunt. Hundreds of thousands. They executed anyone they found with the American items we'd gifted them— cigarettes, playing cards, jerky. That's how thirsty they were to find us. That's how desperate.

Can you imagine them ravaging those paddies, turning over houses? Can you imagine the hate in their eyes? I hope, for your sake, that you cannot.

If I'd known the price all those people

would have to pay for me, I would have waited there in that field. I would have waved those Japanese planes down.

I have confidence in your strength, but if this letter has upset you, forgive me.

William Mayfield ∽

Further Reading

To learn more about the WASP, visit wingsacrossamerica.us, Wings Across America's digital multimedia project hosted by Baylor University, which pays tribute to the Women Airforce Service Pilots by compiling primary documents, records, audio and video clips, photos, interviews, and other resources into a comprehensive historical guide that can be found all in one place, as well as creating interactive materials with which to engage and enjoy. ∿

Discover great authors, exclusive offers, and more at hc.com.